IN YOUR MIND'S EYE

GARY NANSON

DEFIANCE PRESS
& PUBLISHING

IN YOUR MIND'S EYE

Copyright © 2023 by Gary Nanson
(Defiance Press & Publishing, LLC)

First Edition: 2023

All rights reserved. No part of this publication may be reproduced, distributed, or transmitted in any form or by any means, including photocopying, recording, or other electronic or mechanical methods, without the prior written permission of the publisher, except in the case of brief quotations embodied in critical reviews and certain other noncommercial uses permitted by copyright law.

This book is a work of fiction. Names, characters, places, and incidents are either products of the author's imagination or are used fictitiously. Any resemblance to actual persons, living or dead, or locales is entirely coincidental.

ISBN-13: 978-1-955937-82-5 (Paperback)
ISBN-13: 978-1-955937-81-8 (eBook)
ISBN-13: 978-1-955937-83-2 (Hardcover)

Published by Defiance Press & Publishing, LLC

Bulk orders of this book may be obtained by contacting Defiance Press & Publishing, LLC. www.defiancepress.com.

Public Relations Dept. – Defiance Press & Publishing, LLC
281-581-9300
pr@defiancepress.com

Defiance Press & Publishing, LLC
281-581-9300
info@defiancepress.com

CHAPTER ONE
IT ALL BEGINS IN NICKERSON GARDENS

The projects in South Central Los Angeles are not welcoming. If you don't live there, it's best not to venture down those streets. Tonight, two powerful forces collided in those projects, and that collision would shake the foundation of Los Angeles.

The semi-horseshoe design of Nickerson Gardens, supposedly an architectural decision to improve the aesthetics of the gloomy surroundings, served as the perfect place for gang members to hide when shooting at passing police cars. Developed in 1955 and operated by the Housing Authority of Los Angeles, as government housing, it was intended to be a model for affordable housing. Although, it didn't quite turn out that way, and the politicians in Los Angeles never talk about it. Nor do they ever go there.

Lieutenant Jack Adams wasn't surprised when he heard the radio broadcast by a pair of officers in one of his gang details in the projects, in Nickerson Gardens. "Officer needs help! Officer down!" That call for help brought the two powerful forces together and, unexpectedly, the consequent ripples changed lives.

One of the powerful forces believed he was destined to rise to the top ranks of the Los Angeles Police Department, and he was intent on engineering his ascent to the top. The other . . . well, the other was fighting to stay on his path of caring for those who needed help and arresting those who committed crimes. It seemed so simple, so clear, yet that path proved to be far more treacherous than most would believe.

It was early in their shift and as the two LAPD Gang Detail officers drove along East 114th Street from Compton Avenue with the windows down, they argued about where to eat tonight. Sneaking out of the city and driving over to Gardena to a Japanese restaurant on Western Avenue won the battle, and the officers knew that they had better eat before things got busy.

The officers kept the windows down so they could hear and experience everything outside the police car as they drove. They unbuckled their seat belts before they entered the projects; being buckled in with seat belts was tactically dangerous.

As the passenger officer leaned forward and slapped the dashboard to celebrate his dinner choice, his head suddenly snapped to the left. The policeman driving the car felt blood splatter on his face, and he knew his partner had been shot as the man fell against him. It had just happened so fast.

"I got you, man, I got you. Hold on, I got you."

The shooter, a sniper with a rifle secreted behind a second-floor window, merely shot at the windows of the moving police car. The rifle recoiled so sharply that the young man dropped the rifle when it shook from his hands. "Bounty Hunters—motherfuckers! Bounty Hunters."

When the blood hit the side of the driver's face, he instinctively knew to get out of the line of fire. Acting against what most would think was common sense, the driver reverted to his training and hit the gas pedal, jerking the steering wheel to the right and driving directly toward the shooter. The police car bounced over the curb on a vicious path toward the housing units.

At the last second, he turned the police car sharply and put it right next to one of the housing units that protected them from the line of fire. Without even thinking, he had disallowed his emotions and reacted to the situation, a result of having experienced countless life-threatening situations prior. The concentrated experience of a Los Angeles policeman.

The driver's expression was perfectly blank as the car came to a stop and he looked at his partner lying against him. "I got you, man. You're good, I'm getting help for you."

He knew that driving directly at the threat was the best tactical reaction to get out of the line of fire and confront the suspect. He had to give him and his partner some level of cover, then get the radio broadcast out. "Officer needs help! Officer down! 114th Street east of Compton in the projects. Sniper north of our location. Get me an RA unit, my partner's hit." He hoped the fire department rescue ambulance and paramedics would arrive in time.

The officer dropped the radio microphone to the floor of the police car, knowing he didn't have to say anything else. The responding officers had undoubtedly done this before, many times. They would know to be cautious of the sniper's line of fire and to get a perimeter around the scene to protect the officers and capture the suspect inside the perimeter. The air unit would be coming. K9 units would be coming. Everyone would be coming. Drop the microphone, he decided, and let them do their work while he does his.

He pushed his hands under his partner's arms and pulled him across the seat out of the driver's door. He laid his partner on the ground, wedged tightly against the police car, and looked at his partner's face. His eyes were closed. "Hang in there, partner. The cavalry's coming."

He pressed one hand hard on his partner's neck and held it tight, slowing the flow of blood until fire rescue could arrive. He could feel the blood pulse with every heartbeat, but the pulses were becoming further apart. With the other hand he held his gun out in front of him, scanning the area for suspects, for shooters. With his back shielded by the police car, he knew there may have been more than one suspect and that they could come from any direction. Soon he began to hear sirens—lots of them.

#

Lieutenant Jack Adams, the current officer in charge of the gang side of Gang and Narcotics Division, which fell under Detective Bureau, was only minutes away when the shooting occurred. Not believing in sirens, as he had found they never really enabled you to travel any faster, he turned his unmarked police car north toward the projects and stomped on the gas pedal.

Detective Bureau was commanded by Deputy Chief Steve Nelson. Under him was a brand-new commander that Adams had not met yet, Stans Jelenick.

As to the chain of command, Lieutenant Adams usually answered to the commander of Detective Bureau, but for a few months the commander spot had been vacant. During that time, Adams had been working one step higher, directly with Deputy Chief Nelson. Since Adams had not met his newly assigned boss, he reached for his phone and called Deputy Chief Nelson.

Nelson didn't want to be notified of every gang shooting, as he trusted Adams to handle the scene, but tonight was different. Tonight, a police officer had been shot, and Adams knew the deputy chief would want to be notified.

"Good evening, Chief, it's Lieutenant Adams. I'm on my way to the projects in Nickerson Gardens with an officer down. I probably won't be able to call once I get there, so I'm making the call now even though I don't have all the info. I'll take the scene, but it's not sounding good, sir."

"Okay, Jack. I'm home, but I'll be en route to the hospital as soon as I hear where they're taking him—just have to pull my pants on. You've got the field investigation, but notify Commander Jelenick; he needs to get broken in on callouts. I'll probably see you later at the hospital, but if I get a chance to come by the scene, I'll see you there."

The rumor on the street was that Commander Jelenick had been placed in Detective Bureau because there was nowhere else to put him. His work experience being mainly in West Los Angeles and in the San Fernando Valley, he was not a solid leader or a solid decision maker. More of an administrator. Adams wasn't too happy about Jelenick and his reputation showing up at his crime scene, but he was sure that Jelenick would probably go to the hospital, where all the brass would be.

Adams sighed. He didn't really want to make the next call. "Good evening, Commander Jelenick. This is Lieutenant Jack Adams. I work Gangs. We've had a shooting tonight, sir, and a Gang officer was hit by a sniper round in the projects, in Nickerson."

"I see, Lieutenant. Well, I'll come by the scene to meet with you and the officers and then I'll meet with Deputy Chief Nelson to brief him on the situation. Stand by for me until I get there. I'm on another call in South Gate with an off-duty detective injured in a traffic accident and I'm not too far away."

"Roger that, Commander." *Damn it.*

"Be sure to stand by until I get there, Lieutenant."

"Roger that, Commander." *Fat chance.*

#

Spending his years as a Los Angeles policeman in Watts in South Central Los Angeles, Jack Adams had learned to navigate the shadows cast over the city. In fact, over time Adams somehow came to feel comfortable in those shadows that seemed to scare or confuse most people. In his mind's eye, Jack Adams now lived in those shadows. He denied fear.

It was sweltering hot outside. Even though it was early, the projects were a buzz of activity. Everyone wanted to know what was happening and the Bounty Hunters were out in full force. The Bounty Hunter Bloods owned Nickerson Gardens.

Lieutenant Adams was used to rolling in to scenes that seemed violent and chaotic. His job tonight was to lend a sense of control and management as the Gang Detail officers and Southeast Division patrol officers worked together to locate the shooter while playing defense, trying not to become victims themselves. They believed that a rifle had been used in the shooting of the Gang officer.

The Los Angeles Fire Department, LAFD Station 41, was just arriving at the scene of the shooting and Adams followed them in on 114th Street from Compton Avenue. Two black-and-white police cars from LAPD Southeast Division had pulled alongside the fire trucks to provide security. It wasn't safe in Nickerson Gardens for anyone.

The firemen of LAFD never hesitated, driving right into the scene despite the sniper lying in wait somewhere out there. No time to wait for the scene to be made safe; an officer was shot, and he needed help.

Lieutenant Adams went directly to the wounded officer as he was being placed on a gurney by fire rescue. They were working feverishly on his vitals, trying to stem the flow of blood from his neck, but they knew he had to be transported immediately. It didn't look good, and the officer appeared to be unconscious as they worked to keep him alive.

As Adams put his hand on the officer's chest to will life into him, one of the firemen handed Adams the officer's gun belt. "Time to go, Lieutenant. We have to move now. Here's his gun. Please step back, sir."

When you're the victim of a gunshot wound, of a serious life-threatening injury in a tactically dangerous situation, these are the guys you want caring for you. These guys would wade through Hell to get to you. If anyone can save your life, the LAFD will.

Adams looked in the officer's police car, noting the blood on the seats and on the dashboard. The large pool of blood on the ground next to the car seemed to spell doom for the injured officer. Adams struggled internally, transitioning from the worry over the injured officer to the investigation and confrontation of the suspect, but it was time to turn his back on the ambulance and go to work. *Just shut it out and do your job.*

As the doors of the ambulance closed, the lights flashed and the ambulance headed to the medical team that was already assembling at the Harbor-UCLA Medical Center. The closest hospital was the Martin Luther King, Jr. Hospital, but policemen and firemen were never taken there for care. Given the name "Killer King," the Martin Luther King, Jr. Hospital in the Willowbrook area of Watts was a Los Angeles County facility that had been closed in 2007 after countless cases of incompetence, medical errors, and deaths. The attached medical school, the Charles Drew University of Medicine and Science, was also closed after receiving one of the lowest rankings in the nation. The hospital reopened in 2014 under the promise of better medical care, but the reputation held strong.

Adams listened to the ambulance siren fade as he turned to the officer who was locked in place, staring down at his partner's blood covering him. Looking into his face, Adam saw the familiar blank stare. Trauma.

Adams placed his hand on the officer's shoulder and lightly squeezed. "You did a good job. You kept him alive, and I'm proud of you. Now it's up to the doctors to do their part and time for us to get to work. Did you see a shooter?"

The blank stare began to waver. Adams saw some level of recognition in the officer's eyes. "No, Lieutenant. I think I heard a shot, but I'm not sure. But I think the round was north to south and into our car. From those buildings over there."

"Okay, pal. I need you to trust me to take this now. You did your job—now it's time for me to do mine. I'm going to have this sergeant here take you to Southeast Division, where you'll be interviewed once things calm down. This is really important; it builds the criminal case against the asshole who shot your partner, and we need to get it while everything is fresh in your mind. I'll call the watch commander and have him get a steak sandwich and coffee for you. Listen to me, you did good. I'm really glad you were here for your partner, and I'm proud of you."

Adams watched as his sergeants organized search teams and set up a perimeter around the crime scene. The airship was scanning the area but held at a higher and safer altitude with the goal of forcing the suspect to hunker down and stay in place. The pilot and observer knew how important it was to keep the shooter inside the perimeter by limiting his ability to move without being seen.

Adams would wait until they got things more under control before he got involved. He trained his sergeants and detectives to be independent thinkers, decision makers, to be leaders who got the job done. They didn't need him yet. Adams used wipes from the fire department to wipe the blood from his hand, then laid the officer's gun belt in the trunk of his car. He pulled out a folding table, which became a make-do command post, and laid out a well-used map of the projects to sketch out the perimeter boundaries and assigned search areas. The commander's orders for Adams to stand by until he arrived were already forgotten.

CHAPTER TWO
POWERFUL FORCES COLLIDE

Commander Jelenick had never worked with Gangs, and he was excited to be on his first callout. He hadn't actually been to South Central Los Angeles before except for driving up and down the Harbor Freeway, and he was having a little trouble finding his way. As he drove into Nickerson Gardens, feeling a little bit lost, he cruised the streets a moment until he saw police cars grouped together. He was a little concerned, as many of the cars were parked on grassy areas, not legally parked. He would talk to the officers about that. Jelenick parked his brand-new shiny Chrysler 300 as close as he could to the group of dirty beat-up black-and-white police cars and SUVs but made sure to park legally at the curb.

He found what appeared to be a focal point of activity and saw Lieutenant Adams standing in the middle of the commotion. Commander Jelenick had expected Lieutenant Adams to be standing by and waiting for him to arrive, as he had instructed, and he fully intended to take charge of the event. However, as he got out of his car and walked toward the group of officers, he was clearly out of his element. In fact, to the officers around him, he seemed confused and appeared to slow his gait and pause as he observed what was happening. The fact that he was the senior officer on scene and decided to stand back and watch spoke volumes to the policemen standing in the middle of Nickerson Gardens. Even in the midst of chaos, they didn't miss much.

Lieutenant Jack Adams knew it was time for his involvement now. He stood in the middle of the sergeants and officers who had come together at the impromptu command post near his car. A solid perimeter had been set up, and a plan for search teams to move throughout the projects had been agreed on. The shooter was still outstanding and each officer on scene was ready to engage a violent assault that could occur at any moment. Adams held a .45 caliber handgun softly against his chest with the barrel pointed toward the ground. Jelenick was shocked to see a lieutenant in the field with his gun unholstered.

Adams began giving instructions to three separate search teams, two of which had K9 officers and a dog, who were to locate the shooting suspect hiding in the projects. He knew the suspect was most likely holed up within one of the housing units, most all of which were small one-bedroom units, but they had to start somewhere. His hope was that during the search, one of the search dogs would flush the suspect from a hiding place or would, at the very least, detect something useful. There was always the chance that someone would come forward with information helping the officers to find the suspect and the gun that had been used to shoot the officer, but in the projects, that was not very likely.

As Jelenick listened, he thought Adams was being overly aggressive in leading the search for a criminal suspect and decided it was time for him to step in and take control of the situation. He had told Adams to stand by until he arrived, yet Adams was now acting on his own. He would discuss that with Adams later. He was a commander—he was the senior officer on scene. He was in charge, not Adams.

Commander Jelenick knew a perimeter had been set up, and he believed there was no hurry in searching for the suspect. He was an expert at handling situations in such a way that any liability to himself was watered down so that he could avoid making decisions. Decisions were always dangerous to one's career.

There was no hurry to search now that a perimeter was in place and the scene was contained. He could request Robbery Homicide Division or SWAT to respond. They were the experts and could easily take over the scene. They could make the decisions.

That became Jelenick's plan: Step up and exhibit strong leadership and take over. Put the search on hold, then request Robbery Homicide Division, known as RHD, and SWAT to respond and make the necessary decisions. He would oversee the scene. If successful, they would sing his praises, and if something went sideways, well, there would be plenty of other people to blame.

As he stepped through the ring of officers to approach Adams and take command, an officer from Southeast Division suddenly announced over the radio that they had cornered the suspect in one of the housing units. A neighbor reported hearing loud voices and stated that at least one suspect had apparently forced his way in to the unit next door and was threatening the occupants so they would hide him. The people who lived in the unit were reported to be longtime residents of Nickerson Gardens, a man and his wife in their eighties.

#

When three young men forced their way through the front door of the unit, the elderly couple had pleaded with them to leave. They told the three intruders that they had nothing of value, nothing to steal. The three young men pushed them to the floor and ransacked their small home to no avail—except for the hunting rifle that had lay under the couple's bed for so many years, it had been forgotten.

The situation had just changed, and Jelenick stopped in his tracks. A barricaded attempted murder suspect with a rifle, holding hostages in a housing unit with windows facing both north and south, including high-ground windows, second-floor windows, which created a large killing area.

Adams, however, had decisions to make, and only seconds to do it. But his path had always been clear, and the decisions came easily. The suspect posed an immediate danger to officers and firemen, the airship, and all of the people standing outside or driving by. The most prominent danger, however, was to the hostages being held.

Commander Jelenick wasn't quite sure how to handle this new development. He had never been trained to handle something like this and had never been involved in such a tactical situation. Protocol was for SWAT to take the lead. Afraid to speak in front of all these officers, he froze in place and merely listened as Lieutenant Adams ordered a tight perimeter around the building and for the connecting housing units to be evacuated.

Adams then ordered the officers to clear people out of the field of fire north and south of the housing unit, and Jelenick kicked himself for not thinking of that. Evacuating everyone would give him more time to avoid making other decisions! But then Adams began giving instructions to one of the search teams that included a K9 officer and Jelenick began to panic.

Lieutenant Jack Adams knew that the safe decision was to lock everything down and request SWAT to respond, but time was not his friend. He had highly trained and capable policemen on scene, and every second that passed posed more threats. He knew he had to act now.

"Bring fire rescue up and stage them at the end of the building so they're close. We're making entry now—no time for SWAT. No announcement, just hit the door. Let the back door stand unless I call the rear team in. There's not much room to maneuver in there, so let's keep the entry team to five. K9 and two, stand by at the front door and back up the entry team. Bring a couple black-and-whites up to the rear and stage four behind them. Outside teams, watch those upper windows for shooters and jumpers. We know we have at least one armed suspect with a long gun and he's holding hostages, but it's unknown if there are more than one, so stay tight. These doors go down fast; they're cardboard, so no ram. You guys listen up . . . we have an officer down. Watch your backs while we're doing this."

As Adams personally led the team of officers to make a forcible entry and extract an armed suspect to rescue the people in the housing unit, Jelenick again decided that it was time for him to step forward and take over. This was moving too fast, and he feared he may end up being responsible for everything because he was the highest-ranking officer on scene. He thought that once the connected housing units were evacuated and people moved out of the area, they could just wait and have RHD and SWAT respond. He would stop everything now.

Jelenick's uniform was sharp, freshly pressed. His leather gear had been spit shined and his badge literally sparkled. The highly polished stars on his collars identified him as one of the brass to everyone within a hundred yards. *Someone*, Adams thought, *who should not be in Nickerson Gardens.*

"Lieutenant, hold off on those orders. I told you to stand by until I arrived. I want you to strengthen the perimeter around the crime scene and wait for Robbery Homicide detectives to arrive—they'll take over. Request SWAT to respond and deal with the suspect, but they don't move until RHD gives them the orders. I want you and each of these officers to holster your weapons and put those rifles away." With his plan to appear in control but actually kiss off the responsibility in place, Jelenick was anxious to get on his phone and advise Deputy Chief Nelson that he had the scene under control. He would also try and find time to call his wife and tell her that he was in charge of a serious and dangerous tactical situation involving gangs and shootings.

Adams looked at the polished name tag on Jelenick's uniform. He had never met the man before but was aware of his reputation. Adams immediately recognized Jelenick as one of the brass who were more concerned with protecting their jobs than protecting the citizens of Los Angeles. Regardless, Adams knew there was no time to waste and wasn't sure how to even respond to this commander who was interfering in a hostage rescue operation.

"Commander, I'm Lieutenant Adams. We have a long gun shooter who has access to barricaded high ground and may have taken the occupants of this housing unit hostage. The shooter already hit one of our Gang officers, and he's wanted for attempted murder unless our officer dies. Our officer is being transported by LA Fire, who's trying to keep him alive, and I don't intend to transport anyone else."

Adams looked at the upper floors of the various buildings and then told Jelenick, "You might want to stand someplace else, sir, because you're right in the line of fire of those upper windows. We've run out of time, Commander, and we need to hit this place now. Right now."

Jelenick wasn't used to being in the field and he was sweating now. The heat was unmerciful. He looked up at the upper windows and then moved a few steps closer to a metal clothesline pole. He had just figured it out—he was in danger—and suddenly the whole scene changed. Being in danger wasn't his job.

Adams saw Jelenick stepping back, and without pausing for even a second to give the commander a chance to respond, Adams decided it was better to save lives now and worry about him when the time came. Somehow, a spit-shined commander who hadn't the slightest clue about tactical police operations had found his way inside the perimeter.

Jelenick was used to giving orders and having them willingly followed, although mostly in an office setting—a quiet air-conditioned office with a cup of coffee on his desk and spit-shined policemen completing paperwork on their own desks nine to five. Now, he was taken aback by the person standing in front of him. All Jelenick wanted to hear from this lieutenant, who in his eyes needed a freshly laundered uniform, was for him to say, "Yes, sir."

CHAPTER THREE
LEADERSHIP COMES WITH RISK

Leadership is not granted by rank. Leadership is determined by one's actions, and what Jelenick didn't seem to comprehend was that policemen working on the street follow courage and confident actions. Bars and stars on your collar carry very little weight when you're in the heat of the moment, especially in Nickerson Gardens.

Jelenick was unsure of himself now and felt apprehensive in his surroundings. Somehow, he had ventured into a situation in which he was in personal danger. He moved to stand closer to the building as he glanced around at all the windows looking down on him. Large groups of men and women who lived in the projects stood nearby, surrounding him as they glared at him, and he was scared. Jelenick didn't understand this situation at all.

The LAPD helicopter suddenly dropped down directly over the housing unit, and the sound was deafening as Jelenick wondered if the helicopter was supposed to fly that low. He made a mental note to call the commanding officer at Air Support Division later to ask that question.

Commander Jelenick had never been to South Central Los Angeles and had certainly never been in one of the housing projects. He suddenly realized that he wasn't even sure where he was, what the street name or the address was, or even how to get out of the projects. When he had arrived in the area, he merely saw the group of police cars and landed there. It was unsettling.

He looked to the officers on scene for his personal safety but found himself surrounded by officers that didn't look like any officers he was used to. Each of them wore disheveled uniforms and scuffed-up boots, each one with a very serious look on their face. They all needed haircuts. Most of them held guns in their hands. These were serious people, not the spit-shined crew he was used to working with in his comfortable office. Policemen in South Central Los Angeles were a different breed.

The radio was constantly crackling now with officer's communications, but Jelenick wasn't able to follow any of it. He wasn't used to it; it almost sounded like a foreign language, and he struggled to get a grip on what was happening.

The helicopter overhead held an incredibly bright light directly on the housing unit where the suspect was believed to be hiding. The sound of the rotors continued to intensify, which made the scene even more confusing to Jelenick. He tried to raise his voice above the helicopter's rotors and barked, "Lieutenant, I'm giving you an order to stand down! I want everyone to holster their weapons." He immediately knew no one heard him.

No one was listening to him. He had to stop this—he could be responsible.

When Adams gave the orders to move forward, the Gang officers and patrol officers from Southeast Division acted as if Commander Jelenick was invisible. One officer moving toward the front door of the residence collided with Jelenick's shoulder as he passed, knocking the commander to the side.

Commander Jelenick had never been more scared during his entire career with the Los Angeles Police Department. He was in danger, and he didn't know where he was. He didn't know what to do or where to go. He didn't understand the situation, didn't know what was going to happen or how he was going to explain it. And he didn't know who was looking at him from all those dark windows.

Adams held his ground as the events unfolded. A tight perimeter of eight officers formed around the housing unit where the suspect was believed to be. They protected the backs of the officers who would engage the suspect. The LA Fire rescue unit stood by only steps away.

Two black-and-white police cars drove across the grass to the back of the housing unit where four officers barricaded behind the cars. The officers focused on the upper windows and on the back door, which had a barred window covered by a curtain.

The K9 officer and his dog, along with two additional officers, positioned themselves near the front door of the residence, ready to follow the entry team into the residence if they were needed. Jelenick felt a sense of panic as two of the officers trained their Colt AR15 rifles on the upper windows. He needed to stop this but didn't know how. These officers weren't listening.

The five-man entry team staged at the front door lined up along the wall of the building. Each member of the team was focused intently on the barred faded brown door, ready to engage Satan himself if that door opened. Each officer was focused on the door—except, that is, for the fifth and last officer in the line. A very large mission-driven man with a round face and short cropped haircut. A man who had been in that position before.

The last officer on the entry team turned his head to look back over his right shoulder. With absolutely no expression or emotion evident on his face, he stared at Lieutenant Adams and waited. *All the time in the world.*

Commander Jelenick moved next to Adams and ordered him to stand down as sternly as he could muster. Jelenick was yelling now, trying to get someone to hear him. He was a commander—he had power, he was important, and he refused to be responsible for decisions made during a tactical situation. It could always be avoided.

Adams looked at him blankly, trying to understand what this guy was even doing there. He looked up at the airship hovering over the location and then at the line of officers staged at the front door. He thought about the people being held captive inside their home by an armed man who had shot a police officer, an armed man who could fire out of those windows at any moment. And in a fraction of a second, Adams made a decision and those two powerful forces met in a head-on collision.

Adams spoke into the radio microphone clipped to his shirt and said something that Jelenick could not understand. The airship immediately extinguished the bright light shining down on the building. Then, Adams spun his right index finger in the air.

The fifth and last officer on the entry team simply nodded one time, turned his head toward the barred door, and patted the officer in front of him on the shoulder. Each officer followed suit and when the lead officer felt the tap on his shoulder, he moved under the overhang and slid a crowbar between the barred door and the wood frame. When the barred door popped open, he dropped the crowbar to the side and smashed the inner wooden door open with his boot. The entire team disappeared into the unit. Commander Jelenick was invisible. He had no power. He was not important. He was nobody.

Inside, the officers found they were engaging three suspects, not one. The officers passed a kitchen door on their right where they saw two elderly people lying on their stomachs with their hands tied behind their backs. They peered into the living room and the situation was tense, all three suspects crowded into the cramped space.

It was quiet in the house except for the commands barked out by the first officer entering through the door. The other four officers knew to remain silent; only one officer talks. Although none of the suspects appeared to be armed, they ignored the officer's orders to hold their hands up and kneel on the floor. The rifle used by the suspect to shoot the Los Angeles police officer was not visible, but the three suspects were not cooperating with the officer's commands.

The suspects appeared defiant, with the tallest one saying, "Fuck you! Fuck you, motherfuckers. My grandma lives here."

The suspect standing next to him flashed the *B* and *H* gang hand signs and yelled, "Bounty Hunters, motherfuckers!"

A set of stairs on the officer's left created a tactically unsafe situation, and the two elderly people needed to be rescued. Standing motionless while facing the three suspects in the cramped environment was not an option. The entry team moved aggressively into the living room as they maneuvered around the furniture. Speed was critical.

The first officer pushed forward and took the tallest of the three suspects down to the floor. He fought to maintain control and handcuff the suspect in the small space while the other two suspects were also forced down to the floor.

While officers searched and held guard over the three suspects, two members of the entry team moved slowly up the narrow carpeted stairway to the second floor to clear the location of additional suspects, locate weapons, and seek out other victims.

There was no light in the stairway, and it was only wide enough for one person at a time. The stairway made an abrupt turn at the top, creating a dangerous situation for the two officers who both held their guns facing forward. There was no easy way up; their only choice was to just get up the stairs and move around that corner.

The house was cleared and in the blink of an eye, it was over. Adams extended his arm up over his head and held up four fingers to the helicopter—Code Four, under control—and the helicopter banked sharply and cleared the area. Their job was done.

The scene was suddenly quiet as Adams stepped into the housing unit and observed officers cutting the cords from the elderly couple. Policemen can't do their jobs without a strong, quality knife. One of the officers rolled the female onto her back and said, "She's not breathing." One officer placed his hand under her neck and tilted her head back while the other officer began compressions on her chest.

The elderly man looked on in fear. "Oh, my God, help her! She's my wife—please help her! Anita. Anita, open your eyes!"

One of the boys who was now in handcuffs remarked defiantly, "She's old. Fuck the bitch. Bounty Hunters!"

The Fire Rescue team moved into the unit and seemed to push everything aside with their shoulders. They literally made a path through the kitchen by pushing the refrigerator into the living room.

Two firemen slid the elderly man outside and examined him while two paramedics worked on his wife. The paramedics loaded her on a gurney and continued to work on her as they transported her, but she would never return to her home. She died at the hands of the three suspects who invaded her home and took her hostage.

Lieutenant Jack Adams hoped to intervene in this crime and stop anyone else from becoming a victim, but he was too late; he was helpless. Helpless as he watched the paramedics trying to revive the elderly woman who had lived most of her adult life in fear. Adams had seen death many times, and when he looked at the woman's face, he knew she would not be revived.

The three suspects had used a cord from the mini blinds to tie the hands and feet of the two people who lived there. The elderly couple, in their eighties, had cried in fear and begged to be released. They believed they were to be killed. Living in the projects of Los Angeles, they had always lived in fear, but this was occurring inside their home, where they were supposed to be safe from all that transpired on the other side of their front door.

Their small home was cramped. The couple rarely left or opened the door, and their car had been stolen long ago. They had accepted welfare many years ago and now were dependent on it. It wasn't the life they had planned on nor the life they wanted, but they were trapped. And now, everything was worse.

The semiautomatic rifle was found in the hallway closet secreted under a pile of musty clothes. Cockroaches had taken the closet over long ago, and they scampered in all directions when the door was opened. The Remington .308 caliber rifle with a removable magazine was dusty and dry, but it had fired the round used to shoot the officer.

Outside, next to the LAFD rescue ambulance, the elderly man dropped to his knees and cried. It was darker now and the scene was largely lit by flashlights. The firemen attending him tried to console him, but his pain and his sorrow was overwhelming. As Adams knelt next to him and looked into his eyes, Adams knew there was no path to easing his pain. All the man could say was, "My Anita's never coming home."

Just before the man was transported to the hospital where he could be cared for, Adams placed his hand on the man's shoulder and squeezed, trying to take some of his pain. Occasionally, the shadows allowed for some measure of mercy on the streets of Los Angeles. Adams hoped this would be one of those occasions.

The suspects were eleven, fifteen, and sixteen years old. Bounty Hunter Bloods. Gang members. The scene had been intense but did not garner a lot of media attention, as members of the press didn't usually venture into the projects. They got their information from the LAPD media relations staff. There were enough sensationalized violent crimes in Los Angeles, and they could at least avoid putting themselves in danger by not driving into the projects.

CHAPTER FOUR
THE AFTERMATH

The collision between Commander Stans Jelenick and Lieutenant Jack Adams was harsh. It didn't bother Adams much, but Commander Jelenick was furious. After the scene calmed down and the three juvenile criminals were in the back seat of police cars, the full investigation began. Yellow tape went up, and Nickerson Gardens got even hotter.

Bottles were being thrown and broken on the streets. People were seen running in various directions and whistles were heard everywhere. The crowds grew very large at the boundary of the yellow tape; people were loud and vocal, spewing threatening comments and gestures. When two gunshots were heard from the northwest corner of the projects, Adams ordered the sergeants on scene to maintain a strong perimeter to protect the crime scene and provide a strong presence to discourage violence or rioting.

Lieutenant Adams was used to these situations. He stood sentry over the scene and kept control of the big picture. Commander Jelenick, however, saw the situation differently, as being out of control and explosive. At the sound of gunfire, Jelenick burst out, "Request help, Lieutenant, we need more officers! Request fifty officers and five sergeants, Lieutenant."

"We're fine, Commander. We have all of the resources we need."

Jelenick lingered in the background to distance himself from the events that had occurred. He began developing a new plan to divert the responsibility for the entire event, including the woman's death, to Adams. He just needed to convince Deputy Chief Nelson that this was on Adams's shoulders.

Jelenick purposely spoke while other officers were in earshot. "Lieutenant, you and these officers disobeyed my orders, and we can't have that. You're a lieutenant, and I'm sure you realize how important discipline and order is, how important it is for people to follow orders. The result of you disobeying me is the death of that woman." Laying the groundwork to transfer blame to Adams, Jelenick began to feel more confident. He was good at this.

Adams thought about that and knew he shouldn't say one word. Yeah, that didn't work out for him. "Commander, I don't know you. But these policemen that you see here, they're the most courageous people you'll ever know. The Los Angeles Police Department is built on these officers, what they believe, and what they sacrifice. We did the right thing and rescued those people. We caught the bad guys, and they're going to jail. We took that rifle off the street."

"Bad guys? Are you kidding, Lieutenant? They're children—little kids. They don't even know they did anything wrong!" Jelenick appeared animated, a drama queen. "We don't even know if they're the ones who actually shot the officer! And I'm sorry that lady died, but those children didn't know that was going to happen. They didn't intend to kill her; it was an accident, Lieutenant. Don't you get it? They just tied her up—they were scared. You overreacted and ignored my orders, and this is on you. You were insubordinate, and I'm going to recommend you be fired."

Adams turned his back to Jelenick and answered the call from Deputy Chief Nelson. "Jack, I want you to prepare yourself for bad news. Officer Miller was just pronounced dead. They did everything they could, Jack. He just didn't make it."

Adams slid his phone into his pocket. The hectic scene suddenly softened, and all was quiet. The shadows surrounded him as time slowed. Adams felt that the summer air entering his lungs had cooled a little, but he felt tired. His slow deep breaths seemed to draw the shadows more tightly around him, protecting him. He had met Officer Tim Miller's wife and three children, and he thought about them now. Somehow, the families of police officers were always lost in the mix, always discounted. No one ever seemed to think of them when a police officer was injured or killed.

Slowly, Commander Jelenick's voice began to filter through the darkness. "Adams, don't you dare turn your back on me!"

Commander Jelenick just wanted to get away from the scene and distance himself from any responsibility. So much was happening, and he didn't know how to control any of it. He needed to get to his car and leave before anything else happened, head for his office and leave Lieutenant Adams holding the bag.

"As soon as you're done here, Lieutenant, you report to my office." Jelenick was speaking louder now for the benefit of his audience. With that one sentence, he had successfully transferred responsibility for the events to Lieutenant Jack Adams and was now merely a reviewer of the facts. He would not be held responsible for the decisions that were made, and he would be able to sacrifice Adams to save his own image and his place in the police department. He would use this event to his advantage in his promotional interview for deputy chief. Yes, he was sure he could use this to make himself look good.

With a quick turn, he successfully had the last word and was in his car and driving away while thinking about what he was going to do when he got back to his office. How he was going to relieve Lieutenant Jack Adams from duty for insubordination, for refusing to follow his orders. He was a commander, soon to be a deputy chief, and when Lieutenant Adams arrived at his office and sat down in front of his desk, he would impose discipline.

During all of his planning to ruin Lieutenant Adams, Commander Jelenick never gave a thought to visiting the officer who had been shot by the sniper, to consoling his family. He was lost in his thoughts as he drove along 114th Street, making two quick turns on his way to the Harbor Freeway. Not knowing where he was, he found himself transitioning onto Zamora Avenue and suddenly felt lost in the maze of the projects.

The projects were exploding with gunshots and bottles breaking as a result of the arrest of the three juveniles, gang members on their home turf. Jelenick was trying to stay calm just as two bottles smashed against the back window of his car and he heard the shouts of "Bounty Hunters!" Panic welled up inside him as he accelerated along Zamora Avenue, his heart pounding out of his chest. He reached for the radio to broadcast a call for help but then realized he didn't even know what street he was on. He needed help—he was being attacked, but he didn't know where he was.

A large group of men appeared in the intersection right in front of him, and a car blocking the intersection had been set on fire. Jelenick hit the brakes and put his car in reverse, but the street was filling with people behind him—there was nowhere else to go. The men began yelling at him and throwing gang signs as he drove forward into the intersection. One young boy threw a beer bottle that broke on the roof of the police car and Jelenick feared it was a Molotov cocktail, that his car would be set aflame.

He jerked the steering wheel and turned left onto 112th Street, accelerating harshly past 112th Street Elementary School. He watched his windows and mirrors for fire and smoke coming from his car, then he saw a traffic signal, an escape from the projects. He raced toward it and turned right against a red light onto Central Avenue, cutting off another car and barely avoiding a collision. Jelenick accelerated northbound toward safety, to his office in downtown Los Angeles.

Back in familiar territory, he parked in his assigned parking space and held on to the handrail as he rode the elevator to his office. It was after hours, and the nine-to-five crew had all gone home. Jelenick paced back and forth in his office anxiously. It took thirty minutes before he calmed down. *This is all Adams's fault.* Jelenick knew he had to practice his story for Deputy Chief Nelson and be sure that he didn't look weak or not in control. He actually *was* in control, but the problem was that nobody would listen to him. The safe decision would have been to surround the suspects and wait for more help. Deputy Chief Nelson may even have come; the press would have come.

SWAT would have taken over. There would have been more people there to make decisions.

Jelenick was sure that Deputy Chief Nelson would agree with him that Adams had to be fired. Jelenick would redirect responsibility for the entire event to Adams by displaying his own exceptional management skills. *This may actually help me get promoted*, he thought. He was sure of it now.

But as Commander Jelenick played the story out in his head and strengthened his intent to impart strong and swift discipline as a commander should, the story took on a life of its own as it spread through the department like wildfire. But it wasn't the story Jelenick had expected.

The story depicted him as a coward who had attempted to stop a police investigation in Nickerson Gardens that led to the arrest of three gangbanger cop killers and the recovery of the weapon after the murder of one elderly hostage and the rescue of another who had both been tied up inside their home.

And Lieutenant Adams? Why, he came off as a hero to the troops. The lieutenant who had stood up to a commander to capture the gangbangers that shot a Los Angeles police officer, one of their own. The lieutenant who had directed the rescue of an elderly couple being held hostage at gunpoint in their own home.

On another day it may have appeared differently, but on this day Commander Jelenick had been painted a coward. On day three of his assignment as a commander in Detective Bureau, that wrench he had always worried about was finally thrown straight into the system, and Jelenick's goal of becoming a deputy chief took a big hit.

Commander Stans Jelenick had moved through the ranks of the Los Angeles Police Department without much notice. A stout Roman Catholic, he maintained strong connections to the leaders of the Catholic Church in Los Angeles, believing it would be good for his career with the LAPD and his standing in the Czechoslovakian, or "Czech," community.

His wife, Elana, an aspiring artist, had spent her entire adult life chasing her own goal of making it big as a painter in the Czech art community. The Jelenicks lived above their means in a small but trendy home near Fairfax and Pico Boulevard so that Elana could maintain access to the Arts District. In fact, the couple spent most of their free time in the social circles and events of the wealthy Czech arts communities.

Within the LAPD, Jelenick was used to being out of sight and out of mind. He had learned early on the closely guarded secret of those promoted to the upper echelon of the LAPD: that it wasn't necessary for him to excel or achieve any appreciable success to rise through the ranks. He had only to stay in administrative positions and, most importantly, stay out of trouble. To be one of the insiders, it was best to be invisible.

It had worked well for Jelenick thus far. He was content not making waves while in administrative positions, sitting at a desk and quietly getting promoted to keep up with his wife's upwardly mobile desires with his ultimate sights set on deputy chief.

Although many in the command staff dreamed of sitting in the chair of the chief of police, Jelenick wasn't interested in gaining that much personal responsibility; he simply wanted one of the number two spots and to stay out of the limelight. Deputy chief or assistant chief would suit him just fine.

Only three days after being assigned as a commander at Detective Bureau, Jelenick had made a big mistake and veered from his plan. He had ventured out of his comfortable office and encountered Lieutenant Jack Adams on the mean streets of South Central Los Angeles, where everything had gone sideways—at least in his mind.

The following morning, the conversations racing around the LAPD infiltrated the halls of management. Every member of the command staff was concerned, but the issues presented weighed most heavily on the shoulders of Deputy Chief Steve Nelson. Chief of Police Fuller was waiting to be briefed on Nelson's handling of the event.

After listening to Commander Jelenick's account of the evening, Deputy Chief Nelson had an uncomfortable conversation with Lieutenant Adams to gain a more thorough perspective. Nelson was in a tough position.

Behind that massive wooden door, the verbal discipline Adams received from Chief Nelson was clear. Right or wrong, misunderstanding or not, department management would take notice of Adams's refusal to follow the commander's orders. That cloud that Adams oftentimes worked under had just become darker. Adams knew he walked a fine line sometimes by treading on the egos of some in command positions, but on this day, the pendulum had swung in Adams's direction. He knew he would be lucky to keep his job.

Not one person in a command position would support Adams, because they all knew the second secret never spoken out loud: if no one follows you, you're not a leader. They all feared the day that someone would tell them "no."

After reviewing the event and being fed the conversations buzzing throughout the department, Deputy Chief Steve Nelson and Chief of Police George Fuller came to an uncomfortable conclusion.

When Jelenick was summoned to the deputy chief's office, Jelenick knew that Adams would be suspended pending a disciplinary investigation and hearing. As is usually the case with command staff, he would be supported as having imparted wise and patient guidance in his oversight of the tactical event that had been endangered by a reckless Lieutenant.

Commander Jelenick grabbed his cup of coffee and walked down the hallway to Nelson's office. He sat confidently in the chair in front of Nelson's desk, his legs crossed, as if they were the best of old friends. "Chief, I'm sorry we have to deal with this issue. It's uncomfortable, but in the end, Lieutenant Adams will learn from it and we will send a strong message."

In a most unexpected way, and one that took unusual courage, Deputy Chief Nelson kindly and patiently looked across the desk and benched him. "Stans, Chief Fuller and I have discussed this at great length. We've decided, for the good of the LAPD, that we will play this off as a misunderstanding that happened during the turmoil of a tactical operation. Sometimes in the heat of things, communications are not always clear."

Commander Jelenick sat in stunned silence. What no one else understood was that behind the scenes, Deputy Chief Nelson had already been concerned about his new commander before this event happened and had multiple conversations with the chief of police about the situation. Nelson was privy to information that supported the concerns people had about Jelenick, and he was now resolute in his decision to bench him. He personally supported the actions that Adams had taken by taking leadership of the shooting scene in Nickerson Gardens and was shocked at Commander Jelenick's interference—a fact that he was not at liberty to reveal to Adams.

Deputy Chief Nelson had soon realized that Jelenick did not have the command maturity to take on much responsibility in Detective Bureau, comprised of the most senior and most highly experienced LAPD officers who were certainly the hardest types of officers to supervise. These were strong, independent leaders who knew how to do their jobs and did not appreciate being micromanaged. In fact, that's how they came to be selected for these positions.

Deputy Chief Nelson had taken on supervision of these units while the commander's position was vacant and found he really enjoyed doing so. It took him away from the mundane of sitting at a desk with administrative work and allowed him to be involved in police work again. The answer to this particular problem, then, was obvious.

Nelson removed Commander Jelenick from supervising the field units and assigned him to oversee COMPSTAT, computer statistics, the LAPD's data-driven effort to identify crime trends in the city. Statistics—a tool to make the department more efficient, at least on paper. COMPSTAT was known as a dead end, a place to send those with questionable leadership skills. The perfect place to hide them.

"Stans, with you coming into Detective Bureau, my plan was always to give you COMPSTAT, as I've already taken on overseeing field operations while the commander position was vacant. I have to tell you, I enjoy working with the field guys again, and I didn't relish giving it up. COMPSTAT is a very important but very intricate and time-consuming assignment, which I'm finding that I don't have the necessary skills or time for. I think it's best that we stick with that plan and sidestep the turmoil that has occurred."

Jelenick was devastated. As he got wind of the stories circulating through the police department, he knew he had made an enormous mistake. He had stepped outside of his office and gotten involved in a field tactical event, something he never should have done. After all, Stans Jelenick's plan to get promoted to the top of the Los Angeles Police Department had nothing to do with police work. He had violated his plan of quietly moving up the ladder, invisible. Now, his anonymity was at stake. Now people were looking at him and speaking his name. That wasn't good.

Jelenick returned to his office and closed the door behind him, yelling, "Goddamn it!" He blamed Adams and quietly committed to ruining him while bolstering his own career. The two powerful forces had collided, and Adams had a new enemy on the horizon. Jelenick had come too far; he needed to get back in the game. He would be a deputy chief on the Los Angeles Police Department yet, and he swore to get Adams back under control, as he thought the lieutenant was running amok. Actually, there was a little truth in that. Maybe a lot.

Even though the situation was quietly quashed behind closed doors, Commander Jelenick knew this was something everyone in the command staff took notice of. He knew he had to break out of this mold to rise to the next big step. He had to reassert himself as being in charge of special units such as Gangs and Narcotics, and he had to find a way to get there quickly. He had to get out from under COMPSTAT and the reputation it held.

Before the day even ended, Jelenick began strategizing to fight his poor misfortune. He would have to work around Deputy Chief Nelson, maybe even throw him under the bus also. *Collateral damage.* Maybe Nelson and Lieutenant Adams were conspiring against him. He thought he could possibly sell that. Someday, Nelson would be working for him.

Lieutenant Adams, on the other hand, went back to his assignment working directly for Deputy Chief Nelson. Adams was driven, a results-oriented man who believed that the way you got to the end result was important and that he should take the most correct path. Not the perfect path—maybe not even the right path—but the most correct one, which was one of the reasons Adams had become a man who was hard to like. Adams had learned in his life that the correct path oftentimes took him through the shadows, and it was rarely ever a straight road.

CHAPTER FIVE
MONSTERS ARE REAL

Lieutenant Jack Adams was in charge of all gang operations in Los Angeles. He was expected to stay on top of every gang, gang member, and gang crime at any given moment by the police department management and the politicians who tried to run the city, although poorly in Adams's opinion. Somehow, politicians had taken over the control of law enforcement, but the political pressure on his shoulders to stop gang crime was far less than the pressure he put there himself.

He wasn't proud of the events that had happened with Commander Jelenick. He knew a lot of people would be second-guessing him, just as he would be second-guessing himself. Time continued to pass and things had quieted down, but Adams still felt the pressure.

After a long shift, and now with the sun fully up, Adams looked forward to two badly needed days off. He loaded up in his dark-blue Ford Crown Vic that was really good at operating on autopilot. After pointing the car southbound and somehow finding his way back home, everything was right in the world again.

A hot shower and a couple hours of sleep were all he needed at home before he went to spend some time at the ballpark. There were two midmorning games, the first one between the Mustangs and the Dodgers, the second one an ongoing rivalry between the Pink Panthers and the Red Hots.

Between the cheers of the parents, Adams felt his phone vibrating in his pocket. "Hi, Lieutenant, it's Maggie. Hope I'm not disturbing you."

"Hi, Maggie. I've got my soda and sunflower seeds and I'm watching my son's ball game. My daughter's game starts in just a bit. Why are you working on Saturday? What's up?"

"Just catching up, sir, and getting all this paperwork done. I see in your inbox that some consulate person called about El Salvador. Do you know anything about going to El Salvador to talk to the government there about gangs?"

"Yeah, I heard they were requesting me through the chief's office, but I haven't heard any more about it. They approached me after I talked at the International Conference on Gangs two months ago. I think the chief of police nixed it, though. It's a little far from my beat."

"Well, someone from their Los Angeles Consulate is asking to meet with you to set up travel arrangements."

"Okay, Maggie. I didn't even know they had a consulate here. Let's put that on hold. I'll check with Deputy Chief Nelson and see where the department is on this. I'm thinking they can come here and we can talk just as easy. As dangerous as it is in Los Angeles, I think it's even worse in El Salvador. I'm better off staying here 'cause at least I can carry a gun. While I have you on the phone, we have a training day set up with Metro Division for the third of next month on building entries—can you check on that for me? After that, call out to Colonel Graves at Camp Pendleton and see if we've firmed up a date for joint training with them. It's a three-day session on the base. I was hoping to connect it with some days off so I can hang out in San Diego, in North County."

"Hey, Lieutenant? Before I go, I'm glad you're with your kids. I worry about you working too much."

That night, the family enjoyed a rare Saturday night with no callouts from the LAPD. One single call interrupted their movie, but a gang shooting with no deaths didn't require Adams to go to work. He needed time at home with his family, and he needed sleep tonight. Sometimes sleep becomes so precious that every minute counts as a blessing.

The following day went by slowly and quietly. Adams was in a somber mood and worked diligently to count his blessings as he considered the fate of Officer Tim Miller's family while helping his son and daughter with their school projects, enjoying hot chocolate together with dinner, and reading their favorite books into the evening hours.

Adams was off to sleep early, and as precious as sleep was for him, he was used to his son or daughter waking him up. Sometimes he slept so heavily that he didn't hear his phone ringing in the middle of the night.

"Dad, drive-by. A sergeant on the phone says to wake you up."

Jumping in the shower just to wake up, Adams felt fatigued and knew he was going to be dragging tonight. He had really hoped for one more full night of sleep. It was always so hard to pull away from his family and head back to Los Angeles—two very different worlds. Pulling out of his driveway in Rossmoor in the middle of the night, with his son and daughter on the porch wrapped in a blanket as they waved goodbye, was tough. When they couldn't see his car anymore, both kids climbed into their dad's bed and were asleep before Adams crossed that very ominous city line into Los Angeles.

Lieutenant Adams pulled into the shooting scene at 36th Street and Denker Avenue and found the parking lot was closed off by police cars blocking the driveways. Southwest Division Gang Sergeant Ralph McDonough met Adams at the curb outside the yellow tape.

"Hey, Lieutenant, hope we didn't get you up from your beauty sleep; God knows you need it. We've only got one body down, a little gangster from the 43rd Street Hoover Crips. Not sure what he's doing over here, but the obvious answer is probably that he came to stir shit up and got his own shit stirred up. Two bullet holes in his back, one in his foot. Wits reported hearing six or seven shots, so we're still looking for more victims. The body's over there in the parking lot between the senior center and the rec center, under those palm trees."

Evidence markers were spaced on the ground covering expended brass and a sheet covered a body. *Another body.* The LAFD paramedics had come and gone after finding the victim dead. Just then, the Los Angeles County Coroner's van pulled to the curb in front of Adams's car and started unloading their gear. Two Gang detectives inside the yellow tape waved to Adams and looked like they had been there for a while.

"Thanks, Ralph. I'm dragging a little tonight, so I'm just sightseeing. But if I can help with anything, please let me know."

Adams knew this scene would be processed fast and he wouldn't need to be present for very long. Nothing high profile or newsworthy, just another gang shooting. *Just the facts, ma'am.* For him, he'd get the big picture and then be back on the road headed home before the press arrived and the sun came up.

As Adams sat in his police car writing notes from the crime scene, he realized that if he got on the freeway now, he would still have some time to get some sleep before sunup—right up until the radio announced a second drive-by shooting at East 92nd Street and Grape Street. A shooting that, though he didn't know it yet, would change things.

In the hours just before daylight across from 92nd Street Elementary School in Watts, Lieutenant Jack Adams found himself standing next to the LAFD Station 65 fire truck just outside the perimeter of the crime scene on Grape Street. The fire paramedics had just finished washing his hands and arms, clearing them of blood, but the blood soaking through the front of his police uniform became more obvious as the sun rose over Los Angeles.

Something happened tonight. Something different. Lieutenant Jack Adams wasn't able to stop the child's murder from touching his heart. And it hurt. The shadows seemed to sense a weakness as they floated around him, engulfing him, capturing him. Adams tried to step through and free himself, but the shadows were too strong. They held him in place.

"You've got to let it go, Lieutenant Adams." LAPD Gang officer Karen

Aoki tended to look after the rest of the officers, even the lieutenant.

"She was only three, Karen, and I don't even know her name. I was holding her when she died and I don't even know her name. Damn . . ."

"These gangbangers raise their kids to be losers, Lieutenant. That little girl never had a chance, sir. If it wasn't today, it would have been another day. They're monsters, Lieutenant, every single one of them."

"Yeah, well, monsters are real, Karen."

"That's my point, Lieutenant, we know that. We live in this life, and we know they're monsters because we see how they live and what they do every single day. But no one else seems to know it. What the hell, Lieutenant?"

Officer Karen Aoki was used to the violence and to the victims in Los Angeles. *So many victims.* Today she was shaken, but not by the violence; the fatigue she saw on the lieutenant's face unsettled her. He was stability, he was their support. Today, something was different, though she wasn't sure what it was.

"You have the baby's blood all over your shirt, sir. You need to go to the station and get cleaned up. Take one of those marathon showers I hear you like."

"It doesn't really come off, Karen. You would think it would, but uh, it just doesn't."

Aoki continued to sense that something in their world had just changed. She looked at Lieutenant Adams. He seemed different. "I know this hurts, Lieutenant, I know you. Keep things right in your mind's eye, sir. Just like you always tell us. In your mind's eye."

Confident his Gang detectives had the crime scene in hand now, Lieutenant Adams began to think about sleep again. His body craved it, and his mind needed to shut down. Not someone to move very quickly unless he had to, Adams began an unusually slow walk to his police car. *Time to go home.*

Out of the corner of his eye, Adams saw the large blur rapidly approaching him that could only be the press. He was surprised it had taken them so long to get here today.

"Excuse me, Lieutenant. Candace Morgan. Do you care to comment on how the lack of effective gun legislation is killing our children? We were told a baby was murdered here last night by illegally possessed guns. Do you support legislation that could remove those guns from our streets, Lieutenant?"

Candace Morgan held a microphone out in front of her while her cameraman stood slightly to the side, filming.

Adams looked at the large crowd that had gathered at the yellow tape even at this hour. He was amused how they became more animated when the press arrived. The group of young men had pushed their way to the front of the crowd against the yellow tape and stood there flashing the *G* and *W* hand signs for the cameras.

"The sun is barely coming up, Miss Morgan. Why are you up so early? Don't you have a personal life?"

"It's my job, Lieutenant Adams, and this is my beat. Our audience want to know what the effects are of inadequate and ineffective gun legislation. Something has to be done to stop these shootings. Would you be willing to become involved in developing legislation to remove guns from the streets of Los Angeles, Lieutenant? You would be the perfect person to work with our staff and help to influence legislators by the power of the press and to finally enact strong gun legislation to take these guns away. To save the lives of our children! Isn't that what everyone wants?"

Candace Morgan was an up-and-coming reporter in Los Angeles. She was hungry to expand her role to be the new face on the nightly news, and she dressed the part. Although, in the firm-fitting blue dress and black heels, Adams thought she looked cold this morning. Morgan was getting a small spot every now and then, but her goal was to be in front of the camera every night. She was pretty sure that no one read newspapers anymore, and she had an ace in the hole . . . she had a deal.

"You need to get a real job, Miss Morgan. And the first thing you should be reporting about is why we don't prosecute the gun crimes that are already on the books."

Approaching like a middle linebacker, Commander Stans Jelenick was obviously upset and angry. "Lieutenant Adams, that is not an appropriate response to members of our press! A moment, please."

The rest of the police department wasn't privy to Commander Jelenick being benched by Deputy Chief Nelson yet. When the shooting occurred, the 77th Division Watch Commander looked at his notification list and began making phone calls one by one. When Jelenick got the call, he decided to respond and play dumb if Chief Nelson asked him about it. He needed to stay in the game, despite Chief Nelson.

Jelenick walked quickly toward a parked car with no tires on it in front of the homicide location. He turned to face Adams, who hadn't caught up yet, obviously on purpose. "Lieutenant, it's a good thing I came in tonight. You continue to alienate the press, and I'm not covering for you. I'm giving you a direct order, Lieutenant. You go back to that reporter, apologize, and give her a full accounting of this scene."

This was the second time in two days that Commander Jelenick had inserted himself into a field event led by Lieutenant Adams. Although the first time didn't turn out well—an understatement, considering he had been reassigned to COMPSTAT—he had to keep trying. He had to get back in the game; he would be more careful this time and make it work for him instead of against him. Adams wouldn't dare resist a second time.

With his hands in his pockets, a well-known trait of Adams, he spoke slowly and looked to the sky when he responded as if he were trying to find some elusive thought. "Yeah, well, we're not doing that, Commander. I don't work for you." And just that easily, Lieutenant Jack Adams stepped on the toes of a Los Angeles Police commander for the second time, calm as you please.

Adams looked utterly fatigued from his shift. The child's blood on his arms and hands had been cleaned off by the first responding Los Angeles City Fire rescue personnel after they gently removed the child held against Adams's chest where she had died. Adams couldn't quite seem to put her down, but the fire personnel on scene gradually slid her away to provide care and pronounce her dead.

"Are you refusing to follow my orders, Lieutenant?"

Although Commander Jelenick was visibly angry, Adams seemed to ignore the commander's reaction. Looking around the crime scene at the people and the events taking place, he squinted as the sun began to burn his eyes. This was the hard part of morning, and he had hoped to be back home before the sun came up.

"Glad you got a good night's sleep, Commander. All showered up, your suit looks great. All these officers you see have been out here all night, but I'm hoping they'll get a little sleep, too, before they turn around and come right back to work tonight. Some of them have court this morning, though, over at 210 Temple, but they might get a little sleep in the officer's waiting room. By the way, that car you're leaning on is somebody's playhouse."

The abandoned and stripped car had no tires and had been a fixture of the neighborhood for over four years, a literal playhouse for the children living there. It was covered in gang graffiti and all the windows had been broken out long ago. Los Angeles services for picking up trash and abandoned cars left a lot to be desired. Another broken system.

Jelenick grew more furious as each second passed. His breathing was faster and his speech became louder. His face twisted into a scowl as he barked at Adams. "Are you listening to me, Lieutenant? Apologize to that reporter and give her a full accounting of this incident."

Candace Morgan, only ten yards away, overheard pieces of the conversation, excited at the prospect of the commander forcing Adams to give an interview. This may have been the break she needed. Her ace in the hole, her deal, relied on it. She had to get Adams, and she edged closer to the conversation.

Taking a long, deep breath as he looked up into the sky, as if sending a challenge to the sun that was now burning his eyes, Adams slowly turned to face Jelenick. Adams didn't appear tired any longer. He seemed to grow taller and his shoulders widened.

"We have an active crime scene, Commander, with one gang-on-gang murder and multiple attempted murders. There are outstanding suspects and guns, and we're currently following up on the evidence and witness statements to identify, locate, and arrest those suspects. A three-year-old child was killed tonight, and she's on her way to the coroner's office to lie on a stainless steel table in a plastic bag. A child, Commander. A baby. The monsters who killed her are driving around our city celebrating their kill. Anything that we would reveal to the press at this point would jeopardize this investigation and most probably endanger the gang officers and detectives working this case."

"Lieutenant, are you refusing to follow my order?" Jelenick's face was red, and he spat as he talked. He had an irritating habit of moving his feet when he was upset like he was walking in place.

Speaking calmly and softly in his slow manner, Adams responded, "No, Commander, of course not. I'm just helping you not to make an enormous mistake that would derail your career ambitions."

"Lieutenant, who's in charge of this scene? You or me?"

The commander finally figured out how to push Adams's buttons. That question sparked something within him. His response was loud and, unfortunately, overheard by Candace Morgan.

"Regardless of who's in charge, Commander, *I'm* responsible! Responsible that our streets are not safe for a child to be outside, even with her asshole father, and I'm responsible for the lies that our politicians tell everyone. I'm responsible to be here, at this place and at this moment, to clean up all of their lies and failures. I'm responsible, Commander, for the crime that occurred here and for intervening in the series of payback crimes that are bound to happen now while these assholes continue to shoot each other. I'm responsible for that yellow tape you see and for all the citizens on the other side of that tape living in fear. I'm responsible for the investigation of this murder and for successfully prosecuting the criminals that did it. Responsible for the cries of racism because I'm a different race than the suspects who killed that child. And yes, Commander, I'm responsible for what we give to the press and the way they spin it, for the lies and misrepresentations that they'll give to the public regardless of what I tell them."

Adams stepped closer, face-to-face, close enough to make Commander Jelenick very uncomfortable. "But if you'd like to take over, sir, I'll head home and take a shower and get some sleep. I'd love to see my family. You're a commander for the LAPD, and I'm sure you'll do a great job with this crime scene and the criminal investigation and the prosecution. I'm also sure you'll do a much better job than I did in making the press release with Miss Morgan over there. Just nod your head and I'm gone."

Jelenick felt like a bomb ready to explode, and his wrath was about to get the best of him when the conversation was suddenly interrupted.

"Excuse me, Lieutenant, something has come up. Can I talk to you for just a moment? It's an emergency, sir." Officer Aoki walked with Adams back to the yellow tape at the crime scene perimeter.

"Lieutenant, all our Gang guys have been here all night. The Day Watch patrol units from 77th Division are coming on duty now and filling in on the perimeter so Morning Watch can go home. Should I ask Day Watch to get coffee for everyone?"

"That's the emergency, Karen?"

"Yes, sir. I was sure you'd want to address this emergency coffee issue immediately. Before the commander's head blew up."

"Get back to work, Aoki."

"Yes, Lieutenant."

As Commander Jelenick walked away from the scene and passed Adams, the look on his face was pure fury. "Lieutenant Adams, Chief Nelson and I will have a chat about your actions here today! Be prepared for a discussion with both Chief Nelson and myself. I can't guarantee you'll have a job after our discussion."

"Yes, Commander." Adams just couldn't find it inside himself to care about the commander's issues anymore.

Turning to the cameraman, Candace Morgan asked, "Tell me you got that. Wow."

The cameraman was filming the young men throwing gang signs. He looked up from the camera with an apologetic look on his face.

"Damn it! We had him, damn it! Pay attention." Morgan watched Adams get into his Ford Crown Vic and drive away, feeling as though her leverage over Adams had just driven away with him. She had to find a way to persuade Adams to cooperate with her, and they had just missed their first big chance.

The investigation into the drive-by shooting on Grape Street continued through the day. The victim's father, a second-generation gang member from Grape Street Crips, had been holding the child when the shooting started, but he walked away without a scratch. His three-year-old daughter had shielded him and taken a bullet, saving his life but giving hers. The child's mother was in the LA County jail doing a short stint for drug driving.

Gang Homicide detectives were used to the long hours and the string of bodies that fell on the streets of Los Angeles each day. Even children being subjected to violence by their gang-involved parents wasn't enough to faze them after a while. But thoughts and feelings ignored or unspoken are not invisible.

The transfer of the three-year-old child's body was heavily photographed by the press. But even at the Los Angeles County coroner's office, a young child shot in the chest had an unraveling effect on everyone's sense of well-being.

Following the shooting, witnesses were scarce or unwilling to become involved. The car full of shooters seemed to vanish into the night. The streets of Los Angeles have a way of swallowing people up and hiding them.

CHAPTER SIX
THE SHADOWS CAN FOLLOW YOU HOME

Adams headed southbound on the Harbor Freeway with the Los Angeles shadows following right on his bumper. He sped up but still couldn't shake them. This was new, as typically Adams worked diligently to leave them behind in Los Angeles when he returned home. As he pulled his Ford Crown Victoria into his driveway in Orange County, the neighbors were pulling out of their garages before heading toward work and school. It seemed he was in a perpetual pattern of returning home when everyone else was leaving. Even though they were ignorant of the carnage that had occurred not too far away in Watts, they would get the spin on the events from the nightly news. The spin that a child's death had been caused by weak gun laws and that the police were refusing to talk to the press, obviously hiding something.

Adams thought he'd have time to get cleaned up and make breakfast for his son and daughter, who were still dragging their feet about getting out of bed and getting dressed. Seeing those two still sleeping in his bed with the covers pulled up over their shoulders was the exact medicine he needed on this very somber morning. Adams sensed that something had happened, something different. The shadows had followed him home today, something he never allowed.

Taking deep breaths, he walked into his bathroom and took off his leather gear and equipment, placing his Kimber .45 caliber handgun into a small safe. Reaching inside his shirt, Adams retrieved his small backup Kimber .45 from the pocket sewn into his bulletproof vest and placed it in the safe as well.

His boots came next, and then he sat for a moment while the shower warmed up. Water service near the beach was always questionable. Luckily, his home was just over the border into Orange County, where he escaped the political failures in Los Angeles, so waiting for hot water was a minimal concern.

As Adams began to unbutton his shirt, he noticed for the first time the sheer amount of the child's blood that had soaked through. He just couldn't seem to get it unbuttoned. His hands just weren't working right this morning, so after a moment he gave up on it.

Stepping into the shower and hoping to leave the shadows on the other side of the glass door, his uniform seemed to resist releasing the blood staining it. Lowering his head under the shower and leaning forward with his hands held up high on the wall to support him, he closed his eyes and took slow deep breaths.

Everyone has those particular things that soothe them, and hot water was Adams's way of escaping. The longer the water pounded him, the deeper the escape. He just wanted to sleep, to stop thinking, and he began to drift off. Adams didn't know how long he had submerged himself in the escape from all that tried to destroy him, and neither did he notice his daughter standing in the doorway. He never saw her retreat into the master bedroom or her display of inner strength as she pushed the speed dial.

"Grandpa, my daddy is hurt. He's bleeding!"

"Hi, angel. Where is your dad right now?"

"He's in the shower, Grandpa, he's bleeding! There's lots of blood, Grandpa, and I'm scared."

Time stood still as a father's nightmare visited all the dark places, the agonizing worry about a son in harm's way. Taking a deep breath and placing his hand on his wife's shoulder, the reply into the phone was very slow and measured. "Angel, is your dad lying down in the shower?"

"No, he's standing up, Grandpa. He has his police clothes on."

After a short pause, and after coming to the most probable conclusion, words were somehow found. "Okay, angel, don't be scared. I think your dad's okay, and you were very brave to call me. Do you think you could go knock on the shower and tell your dad that I'm on the phone and want to talk to him?"

"Okay, Grandpa."

Bolstering her courage and holding her head high, that brave young girl walked strongly into the bathroom and knocked on the shower door, set on her mission. "Dad, Dad! Grandpa's on the phone."

Fighting to wake up and return to reality, Adams forced his response to his daughter as calmly as he could. "Okay, sugar. I'm coming right now. Why don't you get your brother up and I'll cook some eggs benedict?"

Stripping his uniform off and leaving it behind in the shower, Adams decided he'd drop it off at the cleaners and let them deal with it. He thought about what he had told Officer Aoki about the blood never washing off. *Literally, it seems.*

Wrapping a towel around himself and moving to the phone, he started, "Hi, Dad, everything okay with you and Mom? It's pretty early for you to call."

"Yeah, we're fine, son. Just checking in. How are you doing?"

"Long night, sir. Little three-year-old girl shot in a drive-by up near Jordan

Downs projects. Her so-called father was holding her when she got shot, but he put her down so he could hide. She was breathing when I got to her, so I picked her up and carried her out, but she was gone before Fire arrived."

"Yeah, I'm so sorry to hear that, son. I'll watch for it on the Los Angeles news tonight. There's no answers for some of these things, I guess. There's just a lot of really bad people in this world, people with no conscience. But people like you, son, people like you can stand up to them. It takes your kind of courage. Listen, I won't keep you—just checking in. Take care of your family today. They need a little extra attention."

"Will do, Dad. Thanks for calling. It came at a really good time."

"Hey, Jack, call me anytime you want to talk about something. If something's bothering you, just give me a call."

"Will do, Dad. I have the whole day here, so while the kids are in school I'm going to work on the boat and sleep a little. I won't go back in to work until this evening. Enjoy those mountains; I'm really jealous. Be safe, sir."

"Be safe, son." As he hung up the phone, the look on his face told his wife she could relax. Today wasn't the day.

#

Monday morning had come quickly and Adams busied himself with caring for his family, making breakfast for the kids, getting them dressed and ready for school. The dressing part always seemed to take a while. Adams's son and daughter were both very independent, to say the least, and thus they each had their own style and their own ideas about how to dress for school.

In that other world in Downtown Los Angeles, the fireworks started early. As soon as Deputy Chief Nelson received his morning briefing of the events that occurred over the weekend, he excused his staff but Commander Jelenick remained in his chair.

"Stans, did you have something else?"

"Chief, I want his fucking ass gone! I bore the brunt of this last time and I'm not doing it again. I gave Adams another direct order, and he refused to follow it. Insubordination as clear as it gets. I want him gone."

"Stans, Lieutenant Adams had a baby die in his arms. How would that affect you?"

"I understand, Chief, but we've all had bad experiences. We're police officers; that's what we do. Adams was insubordinate in front of all those officers out there, in front of the press, and he left me looking terrible. We can't let this go—we have to take action. I'm going to write up a personnel complaint against him, Chief. We have to handle this the right way. We need it on paper."

Deputy Chief Steve Nelson, the head of Detective Bureau, sat behind his desk feeling the pressure, and it was mounting quickly. This was a no-win situation for him.

"Stans, you're right and you're wrong. I was clear with Adams that he answers directly to me and you put him in a bad spot by giving him an order. Even so, Adams should have followed your orders and made a press release, even if it was just fluff. But we've all been misquoted in the press and it's disheartening, especially for people like Adams who are out there every night and in the spotlight. Combine that with what he went through last night and we get a pretty cloudy situation. For something as small as not wanting to make a press release on an ongoing investigation—which, by the way, could have been jeopardized by a press release . . . well, I think we'll pass on that personnel complaint, Stans. But I'll keep an eye on this situation. By the way, why were you at the scene? We didn't talk about this, I guess, but you're not on the callout roster any longer. You have COMPSTAT now, Stans."

"Well, I had planned to come in early anyway to complete some things on my desk and when I got the call, I just thought I'd drop by and then go to my office. Once I heard about the incident I pulled in to see if I could lend a hand."

"I see. It's a pretty far stretch beyond the assignment I gave you with COMPSTAT, Stans, but I can overlook that also. Let's try to understand what Adams went through and give him a little understanding. Let's also think about the value, or damage, of press releases. The best that Adams could do would be to say, 'No comment.' But if it happens again, we'll look at it in more detail. Deal?"

Commander Jelenick knew he had no choice. He hated the answer he was about to give. "Sure, Chief, you're the boss. But Adams is out of control, and it's going to come back to bite us."

Jelenick walked out of Deputy Chief Nelson's office fuming. Regardless of what the deputy chief said, Adams was going to pay for this. Maybe even Nelson would pay for it. *That would open up another deputy chief spot.*

CHAPTER SEVEN
A BADGE OF BLOOD

Police Officer Mike Rand, the senior officer of Lieutenant Jack Adams's inner squad of six Gang officers, climbed the stairs to the helipad on the roof of LAPD 77th Street police station. He loathed these jobs, being messenger and interrupting Adams's rare few moments of quiet time.

Rand found the lieutenant standing alone on the roof looking out at the city as the summer sun set. It seemed like they just had watched it come up only a few minutes ago. "Hey, Lieutenant. Deputy Chief Nelson wants to see you at his office."

Lieutenant Jack Adams, without even turning around, responded, "Thanks, Rand. I just need a minute, pal."

Adams had been expecting the call to Chief Nelson's office. He was sure that Jelenick had been bad-mouthing him all day. As he looked across the city, Lieutenant Jack Adams reflected that the police officers he had worked with throughout his career were the heroes of our societies, and he was so proud to be one of them. But maybe his time was coming to an end. The Los Angeles Police Department was changing and all the changes seemed to be bad.

"You know, Mike, these policemen out here amaze me every single day." No one except another policeman can understand the sacrifices policemen make each day. Doing their best to make good decisions, doing their best to help others, and all while trying to stay alive. Every policeman wants to go home safe to their family at the end of each day, but surprisingly, no one seems to understand that. Adams knew the strength and greatness of the Los Angeles Police Department was in the hearts of those officers.

Rand, not wanting to push the lieutenant, knew he had to get him to the deputy chief's office immediately. "I know, LT, but Nelson said he needs you right now. You know how he gets—the guy never sleeps. What do you think he wants you for?"

"Think he wants to fire me, pal. I'm sure the commander has been trying all day to convince him to fire me."

"I hate that guy. He's a sleazebag. How did he get to Detective Bureau anyway? How did he even get promoted to commander? I'm gonna beat the shit out of that asshole." Rand was not someone you wanted to make mad.

Although Adams agreed, he couldn't let the comment pass. "Yeah, let's not talk about a commander like that, Mike. I'm sure he thinks he's doing his job; he just doesn't do it the way we think he should. He's a politician, a climber, and he sees things differently."

"I know you're trying to be professional, Lieutenant, but you don't have to play that with me. You and I know each other, and that son of a bitch needs his ass kicked."

Air 10, the LAPD PM Watch helicopter just coming on duty, flew overhead. It was headed southbound to a request in Southeast Division for a robbery at 103rd Street and Central Avenue. The sound of the rotors drowned out any more conversation, but from the rooftop Adams and Rand heard gunfire breaking out just east of the 77th Street police station.

"I just have to meet with 77th Gangs first and see where we are now with the drive-by from last night. Maybe the little girl's father will give us something. I'll head over to the chief's office right after that. Thanks, Mike."

As he walked down the stairs to talk with the Homicide detectives, Adams's mind drifted again to the three-year-old girl he had held in his arms last night and what her last breath was like. How she slowly closed her eyes and lowered her chin to his chest, as if she knew. Then she was gone.

Pausing on the steps of the stairs, Adams looked down at his chest where she had lain and noticed there was still blood in the crevices of his badge. Like he said, it just never seemed to wash off.

Stepping into the Homicide office, the room was in turmoil as the group of detectives argued. Adams pulled Detective Maddie Hill to the side. "Hey, Maddie. What's the argument about?"

"Just egos, sir. Detective Decker wanted to book the father for child endangerment, but Commander Jelenick was here and told him no. He said the father was sad enough that his daughter was killed and he shouldn't be arrested. Said the district attorney would never file on him, like the DA ever files on anybody! Clearly the guy is clueless. Now the whole office is arguing, and no one knows who works for whom. I've never even seen that commander before. Who the hell is that guy?"

Adams knew he had to fix this, but didn't know how to do it without stepping on a certain commander's toes. Again.

"Hey, everyone. I hear you have some controversies going on. Listen up: you Gang guys work for me, and I work for Chief Nelson. Someday we're going to get a captain, but until then, it's Chief Nelson. That's the chain of command. Me, then the chief, and we accommodate the captains of each division. That being said, whenever any other supervisor gives you directions, absent some emergency situation, I expect you to be polite and tell them you will be glad to do what they ask as soon as you run it past me so I know what you're doing. That takes the pressure off of you and maintains our chain of command. If I decide to not follow their orders, it's on my shoulders, not yours."

Adams was visibly angry at having to reinforce the importance of following the chain of command to experienced senior detectives. "I hear you received some directions from someone else today. Sometimes we have supervisors who display weak management skills at times or who rule by ego, and in violating the concept of chain of command will attempt to give you orders. As I said, be polite and tell them you're glad to do what they ask as soon as you run it past me. That takes courage on your part to respectfully stand up to whoever it is. But you're policemen, for God's sake, and if you don't have a little courage, you shouldn't be here. Everyone good?"

Detective Dave Decker spoke up. "Lieutenant, a Commander Jelenick reviewed my decision to file charges against the father for child endangerment and told me not to do it. I know he works in Detective Bureau, but I've never met him before."

"Thanks for telling me, Dave. That's exactly how this should work and I'll give you my answer: you're the senior detective on this case, and it's your call. If you have a case against the father, file it. Anyone have anything else?" Adams looked around the room and sensed a return to normalcy as the situation calmed. Everyone knew where they stood once more.

Policemen are a rare breed that usually balk at authority. They're strong-willed and don't like taking orders but will willingly follow strong leaders who deserve their loyalty. In police work, loyalty goes both ways. Just as policemen must be loyal to their leaders, leaders must be loyal to policemen.

#

Los Angeles covers five hundred square miles and has a population of over four million people. Overseeing gang details in twenty-one LAPD police stations, along with managing detectives and homicide investigators, task forces, and surveillance details, can weigh heavily on the shoulders of one man responsible for the whole package. A few minutes of quiet time is a rarity. Adams wished he could just have a minute to himself, but duty called. Or at least the deputy chief called.

Deputy Chief Steve Nelson was a nice enough man—very pleasant, actually. With so many connections to politicians and community members, he was also believed to be the next chief of police, a rank only the politically connected could hope to attain. Now that the Los Angeles City Charter was modified and the chief of police was appointed by the mayor, a political appointment, those skids needed to be greased early on.

The current chief of police, George Fuller, who had been selected less than a year ago, bent that rule. Fuller was known as a street officer and not a climber, not a politician. Even so, everyone in the police department believed that Fuller's appointment by the mayor, Gilliam "Gilly" Hernandez, was just a ploy to renew some semblance of positive morale in the LAPD. Everyone knew Mayor Hernandez didn't really care about police officers, but he did care about being able to stand in front of the cameras and tell his voting public that crime was down and Los Angeles was safe.

The other thing the mayor cared about was money, and he needed more of it, so that meant that he wanted police officers writing more tickets. Sounds petty on the surface, but those tickets brought in unbelievable sums to the city coffers and politicians always need money, as much as they can get. Spending other people's money was the primary pastime of politicians in Los Angeles. The political pressure that Hernandez put on the chief of police to write tickets, rolling downhill to police officers, had become stifling and officers were rebelling. Police officers were not stupid; they absolutely realized that tickets were all about money for the politicians. Anyone who thinks that police departments do not generate income for the cities is just naive.

With police morale down, arrests down, and ticket counts falling off, Mayor Hernandez was suffering on all counts. As much as the mayor and the prior chiefs of police tried to spin the numbers and convince everyone that crime was down in Los Angeles, no one bought what they were selling. Most people are not as stupid as politicians think they are.

Taking slow, deliberate steps, Lieutenant Adams headed for his meeting with Deputy Chief Nelson and the looming threat of being fired. He missed the old LAPD headquarters building at 1st and Los Angeles Street. Parker Center was dubbed the "Glass House" by street officers because of the windows that appeared to be glass walls. With Parker Center condemned, the new headquarters just blocks away at 100 West 1st Street seemed like a corporate office, very cold and sanitary. Mostly it had no history, no connection; it was just a modern-looking business office.

Much of the history and tradition of the Los Angeles Police Department was gradually being lost. The Los Angeles Police Academy in Elysian Park next to Dodger Stadium had been one of the venues for the 1932 Olympics. An incredible setting that had caused all who entered to walk under the arches that read "Los Angeles Police Academy" had been largely replaced by a corporate building purchased in West Los Angeles. An ugly large office building.

Housing the command staff and all of those officers who fled street police work for Monday-through-Friday desk jobs, Lieutenant Adams felt like a dinosaur walking through the glass doors of LAPD Headquarters.

Adams couldn't even remember the elevator ride to the tenth floor as he suddenly found himself standing in Chief Nelson's outer office. It seemed so normal to lose small blocks of time that Adams was sure it happened to everyone.

"Hey, Chief, Mike Rand said you were looking for me. Why are you here so late, sir? It's almost ten o'clock. I'm guessing Commander Jelenick persuaded you to fire me."

Deputy Chief Steve Nelson appeared incredibly organized at his overly large desk within his very impressive office. His adjutant, Lieutenant Kathy Moss, had merely waved Adams in as he entered the outer office. Adams was one of those few known persons allowed to enter the inner sanctuary of the LAPD.

Adams wondered why Moss was still at work too. She had a poor reputation in the department, known for being completely incompetent in the field and always looking to hide behind a desk. Her practice was to find one of the command staff to protect her while she tried to climb the ranks. Police officers call it "having a sponsor." Her brownnosing usually stopped at 1700 hours, 5 o'clock p.m.

"Hey, Jack. I'm always here, you know that. Yeah, the commander brought some of his concerns to me. It's starting to be a pattern, Jack. I hope we won't have to have this discussion again." Deputy Chief Nelson appeared calm and easygoing most of the time, a trait Adams really appreciated about him.

"No, sir, I'm sure we won't."

"Good. Now that's settled, I've got a new job for you. I know you're busy, but Mayor Hernandez is putting a lot of pressure on us through Chief Fuller to start some kind of gun confiscation effort to show we're serious about reducing shootings. The anti-gun lobby pretty much camps out in the mayor's office, and he buys them lunch almost every day. He knows they have the press in their pocket and unlimited money to give to politicians, which means he has to buddy up to them. Anything for votes, anything for money."

Adams understood that politics, as usual, reigned supreme in Los Angeles, but he was surprised Chief Nelson felt comfortable remarking about it so candidly. What Adams didn't know was that this new assignment would change his life.

Nelson took a drink from his "LAPD Bench Press" coffee cup, then continued. "The mayor wants a press release with lots of guns on a table and lots of numbers to prance around, so Chief Fuller said the only way to have some kind of appreciable success would be to target gangsters. Think you can convince our local gangbangers to stop playing with guns and turn them in? How many of your gang officers can you redeploy to a dedicated effort to grab guns?"

"Chief, you know how I feel. Continuing to ask Gang officers to drive up and down the streets of Los Angeles and jack gangsters to see what they have in their pockets is not going to get what you want, nor what the mayor should want. We bring guns in every night, sir, but to get what the mayor wants, some kind of publicity stunt to get him more votes, we can actually use that to accomplish something bigger. We just need to work around him. I would suggest looking for a new way to get guns that we can actually tie to shootings and solve some homicides, not just the guns we find in their pockets every night."

"I'm fairly open with how we do this, Lieutenant, but we have to be results oriented, get guns on the table." Chief Nelson was always straightforward, which made him easy to work for.

"Chief, I have an idea about a new operation—an intelligence-based operation. We'd be using detectives and my surveillance assets instead of uniformed Gang officers. Something where we can have a real impact and not just be a publicity stunt for Gilly. Kill two birds with one badge."

Adams knew he was going to tread into sensitive waters now. "Here's the rub: if we run it the way I want, we would have to keep the details under wraps, especially from the mayor. I don't trust him not to leak information when it benefits him politically, and he's too close to these gang intervention nonprofits who keep milking the government for money. We have to keep everything away from those guys or they'll leak the details and put our officers in danger."

Adams asked Deputy Chief Nelson for a couple days to put something together. "How much money is available for this?" Adams asked.

After Nelson laughed, he replied, "Jack, you can't keep asking for more money. There's no line item on the LAPD budget labeled 'Lieutenant Jack Adams.' You have officers and overtime—make it happen. I'll set up a meeting between you, me, and Chief Fuller for Monday. I'll let you know what time, but plan for ten o'clock, ten hundred hours. Have your plan ready, and Jack . . . don't ask the chief for money."

Nelson's adjutant, Lieutenant Moss, interrupted and handed Adams a note. "One of your officers, that big guy Rand, is in the outer office and said to give you this. Guess you two were hanging out on the police station roof and heard gunshots over in 77th. He said the Rollin' 60s just shot a gangster from Big Hazard outside of a market at 77th and Main. He said you know what that means—it sounds colorful. Hey, isn't Rand kind of old for your units? I thought you wanted all young studs," Moss remarked.

"Mike Rand has paid his dues and works wherever he wants," Adams responded.

Moss suddenly stopped in her tracks. "He's the one who got shot about ten years ago. And didn't he get shot when he was really young on the job? What's he still doing out there? We can find a desk for him here."

"Real policemen don't work at desks, and Rand is a real policeman. When you pay your own dues on the streets of Los Angeles, you can question why a guy like Rand is out there."

Deputy Chief Nelson knew what was coming, so he interrupted the looming battle between Adams and Moss to bring the conversation back to the shooting.

"So, Lieutenant Adams. I haven't heard much about the Rollin' 60s in quite a while."

Adams advised Nelson that a race war between street gangs was rearing its ugly head again around Big Hazard, a Hispanic gang, with a history of assaulting Blacks. He offered that they may end up being the aggressor in this shooting with the Rollin' 60s, a Black Crips gang.

Nelson's calm demeanor quickly faded. "Jack, don't even say that! No one wants to hear that shit about brown on black! It just scares everyone and Gilly goes crazy. Play it off some other way." Nelson was visibly upset. This was clearly a sore spot in Los Angeles politics.

"You mean lie about it," Adams responded.

"No. Just play it off some other way. And stay away from the press about that." Clearly this was intended as a direct order.

"Not much worry about that," Adams commented. "Every time I talk to them, they print something else and I find myself in hot water. I don't talk to the criminal bastards."

"Jack, we need the press on our side even though they're never really on our side. It's a weird game. The police will never please the liberal press no matter what we do, but we don't want to make enemies, either. I guess what I'm saying is that even though you need to follow the rules, the rules aren't always clear. In the police department, we have a lot of competing interests, but we have to balance them. Trust me, Lieutenant, the higher you climb in this world, the less clear the rules become as to how we accomplish our jobs."

"It's not the rules I'm concerned with, Chief. It's getting the job done."

"That's my point, Jack. That's why you scare some people. You play the game differently. But listen to me when I tell you this: it puts you in a lot of jeopardy. Jack, I guess it's time we had this conversation."

"Don't you see it, Chief? We're all running scared of the press and of these liberal politicians! It's not right. We, more than anyone else, should do the right thing, and to hell with the politicians. We should be independent,

Chief—we're the police. We fight for the people, and many of them can't fight for themselves. We keep them safe from all the evil in the world. We used to be the heroes of society, but the press has convinced everyone that now we're bad guys. We should call it out for what it is."

Both men immediately realized that words had been spoken that weren't supposed to be uttered, not even in private. It was not allowed by the rules of the game.

With every word, Adams fell further down the well. "Police departments used to be independent, but we're slowly being pulled into all this craziness in politics. Now the mayor appoints the chief of police and turns him into his puppet. Thank God that Chief Fuller isn't going down easy! They don't want us to stop suspicious people anymore, so crime prevention is out the window. All we do is respond when someone calls us, which means the crime has already occurred and all we do is take a report. We're policemen, Chief. *Real* policemen. How do we stand in front of the public and tell them how important it is that they protect themselves because we're not allowed to do it anymore? How do we teach people to never be willing victims, sir? We believe it, we live it. But that comes with being policemen. How do we teach everyone else to fight back, to protect themselves and their families, protect their property, protect their neighbor?"

Deputy Chief Nelson wanted to interrupt, but he knew Adams needed to get this out. "They don't want us to arrest anyone who isn't white, like policing is an act of discrimination. Anytime we use violence to react to violence, we're immediately the bad guy. How many people do we have in Internal Affairs now? We spend more time and effort policing ourselves than we do policing the streets of Los Angeles! They change their name from Internal Affairs to Professional Standards and try to convince us that now they're our buddies."

Adams took a breath and considered stopping, but he just had to continue. He was on a roll to ruin his career, so why stop now? *I'm probably going to get fired today anyway.* Down the well he dropped, right to the bottom.

"Are there prosecutors who do absolutely nothing but investigate and prosecute police officers? How many ambulance-chasing attorneys are there that do nothing but sue policemen? They don't want criminals to go to jail anymore and the criminals that are in jail, they're letting out. And everyone's buying in to this nonsense! People are beginning to believe it. They put cameras on our chests and try to tell us it's to protect us. You and I know that's bullshit—it's to catch us. To second-guess us and use against us. A camera on our chest and a target on our back. Isn't anyone going to fight back?"

Chief Nelson's initial response was anger at the subordinate standing in front of him questioning his authority, questioning all authority. Worst of all, he was saying those things that couldn't be said. It just wasn't allowed.

Nelson wanted to lash out with the power of his position, a deputy chief of the Los Angeles Police Department, but suddenly he felt a heaviness tugging at his heart. He felt the pain that he knew all police officers carry with them. Those men and women who sacrifice absolutely everything to keep people safe only to be berated and attacked.

Then, Nelson felt his own pain, the pain of helplessness, and he hated it. The knowledge that a deputy chief of the Los Angeles Police Department, with all that power, could do nothing to change it. That train had already left the station. To protect his own job, he was relegated to sitting at his desk and not saying one word. He wasn't allowed to fight back, and this caused him to pause, take a few breaths, and lower his voice as he responded.

"Well, Lieutenant, things have changed over the years. But society changes, and we're not in charge. It doesn't mean we don't care, but we're not in charge. We all have bosses that we're expected to answer to. The problem is that we no longer answer to the public that you're talking about. Today, we answer to politicians and a very vocal activist section of society. The average people that you're talking about have lost their voice. They don't count anymore, Jack."

The anger continued to well up in Adams, and he wanted to strike out. *The system is broken. People are suffering. People are scared in their own homes. People are scared at work and at school. People are just scared.*

And Jack Adams? He had begun to feel the things that he'd always chosen not to feel. The shadows.

"Chief, the press never interviews the victims or all the neighbors who live in fear. They only ever interview the mother of the person we arrested. They never publish anything about how terrible the criminal is, only how terrible the police are for arresting them. I can't believe the public really wants this, sir. Not the real public. I understand the people who have the voice of the press behind them make everyone believe this nonsense, but I don't believe the public, as you call them, really wants this. Other police departments have given up; they just do nothing, and crime is skyrocketing.

"The real public—our families and neighbors, the people I talk to every single day—want people to obey the law and go to jail when they don't. That little girl who died on my chest last night wanted people to obey the law, Chief. She didn't want some gangbanging asshole to shoot at her gangbanging asshole father and kill her by mistake. She was three, Chief Nelson. She was three years old and had a fucking Grape Street gang tattoo on her shoulder. I think the real public wants bad people to go to jail. I think they want to feel safe. Do you know anyone who lives in LA who feels safe, Chief? Even one person? Because I've gotta tell ya, sir, I don't know anyone."

And so it came out. Nelson knew the pressure building up on Adams was becoming extreme and knew the incident last night must have affected him greatly. Something had changed with Adams, and it was becoming more apparent every day; the man had talked more in the last five minutes than the entire time Nelson had known him. Even though Adams was someone who held his cards close to his chest, a child's lifeblood flowing onto that same chest as she died would shake anyone.

When Commander Jelenick came to complain about Adams's comments and actions last night, Nelson had tried to educate him about the way people under stress respond, but it seemed to fall on deaf ears. Jelenick had never been in that place.

Chief Nelson let Adams finish, then excused his adjutant. "Lieutenant Moss, would you excuse Jack and I for a moment?" Moss took her cue and left the office closing the door behind her.

"Jack, I know how much this wears on you. I see it, I support you, and I agree with you. But you're letting this in, and that's really dangerous. You have a big heart and I know how much you sacrifice, but you've got to let this go. That time has passed and now we do everything we can . . . but within the rules they give us. We are not in charge, Jack, and the people we answer to has changed. It's just that simple."

Adams was immediately sorry for the outburst and wished he could have pulled it back in. "Yes, sir, it is really simple. I appreciate your support and talking to me. But I just can't promise I'm not going to fight back. Being a victim doesn't sit well with me."

Mike Rand suddenly pushed his head into Chief Nelson's office. "Hey, Lieutenant, sorry for interrupting. We just had a second shooting you need to know about. Good evening, Chief Nelson."

"It's okay, Mike. What do you have?" Lieutenant Adams wasn't too happy about Officer Rand feeling he could interrupt a meeting in the office of a deputy chief, but he worked with it the best he could. He could talk to Rand about it later; in truth, he was actually glad for the interruption. This conversation could go nowhere, and his emotions were showing heavily on his sleeve. He was starting to appear disrespectful, which was certainly not his intent. He only wanted people to obey the law and be held accountable when they didn't. He only wanted people to be safe and feel safe. That was why he became a policeman. His role had become really sketchy now.

"77th Gangs said two Rollin' 60s just got shot up by Big Hazard driving down McKinley at 87th. They think it's Big Hazard retaliating from the first shooting earlier tonight on Main Street. That didn't take them long. Our guys are already on scene—think they were expecting it. One down at the scene and one transported to Killer King with a chest wound. We got two officers from 77th Gang Detail headed to Killer King to guard the door."

Following gang shootings, it's not uncommon for a rival gang to force their way into a hospital emergency room and finish the job they started. Adams had made it standard procedure for Gang officers to immediately deploy a security detail at a hospital receiving a gang member who was a shooting or assault victim, mostly to protect the hospital staff. The same went for gang funerals after numerous drive-by shootings had occurred assaulting the "grieving" gang.

"Chief, I'm going to roll to the shooting at 87th and McKinley. If you need anything, I'll be on my cell. I'll see you Monday morning in Chief Fuller's office. You think he'll have coffee and donuts for us?" Adams loved free food.

"I'm sure he will," Nelson replied. "If you bring them. Free up some of that overtime money you're always making. I'm sure you're making more than me. And Jack . . . be safe, Jack. You can talk to me whenever you have the need. You're a really good man, and we need you functioning. Don't allow yourself to get off track. Just be safe."

As Adams left the deputy chief's office and encountered Lieutenant Moss seated at her desk, he just had to twist the knife. "Hey, Moss, it's already dark outside. If you're scared, I can have one of my Gang guys drive you home."

Nelson was standing at the door to his office and quickly raised his hand up in the air to stop the impending argument. Nelson pointed to the door as Adams obediently made his way out of the office. It always felt good leaving LAPD Headquarters. *Survived one more time.*

Nelson retired to his office and closed the door, worry showing on his face as he sat at his desk. He needed Adams at the top of his game and feared that something had happened. Something different. Adams was feeling pain, and men like Adams never felt pain.

Now it was time for Adams to go where he surprisingly felt safe and secure: on the streets of Los Angeles in the darkness, walking in the shadows. That was his place in the world. The place no one else wanted to go.

CHAPTER EIGHT
THE BIG DOGS

At 87th Street and McKinley Avenue, two officers mid-block on 87th holding the outer perimeter for the crime scene recognized Lieutenant Adams's dark blue Ford Crown Victoria as he approached. "That's the lieutenant's Crown Vic! Make a hole."

The senior officer moved the police car back, leaving room for Adams to drive through and enter the outer perimeter. Leaving his car and walking toward the all-too-familiar yellow tape, Homicide Detective Dave Decker intercepted him.

"Hey, LT, got the crime scene pretty much buttoned down. I've been in court all day, but I was the first one here, so I'll take it."

Gang Homicide Detective Dave Decker took gang shootings in stride. Los Angeles police officers were so used to homicide scenes that by the time the detectives arrived, the scene was, in every case, protected and contained with yellow police tape, dead bodies were shielded from view, medical rescue operations were underway, efforts were made to identify witnesses and suspects, photos of bystanders and parked cars were taken, a log was made of all law enforcement who arrived on scene, and any visible evidence like bullet casings were protected. Any suspect information was immediately acted on by officers with the motto "An arrest is imminent."

These officers didn't need a detective to give them directions about hunting a murder suspect; they only stood down if a detective told them to stop. You want thoroughbreds to stop? Then you have to grab the reins with both hands and pull really damn hard.

The officers in charge of the scene worked hard to keep everyone outside the yellow tape until the detectives arrived, and when they did, the tape was respectfully raised up as the detectives strode under it to take control.

Being a homicide detective in Los Angeles meant something, and Detective Dave Decker was one of the big dogs. A Gang Homicide detective in South Central Los Angeles, in Watts, no less. They carried the largest workload and engaged the most violent criminals in the city. Those with no conscience. Monsters.

When Lieutenant Adams placed both his hands in his pockets, Decker knew it was time to put Adams into play. Strong law enforcement leaders on the streets of Los Angeles hit the ground multitasking, looking at the details while also working with the big picture. That can't be done with cell phones and radios demanding your attention. As soon as you put one of those to your ear, you lose sight of the details and miss the big picture. Adams learned long ago to put his hands in his pockets and focus on the job at hand. Over time, it had become an element of his persona.

Decker was an expert at getting the story out short and sweet when briefing Lieutenant Adams. "Yellow tape is up and the body is tented, LT. Sixteen-year-old from the Rollin' 60s—I think you know him—Short Cuz. I guess his mother is on the way from Carson. They pulled up to the intersection and took rounds on the driver's side from the car next to them, a maroon Monte Carlo with two Hispanics. They sent rounds through the driver's door and window. Hit the driver in the chest and then dumped the passenger, Short Cuz, with a head shot. The driver was transported to Killer King. Some brass in the street between where the two cars were stopped, so the shooter must have shoved the gun out the window as he was shooting."

"Thanks, Dave. Any further info on the shooters or ID on the victims?"

"A little bit, LT. We got three wits and two of them heard the shooter yell 'Big Hazard,' but both wits are juveniles. I hate to involve them, so I'll look for something else. I haven't identified the driver yet; he had no ID in his pockets. He got hit in the chest through the door and paramedics took him to Killer King but said he won't make it. Gang cops at the hospital said he's pretty much KMA, so I'm not going to send anyone else over there. The two 77th cops that are there know to get a statement if he lives."

"KMA" serves as LAPD slang used mostly for dead bodies. In years past, police agencies operated under arcane communications standards when transmitting over radio frequencies. One of those standards was a requirement that once a police officer completed a radio transmission, they had to call out the frequency identification number. The number in South Central Los Angeles was KMA367. The officer would end radio transmissions with "KMA367," similar to a report of "over and out." As time went on, when anything ended, Los Angeles police officers would say, "It's KMA." Whether a computer broke down, a car engine blew up, or a gang member was killed, they were all considered KMA.

"Thanks, Dave. Are we on the same page that this is a Big Hazard hit on Blacks? Or do you know anything about an actual beef they have with the Rollin' 60s?" Adams needed to get right to the point.

"No, sir. Far as I know, it's just Big Hazard doing their racial thing again. Looks like they were involved in the shooting over at 77th and Main a couple hours ago." Detective Decker had already connected the two shootings and knew he was responding to a retaliation following the first.

"The detectives over at that one have a ton of wits. I guess there's brass on the ground from multiple shooters who were all on foot. Big Hazard was on foot when they shot at three of the 60s coming out of the market, then jumped in their ride and split. I think they were in the same Monte Carlo as ours."

"So it wasn't the Rollin' 60s who started things, Dave?" Adams was inclined to believe that it was probably Big Hazard who had initiated the shooting with a racial hit on Blacks.

"Nope, it was Big Hazard who lit the fire. But their plan didn't work out so well when Little Weasel got dumped, though. The Rollin' 60s were too fast on the draw. Rowe only said he *thinks* it was Rollin' 60s by what wits said and that they fled on foot. I don't think they live in the neighborhood—must have had a car somewhere."

Adams noted the growing crowd at the yellow tape and a sudden large commotion. *Mom must have just arrived. Great, here come the cameras hot on her trail.* "Ok, Dave, you pretty comfortable that the crew from this hit are the same as 77th and Main?"

Detective Decker nodded his head while watching the crowd and suddenly began to feel the pressure mounting. His decision to roll on this crime scene after being in court all day was turning into a much larger incident than he had realized. He knew he was tagged to work through the night now. "Yeah, I think it's probably the same. The wits describe the Monte Carlo and the two who left in it. It was parked in the driveway next to the market."

Adams needed to move on this situation for what it was—racial murders, brown on Black—while staying under the umbrella Deputy Chief Nelson had laid out.

"Listen, Dave, if this pans out to be a brown-on-Black crime, just move forward on it for what it is."

Dave Decker, the senior Gang Homicide detective in Los Angeles, knew he would be compiling facts of such a sensitive nature that the city leaders wanted them stifled. Politicians in Los Angeles were never about the truth; it was solely about their image and keeping their votes.

There wasn't a single politician in Los Angeles that would admit to brown versus Black racial strife in the city, as in their minds this would have indicated a failure on their part. An allegation of brown-on-Black violence or vice versa was out of bounds.

Adams knew he was doing the right thing, but for now he would compile facts and sit on them. He had no plans to violate Deputy Chief Nelson's orders. He only wanted to help Nelson have more facts in which to make better decisions . . . or something like that.

"I'm on board, LT, but keeping this quiet isn't easy. I know the mayor doesn't want to hear it, and maybe the chief, too. How far are we hanging out?" Adams wasn't surprised by Decker's question. Every policeman knew, but no one talked about it.

"We're not hanging out if we handle it right. It's just a query at this point, Dave. I'm not going to be disloyal to Chief Nelson or Chief Fuller, or to the department. But if it leaks that we're looking into this angle before we're done, it will look really bad, and it's going to be hard to explain."

Detective Maddie Hill approached with all her usual energy. "Excuse me, Lieutenant. One of the wits got a plate on the Monte Carlo the shooters used, but it's a stolen from over in Rampart Division. I've got Rampart following up on that to see if we've got anything, but I think it's a dead end. The report said the owner came out of his house and his car was gone, and he's nobody. We'll stay on top of any retaliatory shootings tonight, but I'd expect more hits by Big Hazard after Little Weasel got dumped, and those guys are really mobile. They steal cars like I drink coffee—fast and continuous. Oh yeah, the press is arriving. You want to talk to them, or should I?"

Detective Maddie Hill, the youngest and most energetic Gang Homicide detective in the city, was partnered with Decker so he could train her. Hill had proven herself early on to be a self-starter, energetic, and a valuable member of the team. She had a very broad base of experience on the street working in Newton Division and as a detective working juvenile, robbery, and violent crimes. She fit in perfectly with Gangs. Hill was fiercely loyal and driven to win at everything she did.

Because Detective Hill was not privy to the previous discussion, Lieutenant Adams told Decker to make the press release but with no mention of the racial angle. "Just play it to them like always, Dave. Possible gang involvement and we're still investigating, but it's too early to make any conclusions."

Pulling the tent back, Detective Maggie Hill introduced the second gang shooting victim of the evening to Adams. His gang moniker was "Short Cuz." She also pointed out the Glock 9mm handgun that had been in Short Cuz's waistband when he was shot and pointed to the three clear bags holding rock cocaine visible in his shirt pocket.

The gun was moved to a safe location away from the suspect and a police officer was assigned to stand over it and protect it while it was photographed and collected as evidence. The bags in Short Cuz's shirt pocket would be recovered by the coroner's investigators when they arrived, as they held the responsibility to remove items from the body.

Short Cuz was sitting in the front passenger seat, so it was not known whether he had been targeted or had taken a bullet meant for the driver. A bullet wound over the left ear and exiting to the rear of the skull identified the cause of death—a severed brain stem. Sixteen years old and living a life most parents could not conceive of for their children, Short Cuz had been streetwise, disrespectful, and violent. Up until tonight, anyway.

Adams looked at the dead body under the sheet and recognized him from a gang intervention program called Positive Alternatives, a nonprofit organization that employed ex-gang members to intervene in gang activities by "keeping the peace." Positive Alternatives touted their efforts assisting gang members to leave gangs, but there was no clear evidence that they had ever been successful. Adams was well versed in how most such programs manipulated the system to get city, county, state, and federal tax dollars as well as the problems that resulted from hiring ex-convicts and ex-gang members. But most of the long-lasting programs like Positive Alternatives were politically connected, mostly to the mayor or someone on the Los Angeles City Council, so Adams needed to tread lightly. Even so, he and the gang details throughout Los Angeles continually refused to partner with them in any way.

When Adams discussed these programs with other officers, he used the phrase "Keeping them outside the yellow tape" to guarantee they were never provided access to sensitive information.

City politicians and even some of the past politically appointed chiefs of police had pushed for LAPD to partner with the gang intervention programs, but so far it had been avoided. Adams certainly had no intention of ever doing so.

Two months ago, Positive Alternatives had made a pitch for city dollars to fund their efforts, which really meant to help pay their own salaries and keep their payrolls going. They had received an invitation from City Councilman Villanueva, who strongly supported several questionable nonprofit organizations. The city councilman had lobbied for the City Council to fund Positive Alternatives out of the Parks and Recreation budget to work with young people involved in gangs.

At the presentation, the executive director of Positive Alternatives introduced sixteen-year-old Harvey Williams, "Short Cuz," as one of the success stories for Positive Alternatives.

Growing up with a father in the Rollin' 60s, Short Cuz had entered gang life at age nine. The following year, his father had been shot and killed as the result of a gang dispute while dropping him off at 54th Street Elementary School on South Eileen Street. As Short Cuz walked to the front entrance of the school, his father was shot through the car door during a drive-by shooting.

After watching his father die in the family car, fifth grade would be Short Cuz's last full year of school. He was then taken away from an alcohol-and drug-addicted mother and placed in the custody of his grandparents.

As he turned twelve years old, Short Cuz was arrested for armed robbery of a woman who ran a small cart serving fruit bowls at Florence and Van Ness. As a term of probation, Short Cuz enrolled in the Positive Alternatives program where he reportedly left gang life behind and became a rare success story for Positive Alternatives. Executive Director Will Sanchez took Short Cuz to every political meeting he could find to tout their success with this incredible young man who had been transformed into a pillar of the community by Positive Alternatives.

However, Lieutenant Adams was hard to fool, and he knew that one of the scams that some gang intervention programs ran was to go to Los Angeles County and sell their programs as being an acceptable "condition of probation." After an arrest, the court would then assign juveniles to work through the programs developed by them. It made it difficult not to fund them with government dollars when they were servicing government wards of the court.

At the City Hall presentation to beg for money, Positive Alternatives introduced Short Cuz as an example of their success. Reportedly, Short Cuz had left gang life and was mentoring and counseling younger gang members. Positive Alternatives reported that Short Cuz was instrumental in keeping the peace between numerous rival gangs. Personally, he was working his way back into school and completing community service. *As it turns out, not so much.*

#

Detective Maddie Hill took it upon her shoulders to meet with Connie Kester at the yellow tape. "Miss Kester, you know I can't allow you inside the scene to see your son. You could contaminate the crime scene, and then we wouldn't be able to successfully investigate your son's death and prosecute the people responsible. I need you to help us, ma'am, and work with us to solve this crime. We want to solve this crime."

Connie Kester wasn't much interested in listening, only in seeing and holding her son. Her worst fear had come true, although she had always believed that her son's involvement in gangs would take him to the same fate as his father.

The young female with a press pass hanging around her neck, Candace Morgan, standing next to one of the two cameras on scene shouted out, "Detective Hill, why are you disallowing this grieving mother from seeing her dying son?" A fraction of a second before Hill punched her in the face, Hill opted to turn and walk away.

There was no mention of the grandparents who had actually been raising Short Cuz. Connie Kester held the spotlight as the grieving mother and played out the drama as best she could, even though she had not seen her son for over eight months.

Once Miss Kester was done being interviewed by Candace Morgan and the camera lights were turned off, Detective Hill assigned one of the officers on scene to transport Miss Kester to 77th Street Police Station, where Hill had promised to meet with her and answer all her questions. In actuality, Hill was most interested in moving Kester out of the view of the press and then asking questions of her own that may shed light on her son's death. Hill had more questions than answers at the moment.

Detective Maddie Hill, still fairly young in her assignment, had a question for Adams that she should have already known the answer to. "Lieutenant, there's someone here from one of those gang intervention scams, Positive Alternatives. They're over there by the press area and said they had questions about the dead guy, Short Cuz. I guess he worked for them."

"Thanks, Maddie. They stay outside the tape and get no more information than anyone else."

Members of the press battled for position to film the grieving mother and the person they would report as being the heartless detective. Candace Morgan eagerly took her place in front of the camera. She needed her face to be on television.

"Tonight, another lost life on the streets of Los Angeles as the result of weak gun control laws. One Los Angeles Police detective, Detective Hill, stands heartlessly between a mother and her murdered child, only sixteen years old, an innocent victim of gang violence. A victim of lax gun control laws. The LAPD has refused to comment on this situation or the need for stronger gun control as our children continue to fall. This is Candace Morgan."

Adams walked to Miss Kester to give his condolences and apologize that she would not be able to enter the crime scene to see her son. "Lieutenant, you were there—you were at the meeting. He was done with this. He wanted to move back in with me, and I made the couch up for him. He said he was enrolling in school."

Lieutenant Adams reached out and took her hand. How do you tell a parent that their child's criminal lifestyle and choices lent to their death? Can that ever be accepted by a parent? Policemen are not grief counselors and it's not their job to solve societies ills. They simply do their best because oftentimes, there is no one else.

"Miss Kester, I'm so sorry this has happened. To your son and to your family. I can't even comprehend the pain you must be feeling. You already know that we will work hard to investigate this, but that doesn't really help you and certainly doesn't answer very many of your questions. We're going to stay in touch with you as the investigation progresses, but I'm going to ask Detective Hill to sit with you at the police station and give you some contact information for people who can hopefully help you through this."

Damn it. Adams wished there was more he could do. There were so many failed leaders and failed systems in Los Angeles and it was impossible for the police department to clean it all up.

Detective Hill assured Lieutenant Adams that investigators from the coroner's office were en route to the crime scene. Still not fond of autopsies and what she described as a "stainless steel" smell in the coroner's office, Hill had been rebuking one of the coroner's investigators for months. She was afraid that smell would rub off on her. In her mind she tried to make believe the bodies on the autopsy table were not real people, that they were just clues to solve a murder mystery. So far, she hadn't been very successful yet.

"Hang in there, Maddie, it's just another autopsy. Don't let it affect you."

"Kind of late for that, LT. My husband left me for his teenybopper bitch secretary and I chase men away like I'm the plague. I think you're the only person I like, and I barely like you. I don't even know anyone except cops. I can't sleep without three shots of Patron Silver, and I eat my dinner at the bar in the Drawing Room down the street from my house. How do I do change this mess?"

Adams saw the chaos in her eyes. "You change things when you choose to, Maddie."

"Easier said than done, LT."

Didn't he know it.

As two reporters began to shoot questions at Adams that he had no intention of answering, he turned and walked away to answer a call about the first crime scene, where Little Weasel had lain partially on the sidewalk and partially in the street with bullet holes in his stomach and back.

He learned that three Rollin' 60s gang members had walked out of the market and were shot at by three gang members from Big Hazard who were on foot in front of the market and standing at the newspaper rack that had been empty for the last two decades. One of the Rollin' 60s returned fire and hit Little Weasel, knocking him to the sidewalk. The Rollin' 60s had fled around the corner and westbound on 77th Street, then ran northbound up the alley behind the market. Witnesses said one of them was shot, because the other two were carrying him or helping him walk. Little Weasel was identified by the very first Gang officer who arrived on scene. He was well known in 77th Division thanks to a lengthy and violent record.

Two of the Big Hazard gang members ran to a maroon Monte Carlo parked in the drive on the north side of the store and drove away northbound on Main, leaving Little Weasel behind on the ground to die. A chrome 9mm handgun was found on the ground only two feet away from Little Weasel, and there was expended brass from multiple guns scattered across the sidewalk. All seven of the witnesses to the shooting were transported to 77th Street Police Station, and a notification was made to the hospital consortium that a possible gunshot victim may arrive at one of the emergency rooms and that they should contact LAPD. So far, the best witness would have been the one who got shot, if he was still alive.

While Adams stood with Detective Decker, the next and entirely not unexpected call was from Los Angeles City Councilman Gil Villanueva. "Lieutenant Adams, this is Councilman Villanueva. I trust you're safe while handling the scene of the shooting?"

That made Adams laugh. "Yeah, Councilman, I guess I'm pretty safe. What can I do for you?"

"I want to begin by giving you the thanks of the city, Lieutenant, the thanks of the City Council, and my personal gratitude for the work you're doing. I was informed that a young shooting victim, still a child, expired at the scene. Can you tell me what the situation is?"

Adams was way too tired for this; he already knew what Villanueva wanted. Someone from Positive Alternatives had obviously called him and told him that their prize trophy had been shot and killed and that LAPD was stonewalling them. Villanueva funded them, and now his personal credibility was on the line.

"I don't have much more information than you apparently have, Councilman. Two gang members from the Rollin' 60s holding guns and narcotics were in a car together in a high gang crime and narcotic trafficking area late last night and were involved in a shooting with rival gang members from Big Hazard. One of the Rollin' 60s was sixteen-year-old Harvey Williams, whose gang moniker is Short Cuz. He has a strong criminal and violent record. He was carrying a gun in his waistband and bindles of rock cocaine in his pocket. He's dead."

"I see, Lieutenant. I'm sure you're aware that this information is sensitive, and it could easily be misrepresented in a negative light as to young Mr. Williams, who has made incredible strides to rid himself of gang life, and he has been helping others to do so along the way. He is directly involved in one of our city-sponsored organizations to intervene in gang activities. The organization that he is working with, Positive Alternatives, is well thought of and supported by the city leaders. It was reported to me that Mr. Williams was actually on the street this evening representing Positive Alternatives, because that is when he is able to connect with those persons involved in gangs, and that he was working to help members of the Rollin' 60s to leave the gang. Apparently, he was actively attempting to gain employment for them when he was mistakenly involved as a victim in a drive-by shooting.

"I have personally met this young person and this is a tragedy, Lieutenant, that this fine young person was working on our behalf and on the behalf of all of the citizens of Los Angeles when he was targeted. I believe that he may have been specifically targeted because of his efforts to seek peace. Lieutenant Adams, I want to encourage you to address these issues with the press and guarantee that young Mr. Williams, only a child, is recognized as a hero who gave his own life to help in gang intervention efforts."

It took a moment for Lieutenant Adams to muffle his laugh and respond. "Councilman, I'm here on scene, and the facts you've been provided do not appear to be accurate. I don't lie to the press. That being said, it's not my role to spin this one way or the other with the press. I'm also sure that you know the press will report what they want regardless of any information that I give them. My only job here is to investigate the crimes that have occurred and prosecute those persons responsible. Part of this investigation will include the gun that Harvey Williams carried in his waistband, why he had it, and whether it has been used in past crimes. We'll also be looking at the numerous bindles of crack cocaine that he was carrying in his pocket when the gang shooting occurred."

Adams thought that would end the conversation, but one other thought popped into his mind. "But I want to thank you for the information you have volunteered, Councilman Villanueva. Now that you have given me witness information that Williams was actually working for Positive Alternatives, who is funded by the city of Los Angeles, when he was out here with a gun and narcotics and involved in a gang shooting, I'll list you as a witness in the investigation. How did you come about that information, Councilman?"

"I think we've misunderstood each other, Lieutenant Adams. I am not a witness."

"Councilman, when you told me that someone gave you a report that Williams, a known Rollin' 60s gang member known as Short Cuz, was out here while working on the payroll of Positive Alternatives, a city-funded organization, that means he's actually on the payroll of LA City and it made you a witness. I will include that information in the investigation, sir, as I'm not able to hide it or lie about it. As I've said, I'm not able to spin information, sir, I only report it."

"Lieutenant, I'll tell you one more time. I am not a witness. I only called to receive a briefing on this situation, Lieutenant."

Adams thought this was fun now. "There is one other thing, Councilman. When you said you were encouraging me to report to the press what you told me, were you actually telling me to lie to the press, sir? Because if you were, I want to be clear that I would never lie to the press at your urging, nor anyone else's."

"I see, Lieutenant. I'm sure you're doing a fine job at investigating, and I'll discuss the issue with the chief of police. I look forward to seeing you again in Council Chambers. Good night, Lieutenant."

As the call disconnected, Adams remarked, "Yeah, whatever."

"Did I track that call right, Lieutenant? A councilman is telling us what to report to the press?"

"Dave, sometimes these politicians are so used to manipulating things that they think everyone around them can be manipulated by them. All we did was give this guy a little reality check. List him as a witness in the murder book, Dave. He says someone reported to him that Short Cuz was out here working tonight on Positive Alternatives payroll, on the city dime. That's critical information, because it could point to a motive by the shooters. Whoever made the report to the councilman may also have other information about Short Cuz or this situation that sheds light on the shooting. Over the next couple of days, follow up with a phone call to his office and request an interview. I'll let Deputy Chief Nelson know."

After the call, four unmarked police cars arrived carrying Detective Ron "Mac" McClain, Adams's second in command, and the six officers assigned to Lieutenant Adams's inner squad. Although each of the LAPD police stations had a Gang unit, along with the existence of task forces and special details, Adams maintained a senior detective and six officers with him to delegate tasks to, use for special assignments, and to be an extension of his authority throughout the city. As much authority as a lowly lieutenant could have, anyway.

Detective Ron McClain asked, "Hey, LT, we're all here. What do you need?"

"Hey, Mac, good to see you, pal. 77th Division has both these scenes and Dave Decker is overseeing everything. We'll help them later with interviewing wits when they get to that, but I have to eat something. I'm starved," Adams replied.

"I'm thinking Little Tokyo and having the B lunch over at Mitsuru on

1st and Central. I need to get some of those little Imagawayaki cakes to take home to my son and my daughter; it's their favorite. You guys hungry?"

Adams knew Mitsuru was one of Detective McClain's favorite spots for Japanese food. All six officers piped up like they hadn't eaten for a week, and off the caravan went, five Ford Crown Vics in a caravan northbound into downtown Los Angeles. Police officers Mike Rand and John Andrews rode in one car, Julie Barr and Karen Aoki in another, and Jim Halverson and Mark Torres in the third. Detective Ron McClain followed, driving alone.

Before the officers had even arrived at Mitsuru, Councilman Gil Villanueva was leaving messages for Chief of Police Fuller to return his call.

CHAPTER NINE
THE PLAN

Mayor Gilliam Hernandez pushed his chair back and stood behind his desk. He was visibly angry as he put his hands on his desk and leaned over it. "I need this coverage, Dolinski. We're going into campaign mode and I need this money from the anti-gun lobby. They've promised, and I haven't produced. What the hell is going on? Do you know how much money we're talking about here?"

Senior News Editor Kevin Dolinski sat smugly in front of the mayor, a character trait that he often practiced while sitting in his own office barking orders. It made him feel superior and reinforced that if you controlled the news being put out to people, you controlled everything.

Dolinski used his power smartly. The most powerful people in America, in the world, were not the politicians or the millionaires. The one thing he kept out of the media was the veritable fact that the most powerful people in America were those who controlled the media.

Senior Editor Dolinski believed it was best not to throw that out in front of people and risk the chance of calls for regulation, so he only discussed his power behind closed doors. Even though the tech firms were battling incredible resistance and calls for government regulation, the rest of the media continued to skate. Even so, Dolinski controlled a power that few people could ever imagine, and he was an expert at keeping people in his debt, especially politicians.

"We're working it, Mayor. I've assigned this to Candace Morgan as her sole responsibility and she's right on the verge of breaking through to a source inside the LAPD. She almost had their Gang lieutenant the other night, but it slipped through her fingers. We're hitting it hard—we're at every shooting. She sleeps with her clothes on and the production van parks outside her front door with the engine running. But once we do get an inside source in the LAPD, we can blow it up to look like we have multiple sources and present it as a law enforcement perspective, but one that fits our needs."

Dolinski knew that set the hook in the mayor. "Policemen don't believe in what we're selling, Mayor. You may have the chief of police in your pocket, but he's not speaking the same language as the rest of the police department.

But when we get a source in the LAPD, we can spin whatever they tell us and, like I said, play it up like we have we have multiple sources. All we really want are some details that makes it look like we're inside."

"I'm not worried about the support of the LAPD, Kevin. And don't worry about what police officers think; they don't even matter. The chief of police will stand behind me during my press conferences, and the support of his police officers will be assumed. What I need is inside information that entices people sitting on their couches to watch the news. A hook, Dolinski, sensationalism! A panic to outlaw guns. Something that grabs them and glues them to the TV screen and goes on night after night. I need you to create a panic, Dolinski. Not about crime being out of control; that's not it, and that's what I'm getting now—shit. It makes me look bad, damn it.

"I'm telling everyone that crime is down, and you're putting crime on the front page. I need your coverage to sensationalize the urgency of getting guns out of citizen's hands. I need them to believe that once we get rid of guns in Los Angeles, crime will go away and they'll be safe and we'll be able to protect them. I need the coverage to be about guns and video coverage isn't enough, damn it! I need coverage that emphasizes that if gun laws were stronger then these gang members wouldn't have access to them any longer and they wouldn't be able to continually shoot at people. I need you to tell people that no one should have guns and that we can protect them. Tell them to trust us."

"We have a lot of vigilantes out there, mayor. We have to be careful not to let people think they can protect themselves. If that starts happening, we lose a lot of our power, so we don't want to enable these heroes. I've been through this and you have to trust me, this could go sideways."

"Dolinski, you're not listening. You're the only one who can stop vigilantes. Criminalize them on the front fucking page—make them public enemy number one! Put pressure on the district attorney to prosecute them. Make people afraid to protect themselves, just like you make policemen afraid to do their job."

The mayor stood and slammed both hands down on his desk as he leaned forward and barked out what sounded like orders. "Listen to this old dog, Dolinski. Make them believe that if we take guns away, gangs will go away, crime will stop, people will be safe, children will be safe. I want to see the blood on the street before they wash it down, Dolinski, with a gun lying in the blood! And I want the bottomless pit of cash that these anti-gunners have access to. Do you get me, Dolinski? I need sensationalism to get the cash! Then we both benefit."

Sighing, Kevin Dolinski raised his chin to look directly at Mayor Hernandez and spoke as if he were bored. "I understand what the need is, Mayor. But we have to do this right. We don't want this coverage to turn on us. We're building up to it; we're creating the foundation. Then we'll be ready to hit a peak when we get our source inside the LAPD. It will be any day, Mayor, and the timing will perfectly blend into your campaign. One other thing: When will you be ready for the press release on guns recovered by the LAPD?"

"Oh, man, that's another issue. The chief has assured me he's on it, but he's dragging his feet. I pushed as much as I could without playing my hand, but we're just waiting for his plan. I know he's pulling Lieutenant Adams in to get their Gang officers involved, so if you've got Candace Morgan on him, she'd better get serious about it. When we get the guns on the table, the chief isn't going to like the spin you put on the coverage, but I'll blame it on the free press and divert it from my shoulders. For now, I'm hyping it as a press release promoting the successes of the LAPD in recovering guns and making the streets safe. That being said, I need you to be ready with your press release. It has to completely overshadow everyone else's coverage. We're talking *major* sensationalism again. Get your verbiage and your graphics ready, and hit everyone in the face that we need to outlaw guns."

Dolinski was one step ahead of Mayor Hernandez, as he usually was. "We've already got video coverage and archive footage ready to splice in. The talking points are done; we just have to fill in some blanks for the spin and to sell it as an anti-gun campaign in support of reelecting you. We're still sitting on the senator's interview, and she will be icing on the cake. She thinks we interviewed her to support her own anti-gun legislation that she's failed at about a hundred times, the stupid bitch. But her interview is going to do double duty to get you reelected. Everything is just waiting on your ability to get a photo op with the chief of police standing behind a table of guns. I think we could be ready today if you are."

#

It was a short drive back to his office. After Kevin Dolinski was back behind his own desk, Candace Morgan was in the hot seat. "I keep trying, but no one will talk to me."

Senior News Editor Kevin Dolinski wasn't buying it. "Candace, don't give me that. We have a deal; this is your job. If you can't do it, I'll give it to someone else. You had Adams and you blew it. I gave you a break by assigning you gang shootings to emphasize stronger gun laws, and your time is running out. This could blow up to be the biggest show in town, and it's straight from the mayor's office this time. That stupid bastard still doesn't understand that he works for us, but he will. I'm almost ready to pull his leash and educate him as to who is in charge. This can get us nationwide coverage if we play it right. If you can't do this, tell me now, Candace."

Dolinski sat in his large leather chair with his arms crossed over his chest, glaring at Morgan. "Candace, listen to me. This mayor is a worthless piece of shit, a gutless bastard. We already have all the dirt on his sexual exploits, and we can dump his ass out of office whenever we like, but he's becoming more useful to us if we leave him in place. This gun issue is a much better way to control him and get what we want. The end result is us using him—do you get that? If we plan to capitalize on the mayor emphasizing stronger gun laws, he needs coverage from us. No, he needs sensationalized coverage, but right now he's getting vanilla. He's getting crime scene footage that's on every channel as status quo in Los Angeles, just like traffic jams. It makes the mayor look bad; it's emphasizing high crime, and that doesn't get the mayor votes and doesn't get what we want to eliminate guns. Turn that shit around the corner and make it about weak gun laws. Make this mayor beholden to us even more than he already is, and we take control of the city. I'd send a bunch of these photos of him screwing other women to his wife, but it benefits us to keep this dumb bastard in office, and then we win on all fronts. Change the perspective, Candace. That's the power we have."

Dolinski was used to manipulating the news to feed his own ego and his own ambitions. There were a lot of people who owed him and he planned to collect on every single debt, even from the mayor of Los Angeles. "Candace, all we need are a few raindrops and we can make it look like a flood. If Adams won't talk to you, put pressure on him and make him talk. Find a way and put him in a position where he has to cooperate with us. Or just get it from one of the Gang officers and make it sound like it comes from Adams. Get a relationship going with one of those big, strapping men in uniform. This series is important to us, Candace, really important, but you need a partner on the LAPD to make it happen."

"I've tried, but Adams has them trained not to break ranks. They look at me like I have cooties. Those guys are so loyal, it makes me sick."

"Candace, listen to me. If we want to sell gun control, the answer is in gang shootings. We already have the foundation in place to capitalize on these crazies involved in mass shootings, but the volume, the shootings every single day, are with these little gang bastards. That's where the volume is, and that's where we can sensationalize the hell out of it. We're constantly playing catch-up with these gang shootings, which means I'm catching a lot of heat. Arriving at the crime scene after the fact and being stonewalled by the police doesn't work; we're just reporting crimes. It looks like we're telling the public that the mayor is a piece of shit because crime is out of control. We need to find a way to get out in front of this shit. The mayor wants to guarantee this shit stays a police problem and doesn't become a city leadership problem. This is an election year, Candace. The mayor can ride the wave campaigning on stronger gun laws and piggyback on our senator's efforts and get free publicity. But if all he has is crime out of control in Los Angeles, he'll sink. Get it?"

Dolinski knows what he wants to say but realizes he must be careful with his words. Even while sitting at his own desk. Candace Morgan is hungry, and he's learned from past mistakes that hungry people can turn on you if it benefits them.

"I'll get what we need, Kevin. Don't you dare give up on me. You just uphold your part of the bargain and make sure I stay in front of the camera."

"I know you have big ambitions, Candace, but listen to me . . . you're going nowhere unless you figure this out. You need to put Lieutenant Adams in a corner. Make it about him. If he won't tell us what's happening, then make all this shit about him. Find his secrets and use them. If he doesn't have secrets, manufacture them. Love triangles, drugs, drinking, who gives a shit? In the end, if he won't cooperate, we'll force him out and then try the next one. If you can't win the battle, Candace, change the battlefield."

"I'll do my best, Kevin. These Gang officers are a tough crew to crack."

"Candace, time is running out. I heard the *LA Times* is assigning an investigative reporter to link the rise in gang crimes to a weak police response, that the police aren't doing their jobs anymore. The *Times* is working the angle that the problem is a police problem. I'm sure the mayor has had some say in that as a backup plan. If he can't make it about gun control, at least it will land in the lap of the police department and not in his. Looks like he's working every angle so that as a last resort, he can become the crusader to reform or defund the police. The problem with that is the public may connect the story to low police morale and the fact that the politicians don't support the police. We already know that's going to be the response of the police union. Can't blame them, actually. But the morale issue can be directly linked to the mayor, to the City Council and their policies. I'm sure Mayor Hernandez will be putting pressure on the *LA Times*, but that's his problem, not ours."

Dolinski didn't sound as confident as he usually did just then. The pressure was making him start to sweat. "My concern is that the *Times* will get in our way and screw up our efforts. The mayor's all over the map on this, and he could easily screw this up for us also if we drag our feet. We have our own needs to take care of, Candace. We need to get this moving forward, and I mean now. We have to get it out there that the gang problem is a gun legislation problem before the *LA Times* succeeds in painting it as a performance problem of the LAPD. Either one is going to be a tough sell with the public, so whoever gets to the end zone first will win. I intend to win, Candace."

Senior Editor Kevin Dolinski waited until Candace Morgan left and the door closed tightly behind her before dialing the number. His college roommate, and his strongest contact with the anti-gun lobby. "Steve, it's Dolinski. Listen, buddy, it's time we really stepped this up. Where are we at with the funding you promised me?"

#

It was no easy task to squeeze eight police officers dressed in wool uniforms with all their gear into a small Japanese restaurant with only a handful of booths made to economize on space. The amount of gear officers lugged around on their Sam Browne, the leather belt upon which everything was attached, had become heavier and heavier over the years. Adams started in the LAPD with a holster and gun, an ammunition pouch, and a handcuff pouch. But as litigation against police officers increased, so too did the amount of equipment they were required to carry.

"Listen up, knuckleheads. We need to put something together to take guns off the street for your favorite mayor."

Julie Barr spoke right up. "He's not my mayor; I didn't vote for him. I don't even live here."

Mark Torres just had to pipe up. "Are you sure, Julie? I hear he hits on every woman in town. You sure you don't have a special arrangement with Gilly?"

Barr's eyes shot daggers. "Torres, my balls are bigger than yours, and I'll punch your brain right out of your head if you say that again."

"Can we get on with this?" Adams didn't feel like being entertained at the moment. "I have to meet with Chief Fuller on Monday to recommend a plan, so I don't have much time. Anyway, I'd like to develop some kind of undercover or buy-back operation where we can take the guns out of gangsters' hands, but without them knowing it's us. I'm looking for the guns we don't normally get when we're rummaging through their pockets when we jack them. I'm interested in the guns used in shootings. Behind the scenes, I want to run forensics on everything we get and try to match them to open homicides. If we can get guns rolling in and match them to open crimes, then other cases may open up for us. But listen really clear: I want a plan to specifically target the guns used in shootings that are hot."

Adams looks around the table for input but everyone is playing the silent card, not wanting to be the first to comment. "Mac, I need you to head this up. I may pull you off other responsibilities and just work this full-time; we'll see how it goes. Let me know what you think as we put it together."

Mike Rand was the muscle for the unit, a loyal soldier, but not always the detail guy. "We're doing that now, LT, with the guns we bring in every day," Rand commented. "If we put undercovers out there buying guns, we'll need guys for each race, each gang, and in each part of the city. Then they have to make their way into each gang . . . man, that's monumental. And then they're just going to get robbed and probably shot."

Jim Halverson, one of the more silent officers, talked about growing up working in his father's pawnshop in the old part of Reno on Virginia Street. He laid out how they had bought guns over the counter, which sounded promising.

"Think like a gang member, you guys," Karen Aoki added. "They're not going to bring a gun in and sell it if they need to show ID. Most of the guns are stolen or are shooters. We need to give them a way to sell the gun to us, but it has to be anonymous and under-the-table. And it has to be worth their while. Right now, they just send them south of the border, hand them off, sell them to other gangbangers, or dump 'em."

Julie Barr, supporting her partner Karen, added, "We need a business, LT. Somewhere gangsters can come in and sell a gun under-the-counter and think it will never come back to them. Maybe a spin on what Halverson said, like a crooked pawn shop. Let them come to us."

Adams agreed and added that a physical location, a business, would allow them to engineer a higher degree of safety for the officers and foster the ability to record gun transactions on audio and video by prewiring the location.

"Ok, let's run with that. Too dangerous to piggyback on an existing business, so we're going to be businessmen. Or businesspersons. We'll open a business, buy guns under-the-counter, pay a lot for them, and assure the gangsters it won't come back to haunt them. Maybe we'll tell them we send them out of the country," Adams thought out loud.

"We'll have to get the word out somehow to draw these gangbangers in. I have an idea how to do that," John Andrews added. Andrews had a lot of undercover experience in both Vice and Narcotics. "Once we have a location, we can send Vice undercovers out to pick up prostitutes, then bring them to the location and pretend to sell a gun in front of them. We'll flash a lot of cash and lay a story on them. Then the undercover can get a call and tell the prostitute they have to run, throw her a couple bucks, and dump her back on the corner. Let the working girls get the word out. Maybe tell them they'll get a tip for bringing customers in that want to sell guns. If we're going to be businessmen, we have to do marketing. That will get word out on the street really fast."

Everyone was quiet, wondering what Adams's response would be. "Let me think about that," he remarked, thinking that plan raised all kinds of concerns.

"I can be the guy to pick up the girls. I'm the best-looking one here," Mark Torres threw out.

"Yeah, well, you better carry a lot of money with you if you think you're going to pick up girls. You'll need it," Julie added.

"Well, I know a guy," Adams joked. He said he would meet with a friend of his to discuss an idea and then brief the unit.

John Andrews was the first to finish eating. "LT, I got a call from one of my snitches in the Hells Angels. He's a parolee and he's already signed up as a confidential informant, a CI. He's working at a machine shop over in Hollenbeck Division and said his boss approached him about killing somebody. Guess his boss hires a lot of parolees. I was hoping to meet with him tonight, if that's okay with you."

"No problem. Take your partner with you. After we eat, I'd like the rest of you guys to work with 77th on the shootings tonight. See what help they need finishing interviews. Keep an ear out for the 60s tonight; they might be shooters or victims. Don't forget to listen for a gunshot victim to show up at an ER room. If one of the 60s was hit at the first shooting outside the market at 77th and Main, he may be showing up somewhere. Mac, can you meet me at our office?"

After dinner, Adams settled into his dark blue Crown Vic, his mobile office, and called Alcohol, Tobacco and Firearms (ATF) Special Agent Dan McVay. "Hey, Dan, it's Adams over here at the real police. It's late but listen, pal, I'm developing a gun-grab operation with gangbangers and hoped I could get you to saddle up with us. My purse strings are getting pulled tight and I could really use some of your toys. Audio, visual, and a good connection to a US attorney that likes guns."

Many gun violations could be prosecuted under federal statutes, which provided for stronger penalties, but finding a US attorney to do it was tough. Even though one crime violated the law, most US attorneys wanted three crimes to be committed before they would agree to prosecute. They wanted to guarantee their successful prosecution rate was high. More politics.

McVay was always looking for ways to promote his unit but wasn't always that excited about partnering with other agencies. Adams was the exception, and McVay quickly opened the door for this effort. "Sure, Jack, it sounds interesting. When are you up and running, and what part of the city?" Adams told him the plan was being developed and promised he'd get back to McVay next week. *Next, the most important call . . .*

"I know it's almost midnight, Jesse, sorry to wake you up. Tell your wife I apologize; she told me the only time the phone rings late at night is when I'm the one calling. I'm putting something together, and I have to move quick. I need a business office to rent. Rent for free, actually."

Jesse Levin was a businessman in the San Fernando Valley north of downtown Los Angeles, but he had his fingers in enterprises across much of the city. He rented equipment to filming productions along with Paramount, Universal, Santa Clarita, and Warner Brothers Studios for filming offstage, such as lights, generators, tents, tables, and chairs. He also rented stake bed trucks, shuttle vans, and even a gas truck for refueling other vehicles and generators. Jesse also owned commercial real estate in a number of spots throughout the city, and that was precisely what Adams needed.

A likable man with a big heart, the kind of man you're proud to have as a friend, Levin was considering getting out of the business. Levin was in fairly constant disputes with the Teamsters, whose workers populated most of the filming locations.

Studios rented absolutely everything for filming offstage. The Teamster captains and coordinators, who were supervisors on the film locations, had a high level of input as to what equipment was rented. The rub was that they all seemed to have their own personal equipment that they rented to the studios, whether they needed the equipment or not.

The corruption of the old days seemed to still be reflected in this organization that allowed individual Teamster supervisors to make the decision to rent their own equipment. Equipment that may not be needed, equipment that may not even work, and equipment rented to multiple shows at the same time. The Teamster supervisors also decided how much the studios would pay them to rent their own equipment. Quite the scam.

Someone else owns equipment to rent? Well, if they want to see their equipment on a film production, then they better make nice with the Teamsters supervisors, whatever that may mean. Levin, running a legitimate business and being on the outside, constantly battled the "insider trading" scams of the Teamsters and ongoing efforts to cut his fees. Some of the Teamster captains and coordinators even rented equipment from businesses like Levin's, then re-rented the equipment to the studios for a higher fee, the difference, of course, finding its way straight into their pocket.

After being on the set of a movie being filmed in Manhattan Beach, Levin finally reached the point that he was considering retiring and turning the business over to his son-in-law.   At the set, he observed the Teamster driving his gas truck filling the gas tanks on Teamsters' personal trucks. Levin asked the driver who had told him to do that, and he responded that one of the Teamsters' transportation coordinators always told him to fill the gas tanks on personal trucks and cars for the people working on the set. Levin had enough. Whether the gas was paid for or not by the studio, theft was theft, and he was done. Levin was working his way out of the business.

"You know I'll bend over backwards for you, Jack. But you want me to rent you office space? And for free? Why would the LAPD want office space?" Adams laid out a rough plan to his friend for opening a business for an undercover operation but was careful not to say too much and unnecessarily involve Levin. Adams told him it may take up to a year to complete the operation.

"Jack, I've got two warehouses that are almost empty over in Echo Park off Benton Way. Then, let's see . . . I have an empty office in Burbank that sits over an electrical company, but I think there's an approved application for that one. If a small warehouse works, I could move some stuff and empty one of the Echo Park locations for you. But it's just a warehouse with one glass door and one roll-up door. It's pretty small and just one big open room. It has a bathroom, though. I just use it for storage of small generators and portable lights that USC always rents. We call them GloBugs."

Adams thought it sounded perfect, mostly because it was centrally located in the city. "Thanks, Jesse. I owe you, like always. I'll plan on it and get back to you with specifics about time frames. But I'd need to get access to it as soon as possible, Jesse. Go back to sleep, pal. It will all seem better when you wake up."

The doors for the plan were now open. At last, Adams saw a pathway to juggle what the mayor wanted—to steal more votes—with what the Chief wanted and what could actually make a difference in reducing gang violence and putting criminals in jail. Adams's path continued to be straight; he just needed to fight through all the walls along the way. Perhaps most importantly, the plan thus far was also self-funded.

CHAPTER TEN
THE VALLEY ROBBERIES

Adams went to his office in the Central Division Police Station at 6th Street and Wall Street to visit his desk and see what Maggie, his secretary, had left in his inbox. During her Day Watch shift, Maggie was a champ at handling as much paperwork as possible and keeping the mundane away from Adams. She was really good at signing his name.

Maggie didn't physically see Adams very much since he rarely came into his office especially during daytime hours, but they talked on the phone constantly. Maggie was also an expert at reciting, "Lieutenant Adams is in the field right now, but I can take a message for him."

Adams had a second office, although it was temporary, in the Federal Building on Wilshire Boulevard in West Los Angeles, the Los Angeles FBI office. Adams oversaw multiple gang task forces comprised of FBI agents, and according to FBI charter, they could only take direction from FBI supervisors. As such, Adams had been sworn in as a federal agent by the FBI.

He had an assigned desk there but, having a fairly low security rating within their agency, he had very limited access to federal data. And of course, the cherry on top: the FBI provided him a plain car to use in an undercover or surveillance capacity. Currently, he had a silver Ford Explorer with a roof rack and aftermarket custom wheels. The small decal in the rear window that Adams had applied read "Encinitas Surf."

Not one to be beat out, Dan McVay at ATF was also able to provide Adams with a plain vehicle to be used for surveillance. ATF personnel and operations were plainclothes investigators mostly in an undercover capacity. ATF had a restriction that Adams could not take the car to his home and must leave it parked at a city facility when not in use. There was some kind of odd home garaging restriction the ATF employed, while the FBI car had no such restrictions. Although, the ATF had given Adams a much more fun black Ford Mustang GT with dark tinted windows and a manual transmission that he kept at the Rampart Division Police Station in the center of the city. A car like that makes you twenty-one years old and stupid again. *The best.*

Getting to Adams's office and navigating the streets of downtown Los Angeles near LAPD Central Division at 6th Street and Wall Street at night was a near impossibility, but not because of traffic. As the sun set, the homeless moved from the sidewalks and alleys to take over the streets. The city occasionally publicized the number of homeless in Los Angeles, but at the end of the day it was only a best guess, and no one from the mayor's office or City Council ever came here at night. Only policemen and firemen.

The LAPD Central Division was built like a fortress in a hostile land, with tall concrete walls and few windows. The building sat on one complete block, and the officers there used to be good at keeping the homeless on the other side of the street and disallowing them from living next to the police building.

But times change. Pressure from homeless activists, the mayor, and City Council didn't allow that now, so the police building had essentially become a primary encampment location, especially anywhere where there was a nook or cranny that a body could tuck into. It was more colorful now, however, with the tents that sat where the sidewalk used to be. *Adornments for the drab gray building.*

It was heartbreaking, but clearly not a problem the police department could resolve, even though certain members of the public or politicians tried to put it on their shoulders. Even so, after the failures of society and the politicians of Los Angeles reached a breaking point and the public complaints eventually exploded, the police department was always called in by the city leaders to carry out some designated action to clean the problem up, if only temporarily, because there was no one else to call.

The goal of the action is always the same: making the homeless disappear from the location where the complaints are highest. This always happens under the watchful eyes of the press, after which the police immediately become the bad guys. Not a politician in sight as the police carry out their orders. According to the press, the police are the problem. Everyone lies in Los Angeles.

Someday, Adams had hope a chief of police would be selected who had the courage to refuse to shoulder the burden of providing police services to resolve social issues, such as those of the homeless, and cause the services to be provided by the appropriate social services and mental health teams. It takes courage to tell politicians "No," especially when they're the ones who appoint you to your job.

The LAPD Central Division building was largely empty at night. A skeleton crew of one or two PM Watch detectives might occasionally be around, but not so much on weekends. Even Narcotics detectives, who largely only worked Day Watch hours on weekdays, had gone home. As if drug deals only occur during banker's hours.

Adams sifted through his inbox and phone messages, completing as much as he could in as short a time as possible. The LAPD ran on paperwork shuffled from desk to desk.

During Chief William Bratton's appointment as chief of police, Bratton initiated COMPSTAT, computer statistics, and did a great job in causing the police department to be held more accountable for quantifiable results. Bratton singlehandedly changed the culture of LAPD management to be more efficient, more effective, and less ego driven. The negative aspect of this effort was that the pendulum eventually swung too far and the LAPD morphed into an agency in which decisions were made based solely upon statistics and numbers. What followed was the expected subsequent trap that numbers can be made to say whatever you want them to say. Find a way to modify the numbers, and you can achieve the necessary results. Sort of.

What the LAPD experienced was that the more pressure you put on someone, mostly captains, to cause numbers to either go up or down to reach a specific goal, the more imaginative they got at finding ways to make those numbers move. Even if the goal was never actually reached, the numbers were moved, and everyone was satisfied. Always a paperwork-heavy environment with tons of duplication, after Chief Bratton the administrative tasks multiplied.

Detective McClain came into the Gang office with his permanent smile. "Listen, LT, we need to set up a detail out in the valley in Van Nuys. Two guys are hitting all the little taco stands on Sepulveda. One guy reportedly has a big 'BP' Brown Pride tattoo on the back of his left calf, but their turf is over on the other side of the 405 Freeway. They're not really a gang, but sort of, I guess. They have a lot of taggers. The weird thing is they keep yelling, 'San Fer!' as they walk out after the robbery. I don't know what's up with that." McClain had an entertaining way of talking and always had a positive, fun attitude.

"Anyway, the Bureau Chief out in Valley Bureau kicked it to us as a gang issue. I'm thinking they're Brown Pride wannabe gangsters crossing the 405 Freeway to hit these taco spots, then running back home. At first I thought they were probably yelling 'San Fer' to shift blame away from them, along with hitting in San Fer's area. But in reality, they probably know that if they yell 'Brown Pride' that everyone will just laugh at them. I'm guessing that they think no one will see the BP tattoo on the back of the one guy's leg. Gangsters aren't the sharpest knives in the drawer. They're flashing a gun, but no shots so far. It's only a matter of time, though. All the hits have been on Wednesdays and Thursdays, which is weird, and right at sundown around eight or so. It's like they want to get caught."

Adams asked McClain what he recommended and they decided on a short surveillance detail by the in-house crew, working Wednesday and Thursday nights for two weeks, then they would reassess. They put the three teams out to sit on three locations at a time. If they observed the robbery, they could call in the troops.

"Ok, call out to Van Nuys and Devonshire Gangs and coordinate with them," Adams said. "Let them know we'll do the surveillance, but I want their buy-in. Let's don't step on their toes if they want to do it. We have the plain cars so it's easier for us, but they can have it if they want. And Mac . . . I'm concerned about this pattern of only Wednesday and Thursdays. Keep our guys grouped fairly close together in case it's some kind of setup." Adams had a knack for seeing the big picture while others got caught up in the details.

"Why don't you ride with me, Mac? Let's run over to Rampart Division. I want to look at some of the warehouses on Benton Way in the industrial area for an idea I have about this gun-grab detail we're getting roped into by your buddy the mayor."

McClain laughed and blurted out, "He's not my buddy! But I have heard the two of you have an understanding."

"We have an understanding, all right," Adams declared. "We understand that we don't like each other."

CHAPTER ELEVEN
SELLING THE PLAN

Chief of Police George Fuller, a South Central Los Angeles policeman who rose through the ranks but always maintained his contact to street police officers and held mostly operations commands instead of administrative positions, was one of the last true policemen in the upper ranks of the police department.

As a political appointment, Mayor Hernandez had appointed him and apparently believed Fuller would be able to do his bidding while still showing a positive face to the officers. After a handful of prior chiefs under the new mayoral appointment method had failed the department and the city, Mayor Hernandez was between a rock and hard place to select a chief of police that could work successfully in both arenas.

The mayor also needed someone he could mold to carry out his personal agenda, someone who would help to achieve his ambitions. The rumors of a run for governor had persisted for some time but seemed to be derailed, even in his own party, by the leaks of his womanizing lifestyle.

The police officers from Metropolitan Division assigned to drive and protect the mayor were sworn to secrecy about his activities. However, people are human, and continually driving the mayor to meet with various women was bound to slip out sooner or later. It didn't help that Senior Editor Kevin Dolinski had hired a private investigator to find dirt on the mayor, along with most other Los Angeles politicians. That private investigator had a knack for having his camera pointed in just the right spot, and Dolinski filed the photographs in a locked cabinet in his office marked "Insurance."

The historically liberal agenda of the political leadership in Los Angeles certainly did not marry well with the conservative ideals prominent in law enforcement communities. While most sheriffs were elected by the public, many chiefs of police, like those in Los Angeles, were now appointed by the political leadership instead of competitively moving up through the ranks. Darryl Gates, the last LAPD chief of police to achieve rank through a competitive civil service process, had been protected from political interference and could only be removed from office or disciplined based upon misconduct, just like any other police officer.

Chief Gates stood strong in his beliefs and refused to be unduly influenced by then-Mayor Tom Bradley and the Los Angeles City Council. That continuing conflict came to a head after the 1992 Rodney King arrest and rioting. Although many people believed that the ensuing televised speech of Mayor Bradley lent to the violence, the brunt of the riots was placed solely on the desk of the chief of police.

As is common across the United States with most every major police event that is viewed negatively, the chief of police, as a result, stepped down. Chief Gates followed suit and resigned. The political backlash resulted in a change to the City Charter providing that chief of police would henceforth be appointed by the mayor, both a political appointment and a disaster for Los Angeles. The LAPD would never be the same.

In Los Angeles, that meant that the chief of police was in a very precarious position. As a political appointee, the chief must agree to support those same ideals and values of that mayor in order to be selected. If the mayor had a liberal agenda, as is historically the case in Los Angeles, the ability for the chief to support the mayor's liberal agenda while leading a largely conservative force of men and women to protect the public would be incredibly difficult.

The mayor of Los Angeles, while standing in front of those press cameras presenting his agenda, oftentimes needs the police department to support him . . . but not really. The mayor only needs the politically appointed chief of police to stand on the stage with him to signify support, so that he is able to say he has the support of law enforcement. Someday, when the public hears that law enforcement supports something, they will know to differentiate between the politically appointed chief of police and the rest of the police department.

#

After riding the elevator to the tenth floor and entering the outer office of the chief of police, Deputy Chief Nelson appeared in the doorway of Chief Fuller's inner office. "Lieutenant Adams, come on in. Chief Fuller is ready for us."

Adams followed Nelson into the office and observed Chief of Police Fuller sitting at the large round conference table in his office. The chief's office was one of the few with windows and oversaw downtown Los Angeles. *Think that the office makes the man?* This office had a terrace facing City Hall. The chief was accompanied at the conference table by a young woman professionally dressed that Adams did not know.

Walking into the office of the chief of police was daunting for anyone in the police department. The office was very formal with minimal personal accoutrement. Always an "Ozzie and Harriet" family picture, a few pictures with political heavyweights, one of which must always include the mayor, and a group of professional commendations. Sparsely furnished, quiet, and without interruptions. Once the door closed, you certainly felt the pressure.

"So, Lieutenant Adams, you've been doing great things in the world. You may not know it, but I follow what your Gang guys are doing very closely," Chief Fuller commented. "I think Deputy Chief Nelson briefed you on a request from the mayor's office to develop a program to remove guns from the streets of Los Angeles. The mayor is looking for the effort to terminate in a photo op, which he will personally host, to give the public a sense of peace that we are doing our job and that crime is down in Los Angeles. You're the expert, so I'm relying on you to set this up. I'm hoping you've given it some thought and have some recommendations."

"I have, Chief, but I haven't met your guest." Fuller then introduced Deputy Mayor Sarah Holly. Without missing a beat, Adams went on, "Chief, I have some confidential personnel issues to discuss that would bore Miss Holly. I'm wondering if we could start with those issues and then move into the mayor's request. It's fairly important that I get this out right away because it's time sensitive."

Chief of Police Fuller raised his brows and then said, "Sure, Lieutenant. Sarah, would you excuse us for a moment? You can have a seat in the outer office. Can I get coffee or something to drink for you while you're waiting?"

Deputy Mayor Sarah Holly, appearing as if she knew something else was going on and that she had just been dismissed from the inner sanctum, hesitated and then stood. Walking out of the office, she said, "No, thank you. If your meeting will be long, please let me know so I can get back and brief the mayor. He's anxious about your plan." Throwing out that veiled threat, she stepped into the outer office. *It's funny how fast people adapt to the power of political office.*

Over in City Hall, Mayor Gilliam Hernandez anxiously waited to be briefed by Deputy Mayor Holly about the LAPD plan to develop a gun confiscation program that would support a major press conference. The funding from the anti-gun lobby he so highly coveted as he went into election season depended on the LAPD giving him the tools he needed. The chief of police wouldn't be happy with the ulterior motives he held to promote anti-gun legislation, but Mayor Hernandez didn't give that a second thought. Although he was already manipulating the presentation for the press release to support his promises to the anti-gun lobby, time was getting short. He needed results from the LAPD, and soon.

"I didn't know we were going to discuss something else this morning," Chief Fuller commented to Deputy Chief Nelson.

"Neither did I, sir. Jack, what's up?" Deputy Chief Nelson appeared confused.

Adams was not someone to rehearse a presentation, but he was quick thinking on his feet. "I've put something together, but it's not something for public disclosure. The confidentiality of this operation, if you approve it, is critical to assure the safety of our officers. If, after you hear my proposition, you feel it's necessary for the mayor's office to be briefed in, I'll respect that, and I have an alternate recommendation on how to handle this photo op request."

Although Chief Fuller appeared open to this discussion, Deputy Chief Nelson was clearly in the hot seat, concerned that this was going sideways. His greatest fear was that Adams was on the verge of being disrespectful to the chief of police of the Los Angeles Police Department. Being that Adams was his responsibility, Nelson knew he would bear the brunt of such an outburst.

"Lieutenant, what this department communicates with the mayor's office is not your concern and clearly above your pay grade," Nelson interjected.

"Give me the alternative plan first," Chief Fuller ordered, "then give me what you really recommend."

"Yes, Chief. The alternative plan involves no confidentiality issues and can certainly be shared with Mayor Hernandez and Deputy Mayor Holly. We have our Gang officers, citywide, continue to do what they do every day on the streets of Los Angeles. We recover a lot of guns every week, so we give it a month and then set up a table and display all the guns we recovered citywide for that whole month. It will probably be fifty or sixty guns, maybe more if we have recoveries from search warrants we may serve. The mayor gets what he wants, and in only thirty days."

"Hmmm. No change from business as usual," Chief Fuller commented. "The mayor would have his press release, but I'm not convinced that's the best we can do. I'd be interested in an effort that actually has an appreciable effect on public safety. What's your bigger plan, the one that I would have to tell Mayor Hernandez that he's not trustworthy enough for me to brief him in on?"

"Yes, Chief. I would like my in-house squad to open a business—a gold and jewelry pawn shop. You've seen those signs, 'We buy gold and jewelry.' That's a very limited scope compared to a regular pawn shop, and we wouldn't have many people coming in."

"Open a business? What the hell?" Nelson commented.

Fuller smiled and said, "This is getting good. Give me more details. I can't wait for this one."

"Chief, I would use my contacts and drop your name to grease the skids with the heads of city licensing departments and temporarily insert paperwork in the city files that we are a real and licensed business. These gangbangers have girlfriends and relatives in city jobs, and I need this to look real if any of them pull the files to check on us. I think you'll see why we can't involve Miss Holly or the mayor's office."

"Ok, Lieutenant. Keep going, give me the meat," Chief Fuller added.

"We set it up as an international business, and in our marketing we advertise that we buy and sell in other countries. In a nutshell, we convince gangbangers that we're not completely legit and that we black-market guns by buying them under-the-counter and send them in our jewelry shipments out of the country for sale. Once a gun is used in a homicide like the two deaths the other night, gangsters usually dump the guns so they don't get caught with them and tagged for the murders. If they know they can sell them for a high price instead of tossing them and think they'll get sent out of the country, I think they'll be tempted to sell to us."

"It sounds easy enough, but how do you get them to sell you guns? How do they even know this grand business even exists? And how do you open a business, Jack? Or do you go into an existing business and operate with them?" Chief Fuller asked, getting pulled into the details.

Adams, thinking that the chief was on the hook, threw out a little at a time. "Chief, we can't work with an existing business because we can't trust everyone who may work there, and in the end, it could endanger them. Even in the aftermath, they would probably become a target. I would rent an office, configure it for our needs so our officers are tactically safe inside, and make it look legit. We would need desks and computers and other props, and we'd need to put up signs, run ads, and get all the paperwork in place. I would wire it inside for audio and visual to record the transactions because I'm planning on federal criminal filings. Then we'd wire it outside for visual so we can scope cars and license plates coming and going."

Seeing the wheels turning for the two chiefs, Adams continued without any follow-up questions. "I'll have my in-house detective and six officers run the inside. In the background, I'll have one of our surveillance teams on-site, although not in full strength—probably just two or maybe three units to take suspects away from the location after they sell a gun to identify where they live, work, or hang out. We won't be asking for identification, so we'll need a system to properly identify who they are. We'll identify anyone else in their car and any associates they meet with. Our Gang detectives will do the follow-up investigations on guns we buy, including ordering forensics to see if we can match the guns to open homicides. We'll keep an eye on opportunities for pen registers and content wiretaps on cell phones, say, when we do connect a gun to a homicide."

Nelson appeared more nervous the more Adams talked. "We can't be doing wiretaps on people, Jack. That's not what the mayor asked for. I'm not even convinced we can do it. I think we're moving too fast."

"Chief Nelson, we did the first local law enforcement RICO prosecutions on gang members in the United States. LAPD was the first and the trendsetter. I think we can do the same thing here. Since I started doing federal RICO prosecutions, organized crime prosecutions against street gang members, I've been sworn in as a federal agent with the FBI. Since LAPD was the first to enlist federal RICO prosecutions against gangs, this intelligence-based investigation would just be an extension of that effort and keep us in the forefront of federal gang prosecutions. We're LAPD, and we should lead the pack, sir." Adams knew that comment would resonate with the chief of police.

"With a US attorney on board, I have a much broader scope of authority to write warrants on phones, sir. I'd also bring in ATF to give us a hand. They're the gun experts and they can assist with federal prosecutions." Adams was comfortable with the level of details he was providing but gave a little at a time, cautious not to reveal too much.

"Chief Fuller, our gang officers are going to take guns off the streets whether we do this or not. And a photo op for the mayor to take credit for it is no problem, but this effort gives us an opportunity to grab guns we wouldn't normally have access to. Very probably, it would give us access to guns used in homicides. That's the core of this plan—getting guns we wouldn't normally have access to and connecting them to homicides. This plan would give you what we want: an investigation that would have an appreciable effect on public safety."

The two men before him appeared interested in the plan. "Chiefs, this would be an intelligence-based gang investigation supported by federal criminal filings, in contrast to what law enforcement does across the country by policing gangs with uniformed officers. We would reach those gangsters that usually remain invisible to us, along with guns we normally never have access to. We will probably be buying the gun directly from the shooter, which strengthens our criminal case against them. Today, many of the hot guns are sent into Mexico, where they're used again. Some get dumped, some get handed off to other gangsters. The way we're setting it up, it would be very attractive for these gangsters to specifically sell us guns that are hot from a shooting, and it's very probable that the shooter will be the one selling the gun.

"Not only will those guns no longer be available for other gangsters to shoot people with, but those are the guns we're after, Chiefs, before they cross the border or get dumped. It's not just taking a gun out of some gangster's pocket that we would have gotten anyway. My way, we can match these guns to shootings and solve some homicide cases. My way, the LAPD stays at the forefront of law enforcement operations and creates a model for all other law enforcement agencies, including the feds. I fully believe that if we show the feds the way, sooner or later they will have to jump on the bandwagon and deploy their assets to police street gangs at the federal level. Chief Fuller, you would be the LAPD chief of police that continues to revolutionize law enforcement in America."

The room went quiet. Chief Fuller walked out to the terrace and looked out at City Hall, at the office of Mayor Hernandez. Adams began wondering whether the mayor ever looked out of his office at the police headquarters.

Returning inside, Fuller walked to a coffee setup near the inner door to his office. "Steve, can I get you a cup?"

"No thank you, sir. I've had mine," Nelson responded. He wasn't sure, at this point, whether he was in trouble or not.

While pouring coffee, Fuller asked, "Jack, how do you like yours?"

Adams, feeling that he might have a chance to get the chief's approval, responded, "I like a little bit of coffee with my cream and sugar, Chief." Chief Fuller laughed and told Adams that he'd better make his own.

While Adams made his coffee with his back to the two chiefs, Fuller and Nelson sat at the large conference table and engaged in conversation at a level above Adams's position in the department.

"Steve, what do you think? Is it doable? And how would we keep Gilly out of the loop? This is something that's really volatile, especially the wiretap issues. One slip of this getting out would be disastrous."

"Chief, I have full confidence in Lieutenant Adams, but I think we're getting in over our heads. This isn't what Gilly asked for."

"No, it's not, Steve, but I like it. I particularly like that we would be taking a new tack toward policing gang crimes and developing a new model. What we're doing now certainly isn't solving anything. I think Lieutenant Adams is the right person at the right time."

Chief Fuller looked at Adams as he sat at the table. "Jack, don't we need money to rent an office, build it, and all the other things you mentioned? What are we looking at?"

With Nelson looking directly at Adams with a threatening stare, Adams explained that he had already arranged to acquire a location for free for approximately one year from a Los Angeles business owner. "I'll personally buy any lumber or drywall we need to build it, and I'll do the construction myself with the knuckleheads on my crew. I'll send my guys to City Salvage to find desks and props; that shouldn't be hard. I still have to reach out to some folks for some costume jewelry and fake gold for display, and I need to find a big safe to put in the office to sell the con. I can rely on ATF for tech equipment, audio, and visual. My friend Jon has a sign company and I'm sure he'll help us with signage, though I haven't asked him yet. I'll need some cash on hand to buy guns, but I think I can get funded from Narcotics Division with your ok."

"So besides personnel costs, including overtime, we don't need additional monies that Adams hasn't already planned for," Deputy Chief Nelson assured Chief Fuller.

"Well, not exactly sir," Adams replied to Chief Nelson. "I think my contact will pay for utilities, just water and electricity, because they're already hooked up. But we would need a minimal amount for a phone with a business 1-800 number. It's such a minimal cost that I'm sure I can fund it somehow. I can possibly get the signage donated also."

Adams, not finished with his response, took a deep breath and remembered the order Nelson had given him as to not asking Chief of Police Fuller for money. "There is one more thing, sir, and I'm sorry to bring it up. If we move into pen registers and content wiretaps on cell phones, I'll need money for that. We'll need to pay the phone companies for what they do on their end and rent space and hire federal monitors to listen and record the taps at one of the federal centers."

"That sounds like it could be expensive," Fuller commented.

"Yes, sir, I don't want to mislead you. If this grows to the scope I think we're capable of, it could be a few hundred thousand dollars. Maybe more."

Silence filled the room. Deputy Chief Nelson, standing, placed his hands behind his back and paced back and forth behind Adams. *Damn. He's going to lower the boom now.*

"And where does that money come from, Lieutenant Adams?" Nelson calmly asked. *Surprisingly, he doesn't seem angry.*

"I'm committed to finding the money myself, sir. I'll hit all my governmental contacts and raise it. If I can't, we'll cancel that part of the operation and rely on routine investigative practices."

"Jack," Chief Fuller interrupted. "I'm leaning toward allowing this. There's a lot on the line between myself and Gilly and this could go sideways really easy. Word of this doesn't leave this office. No one else besides the three of us, and your staff, of course, Jack. That being said, the safety of our officers would be my highest priority, politics be damned. I never thought I'd be in this job very long, anyway. I'll find a way to deal with the mayor's office. The carrot will be the table full of guns that we normally wouldn't have access to and the ability to solve homicides. But no matter what I do or say, Jack, know that it's not going to go over well with Mayor Hernandez."

"It's a go, Chief?" Adams excitedly clarified.

"It's a go, Lieutenant Adams. How long for you to be operational? And how long before we see results?"

Chief Fuller gets right to the point.

"I'll be operational in about two weeks, but I think it will start slow. We have to get the word out, and that will take some time. Once we start buying guns, I think it will speed up quickly as the gangbangers begin telling each other. As to how long before we can have a press conference for the mayor, that's a little gray."

Chief Fuller leaned back in his chair and crossed his arms. "Get to work, Jack," Chief Fuller commanded. "Steve, good job. Keep a close eye on this. I don't need daily updates, but keep me in the loop with highlights or concerns as they occur. If I need something, I'll reach out to you. And Jack, all our old evidence lockers, which are essentially big safes, that were in Parker Center were replaced when we closed the building down and moved over here. We have two of those old safes that were used for storing narcotics and cash over in Salvage. They're both the size of a large refrigerator, give or take. You can use both of them. Tell Salvage that you have my approval."

Fuller stood and walked to his office door. "Jack, do I need to know where this is happening?" he asked as if in closing.

"No, sir, I know where it is. I'm a lieutenant, for God's sake. If the need arises, I'll brief you."

"There is one other thing, Lieutenant," Chief Fuller added. "Something about Councilman Villanueva being a witness on one of your gang homicides."

Adams had known this was coming sooner or later. "Yes, Chief. The councilman called me while I was at the scene and asked me to make a press release that wasn't exactly accurate. He also gave me some information that was pertinent to our investigation that we can use as witness info."

"I see. Well, let's see if we can avoid placing the good councilman on the witness list, shall we?"

Chief Fuller opened the door to indicate the meeting was over and that it was time for Lieutenant Adams and Deputy Chief Nelson to leave. In the outer office, there was no sign of Deputy Mayor Sarah Holly.

"Excuse me, Chief Fuller," interjected the adjutant to the chief of police. "Mayor Hernandez is on line three for you, sir."

CHAPTER TWELVE
THE PLAN GETS A HOME

"**H**ey, LT, it's Maggie. Are you free to talk?" Maggie had come to learn that Lieutenant Adams rarely had moments to himself, or free time at all, and she was overly sensitive about disturbing him unnecessarily.

"Sure, Maggie. Just left Chief Fuller's office."

Always a sensitive issue, she thought. "Are you okay, Lieutenant?" Smiling at her concern, Adams assured her that he was fine. "LT, don't forget you're teaching at USC tonight at six o'clock. You were pretty late last time, so the dean of the Sociology Department called to remind you that class starts at six o'clock."

"I'll be busy all afternoon setting up a special detail. Be aware that Mac will be running it, and all six knuckleheads will be involved. They won't be coming into the office for a while, Maggie, so you'll need to forward their messages and paperwork to them through me. Just set up a 'Transfer' box and any time I come in, I'll pick it up and take it to them. Please ask the subpoena control officer to call me so I can have him continue any court cases these guys have. I'll fill you in when I see you."

Adams connected with Jesse Levin to obtain the specific address of the warehouse off Benton Way, just west of downtown Los Angeles. Heading to the warehouse to meet one of Levin's employees and obtain keys, Levin assured Adams that the warehouse would be emptied before the end of the day.

#

Pushing the flashing Accept button on his phone made Chief Fuller cringe. He was the chief of police and hated the feeling that he answered to someone else. Especially to Mayor Gilliam Hernandez.

"Good afternoon, Mayor, I expected your call. Deputy Mayor Sarah Holly was here earlier, but I'm guessing she ran out of time, because she left before we could adequately discuss your request."

Chief of Police George Fuller hated the situation he was in with the mayor of Los Angeles, but he had committed to work together as a team in order to be selected for the position. Although Mayor Hernandez fully expected to direct the chief of police in the running of the Los Angeles Police Department, George Fuller had other ideas. Play the game, get some time behind the chief's desk, then move on to another police department as chief of police. A department that was not run by politicians.

"Chief, I need to stress the importance and time-sensitive nature of this request. We, as a team, have a need to display to the citizens of Los Angeles that we are working together to make the city safe. One of the best ways to do that is to address the issue of guns on our streets. It benefits us both, Chief. Where are we with this?"

"Mr. Mayor, we are moving forward with a plan that we will be deploying immediately. I gave approval of the plan and met with my command staff who will be overseeing the project. Due to the sensitive nature of this particular effort, I'm reluctant to reveal the details at this moment, but rest assured I am aware of the priority nature of your request and that I am directing department assets to achieve what you are asking for."

Mayor Hernandez didn't like the sound of the chief's response, but he was used to working with powerful people who oftentimes had conflicting needs. "Thank you, Chief. Please brief me on the project as soon as you're able. But in the meantime, can I assume that you are moving forward immediately?"

"Absolutely, Mr. Mayor."

#

Los Angeles streets are crammed midday. Well, they're crammed all the time. Lots of cracks and potholes that beat everyone up and tend to destroy the cars driving over them. The curbs are broken and most of the faded painted lines and painted curbs are not visible any longer. The worst thing is that there's more trash collected on the streets than anyone would ever expect in a major city in the Unites States. The term "third world" comes to mind when driving Los Angeles streets.

Trees and bushes on Los Angeles streets and lining the freeways are either dead or overgrown. Nowhere in the city can you find landscaping that is well cared for except in front of political offices. Graffiti marks everything and even though some very misguided people in Los Angeles call it art, it's a plague.

Sidewalks have become a major obstacle to living in Los Angeles. They are cracked, broken, and dangerously raised in spots mostly by ignored landscaping and tree roots. They are certainly not usable to walk on anymore and most are blocked by street vendors, trash, and homeless encampments. Some of the Los Angeles politicians have determined that residents and business owners are personally responsible to repair and maintain the city sidewalks that run in front of their properties. Absolute craziness.

Cardboard, tents, and lean-to encampments have taken over many of the sidewalks, leaving only the street and gutter for people to walk as they try to avoid getting hit by passing cars, trucks, and oversize buses. Los Angeles buys mass transit buses that are too wide for the traffic lanes and are usually mostly empty. Yet, walking in the street and gutter is not quite far enough away to avoid the taunts, threats, sexual remarks, and actual assaults by the resident homeless. The current topic in City Council of spending many millions of dollars on bicycle lanes in Los Angeles just added to the humor of it all.

Adams laughed out loud as he pulled behind a white Toyota Prius with a personalized license plate that read "HATE LA." The sticker on the rear window that read "No Incumbents" probably summed up the driver's opinions about the state of affairs in Los Angeles.

Echo Park and Westlake, areas just west of downtown Los Angeles, were largely policed by LAPD's Rampart Division. Many years ago, the area was a special place. MacArthur Park was a beautiful spot with a lake, rental boats, and swans. Movie stars were often seen there. Dodger Stadium was built and became a source of pride for the residents—after they got over the anger of the city taking all of their houses in Chavez Ravine.

Then gangs completely took over Rampart Division. 18th Street gang, which split off from Clanton 14, had been largely a Hispanic gang until they allowed other races and ethnicities within the ranks. Many believed this was what had actually caused the split.

The group that split from Clanton 14 originally claimed the area around 18th Street and Union Avenue in Rampart Division. They had a strong foothold in the area, after which Mara Salvatruche (MS13), a Salvadoran gang, moved in and the entire area became a crime-ridden ghetto. 18th Street and MS13 were known in the United States and in Central America as being among the most violent street gangs in existence and continued to be bitter enemies.

In the late 1990s under Chief Bernard Parks, the political appointment of Mayor Richard Riordan and the Rampart CRASH scandal rocked the city. CRASH, which stood for Community Resources Against Street Hoodlums, was the name of the LAPD Gang Detail at the time.

The Rampart CRASH scandal involved approximately seventy CRASH officers who had been implicated in many crimes. The ensuing corruption investigation became the largest case of police corruption in the LAPD and possibly across the nation.

At the time, many believed there was an LAPD coverup of the investigation led by Chief Parks, who was said to be overly conscious of his personal image as chief of police. The City Council lost faith in Chief Parks and signed on to a federal Department of Justice (DOJ) consent decree that resulted in the DOJ stepping in to monitor reforms in the LAPD. Parks was not reinstated to his position as chief of police, but he was successful at moving on to become a City Council member.

A number of movies and television series were made to sensationalize the Rampart scandal, the studios, producers, directors, and actors getting rich while drawing young persons into the gang life they sensationalized. *You have to wonder how much more money Hollywood and wealthy actors really need.*

While driving to the warehouse in Rampart Division, Adams couldn't help but notice that the area was changing. Some tiny art galleries, some yuppie eating spots and coffee houses were popping up. The gentrification of the area was beginning, but it was going to be a tough road. Most of the businesses would fail. Many of these well-meaning people moving into the area, or people with a sense of adventure, would become victims. Being that Los Angeles public schools were rated among the worst in the nation, their children would attend schools providing a poor education. More importantly, schools where they were in danger.

Pulling up to the warehouse located in Rampart Division, Adams secured his keys to the front doors and thought to himself, *So it begins.*

Adams made his first call from the new office. "Hey, Mac, can you and the six knuckleheads meet me at the Salvadoran restaurant on Benton Way and 6th Street? I'd like to get moving on this warehouse project right away." Adams knew he was on a short timeline, promising Chief of Police Fuller that the operation would be up and running in two weeks. Right now that sounded impossible.

The next call went to Dan McVay at ATF. "Hey, Dan, how's ATF treating you today? Think you can meet me at 6th Street and Benton Way? I'll be at the Salvadoran restaurant for a bit. If I'm not there when you arrive, grab a bite and then just call my cell and I'll direct you into the warehouse. I recommend pollo guisado, the Salvadoran chicken."

Adams surveyed the warehouse before heading off to the restaurant, a big empty room with one walled-off bathroom, a swinging glass entrance door, and an overhead roll-up door. There wasn't much to it, but a lot of the connecting warehouses had opened businesses in them.

Adams had hoped to use the downtime at the restaurant catching up on paperwork, but Detective McClain and the six gang officers arrived faster than he expected.

"Mac, I need you to get over to the City Office of Finance and talk personally to the director. Drop Chief Fuller's name. Our goal is to complete all the business licensing paperwork and have the director personally insert it into the files; that will assure us that no clerical or administrative staff gets wind of this. You'll need a business name, and I also need you to get us a 1-800 number for the warehouse under the new business name and get a phone installed asap. Then we need a plan to design the inside of the warehouse to fit our business. I want public access only through the single glass door, not the roll-up, and I want people to walk into a walled-off office. We can build the walls to separate the office from the rest of the warehouse. Design it so that we can have backup tactical officers in the warehouse on the other side of the wall to keep an eye on things. Be sure that if we're forced to engage someone with a gun inside the location that we don't design the floorplan so that we're in a crossfire situation."

Adams instructed the group to go to the warehouse after lunch, start working on a design plan, and then meet back at the warehouse the following morning at 9 o'clock with work clothes on. "I think you guys will be working Day Watch for a while until we get this built and running, so get used to the sun being in your eyes. Anybody have carpentry skills? Build walls, drywall?" Silence. "Yeah, well, we'll figure it out."

Mac asked about a name for the business and John Andrews recommended, "Gold Rush! I love that show." Everyone traded looks and the name was selected. "Gold Rush, Gold and Jewelry, International."

"All right, you guys, get over to the warehouse. Mac, Dan McVay from ATF will be coming by. Let him know what you need for audio and visual inside and outside. See if he's got a US attorney for us yet. When he does, I'd like you to go with Dan to meet with the attorney and lay out our operation. See what he needs to prosecute and build it directly into our operations plan. I want to plan to succeed from the very beginning, and we want all federal criminal filings."

Adams told the group he was going to work on signage for the front of the business and then he had to get to USC for a class.

McClain immediately began considering all the administrative tasks that should be accomplished with an operation like the one they were taking on. "Lieutenant, do you want me to notify the commander in Central Bureau so they know we're setting up shop in their territory?"

The Central Bureau commander was not high on Lieutenant Adams's list. His claim to fame was that he had worked Gangs at one time, but he'd had a poor reputation then and an even poorer one now. He was largely believed to be a tactical moron who screwed up everything he touched.

The LAPD had been taking a lot of hits for the police response to riots and protests in downtown Los Angeles in Central Bureau, and the reason sat squarely on the shoulders of the Central Bureau commander and the poor decisions he routinely made. LAPD had a history of assigning major events to people because of their rank and not based upon their experience and leadership ability. The result was a lot of embarrassment on the front page of the *LA Times,* which never missed an opportunity to bad mouth law enforcement.

"No, Mac. This is need-to-know stuff, only us and the two chiefs. You know the commander in Central; he screws up enough stuff. We don't need him screwing up our stuff."

"It's going to be tough to keep working around him, LT. How long do you think we can keep it up?" McClain was hoping that Lieutenant Adams would agree to take the blame if the Central Bureau commander started complaining, but no luck.

"I'm guessing that sooner or later LAPD will promote him to deputy chief, Mac. That's what they usually do. At least he'll be out of our hair then."

#

"Pacific Signs, can I help you?" Pacific Signs was a small but successful sign company in Pasadena, just north of downtown Los Angeles. Jon Moser had accounts throughout the entertainment industry and with theme parks, which kept him very busy. His work was amazing.

"Hey, Jon, it's Jack Adams. What's up, big boy?" Moser spoke with a British accent and was occasionally a little hard to follow. When Adams couldn't quite understand his reply, he decided to jump right in. "Listen, pal, we're doing an undercover operation that I can't talk too much about, but I need some signage for the front of a business and I'm low on cash. It's a small warehouse with one roll-up door and one glass door."

Moser seemed interested in the project, even after the comment of not having money to pay for it. "Man, I'm in, Jack. Sounds like you need me to paint the signage on the glass door and maybe a hanging sign. You should probably have some kind of signage inside also, and how about business cards? I can do those."

Wow. More than Adams had expected.

"That sounds perfect, pal. This is a really sensitive operation and the chief has me sworn to secrecy. You'll know what the address is, but I need to swear you to secrecy also. And Jon, this may be dangerous, so the secrecy part is critical." Adams hated putting it like that, but there was no other way.

"Yeah, that's no problem. Get me the info and sizes, and I'll design the signs and then some stuff for the walls inside. I'll get a box of business cards for you, too."

While walking out the door, always in a hurry, Adam told Moser that Detective Ron McClain would be contacting him with the details and that McClain would be his contact person.

CHAPTER THIRTEEN
CULTURE CLASH

Adams pulled out from the warehouse and stopped at Phillipe's over on Alameda. It had only been a few hours, but he figured he'd better get a light dinner before heading to USC. *Once class is over, it will be dark. No telling when I may be able to eat again.*

A French dip sandwich, purple pickled egg, and potato salad with coffee. Oh, and apple pie. Adams picked an empty spot at one of the shared high tables and waded into the mound of paperwork he had to finish.

#

"Hey, Mac, it's Jack. I'm done doing paperwork and I'm off to USC to give a class, so I'll be out of play for a couple hours. You've got the helm, but I'm on my cell."

Parking at USC was tough, but Adams flashed his badge and got a faculty pass at the guard shack. Presenting to the graduate students in the Sociology Department while dressed in plain clothes instead of a police uniform would hopefully soften the perception of him being arrogant, as many police officers displayed. A byproduct of "being in charge."

The stadium seating was great for the students, but instructors were always straining their neck looking upwards. Tonight, seeing the students in the upper levels of the class was tough. The room seemed pretty full.

"Good evening, sociology warriors. Last month we talked about the negative effect of gangs on the quality of education in K-12 schools. We had a pretty heated discussion, but we left out one aspect of school management that I wanted to hit on before we move forward with tonight's discussion."

Adams stepped around the podium. "We talked about gangs in schools, but tonight let's touch a little bit on the negative impact that some school principals and administrators have on the situation. School principals and other school administrators receive annual performance evaluations, their job rating, and it commonly includes an evaluation of the administrator's ability to provide for a safe campus. As such, those administrators may be reluctant to notify the police department or other social service agencies that record statistics when crimes or concerns are reported by students. Those statistics of crimes on campus work against the school administrators. Do you see where I'm going with this?"

Adams looked across the room to make eye contact with the students. "What do you think the results are when the school principal or administrator makes a decision not to call law enforcement or an appropriate social service agency and attempts to handle the problem themselves in order to skew the statistics?"

One of the older students in the class, a woman sitting in the front row directly in front of the podium, burst out in a very loud and angry response. Her buttons had just been pushed, and she began firing off.

"I have two kids and they've gone to the principal like I've told them and reported being bullied and having their things stolen, but the principal refuses to call the police! She says that it's her policy to handle problems in-house instead of involving police agencies and that the school district supports it. I know she's lying. They even have their own school police, but they won't even call them. It makes me so mad. They never do anything, and it makes everything worse. Not only are they teaching my kids things that should only be taught at home by parents, my kids are scared in school. Can't I do anything about this?"

Wow, lots of energy in the first two minutes of class. "Actually, you or your children can call the police department instead of reporting to the school administrators, or do both. You don't have to abide by what the school staff tells you. That's what I tell my children—that they should always call me and then call the police."

This caused the entire class to engage in a fairly spirited discussion that school administrators, in "covering their own butt," create a lot of problems and trauma by persuading students and parents to allow the school to solve the problems.

"Lieutenant, doesn't anyone hold them accountable?"

"Well, think about that. The entire chain of management within the school district benefits from hiding crimes that occur on their campuses, whether it's K-12 or colleges. They want public support. They want parents to send children to their schools. Think about the competition between public schools and charter schools. They want government money. They want to keep their jobs."

It always surprised Adams how people could appear so involved and so upset at something that had existed forever. Like they had just heard about it. *Where has everyone been?*

"Have you heard of the Clery Act? Well, in the late 1980s, the Clery Act was passed and mandated that universities receiving federal aid report crime statistics on their campus. But universities have been fined for not accurately reporting these statistics. Even under the umbrella of law, school administrators avoid reporting crime on their campuses."

"Lieutenant Adams, I would think that the school administrators know what they're doing; they do this their whole careers. Maybe people don't want the police involved. They don't want to have records."

"That's certainly possible, and everyone has the choice. You can have the principal handle it if you like; it's your choice. But what about the student, possibly a very young person, who goes to the school office to report a crime and they are unduly convinced that the school administrators will handle the problem? What if that situation worsens because of that choice?"

A student who had never spoken during Adams's presentations raised her hand. *Very polite.*

"I would never involve the police. They don't care about us and they just fuck everything up. I'd trust the school way before I'd ever trust the police."

Not a fan of the police. "I'm sorry you feel that way, but sadly policemen sometimes give that impression, like in the old show *Dragnet*. Just the facts, ma'am. I think sometimes we get so busy and get so involved in our paperwork that we don't show the empathy, the compassion we should, and I'm sorry for that. Kindly remember that school principals and administrators are not trained to conduct criminal investigations, and they have no resources to prosecute crimes. Only law enforcement professionals are trained and have the resources to professionally resolve the problem, but you always have a choice. Back to the point, what we want to consider is whether the refusal of school administrators to involve the appropriate law enforcement or social service agency to protect their personal or organizational performance evaluation affects the overall, or long-term, environment on school campuses."

A comment came from Adams's far left, a student sitting alone with his arms crossed across his chest. "So do you think we should pass a law that mandates that school administrators call the cops whenever someone comes in the office to report a crime?"

"Well, again, that's the role of legislators, but we already have mandatory reporting laws in place, such as with child abuse. The California Penal Code identifies those persons who are mandated to report child abuse, and that includes teachers and school administrators. So that type of legislation already exists, but it does not include all crimes."

Time to move the class on. "Back to gangs. Police officers engage in what's called 'gang suppression,' policing gangs to investigate criminal activity and to suppress gang crime. Tonight, we're addressing a different perspective and talking about gang prevention and gang intervention efforts, so let's make sure our definitions are clear, because this is more in your wheelhouse as Sociology students." Adams paused as two new students entered the classroom. "Gang prevention refers to preventing someone, usually an at-risk youth, from joining a gang. Intervention refers to the process of assisting someone already in a gang to get out of the gang and shed gang life. Are any of you looking to include working with at-risk youth in your career goals? With youth who are rebellious or involved in narcotics, gangs, or committing crimes?"

Impressively, at least half of the class of forty-six students raised their hands. Adams would have expected that in a psychology course, as many entering that field felt protective of the most vulnerable, but it was a little surprising in a sociology course. At the graduate level, this group usually trended toward research fields.

"This is something we can talk about for hours. I'll try to keep it short and present it in an easily digestible way. So, here we are: gang prevention efforts, even by moderately professional organizations, consistently enjoy over an eighty percent success rate. That means that when we work with at-risk youth to prevent them from joining a gang, we consistently keep over eighty percent out of gangs. That's really high. How many things do we do in such a volatile arena that we succeed at over eighty percent of the time?"

A young man from the back of the class at the very top of the tiered seats that Adams could barely see commented, "Any time you can step in early and stop someone from doing something before they start, show them the error of their ways, and give them better alternatives that they feel good about, you're going to succeed."

Adams smiled at the answer pulled directly from one of the student's sociology books. "Good answer. Common sense, right? Now let's look at intervention efforts. For gang intervention programs, what do you think the average percentage of success is of getting gang members out of gangs?"

After receiving a handful of guesses, Adams dropped the bomb. "The answer is . . . almost never. Although programs vary, overall, the number is so low that we can't even assign it a percentage. In fact, most every gang intervention program shields their successes and failures in rhetoric, not in measurable formats. How scary is that?"

"But Lieutenant, we talk about gang intervention programs and they're all over the city. We've even had some of them come to our lectures and tell us about all the great things they do! They say they get people out of gangs and that they go out and talk to gang leaders and convince them to keep the peace and not fight with other gangs. They even invite students to come and work in their programs. With all due respect, Lieutenant, they can't be as bad as you say. If they're all a big failure, what are they doing? How do they stay in business? How come no one talks about them failing?"

Adams had met this student before class on the first day he presented to them. *She is all business and no nonsense. And she has lots of opinions.* "Good question, Shannon. The first thing to ask is where does their money come from, and how do they spend it? These are nonprofit organizations, and most are led by supposed ex-gang members and ex-convicts. They can raise money basically three ways. They can accept donations, they can sponsor fundraising events, and they can get free money from the government through grants, which is where all, or almost all, of their funding actually comes from. Although, it's not really free, is it? It comes from the taxes we pay, right?"

"But why does the government give them money if they don't do much? Don't they have to prove that they're successful in order to get money? Do they have politicians in their pocket?" Adams noted how impressive it was that students could become engaged in a topic that touched them and suddenly start to see the big picture.

"Well, many gang intervention programs generally profess that what they do cannot be tracked in a quantitative manner, which helps them to avoid the issue of discussing whether they are a success or failure. Additionally, they sell a very subjective idea that they keep the peace between gangs, but how would we know that's true? Is there a score sheet? You guys live in or near Los Angeles and you go to school here at USC in the middle of high gang crime neighborhoods. Do you see peace between gangs? I'll tell you that LAPD Gang officers see almost no evidence of what most of these gang intervention programs profess to be doing. But I'll leave you to make your own determination."

Adams decided not to avoid the sensitive question about relationships with politicians but rather to answer it tactfully. "There's a lot to think about when you ask the question about politicians providing public tax dollars to nonprofit organizations that may not be providing a valuable service. Are those politicians accountable for their actions, the same as whether the nonprofits are accountable for the value of the services they provide?"

"I think they do whatever they want. They never listen to us, and that's why I don't vote." Shannon was grumbling now.

Feeling the discussion was getting off track, Adams changed course with a little more advanced look at gangs from a sociological perspective. "Let's put it in a broader perspective. Everyone has an idea of what a 'gang' is, but not really, so let me tell you. Gangs are a culture. Note that word—'culture.' The term 'culture' refers to social behavior and norms found in certain groups such as religions, like being a Christian, or to ethnicities, like being Chinese or Hispanic. Within cultures, there are accepted societal norms embodied in things like arts, customs, music, dress, food, beliefs, and language. Gangs are a culture." Adams let this sink in for a moment.

"Gangs display those same types of societal norms and customs as reflected in other cultures. Very importantly, do you see how this concept of gangs as a culture applies to those involved in gang intervention efforts?"

"So what you're saying, Lieutenant Adams, is that if gangs are a culture, then it's as hard to get them out of their gang, out of their culture, as it would be to get a Christian person to quit being Christian, and so on?"

Ah, Shannon is also a critical thinker. Adams enjoyed seeing students learn through his technique of presenting information and questions to generate discussions among the students. He would rather challenge students to think and make personal decisions rather than lecture them.

The student in the far back row responded, "Everyone knows they're more than a club or more than being in the Boy Scouts, but I never really thought of them as being their own culture. That seems like you're stretching it to me, Lieutenant."

Adams enjoyed this class, relishing that students at the graduate level were more engaged in the learning process. "If we can accept or even just entertain that gangs are not a club, like you mentioned, or a group of buddies hanging out together but are, in fact, a culture, then I think we can also accept that efforts to cause them to leave that culture and be someone else are probably not going to be successful. It's not surprising that these gang intervention programs largely fail. From a sociology perspective, what would you do to get a gang member to stop being in a gang?"

"Shock therapy" was the first answer thrown out.

Walking toward a student, Adams asked, "What nationality or ethnicity are you, if you don't mind my asking?"

The student answered, "I'm Japanese."

"Okay, if my goal was to get you not to be Japanese any longer, what could I do to convince you?" Adams decided to pose this harder, more personal question to move the discussion along.

"Well, I couldn't *not* be Japanese. I *am* Japanese."

"Exactly," Adams agreed.

"Lieutenant," a new student chimed in. "I don't understand how they can have their own culture. I thought gangs were neighborhood-based groups, gangs of people protecting their neighborhood. Can't they just move?"

"Good question, but you're missing the crux of the concept that gangs are a culture, not merely a group of people who happen to live in the same neighborhood. That being the case, where they live has minimal if any effect on their strength of affiliation to a gang. Even so, I'll tell you that historically gangs were somewhat neighborhood based, to use your term, in that similar races or ethnicities tended to congregate in the same neighborhood and they easily bonded because of their cultural similarities. But, from the very beginning, the foundation for their gang membership could be argued to be cultural."

Adams's goal was to challenge the students' understanding of what a gang member really was. "Early on, people commonly formed a group to defend themselves from other groups and to help them through periods of poverty and possibly discrimination. But that began changing early on. For example, during the late sixties and early seventies we began to see much more rapid change. One of the reasons was that gangs became more prominent in selling narcotics and their profile began to change; they actually went into business."

Adams purposely took a drink of water to pause for effect. "I'll tell you a story from my past. In the mid-1970s, an apartment building in LAPD's Southwest Division became known as 'Sherm Alley' and exploded with PCP sales in Los Angeles. Phencyclidine. The apartment building was near the corner of Coliseum and Santa Barbara Boulevard, now called Martin Luther King Boulevard. Shortly after, rock cocaine came on the scene, and everything changed. Street gang members became businessmen. They no longer said, 'This is my neighborhood.' They said, 'This is my corner to sell drugs. This is my business location, my office.' Gangs morphed into businesses with management, distributors, salesmen, transportation, accountants, the works."

Time to issue a challenge. "Can you see that, as these gangs became businesses, they would naturally continue to evolve beyond being a street gang protecting their neighborhood?"

Shannon grabbed that question immediately. "Of course, Lieutenant. To be a successful business, they must expand. I've read that Los Angeles gangs are all over the world now. They're selling guns and drugs and moving them all over the world. The article talked about Los Angeles Crip gang members in Amsterdam and Brussels . . . I can't remember where else. But they were certainly not in their own neighborhood."

"Exactly," Adams agreed. "We've exported our gang problem and the gang culture to other countries. And in so doing, we've allowed other countries to export their gang problems to America, a large problem with illegal immigration. It obviously doesn't matter where a gang member lives. Although, Shannon, and everyone else, you should be careful with what you read and continue to be critical thinkers. There's a professor at Cal State Long Beach who is still promoting the fact that gangs are neighborhood-based groups, and he's more than fifty years behind the times. He professes that because gangs have some level of discernible boundaries in each of our cities, and that there are areas or neighborhoods that they claim to be under their control, they are neighborhood-based groups. He completely misses the foundation of the gang culture. Why is that?"

"Well, Lieutenant, maybe on a college campus he doesn't get to see the real picture. We're pretty isolated here."

Adams laughed. "That may be part of it, but many professors on college campuses, PhDs, do not conduct original research, and that's the crux of many failures in academia. Unoriginal research. They're trying to understand the issue by studying the works of other professors and then writing a new unoriginal paper on what they've read."

This was moving to a fairly controversial place, being that Adams was standing on a college campus. "Secondly, some professors on college campuses representing themselves as gang experts are somehow actually connected to the fields of social welfare, which tends to look at gangs in a completely different way and believes that they are victims of their environment. They address the issues of social justice, but they miss the entire concept that gangs are a culture."

"Lieutenant Adams, what do you mean they're not doing original research?"

"Good question, Shannon. There is very little original research in the field of gangs, and it's not uncommon for college professors to review multiple sources of existing research—what has already been written. If you look at the bibliography of whatever they are publishing, there's usually a stream of papers other professors have previously written on the subject and it's oftentimes fairly old products. They compile a bunch of previous research and literature, study them, and then form their own new opinions about what they've read and write another unoriginal paper. Some of the more energetic reach out to conduct some level of research, but not to the level required for them to see the big picture. Their research is not original but a conglomeration of research that has already been conducted."

Finally, the lady in the front row got involved again. "Clearly the stuff they use in their report may not be accurate and it may be old. If every one of those guys are merely regurgitating everyone else's work, the opinions they present have to be skewed sooner or later. And it really gives them an open door to present whatever their personal opinions are and hide them in whatever research they can find to support them. They may even ignore other research that doesn't agree with their personal opinions. This is sociology, Lieutenant Adams. One of the things we study is how fast people, humanities, and societies change and how that change occurs. You would think professors or whoever they are in the academic world would do their own original research with current information and good sources! If they're merely reorganizing and rewriting other stuff that they're able to pick and choose from, there's no way it can even be accurate."

"Great point. I want to reinforce that you be cautious about your research into gangs and understand that the most accurate and timely research may not come from the academic community. Gangs are a culture, so the best way to research this aspect of gangs is study the overarching concept of cultures. As sociology graduate students, study the foundations and historical developments of other existing cultures to identify whether similarities exist that support my beliefs of a gang culture. That may be one of the best tools available to you. Societal change affects gang cultures in the same manner as other cultures. Keep your eyes open to recognize the change that has already occurred and, even more importantly, the change that you believe will occur in the future. The gang culture is still evolving, as is most every other culture.

"By the way, change occurs in stages, right? So as we look at gang cultural change, we may not see one hundred percent change in every case. As an example, older gang members will most probably have moved on to a more advanced model of gang activity, while younger members may still be standing on the street corner flashing gang signs. Gangs in Los Angeles may display an advanced stage of cultural evolution, whereas gangs in smaller towns may not be there yet. However, although we see incremental changes, those changes are all focused in the same direction."

Adams was actually enjoying the class tonight. "Although we in law enforcement rely heavily on the information I'm giving you, we know it instinctively by working with gangs every single day and watching the changes that occur over the years and decades. That being said, I'm not aware of even one professor developing a research effort that addresses all of the factors affecting the evolution of gangs. The culturalization of gangs. What's wrong with that? Why aren't those in the field of cultural anthropology developing an interest to do that?"

"Maybe no one cares, Lieutenant. They're just gang members."

"Well, maybe. But let's hope we see some advancement in original and appropriate research in the near future as to the culturalization of gangs. That just may cause the responsibility for many of these problems to be addressed by the appropriate resources, not just law enforcement. For years, the failures of others have been passed on to police departments to solve. Police officers are supposed to prevent crimes largely by their presence and investigating suspicious persons or circumstances, along with investigating crimes and enforcing laws to keep society safe. I think we can agree that it is not the role of law enforcement to solve the homeless problem, solve the problem of young people joining gangs, or resolve mental health issues. Somehow, when others fail in their responsibilities, they hand it to the police departments. Those of you in the field of sociology, I want you to think about that."

CHAPTER FOURTEEN
TRUTH HURTS

After a short break, Adams continued to move the discussion forward. "Your comment about societal and individual change is very interesting, so I'm going to present to you a bit of a bigger piece of the picture now. I don't want you to get stuck on the fact that gangs are no longer neighborhood based, whatever that term may mean, and are now a culture of their own. Nor do I want you to get stuck on the knowledge that most gangs now mimic very familiar business models, although a criminal business model. There is still more happening in the gang world that you need to consider."

Time for the class to take another step.

"Gangs are in the next very natural evolution of gang life and gang crime. For us to believe that gangs are, in fact, their own culture, we also have to recognize that they support somewhat of a business model, although a fragmented and violent one in most cases—a criminal business model. I think we can certainly accept that model will not hold forever, either."

Adams knew he was holding the students' attention now and tried to keep the discussion within the realm of their studies: sociology.

"Gangs are now evolving into a model of organized crime. They are becoming involved in white-collar crime, identity theft, business extortion, human smuggling, and human trafficking, among other crimes."

"Wait, wait, wait, Lieutenant Adams. Aren't they standing on corners selling drugs? That's what I see."

"Great question, but let's start by looking at something that's essentially not visible. For gang members to continue to evolve into a model of organized crime, including the commission of white-collar crime, they can't look like gang members any longer. It's probably hard to pass someone's credit card with an '18th Street' tattoo on their neck. So, no more visible tattoos, baggy pants, and white T-shirts. What we are seeing is gang members shedding what we call the 'physicalities' of gang membership."

The class seemed to perk up again as Adams continued this thought. A new buzzword for them to use in their assignments. "In regards to shedding the physicalities of gang membership, we're seeing fewer and fewer gang members hanging out on the street and being visibly identified by their appearance, their clothing, and tattoos. Mostly, we only see very young kids still on the street looking like gang members. Why is that?"

"Lieutenant, excuse me." More students continued to join the conversation—a good sign they were interested in the topic. "I'm actually a business major and I guess I'm looking at things a little differently. I appreciate the field of sociology, but I'm pretty numbers oriented. The bottom line. If gang members are doing different types of crimes now that are nonviolent, like white-collar crimes, they probably don't get arrested as much, so I'm guessing it's a learning curve. Don't look like a gang member and stay off the street, then make more money without getting arrested. We always hear that white-collar crimes have really low punishments." The young woman sitting next to the business major gave him a big smile.

"Exactly. They're getting rid of gang clothes and cars. They stop hanging out on the street corners. They go to one of the well-meaning free tattoo removal places but only have visible tattoos removed. Just the ones on their face, neck, and arms, not the ones on their chests or backs. Remember, their goal is not to quit being in a gang—it's to *hide* that they're in a gang. Just the opposite of what they believed only a handful of years ago when they brazenly stood on street corners flashing gang signs."

Lieutenant Adams knew he was continuing to push boundaries but believed that sometimes that was necessary in order to educate. "I have another example that may help you understand this trend. Let's see if I can put it in a business perspective for our business major."

Adams reached out for another example, hoping to reaffirm his original comments. Teaching is a challenge that can have incredibly strong results, but only if you're able to reach people. "In Hollywood, prostitutes used to be everywhere and easy to visibly pick out, right? Anyone driving down the street on Hollywood or Sunset Boulevards, Santa Monica Boulevard, Western Avenue, and others in Hollywood could easily point out prostitution activity. It was easy for the police to identify prostitutes and arrest them because they dressed and appeared like the traditional model of what people believed prostitutes looked like. Similarly, they acted the way people believed prostitutes acted like. That was their marketing plan, the foundation of their business plan. They wanted prospective customers who were driving by to know that they were prostitutes, so they had to look and act the part. They had to be very visible to the public, to their prospective customer base. Can you guys buy that?"

"It's a common business and marketing plan," the business student smugly added, then smiled at the young woman sitting next to him.

"You're absolutely right, business major. But then came the age of the internet. With the internet, prostitutes learned they could advertise on the internet and come into contact with even more customers, make more money, and reduce their exposure to being arrested. So, they learned not to go out onto the street, where they were very visible and risked coming into contact with police, where they reached less customers, and where it was more dangerous." Adams observed a lot of nodding heads.

"As such, they modified their business and marketing plans so that it no longer required that they be in a public place and look and act like the prostitute model we talked about. To the contrary, it now benefited prostitutes to no longer maintain that appearance. Prostitutes under the new 'internet marketing model' are not picked up by customers driving by in cars. Instead, they meet customers through internet communication, either on designated prostitution websites or by discussing dating or prostitution on dating sites or social media. So, we can see the 'physicalities' of prostitution changed, similar to what we see going on with gangs. With prostitution, risqué clothes and outrageous public behavior were no longer a necessary component of their business marketing model. It was also no longer necessary to be visible on the street—just like our new model of gangs."

Adams moved from the front of the class, walking to a corner of the room to give students a moment to digest this information. He saw the understanding sinking in from their expressions. "So, now that prostitution is less visible on the streets of Hollywood, do you believe that we've finally solved the problem? That prostitution is no more? Do you think that all the people who complained about visible prostitution activity in their Hollywood neighborhoods should be happy now? Or, on the other hand, can you accept that prostitution today is many times bigger than it ever was? That many more people are attracted to the field because there is less danger of being arrested now and less danger of being identified as a prostitute to one's friends and family? Similarly, on the other side of the coin, can you accept that there are also many more customers now willing to engage someone in discussing prostitution because it is more anonymous, no longer a public or visible action?"

The business major commented, "So, Lieutenant . . . we don't even know how many prostitutes there are?"

Adams nodded. "Can you accept that it's much harder, or even impossible, for us to identify the number of prostitutes in our cities? Can you also accept that we can't determine how many customers there are willing to engage in an act of prostitution because it is less public, less visible now? Just like gangs, can you accept that prostitution has gone through a new evolution and that prostitution will most probably continue to evolve?"

"Lieutenant," chimed in the mother in the front row. "We live in Hollywood, and I've heard our city councilman take credit for his efforts to eliminate prostitution from Hollywood. Is he lying?"

"Well, that's not a question for someone like me to answer. I'm just a lowly police lieutenant. I offer to you that prostitution has gone through a very natural evolution based upon the development of the internet transforming those involved from highly visible street activities to a less visible internet-based business model and that, most probably, your city councilman had no real effect on that evolution. I would also offer that prostitution is many times larger than it ever was when the crime was a more public and visible one, and that no one at present is able to determine the true number of prostitutes or the number of customers. Obviously, my position is that the prostitution problem has not been resolved, only modified to be less visible and to increase both the customer base and the number of prostitutes. I would add that the result is an enormous and unquantifiable expansion of the prostitution problem."

He heard a lot of quiet comments and saw nodding heads in the audience. Adams had actually expected more disagreements during his lecture today, but the class was going easy on him. "I encourage you, as always, to use critical thinking and your common sense to look at this situation and make your own conclusions. Drive through Hollywood and tell me whether street prostitution is as visible today as it was in years past. Then identify whether prostitution exists in an expanded marketing format on the internet—on site-specific formats, on social media, or in chat rooms or other forms of private communications. And if you find prostitution activity actually is less visible today than it used to be on the streets of Los Angeles, then decide whether the prostitution problem has actually been resolved. If you believe it has been, then decide whether your city councilman was the one who resolved the problem."

"So what you're saying is that criminals adapt so that they can still make money and victimize people, but not get arrested as much?"

"Well, that's part of it. Remember that in each of these models, gangs and prostitution, by not announcing who they are by the way they look and dress or where they hang out, the personal danger to them also goes down. They are not visible on the street to be arrested or victimized. Very importantly, it also allows them to commit a whole new set of crimes and a greater volume of crimes, which is paramount to this new model. With gangs evolving to commit white-collar crimes, the results of these crimes usually yield more profit, and the crimes oftentimes result in less criminal penalties if they get caught. This reinforces the benefits of the current evolution of gang crimes and gang membership."

Now to tie the discussion in to the students' field of study. "Again, don't get too caught up in these examples. The point we want to grasp is that criminals evolve, cultures evolve, just like all the other groups and societies that you study in sociology. And if that evolution results in criminals being less visible or committing different types of crimes that are less visible, there may be people in government offices who take that opportunity to step in front of the cameras and take credit for solving that last older, more visible model. Now, I hope you can see how unethical that is. Prostitution still exists and has in fact grown much larger, even though it is far less visible in a public setting. Gang activity still exists and has grown immensely larger. It is international now, even though it is far less visible and gang membership numbers have grown."

"Lieutenant, how many gang members are there?"

"Well, that's such a good question. Let's talk for a moment about the number of gangs and gang members in Los Angeles County, where we are right now. Does anyone know how many gang members there are in LA County?" Lots of numbers were thrown out, but all were guesses. Then came the answers from frantic Google searches.

"You're right, available literature will tell you that there are approximately four hundred fifty gangs and forty-five thousand gang members in Los Angeles County. Can we rely on those numbers?"

The business student immediately raised his hand. "Sir, I'm sure that the people who provide those numbers use a business and accounting model to recognize, measure, and record the number of gangs and gang members with an acceptable error range. An acceptable plus or minus." He gave a big smile to the girl sitting next to him. She even smiled back this time. He was on a roll.

"Good point, and you would think so. But no. We have absolutely no idea how many gang members there are. Not in Los Angeles, the county, the state, or anywhere else. When the city or county of Los Angeles or the State of California put those numbers out that you're seeing on your cell phones, they're not even in the ballpark." That clearly upset the business student.

"Let's look at that business model you're talking about to count the number of gang members. Gang members are actually counted by street police officers as they talk to people during the course of their work shift. The first step in accurately identifying the number of gang members in any jurisdiction would rely then upon police officers contacting every single person in the city, county, or wherever and accurately determining which of those persons are gang members, which is impossible. Think about that. Can the government even get an accurate census as to how many people live in Los Angeles County? How can we ever know how many gang members there are?"

Adams gave a moment of silence for this to register. Common sense is oftentimes enlightening. "And in today's climate, in which policemen are getting out of their cars for proactive police work less and less, it is becoming practically impossible. The more pressure and criticism placed upon police officers, the less proactive work they do, the less people they contact."

Adams let that sink in a second before continuing. "It also assumes—incorrectly—that police officers in every case are able to clearly and accurately identify whether a person they have contacted is, in fact, a gang member. And then, it's usually only officers specifically assigned to gang details that will record and submit a report of a gang member. Most every other police officer will usually avoid the paperwork or may not have the experience or expertise to make that determination. How about smaller police departments across the US that do not participate in the identification and recordation of gang members at all?" As the students processed his words, the numbers on their screens began to look questionable.

"Keep in mind what we've been talking about. Gang members are less visible today, less identifiable as gang members than in the past. Police officers assigned to gang details may not even know to stop them for a gang investigation because their appearances are largely different today."

Adams still had so much to tell these students, but there wasn't enough time. *This has to be abbreviated and kept in the realm of sociology.* "Here in California, law enforcement officers submit those records of gang member street contacts to the State of California for inclusion in a database called Cal Gang, and that's where we draw the numbers from. Cal Gang is the source for what is considered the official count of gangs and gang members in California, while other states may have no such tool. However, the Cal Gang database was never designed to 'count' the number of gang members. It was designed as a research tool to assess the involvement of persons in gang crimes either as a suspect or a victim. Do you see the problem here? It's impossible for law enforcement officers to contact every person in the state, and it's impossible for them to accurately identify which persons they do contact are gang members or not.

"The icing on the cake is that the database that we use to count gangs and gang members was not even designed for that purpose, so it does a terrible job of counting them. So your belief, business major, that a stable business model must be in place to accomplish this task is just not supported by facts. We use street police officers to record the number of gang members they contact because it's the only thing we have. We use the Cal Gang database to count gangs and gang members because it is simply the best we have at the moment, even though it was never designed for that purpose and does a terrible job at it. So, to address your comment that an appropriate statistical model was probably employed to count gang members . . . well, not really."

This drove the business student crazy. His credibility had just taken a hit; the girl sitting next to him suddenly seemed far less impressed. "Lieutenant Adams, you mean there is no business, statistical, or accounting model within which accepted parameters are applied to guarantee an accurate count of gang members?"

"Exactly right. I guarantee you that the published number of gang members in the city or county of Los Angeles is the tip of the iceberg. Listen to my next comment: those numbers being presented that you're reading on your cell phones bear absolutely no resemblance to the factual situation."

"Sir, that's crazy. No one would do that. How do you make decisions on how to fight gangs when you don't even have the right numbers? This is crazy."

Nice kid. "It goes further, young man. Not all law enforcement agencies even make an effort to identify or count gangs or gang members, or even gang-related crimes. So the count could actually be even less accurate in other cities, states, or countries than it is here in Los Angeles."

"So, the numbers we're seeing about the numbers of gang members are basically a joke?"

"I'm sorry to agree with you, son, but yes they are. An absolute joke. Again, the statistics bear absolutely no resemblance to the factual situation. So, as we are developing strategies to have a positive effect on gang membership and gang crimes, law enforcement managers commonly develop plans based upon those incredibly flawed numbers. Meanwhile, we in law enforcement at the operations level who actually work on the streets and fully accept that we cannot even consider these numbers . . . we try the best we can to work with the decisions made by others."

Adams immediately felt bad about his last comment. That just wasn't something you publicly stated, even though it was true. *Time to divert, quickly.* "Understand that there are persons in academia who represent themselves as gang experts and lecture you or develop academic papers or studies for you to read, and they may very well accept these numbers as being factual. How accurate do you think these professors are in developing position papers for you to read about gangs? How much can you rely on their lectures and their opinions as to studying or solving gang issues?"

Taking another swipe at engaging their brains, Adams added, "Law enforcement is in a place today in which most decisions are based upon statistics, upon numbers. I'm sure you've heard the term 'police intuition.' Well, that's a thing of the past. In fact, using that term as a basis for taking a police action will get you into trouble really fast. Today, we are numbers driven. Given that numbers can be made to say what we want, purposely manipulated, or just be wrong, such is the case with the count of gang members or prostitutes, can you accept that decisions being made to address gangs may be bad or baseless decisions?"

Another student up in the cheap seats asked, "Even though we don't know how many gang members there really are, are we really able to count how many crimes gang members commit? How is it that we hear from the Los Angeles mayor, and I think from the chief of police, that gang crimes are down in Los Angeles? If you don't know how many gang members there are, how do they know how many crimes are committed by gang members? How do you know that gang crimes are down?"

"Well, good question, and it hits on two different foundations. The first is that you're correct, we factually don't know how many gang members there are, so we can't possibly know how many crimes are committed by gang members. But it goes a step further, and this is embarrassing."

In that moment, Adams wished the rest of the general public would ask these same questions. "Even of the gang members we do know, we obviously can't know all of the crimes they commit. And of the crimes we *do* know they commit, we don't count all of them. How does that sit with you? Try this one on. Even of the crimes we do know that have been committed by gang members, we only count what we call Part I crimes—murder, robbery, burglary, rape, auto theft, assault, theft, and arson. What about crimes such as narcotics or weapons charges that we don't even count? Remember the comment about gang members standing on the corner selling drugs? Yeah, we don't count those crimes. And remember that we talked about gangs evolving into other crimes such as selling guns, extortion, credit cards, human trafficking, prostitution, and others? Well, we don't track those either. Just as the state's Cal Gang database was never designed to count the number of gang members we have, the system of tracking gang crimes was never designed to track all crimes committed by gang members."

The class began going crazy and talking among themselves. Some were even laughing out loud, which hurt Adams's heart. He knew we as a society could do better. Adams took no pleasure in telling them they were being lied to but believed that sooner or later, we needed to develop a new and well-educated group of people engaging the problems of society. Who better to engage these issues than sociology students emerging into society as professionals? Political leaders along with many, if not most, law enforcement leaders were certainly not doing it.

"Let me ask you this, a common-sense question. If someone in government service, whether it be someone in law enforcement or someone in politics, reports that gang crime is either up or down when we know that the numbers are wrong, what could be their motive in making those statements? The press, the media, hold an incredibly strong influence over all of us, so how about when the press reports that gang crimes are up or down?" Adams posed the question and waited, wanting students to come to their own conclusions.

The business major was the obvious person to respond. "Well, it means they're lying and using those numbers to influence people. Like you said, Lieutenant, numbers can be made to say whatever we want them to say. And if they use numbers that aren't true, that aren't accurate, then they can really use them to say whatever they want and influence people to believe whatever they want. Telling people that crimes are down can get them reelected, or saying that crime is up can make someone else look bad. This is crazy."

Feeling as though he'd stirred the pot enough on that issue, Adams decided to leave the discussion where it was and move forward.

"Sir, this doesn't make sense. How do you do your job? How do you develop plans to fight gang problems? How are all these politicians taking credit for stuff that's not real?" The business student was so frustrated he was becoming angry. *His parents would be proud. He's actually engaging and learning something.*

Adams had dealt with these frustrations for so long that it became second nature. "It's certainly a challenge, but in law enforcement we enforce laws and don't legislate. So, in our eyes, it's what they give us, and we do our best to keep you safe. That's the bottom line: keeping you safe. Officers assigned to gang units understand that decisions made by politicians and law enforcement management based upon statistics may be flawed, but they push forward and try to do the best they can. I understand that some of you do not think kindly of police officers, but trust me, these officers are incredible people with enormous hearts and they're dedicated, through all their efforts, to keeping you safe. I want you to think about that when policemen are criticized. Through all the block walls placed in front of them, these officers are still dedicated to keeping you safe."

Adams tried to keep moving the class along. These discussions were taking much longer than he had planned, and he'd probably take some heat, potentially a lot of it, for some of the comments he made. There always seemed to be someone who felt a need to call the police department and complain whenever policemen said something controversial, although the complaint was commonly made anonymously. Even though Adams's comments were truthful, there were a lot of people who did not want them uttered.

"I want you to grasp that gangs are in a different place today than where they used to be and that they are still evolving into new models. Gang members are becoming less visible to the police and general public. They are committing a new class of crimes—let's call them white-collar crimes for lack of a better title. Gangs are still violent and are now international. So, have we solved the gang problem because it is no longer as visible as it used to be?"

Adams looked across the room and wondered if there was at least one person who felt determined to make a difference in what they were learning about. "If gangs are less visible, can we really believe and accept that gang membership is down or that gang crimes are down? Are we actually solving the gang problem? Many of the violent crimes such as shootings by gang members are gang-on-gang. And as gangs evolve into having a less prominent presence on the streets and are less visible targets, those gang-on-gang shootings are going down. So, have we solved the gang problem if the level of violent crime they commit on one another has gone down? Have traditional gang-committed crimes been replaced by a new type or category of crimes? Can we accept the word of the media, of law enforcement leaders and politicians that we have achieved success in Los Angeles and other cities because shootings are down? Can we accept when they take credit for gang crimes going down? Just like the city councilman you talked about who takes credit for solving the prostitution problem in Hollywood, can we buy into what the gang intervention programs are telling us—that they are actually the ones successfully keeping the peace between gangs? That they are the ones responsible for gang crimes going down?"

The silence in the room was impressive. Students were usually much more vocal and willing to challenge him.

"If you can gain this perspective, maybe you as sociology students can accept a responsibility to address the culturalization of gangs, to identify evolving gang trends and address the expected or projected effects on society. In my humble opinion, it's not enough to look historically at the societal changes Shannon mentioned earlier. Looking to the future is much more important."

The business student had one last thought. "Sir, if we do not know the number of gang members in our midst, nor the number of crimes they commit or what kind of crimes they commit because both processes used to facilitate tracking and recording those figures are flawed, why hasn't there been an effort to correct that situation?"

"Well, again, I'm not able to fully answer that question because it's not something in my wheelhouse. I'll brag to you that I am one of the predominant gang experts in the country, and I have certainly made those efforts to educate people in positions of authority. But what you're asking requires efforts or legislation at the city, state, and federal levels, which law enforcement are not always included in. Most importantly, it requires the will to do it. Certainly, we would be a good source for legislators to rely upon, but the effort is theirs to initiate. Remember, this is an effort that would be necessary to address nationwide. Such a broad brush takes someone high in government circles, certainly not a lowly lieutenant on a city police department."

Adams's time was up. Before he went back to police work, he had one last thought to leave with the class. "Lastly, do you remember what we discussed about school administrators not being willing to accurately report crimes on their campuses because it would negatively affect the way they are personally evaluated? Even though they sacrifice the well-being of so many students, so many young people. Well, a similar follow-up question could be addressed about whether our law enforcement and political leaders even want an accurate accounting of gang issues. A stronger foundation of accurate information that could be used in effective problem-solving strategies would reveal a substantially higher number of gangs, gang members, and gang crimes. Understand that the result of what you're asking, an accurate accounting, will make them look bad. Knowing that, do you really think that will ever happen?"

CHAPTER FIFTEEN
HELLS ANGELS

Another day kicked off, and the two-week deadline to get Gold Rush up and running weighed heavy on Adams. Adams made breakfast for his son and daughter and drove them to school. They loved riding in the police car. As he walked to the chain-link fence and watched them run onto the playground to play with their friends, he realized how blessed his life was. In this moment, it felt like Los Angeles was on the other side of the world.

Adams found a few moments back at home to make calls and enjoy the cool morning weather. The marine layer was holding late into the morning this time of year, and it was a great time to be in the backyard with coffee. Looking at the old boat he had bought a few years ago with the intent of fixing it up, a twenty-six-foot Skipjack, reminded him that he had a lot of projects lined up to finish. Maybe he'd get back to it next weekend. He had lots of dreams about adventures on the water with his son and daughter.

As Adams settled into a chair in his yard, he was surprised by the phone suddenly ringing. "Hey, Lieutenant, it's Roger Leigh over at Wilshire Gangs. Listen, Wilshire Division had two jewelry store robberies a couple months ago and they just linked a carjacking to one of them. Apparently, the suspects jacked a Jeep Cherokee outside a 7-11 about two hours before the robbery and used it as the getaway vehicle."

Detective Roger Leigh got right to the point connecting the crimes to gangs. "When the Robbery detectives followed up on the car and it came back to a Wilshire Division stolen, they found out that the camera outside the 7-11 captured the carjacking in the parking lot. It caught a really clear view of one of the suspects, and two of our Gang officers who work the Jungle identified him as a kid called 'Lil Sweet' from Black P. Stones."

"That was some good luck; those cameras are usually the worst. So I'm guessing you want to take it as a gang crime?" Lieutenant Adams had recently led a joint LAPD and FBI Narcotics investigation targeting the Black P. Stones in the Crenshaw neighborhood of Baldwin Village, a neighborhood known as the Jungle. Adams was always looking for a reason to get back on the Black P. Stones.

In the late 1960s, a young member of the Black P. Stone Nation living off

47th Street in the slums of Southside Chicago moved to Los Angeles with his mother. That one young boy exploded upon the scene, and Los Angeles became the host to a new arm of the Black P. Stone Nation gang, which affiliated with the local Blood gangs.

"Sort of, Lieutenant. Wilshire detectives actually approached us to take over both investigations, but I wanted to check with you first. Same suspects on both crimes, and Lil Sweet is right in there. They wore hoodies but it's obvious. Three males and a tall stocky female. The robberies were takeovers, then they smashed the glass cases. All the suspects had handguns except the female, who had a shotgun in both robberies."

"Sure, Roger, that's a no-brainer if we've already got one identified. I wonder why Wilshire Robbery doesn't want to run with it . . . unless they're really swamped right now. Hold off a bit on picking up Lil Sweet until you have a really good feeling for this. Remember that the Black P. Stones are partnered with most of the other Bloods, and they're usually cliqued up pretty strong with the Rollin' 20s. The rest of this robbery crew could be a mixture of Bloods running together, and that may cloud your investigation as you attempt to identify all the players."

"Got it, Lieutenant. What are you thinking about the jewelry? Are they pawning it?"

"You're probably right, Roger. Gangbangers are low-hanging fruit, and they usually don't have access to quality fences that can handle jewelry. What are they doing with it? There's some pretty low-level pawnshops in the Crenshaw area, but they could have someone inside one of them who's working with them on the jewelry. I'm also wondering if there's more robberies. Could be we haven't linked all of their robberies, so we need to look at other crimes across the city. The tall female with a shotgun is pretty distinct; you might start with that. They could also be hitting outside of LA, because they sound pretty brazen. Like they've done it before and now they're pretty cocky about it. Let me know what you find out."

"Will do, boss. Be safe, sir."

Detective Roger Leigh of Wilshire Division Gangs was excited about the opportunity to take on two easily solvable crimes and beef up his case clearance rate. As he hung up the phone, he got the feeling that it was going to take more work than he first thought. *Maybe that's why Wilshire Division Robbery detectives didn't want it.* His first task: look at every robbery in Los Angeles over the last couple of years. In a place like Los Angeles, that's a lot of robberies.

#

Work beckoned and Adams dialed his first number of the day. "Good morning, Mac. I know you're busy getting the warehouse ready, but what's in the works for the taco stand robberies tonight and tomorrow? It's a bad time because we've only got two weeks, less now, to get Gold Rush up and running, but we've already committed to doing this taco stand robbery detail."

He continues to get work done through others by delegating authority. So much happens on the streets of Los Angeles that Adams continually used the leverage of delegation to accomplish the work.

"Yeah, I know, Lieutenant. I've already told everyone that we're starting midmorning at the warehouse today, and then we'll pull out and run the surveillance on the Sepulveda Boulevard taco stands this evening. I've already selected three taco stands, two new ones and one they've already hit—the one where they got the most money. Van Nuys Gangs will be on the radio to back us up and I'll brief the Van Nuys Patrol Watch Commander when we get out there. All three taco stands are close together, like you asked for."

Detective McClain could always be counted on to run with Adams's directions. Through all of his strong points, the fact that Lieutenant Adams only needed to tell him something one time and knew it would get done was McClain's greatest value.

"There's one other thing, Jack. Commander Jelenick cornered me yesterday to ask about the taco stand detail. Apparently, the commander in Valley Bureau called Jelenick to make sure we were on top of it. He told Jelenick he hadn't heard from us, so I told him we're on it but hadn't finalized the plans yet. I didn't know if you had told him anything, so I didn't want to step on your toes. I didn't think anything about it but then he asked about the 'special detail.' I'm sure he meant Gold Rush, but I didn't think anyone was supposed to know about it. I told him I'd have you call him about it."

"Good job, pal. I'm betting Chief Nelson told him that we're on a special detail for a while but didn't give him any details. Jelenick doesn't like us answering directly to Chief Nelson and cutting him out, so I think he takes it personally. He was probably just fishing to see what you'd tell him. We should be respectful, but he's outside the yellow tape on this."

McClain knew he was on shaky ground sometimes. "Okay, if it comes up again I'll just avoid it somehow."

"Okay, Mac. Tonight I'm planning on being down in Harbor Division with Surveillance to work Rancho San Pedro, but I'll be on my phone and I'll hook up with you in the Valley later on this evening. I think we tied Rancho San Pedro to a Mexican Mafia-ordered murder, but we still need to tie up a few loose ends. You'll have the taco stand detail tonight, but I'll try and team up with you before the night's over. I should be with you tomorrow night."

"Sounds great, Lieutenant. You get to go to the beach and I have to stay in the city—I'll sure be glad when I'm the lieutenant. Oh yeah, we put together a list of lumber and drywall and nails for the construction. How do we pay for it?"

"I told the chief I'd pay for it. It won't be too much, I'm sure. Go ahead and get everything, Mac, then get it inside the warehouse and I'll reimburse you. See you there around eleven? I'm leaving home in a few, but I have to stop at Hollywood Division and talk to the Area captain. He wants to use Gang officers for a Vice sting Friday night."

"He wants them to work Vice? Misdemeanors? Serious? What did you tell him, Jack?"

"Yeah, we're not doing that, Mac. Listen, when I'm done at Hollywood I'm going to drop down to Canter's Deli on Fairfax and get some coffee. I just need a minute to get caught up on some paperwork, then I'll meet you at the warehouse."

„Okay, Lieutenant. We'll have everything at the warehouse by the time you get there. Dan McVay called from ATF and I asked him to meet us there."

#

Sitting in Canter's was always an experience. The place was loud with a lot of controlled chaos all around you. A little hard to get paperwork done, but the food was so good it was worth it. As the waitress who had been there as long as Adams could remember set his coffee on the table, his phone began vibrating. "Hey, Lieutenant, it's Roger Leigh at Wilshire Gangs."

"Good morning, Roger. Listen, I just need a minute. I'm treating myself at Canter's and I just sat down to eat. Can I call you back?" Adams carried two phones and two radios for everyday use. He usually wanted to toss them out the window of the police car just to watch them smashing apart on one of the potholes on the crummy Los Angeles streets.

"This will only take a second and it's pretty important, sir. Remember the two jewelry store robberies we bought from Wilshire detectives? Right after we talked this morning, we found another robbery down in Chula Vista last month, south of San Diego close to the border. Same suspects and same MO. Now this morning, I found out that the suspects probably hit in Portland just a couple days ago. A detective from Portland Police called Robbery Homicide Division, RHD, and said their getaway car had California plates that they traced back to a Thrifty Car Rental over by LAX. Actually, it looks like they drove the rental car from LA to Portland. They stole a car in Portland and used it during the robbery. Afterwards, they left the jewelry store in the stolen car, drove three blocks, and changed cars to the LAX rental, leaving the stolen at the curb and drove the rental car back to LA. Somehow, Portland came up with the plate on the rental as they fled. I'm not too clear on that yet. It rang a bell with one of the RHD detectives and they transferred it over to me. I watched Portland's store security camera video, and it's our guys. What do you want to do?"

"Roger, get everything from Chula Vista and then hop on a plane and head to Portland as quick as you can. Get everything you can, especially pictures of stolen jewelry if they have it. I'm mostly interested in that LAX rental car. Don't spend any time on the Portland robbery; it doesn't affect us and will be a dead end. Let's help Portland serve a warrant on the LAX Thrifty Car Rental and get the rental information, but be sure to get the video at Thrifty to get a visual on whoever rented it. Sometimes they have cameras outside, so let's see what car they arrived in."

"Sounds good, boss. Do I have Chief Nelson's permission for the travel authority?"

"Yep . . . get going." After he ordered his breakfast, Adams called Chief Nelson's office to let him know Detective Leigh was traveling out of state.

The waitresses were all used to seating Adams in the rear of the room with his back to the wall watching the front of the restaurant. Pastrami and eggs pancake style with lots of coffee. After getting some paperwork done and returning some calls from the booth in the back of Canter's, Adams was ready to push the warehouse project forward.

It was a short drive from Canter's to the warehouse off Benton Way. "Hey, guys, you look like people with real jobs!"

Julie Barr had an old leather tool belt around her hip with about fifty pounds of tools. "It's my dad's. He said we could borrow it, and he'll come by and help if we need him."

Mark Torres was flipping a hammer in the air and catching it while John Andrews moved to the other side of the room, trying not to get hit. Adams surveyed the inside of the warehouse and saw the stack of drywall and two-by-fours. "Mac, where are we with a design for this place?"

McClain had set up a folding table and had plans laid out to build two walls to enclose an office area around the single glass entry door. He planned for a counter that separated the customer area from the employee area. There was one door into the bathroom and a side door into the warehouse. This allowed prospective customers to walk through the glass door into an office space with a counter.

"We have it set up so we can stage some backup officers in the warehouse, and they can enter the front office from this side door if we need them. We can trojan horse them into the warehouse through the roll-up door in case anyone has eyes on us. I checked a van out from Transportation and told them we needed it for three months. They didn't like that at all and only approved one week. I gave them your name, LT—hope that's okay. At the end of the week we'll have to talk to them again. They didn't like letting it go for even a week, so you may have to go there yourself, LT, and push a little weight around."

Mike Rand, always the soldier and thinking tactics, mentioned, "I think we should line our side of the counter with sandbags. Worst case scenario, whoever is behind the counter can drop down and the tactical guys coming in the side door can have a clear field of fire over the counter."

"Mac, if that works for you, I'm good with it. Let's also fortify the one wall that would receive our fire so we can stop any rounds right there and have a solid background. For the van, just forget about it for now. We'll deal with it when they find it's missing and start calling us. I'm betting some time will go by and they'll want to call our boss, but calling a deputy chief is not a pleasant task. Well, let's get to work. Mac, I set it up for you to call my friend Jon and give him whatever you need for signs or anything to put on the walls. Remember the two safes from Salvage are coming in, so figure out where you want them and where you want to put desks and chairs. Get everything you can from Salvage and let them know it's approved by Chief Fuller," Adams ordered.

Mac frowned and said, "I thought the chief just approved the two safes?"

"I'm sure he meant to approve anything we need, Mac. But he's really busy, so I don't want to bother him with details. He's the chief of police; he can't be bothered with a bunch of details."

Adams watched as Torres missed the hammer on his last flip and it bounced across the room. "Torres, if you could not hurt anyone with that hammer, I'd appreciate that. Julie, you have enough tools for all of us, so I think we're good there. I've got a skill saw and drill in my trunk. Dan, what do you need?"

"This is easy, Lieutenant. I have a box of stuff for you. Pinhole cameras for the inside and wall-mounted exterior cameras for the front of the warehouse and in the alley. The exterior cameras are longer range because I figured you wanted cars and not people on them. I'll set the microphones up on the counter so it's close to the conversations. I've got the cameras and mics for Andrews's gig also. If you don't use them, I've got some body wires if you need 'em."

"Great, Dan. What is Andrews's gig?"

McClain stepped right into the conversation like he was putting a fire out. "That was my call, Lieutenant. Andrews met with his confidential informant we talked about, the Hells Angel, and laid out a case I think we can work, so I asked Agent McVay to bring some extra gear. I hope that's okay with you."

"Of course it is, Mac. I appreciate that you made the call. Lay it out for me."

"So, Andrews meets with his informant who says he's been working at this machine shop over by El Tepeyac in Hollenbeck ever since he paroled from Folsom. The owner is apparently a pretty decent guy who treats the informant pretty damn good. I guess this owner has a partner in the machine shop who's been taking more than his share of the profits. That wasn't really the end of the world, but then he found out that his partner has this thing going with his wife."

McClain shakes his head. "The informant said that his boss didn't mind so much about his partner having the affair with his wife, but stealing his money really pissed him off. So, he asked the informant to have one of his Hells Angels buddies kill the partner and said he'd pay him. The informant seemed pretty certain that his boss was serious and told him that he'd feel things out and get back to him. What do you think?"

Adams smiled before responding. "Well, I think the same thing you do, Mac. That's why you had McVay hook you up with tech gear. You're either going to wire the informant or wire a location and have the informant meet with his boss and capture the offer of money to kill the guy's business partner."

McClain breathed a sigh of relief that he was on the right track. "I know we're busy, Lieutenant, but it seems like a quick operation as long as the informant cooperates. Should we have Andrews set it up?"

"Absolutely, Mac. Let's get in and get out and move on. Let me know when you finish the background work on the suspect and get something scheduled. Let's run it past the district attorney's office and make sure we're putting together a prosecutable case."

McClain looked uncomfortable. "Actually, we have an opportunity this afternoon, LT. Andrews has already done all the legwork on the suspect and the intended victim. The informant got a call from his boss last night and they're supposed to meet today. Andrews had the informant tell his boss that he was meeting with some of his criminal buddies today about killing the guy's partner and that he was available for a meet this afternoon—pending your approval. I wanted to prewire a location for audio and visual, but it's going to involve a lot more planning and time. Now I'm thinking we'll be good just putting a wire on the informant and having one of our crew nearby to video. If you're good with that, I say let's have the informant give his boss the meet spot that we choose and make it happen. The conversation may or may not go where we think it will, though. I was thinking we'd just do it in the parking lot of El Tepeyac because we could use their office, but then I figured one of our Hollenbeck units will probably be eating there and the police car in the parking lot wouldn't work. So now I'm thinking somewhere with outside tables so we can set up in cars in the parking lot."

Lieutenant Adams looked around the room when he noticed the whole crew was standing by waiting for orders, ready to go to work on the murder-for-hire case. "Ok, let's set this up and see what happens. I'll let the chief know. This is something he'd want to know about."

Adams moved to the back of the warehouse while McClain started setting things in motion.

"Hello, Chief Nelson. Just a heads-up that we have a small side mission to complete today. One of my officers, Andrews, is our resident motorcycle gang expert and he has an informant from the Hells Angels. Apparently, the informant's current boss at a machine shop over in Hollenbeck knows that he's a Hells Angel and approached him about killing his business partner. Guess he thinks the Hells Angels may not be the most upstanding of citizens. McClain has been working this and did a great job setting it up. The plan is to engineer a meet between this guy and Andrew's informant wearing a wire and capture a murder-for-hire offer. We'll get video if we're able. If the conversation pans out, we'll make a quick arrest and move on. We have that taco stand detail tonight out in the San Fernando Valley, so hopefully we'll finish this and move right over to that one. I have to run down to San Pedro, though, to work a Harbor Division murder involving the Mexican Mafia. But after I'm done, I'll team back up with my guys out in the Valley."

"Sounds pretty simple, Lieutenant, but you have a busy day. Do you need anything from me?"

"No, sir. The players in the murder for hire are nobody important, and the arrest shouldn't attract any press. We have a small window of opportunity this afternoon to make it happen, so we'll move forward and get this done so we can get back to work on the taco stand detail. We're greasing the skids with the district attorney's office on the murder for hire, so the arrest should go fast and easy."

"Be safe, Lieutenant. Let me know how this pans out, then back on the gun detail for the mayor's photo op."

At 3rd Street and Gage, the confidential informant, Big Will Stevens, sat at one of the two outdoor tables at Starbucks directly blocking the front door. There were only three parking spaces, but the informant was able to park his 1947 Harley Davidson knucklehead right next to the two tables. He had blacked out all of the chrome on the motorcycle except for the springer front end and the wire wheels.

Julie Barr and Karen Aoki put the lieutenant's black Ford Mustang GT in one of the parking spaces across the drive. Karen Aoki was the smallest of the two, so she got the job of squeezing into the small back seat to set up the video camera. She had to film through a white metal railing, but it was the best they could do. Julie Barr was set up to listen to the conversation between the two men as they ran the video.

Big Will Stevens was nervous wearing the two devices that had been attached to his belt by ATF Special Agent Dan McVay. He certainly looked the part. Six foot four and almost three hundred pounds, his beard carried down to his chest. He chose to wear his colors today, the sleeveless vest that identified him as a member of the Hells Angels—something he hadn't worn for over nine years, since before he was sent to Folsom. Parole didn't allow wearing it, let alone socializing with his buddies, but McClain knew it would set the scene and got permission from Stevens's parole agent.

The black Cadillac STS parked right next to the Mustang GT that Julie Barr and Karen Aoki were stationed in. The man who sat down in front of Big Will Stevens was outwardly nervous; he was sweating through his shirt. Although he kept looking over his shoulder, the look on his face showed that he remained committed to his path. "Will, I want him dead, but it has to happen fast. I'll pay you seven thousand dollars to kill that bastard, or to get one of your buddies to do it, but it has to happen over the next couple days. Here's all the information you need, but nothing can happen around the shop."

Big Will Stevens picked up the photograph and the piece of paper. The photograph, the name, the address, two cars—it was all there.

"Here's the money—seven thousand dollars. Seven grand, Will, but you have to do it right away. Can you do that?"

After Julie Barr gave the takedown signal, Rand and Andrews were the first to pull into the parking lot from Gage, followed by Detective McClain and Lieutenant Adams riding together in McClain's car. Coming in from 3rd Street, Halverson and Torres pulled in and gave a little shot with the siren to put everyone on notice, but in their haste they parked in front of the Mustang GT, blocking the video camera. No great loss.

The informant and his boss—ex-boss, really—were placed on the ground, handcuffed, and arrested. Before they were placed in separate cars, the owner of the machine shop already knew his fate. Screwed by his wife, screwed by his partner, and now by Big Will Stevens. The icing on the cake was when he was served with divorce papers during the preliminary hearing.

And Big Will Stevens? On a deal between the district attorney's office and California State Parole, Stevens would be relocated to Auburn, California, between Sacramento and Lake Tahoe, where there were aerospace engineering and machine shops.

Adams swapped cars back to the black Mustang GT and left to fight LA traffic, headed to San Pedro to meet with one of his surveillance units and the Harbor Gang Detail. Detective McClain left the scene of the arrest and drove to Figueras Road and San Bruno Drive in La Mirada, where he met with the intended victim to advise him of the arrest of his business partner.

It took Andrews and Torres just over an hour to book the suspect on a felony murder-for-hire charge. The arrest report was short and sweet.

Time to head for the Valley.

CHAPTER SIXTEEN
THE COLLISIONS CONTINUE

Commander Jelenick was intrigued when Deputy Chief Nelson told him that Lieutenant Adams was overseeing a new special detail, one that was confidential. Jelenick understood that Chief Nelson was keeping it under wraps, and that meant it might be something important that Jelenick could leverage to get back in the game. He had asked Detective McClain about it but the detective played dumb. He knew he couldn't go directly to Adams, but he was committed to finding out what this special detail was.

Maggie was completely immersed in paperwork at the Gang Detail office. The phones just would not stop ringing today. She prided herself on getting more than her share of work done, along with most of Lieutenant Adams's administrative work, but today everyone was getting on her nerves. A phone call from Commander Jelenick was the last thing she needed—or expected. "Good morning, Commander Jelenick. Is there anything I can do for you, sir?"

Jelenick always came off as being a little bit weird. Maggie was not necessarily a fan of his. "Good morning, Maggie, or late morning, I should say. How are things in Gangs? Are they treating you well? It sounds like you're there by yourself a lot."

"Oh, sure, Commander. If I go in the lieutenant's office I can even see out a tiny window and watch all the homeless urinating in the street. Life is great."

"I've been thinking about expanding my staff a little, and I'm considering bringing you over to my office, Maggie. Would that be something you're interested in?"

Man, did that catch Maggie off guard. She would never leave Lieutenant Adams and Gangs. "Well, that's nice to think of me, Commander, but I'm pretty set in my job here."

"Okay, Maggie, but give it some thought. The working conditions on my staff are pretty good. Long lunches. By the way, how is that special detail going?"

"What special detail, sir?" Now Maggie felt like she was being played, and she didn't like that at all. *Commander Jelenick never calls the Gang office, and today he's playing like old friends.*

"It's a new detail Gangs is working up, but maybe you haven't been briefed on it yet. Oh well. Have a nice day, Maggie. Call me if you're ever interested in moving over here to my staff."

"Same to you, Commander."

"By the way, Maggie, would you have Lieutenant Adams call me? I have something for him."

Maggie considered ignoring the request but thought better of it. "I certainly will, sir."

Hanging up the phone, Maggie couldn't dial fast enough. "Lieutenant, this is Maggie. Commander Jelenick just called on the inside line asking about a special detail. Is there something you want me to tell him? And he told me to have you call him."

"Thanks for the heads-up, Maggie. I can always count on you. No, he's not in the loop, but I think he's fishing."

Pausing and thinking back to the conversation, Maggie replied, "I think that guy just tried to bribe me. He asked me about coming to work in his office and said that I could have long lunches. Then he asked me about a special detail Gangs is working. What the hell?"

"It's okay, Maggie. He's a commander, and we'll always be respectful, but he's not in the loop on this detail per Chief Nelson. And talking about long lunches—you get all kinds of perks! Didn't I bring you a bagel from Starbucks last Friday?"

"You sure did, Lieutenant. I asked for it on Wednesday, it sat on the front seat of your car for two days, and when I got it on Friday the cream cheese was rotten. But it was the thought that counts."

"Exactly, Maggie. That's what I always say. See ya, kid."

"Be safe out there, Lieutenant. Don't forget to call Commander Jelenick."

#

Commander Stans Jelenick was consumed with fighting his way back and securing that next promotion to deputy chief. The promotion was all that mattered, and he had to get out of COMPSTAT and back in the game. He needed to renew his position in charge of special details within Detective Bureau. Specifically, he needed to take charge of the Gang Detail.

After being informally approached by the archbishop from the Los Angeles Archdiocese, Jelenick saw a pathway that gave him hope he could still develop some level of control over Gangs and Lieutenant Adams. And, in so doing, translate that control into a role that strengthened his position in the police department.

The archbishop oversaw three Southern California counties and was responsible for 214 elementary schools and 51 high schools with over 70,000 students. The archbishop had asked for Jelenick's help in expanding the church's role to work with and support at-risk youth through new church programs he planned to develop. Jelenick believed that the influence the archbishop possessed over this incredibly large population could be translated into more power and influence for himself. Jelenick would assign Lieutenant Adams to the task . . . and supervise him.

#

After hanging up with Maggie, Adams thought he might as well get the phone call over with. He had already been briefed that he worked directly for Deputy Chief Nelson but figured he would be constantly walking a tightrope around this situation with Jelenick. "Commander, this is Lieutenant Adams. Maggie asked me to call you. How can I help you, sir?"

"Good afternoon, Lieutenant. I'd like you to meet with the archbishop at the Los Angeles Archdiocese. The office is over on Wilshire Boulevard, but you can get the address when you call to make an appointment. He has a project we would like you to take on."

Adams's intent was certainly to avoid Jelenick, especially since he was under the belief that he no longer worked for him. "Commander, the Catholic Church? What can I do for them? Has Deputy Chief Nelson been briefed on this?" Adams was not one to violate the chain of command, nor allow anyone else to.

Jelenick felt the excitement grow as he embarked on this new effort that had success written all over it. He spoke quickly and authoritatively as he began to lay the plan out to Adams. "The archbishop is planning to expand the work the church does in their elementary and high schools, and in the parishes also, by working with at-risk youth. They're looking for some guidance from us, and you're probably the person most immersed in this field. Your gang-prevention programs would be a perfect model for what the archbishop is planning to build. I'd like you to meet with the archbishop and develop some type of training or guidance program that you can provide to their staff to bring them up to speed on this subject. We would like you to help them develop the program. Once you have the program in place, give me a written briefing on the plan and how you intend to follow up on their efforts. I want you to be an integral part of their team to build and implement this project, Lieutenant. This is an opportunity for us to permanently partner with the church in a community support effort. A community policing effort. I will personally brief the mayor and city council on this effort."

Adams was offended by the request. Adams oversaw a youth gang-prevention detail in each of the LAPD police stations that provided local at-risk youth an opportunity to be mentored by specially trained police officers.

"Commander, we already partner with the faith community on many different levels, including the various Interfaith Councils and the Interfaith Council of Religious Leaders. Has Deputy Chief Nelson been briefed on this? Does this have the support of the chief of police?" Right back to the chain of command.

With a clearly irritated tone of voice, Jelenick asserted the importance of his request. "I understand that, but this provides us a stronger presence in directly supporting the faith community while strengthening their own ability to serve their parishioners. The end game is that the church will assist in keeping young people from committing crimes and out of gangs, which benefits us all, Lieutenant."

Adams decided to move forward tactfully. "Commander, at-risk youth are commonly very vulnerable at many different levels, and we need to be careful involving the police department in a situation where we will have no control. If anything went wrong, any allegations of abuse, it would come right back on us. I think we need to run this past Chief Nelson and probably Chief Fuller. I think we should consult with the City Attorney's Office also as to our exposure to liability. Has Chief Nelson been briefed on this?"

"I will communicate this effort to Chief Nelson, Lieutenant. You keep moving forward on this assignment unless I tell you different. I expect you to meet with the archbishop before the end of the week."

Jelenick hadn't expected Adams to balk at the assignment but felt as if he had just won the battle that would reassert his ability to promote within the LAPD. Jelenick decided to initiate some level of supervision over Adams and the Gang Detail and resume his role a few small steps at a time. For Jelenick, his level of importance within the Catholic Church could grow by leaps and bounds. He was becoming very excited.

Adams, however, decided to put this on the back burner for as long as possible. He wasn't moving an inch without consulting with Deputy Chief Nelson. Even at that, Adams knew in his heart that he couldn't play a role in this plan. Placing vulnerable youth in situations that could injure them was not what policemen do.

CHAPTER SEVENTEEN
WATCH YOUR BACK

Lieutenant Adams made the drive to San Pedro in the Mustang GT. San Pedro always felt like a different world from the rest of Los Angeles, a working- and middle-class area built largely on a sloping point jutting out to the ocean. San Pedro butts up against the more expensive area of Palos Verdes on one side and against the highly polluted commercial Port of Los Angeles on the other.

The last time Adams was in San Pedro, it happened to be the Croatian Independence Day weekend. Adams had been taken to an incredible Croatian restaurant, and he hoped he would have the opportunity to hit it again tonight. As Adams pulled into the Harbor Division Police Station to meet Sergeant Mark Farr of Harbor Gangs, he was eyed suspiciously by four uniformed officers in the parking lot. Harbor Division was a small and very tight station, and these officers knew Adams did not work there. He immediately opened his badge wallet and held it up for the officers to see, then draped it over his belt with the badge hanging visible on the outside.

The image of officers wearing a badge hanging on a chain around their neck is an East Coast thing. In Los Angeles, that only lasts until the first fight the officers get in when the suspect grabs the chain and pulls their head down or chokes them with it, or after it gets caught on the first fence they climb over. Officers in Los Angeles learn fast that what looks good on television doesn't always work on the streets of Los Angeles.

"Sergeant Farr, how are you? Can you brief me on what's happening down here? I understand you have a link between Rancho San Pedro and the Mexican Mafia, La Eme."

Sergeant Mark Farr was a fairly young sergeant to be working in a specialized unit. He seemed uncomfortable talking with Adams. "Hey, Lieutenant Adams. Yes, sir, it looks like our murder is tied to not paying taxes to the Mexican Mafia."

#

As Adams met with Sergeant Farr down in San Pedro, Detective McClain and his six Gang officers began developing their plan for the evening surveillance on three taco stands, hoping to engage the robbers who had been hitting in the area.

The surveillance was being set up wholly in Van Nuys Division where each of the prior robberies had occurred. The rub was that one of the suspects sported a "BP" tattoo on the back of his leg. Brown Pride was a gang of sorts in the neighboring Devonshire Division, on the other side of the 405 Freeway.

LAPD has twenty-tone police stations called "Divisions" or "Areas." Devonshire Division of the LAPD is in a middle-class area north of downtown Los Angeles. People call it the San Fernando Valley, or the "Valley" for short. Female support staff in the captain's office once dubbed the division "Club Dev" many years ago, and they had fought hard to keep the name. For some reason, the female support staff seemed to have a lot of pull with the two captains. Some believed it was due to one of them being married to a retired captain. Granted, Devonshire was a mostly quiet, low-crime area, but most officers hated the Club Dev title, because it certainly didn't support the mentality of LAPD officers.

Gang crime had been growing for years in the Valley and the once-safe bedroom community of Devonshire Division was being infiltrated by Armenian, Hispanic, and Asian gangs, along with the resident biker gangs in the far north end. The Hells Angels and the Vagos had become permanent fixtures. The Asian Boys were from mostly wealthy families and were hard to identify as gang members. They were low profile in the realm of LA street gangs but were known to prey upon their own. Their strong presence in Porter Ranch, a housing community within the Devonshire Division, went largely unnoticed by other residents.

The gangs in the Valley were still a far cry from South Los Angeles gangs. Brown Pride, a resident gang of Devonshire Division known for being mostly taggers and what police called "wannabe gangsters," struggled to compete but had a growing relationship with Mara Salvatruche, MS13. Mara Salvatruche was slowly revealing a growing presence in the Valley, which changed the landscape, and violent crime was increasing.

#

"Fuck them! Fuck those motherfuckers, those CRASH motherfuckers. We'll kill every one who shows up!" Takster, a Brown Pride gang member for the last eleven years, was working hard to move into a shot caller position. "They call us taggers and bullshit. We'll show them! We been doing this 211 shit for two weeks—they'll be on us now. So be ready."

"Yeah, but how many will show up? I ain't going back to lockup. You guys all gotta be in, *all* the way in," AlleyDog replied.

"We got a plan and if they show, we kill their fucking asses. We hit whoever shows up first, and then we're gone," Takster directed. "If they don't show tonight, they'll show tomorrow. They can come after us and we'll kill more of 'em. But tonight, fuck 'em! We rob those fucking mojados, and then we kill those fucking La Houda."

Takster believed that ambushing and killing LAPD gang officers would push him into a shot caller position. DogDayz, also known as Big Dog D of MS13 over in North Hollywood, had told him, "Kill the police and we can talk."

Takster saw a liaison with MS13, Mara Salvatruche, as his pathway forward, a way to get more respect for Brown Pride. Killing the police would be his way to get there, to be a shot caller. He didn't have the courage to do this himself, but he was sure he could set it up to order others to attack the police and get all the credit with DogDayz.

#

"35G11 to 35G10." At 2000 hours, the designation of time for 8 o'clock p.m., Detective McClain, call sign 35G11, contacted Lieutenant Adams, call sign 35G10, on the radio. "We're in place, Lieutenant, and setting up now." The sun was setting, and the heat of the day was starting to ease up.

The number 35 referred to a citywide unit and the *G* signified a gang detail, while lieutenants were always 10. Thus, 35G10. Detective McClain, second in command, assumed 35G11. In LAPD lingo, each letter of the alphabet is assigned a word. The letter *G* is George, so it's pronounced "35 George 11."

"35G11 to G12, G13, and G14. Everyone in position?"

35G12 was the unit designation for Mike Rand and John Andrews, 35G13 was Julie Barr and Karen Aoki, and 35G14 was Jim Halverson and Mark Torres. LAPD Gang officers always work as a pair, never alone. Tonight, this was a surveillance detail, and the officers were all in plain clothes and driving their unmarked Ford Crown Vics. Not really surveillance cars or undercover cars, but they worked for the task at hand.

"35G12 is set on our location. We have a clear eye on the street and front entrance. There's no parking lot." Officers Mike Rand and John Andrews set up on a small fast food Mexican restaurant on Sepulveda Boulevard within sight of the Van Nuys Division Police Station. They positioned their car so that it would be difficult for anyone to approach their car from behind without being seen.

Rand, driving the car, had placed his AR15 rifle on the floor under his legs. Andrews set his 12-gauge shotgun on the floor sandwiched between the side of the passenger seat and the door so that he could open the door, grab his shotgun, then step out of the car with the shotgun in front of him.

"35G13 is set." Officers Julie Barr and Karen Aoki set up on the Mexican restaurant near Sepulveda Boulevard and Nordhoff Street that had been hit last week. An open-air stand with outdoor seating, the smell of the meat cooking drifted clear to their police car. A barbecue was set up outside to cook street tacos, which was the main draw. The street tacos occasionally created a line down the sidewalk late at night, and the restaurant stayed open as long as there was anyone walking or driving by.

The officers set up on Sepulveda Boulevard almost a full block south of the taco stand in a dark spot under a tree that partially masked their presence and their movement inside the police car. Not much, but the best they could do while still keeping eyes on the front of the business. Moving their mirrors so each officer could watch to the rear and down their side of the police car, both officers held their semiautomatic handguns in their lap. Julie Barr sat in the passenger seat. Although right-handed, she held her gun in her left hand and pointed it at her open window, guarding her side of the car.

"35G14 is set." Officers Jim Halverson and Mark Torres set up on the Mexican restaurant near Roscoe Boulevard and Parthenia Street. A little outside the target area on Sepulveda, but fitting the target profile and only a few blocks away. Both officers placed a 12-gauge shotgun on the floor sandwiched between the seat and door, a common tactic by 35G14. Seeing two fearless gang officers exiting their car both armed with 12-gauge shotguns was a fearsome sight. Torres, the driver, also slid his semiautomatic handgun under his left leg and pointed it toward his driver's door as they sat in the car.

During tactical training, Lieutenant Adams constantly referred to a police car as a "coffin." He taught the officers that during stops, the officers had to get out of the car before the suspects got out of theirs. Being captured in the front seat of a police car during any tactical situation with nowhere to go was a certain death sentence. If caught sitting in a police car during any tactical situation, the officers would have to fight their way out of the car. Adams's gang officers were constantly prepared to engage armed suspects while they were inside their "coffins."

Surveillances, sitting and waiting for something to happen while trying not to be obvious, were usually boring and draining . . . and incredibly risky. There was always the chance of getting robbed or carjacked. When in uniform or identified as police officers, the added danger of a drive-by shooting to assault the officers was high. Any time policemen in Los Angeles sat in the same spot for any length of time, they drew a lot of negative, very dangerous attention.

#

Takster was seated in the front passenger seat of a car they had stolen three hours earlier from Panorama City, a blue Ford Escort. Takster saw the gray Ford Crown Vic with two females inside pull onto the curb on Sepulveda near the taco stand. "Those are Gang cops. They're on us. We're gonna kill those motherfuckers tonight. We're killing police bitches tonight!"

Takster was excited to set his plan in motion—kill police officers and cement his place as a shot caller with the backing of MS13. He was impatient to get AlleyDog in place along with Felicia, their getaway driver. "Homie G, it's me. Answer the phone when I call, motherfucker. That's like ten fucking rings! Gang cops are fucking here watching the taco stand. Two bitches. We're just gonna drive-by their ass right now." Takster was becoming more impatient with each moment that passed and began modifying the plan, dictating it to AlleyDog.

"Fuck that, T. We got it, we're ready. Just do what we said. Pull 'em in the front, then get out the back. I'll get Felicia there waiting for your ass. Just fucking do it when I say." AlleyDog, cruising with three other Brown Pride gang members, sat in the rear seat of a silver Camaro stolen two days prior from California State University at Northridge. "We're up Van Nuys Boulevard at Burbank. We'll be there. Wait. I'll tag Felicia."

AlleyDog began to set the plan in motion as he called Felicia. "Chica, we're at the taco stand down from Nordhoff. Remember the back?"

Felicia sat in the car alone, laughing at the plan for Takster to go in the front so the police officers would follow him, then escape out the back. She was to drive down the alley to the back door and spirit Takster away from the scene while the others did a drive-by and shot the police officers in front of the restaurant. Then, Takster would get all the credit. She was always amused at his combination of bravado and stupidity. "Yeah, motherfucker, I'm not stupid. I'm only down the street." Felicia started her car and headed for the rear of the taco stand.

AlleyDog pushed to take the reins and set the plan in motion, even though he knew it made Takster mad. AlleyDog wasn't ready to give up the ship. "Hey, T, Felicia's waiting for you in the alley. Get in there and don't fuck around. Police will see you on the sidewalk when you're walking in. Flash it then."

"Don't tell me what to do, Dog, this is mine!" Takster yelled through the phone at AlleyDog.

"Just do what we planned, T. Don't fuck it up," AlleyDog replied. "You want this done and we're ready. Do it right."

Julie Barr, sitting in the passenger seat and looking up the sidewalk toward the taco stand, watched two Hispanic males getting out of a small blue compact car and walking toward the outdoor barbecue. She was surprised when the taller male held a silver or chrome semiautomatic handgun up in the air with his right hand. "Karen, look. Got two suspects and one semiauto going into the taco stand. Why's he holding it over his head?"

Three customers at the outdoor taco stand immediately ran northbound up the sidewalk. Barr picked up her radio and began broadcasting on a tactical channel. "35G13 requesting a backup, Sepulveda south of Nordhoff. Two possible 211 suspects entering our location, the taco stand. Armed male Hispanics, twenty to thirty, dark clothes, one armed with a silver handgun. Parked their vehicle northbound at the curb, a gray or blue compact two-door Ford."

"35G14 en route." Torres hit the gas pedal and raced westbound on Roscoe toward Barr and Aoki's location. Knowing that they were the closest unit, Torres and Halverson began talking with each other and developed their plan to drive to the rear of the taco stand and contain the suspects in the location while Barr and Aoki secured the front. "35G14, we're taking the rear."

"35G12 en route, two minutes." Rand slammed his police car into gear and began flying northbound on Van Nuys Boulevard toward Barr and Aoki. Everyone knew the drill—no lights and no sirens. Based on their training and formed from their habits, Rand and Andrews began discussing their tactical plan. Initially, they were prepared to arrive at the location in a rescue operation. The plan: locate and protect Barr and Aoki at all cost. They decided to stay shoulder to shoulder and not split up.

Detective McClain had gone into the Van Nuys Police Station to remind the Patrol Watch commander of their Gang Detail surveillance in Van Nuys Division. Upon hearing the broadcast from Barr and Aoki, he passed by the elevator and ran down the stairs sprinting to his car in the rear parking lot. McClain pointed his car northbound on Van Nuys Boulevard and began taking control of the situation. "35G11, responding from Van Nuys station. 35G11, requesting a perimeter at the location."

"9G27 responding from Van Nuys station." The only Van Nuys Gang unit available to respond heard the backup call as they left the police station and saddled up in their police car. Van Nuys was division number 9 in LAPD, the *G* standing for Gang unit, and the number 27 identifying the officers assigned to that unit: 9G27.

Officers Barr and Aoki agreed they should move their car closer, leave it at the curb, and move closer to the location on foot. The two officers cautiously approached the location driving slowly northbound on Sepulveda Boulevard with their lights out, waiting for backup officers to arrive. They pulled slowly to the curb and stopped, five cars behind the suspect's car. It was fully dark now when both officers got out of the car with dark-blue jackets that said "Police" on the chest and the back, handguns held close to their chests. The officers began walking slowly up the line of parked cars, agreeing to wait for backup officers to arrive.

Karen Aoki stayed in the street and crept forward along the parked cars while Julie Barr slid along the sidewalk on the other side of the parked cars. Aoki was the first to get to the suspect's car and signaled for Barr to hang back a few steps. She carefully moved along the side of the car to guarantee it was empty. No keys, and the ignition was punched. A stolen.

Standing next to the suspect's empty car, Aoki carefully peered over the top to see inside the taco stand but she could not see the suspects. She whispered to Barr, "Let's hold here until backup shows."

„35G14, we'll take the rear."

"35G12 approaching."

"35G11, stand by G13 until we all arrive. Let's be careful with this. G14, let me know when you're set up to the rear."

Lieutenant Adams heard the activity on the radio and headed for his car. "Mark, my guys are moving on something out in the Valley, so I'm going to head that way. If it doesn't pan out, I'll turn around and head back your way." Adams knew that at this point in the operation he should stay off the radio. *Let the warriors do their job.*

Driving up Sepulveda Boulevard and expecting to see the two female officers seated in their unmarked police car, AlleyDog sat in the front passenger seat and yelled, "There they are! They're walking in the street." None of the four persons in the stolen Camaro saw Officer Julie Barr on the sidewalk as she crouched down and approached the suspect's abandoned Ford.

AlleyDog held a shotgun in his lap. Arturo Mejia, a distant cousin of AlleyDog, sat in the right rear seat behind AlleyDog and was armed with a semiautomatic handgun. He was to be the second shooter. The driver, a dangerous and violent young man named Tomas Perales who everyone called Little Clown, was on probation for drug violations. The passenger in the left rear seat, Felix Olmos, armed with a semiautomatic handgun was there in case more police officers showed up at the scene. He was backup, but as they started rolling up on the scene, Felix Olmos began wondering how he was going to get out of the tiny back seat of the two-door car. He muttered to himself out loud, "Think we should have planned this better."

As the silver Camaro drew alongside Karen Aoki, AlleyDog pushed the shotgun out of the window. AlleyDog had cut the butt short into a pistol grip like he had seen on television. It made the gun far harder to shoot and made it more difficult to hit a target, but it looked good.

As he pointed the barrel at the female officer's back and squeezed the trigger, the gun kicked harshly upwards, hitting the bottom of his chin and leaving a nasty cut. By the time he recovered, the Camaro had already passed the officer and he wasn't able to fire another round.

Arturo Mejia, seated in the rear seat, fired his handgun out of the tiny rear window but was not sure whether he hit the officer or not. With AlleyDog leaning out the front passenger window, Mejia had no room to maneuver his shot without hitting AlleyDog. He just shot the gun and hoped to hit something.

LAPD Gang Detail Officer Karen Aoki heard loud, thundering noises behind her, the kind of noises you feel in your chest and your stomach at loud concerts. The noises were so loud that they pushed her violently forward against the blue Ford Escort and then knocked her to the ground. She didn't feel pain, not yet. Just blunt force trauma. She couldn't understand what could be so loud. She only felt confusion.

Barr heard the report of gunfire from multiple weapons and saw her partner fall. The thought "drive-by" registered in her mind. Barr keyed her microphone as she moved between the cars and toward her partner but didn't finish the transmission as she engaged the suspects. "35G13. 35G13. Officer—"

Barr stepped between the parked cars and dropped her radio on the back of the Ford Escort. She raised her handgun and fired five rounds at the slow-moving Chevrolet Camaro after she saw a shotgun and a handgun extended out the passenger side windows.

Aoki was lying in the street on her left side but somehow managed to draw her weapon and fire two rounds at the Hispanic man looking back at her from a passenger side window of the Camaro. He had a shotgun pointed out the window. Aoki held her gun with one hand and could not sight down the barrel; she was only able to point her gun and fire instinctively directly at the threat. Directly at the face of the person who had shot her. The fight is never over.

As the Camaro slowly continued past Aoki, Arturo Mejia turned in his seat to look out the rear window and saw Aoki struggling on the ground. They had shot her. "She's dead—we shot her!"

Mejia never saw the rear window break, never felt the round fired by Julie

Barr enter his cheek and exit the rear of his neck. He dropped his gun and died even before Tomas Perales, Little Clown, pushed hard on the accelerator and steered the car away from the scene.

The Camaro accelerated and gained speed northbound on Van Nuys Boulevard, and Barr realized they were still next to the other suspect's car. She worried the suspects they had seen entering the taco stand with a gun would come out of the taco stand and head for their car, directly toward them. Holding her attention on the front of the taco stand, Barr yelled at Aoki, "Watch the street, Karen! I've got those other assholes when they come out."

Barr looked down at Aoki and realized she had been shot. She grabbed Aoki and dragged her between the parked cars and out of the street. She saw blood running on the ground under Aoki's body. A lot of blood.

Barr pulled Aoki up into a sitting position and braced her against her left leg to hold her up and sense where she was. Then Barr stood in a combat shooting stance, prepared to engage the two armed suspects when they exited the taco stand. She would not abandon her partner, but she also would not retreat from the armed suspects. Police officers never retreat. "Karen, how bad is it? Can you wait for backup?"

Aoki, with her legs partially in the roadway, lay back against her partner and used both of her hands to hold her gun up, pointing toward the street. She saw a pool of blood immediately forming under her and began to feel pain that weighted her down. Pain and fatigue.

Lieutenant Adams had taught them that when you get shot, you just want to rest for a while. You just want to give up and rest. That was shock setting in, and then you're not functional. To herself, she recited out loud, "It's just blood, I'm not dead. I'm still in this. Fight, Karen."

Julie Barr heard Aoki and knew that time was not on their side. "I've got you, Karen. Just stay in the fight a few more minutes. Backup is coming. Our guys are coming, Karen, just hold on a few more minutes!"

Aoki felt the burning pain and watched the blood pooling under her. She yelled back to Barr, "I'm okay. I'm bleeding, but I'm okay—I think they hit my vest. I think it's only my leg, but I can't stand up." As each second passed, Aoki felt overwhelming fatigue setting in and it was hard to hold her gun up. She fought against it, shaking her head back and forth as if she was fighting against losing consciousness and reciting to herself, "Fight, Karen."

Each of the teams heard the partial transmission by Barr. Halverson on 35G14 was the first to respond, "35G14, go again G13."

"35G14, go again G13."

Finally, after an eternity had passed, Barr picked up her radio and keyed the microphone. "35G13, officer down! Officer needs help. Karen's hit!"

Detective McClain added, "Everyone go to Van Nuys frequency." He switched frequencies and rebroadcasted the call for help.

The radio dispatcher began to broadcast, as calmly as possible, the "officer needs help" call. "All units, all frequencies stand by. 35G13 is requesting help, officer down, on Van Nuys frequency. Sepulveda and Nordhoff. Two armed suspects. 35G13 come in." The dispatcher was aware of the backup call involving the two suspects entering the taco stand but was not aware of the suspects in the Camaro yet. Multitasking, she dispatched Los Angeles City Fire Department rescue units.

"35G12, we're here. We're Code Six. We see your car, Julie, where are you? Julie, Karen, answer up, where are you?"

Julie Barr kept her eyes on the front of the taco stand, expecting the two armed suspects to come out at any second. "I'm on the sidewalk in front of the taco stand. Karen is hit. It was a drive-by. A silver Camaro, Hispanics. Two more inside the taco stand. Silver semiauto."

Officers Rand and Andrews parked in the street next to the parked police car and bailed out, running up along the parked cars toward the taco stand to Barr and Aoki, who were hunkered down between two parked cars.

Mike Rand put his AR15 to his shoulder, stood up tall like a mountain, and swung his rifle in all directions, looking for targets while providing cover for the other officers. Rand was committed that no force in the world would get through him. He had to find the suspects who shot Karen Aoki.

John Andrews roughly grabbed Aoki under her arms and dragged her south along the sidewalk to the rear of the police car. "I've got her, Julie. Watch our backs."

As Aoki was pulled backwards along the sidewalk, she held her gun out with both hands, protecting their rear. Aoki continued reciting to herself out loud, "I'm still in this. Fight, Karen." But she was fading, and her fight was against shock.

Andrews ordered, "Julie, watch the street! Hold our back." Andrews was struggling to comprehend the situation. "Was this a drive-by or a robbery? Where are the two suspects who went in the taco stand with a gun? Where's the Camaro?"

Barr stepped between the cars and to the edge of the roadway blocking Aoki and Andrews with her body, ready to engage any threat on the street. Watching for the Camaro, she shouted, "There's still two in the taco stand. A Camaro went by and shot Karen. I put four or five rounds in the Camaro, John. Not sure who I hit, but I know I hit the car. I tried, John, but not sure what I hit."

Andrews asked, "Where's the other two? Who's in the taco stand?"

"They're still in there, John. Different suspects were in a Camaro. It was a drive-by." A clear picture was finally starting to come together.

Andrews yelled for Mike Rand in the roadway. "Rand! Drive-by hit Karen and they're gone. Silver Camaro. Two other shooters from the Ford Escort are still in the taco stand. Julie and I have the street, you've got the taco stand." Rand stepped behind the suspect's Ford Escort and focused his attention—and the barrel of his Colt AR15—on the front of the taco stand.

Andrews unbuttoned his shirt and pulled a trauma compression bandage from inside it, holding it on the obvious injury to Aoki's left thigh. "I don't think it's the artery; I think she's okay. You're okay, Karen. Just relax, we've got you. Where do you hurt?"

Aoki looked at Andrews as he held pressure on her leg. "It's a silver Camaro, John. Four people, I think. Hispanics. It was a drive-by, John. I was in the street creeping down the parked cars. LT's going to be so mad. I should have been paying attention behind me. Damn it." Her words were slurring now.

Karen Aoki, her handgun in her hand, pointed down the sidewalk as she lay at the rear of her police car, never giving up, knowing the fight is never over. She began drifting out of consciousness, even as she fought to stay alert. Her gun slowly lowered to her lap.

"Ok, Karen, I got it," Andrews assured Aoki as her eyes closed. "35G12, what's the ETA of the rescue ambulance?"

"35G12, be advised that the RA is two minutes out."

"35G12, get them here now, we're out of time! 35G12 to G14. First two suspects entered the taco stand and they're still inside. We got the front if you're on the rear. Additional Hispanic suspects in silver Camaro hit Karen with a drive-by and fled northbound Sepulveda. Drive-by shooting. Officer down."

Rand couldn't see Andrews or Aoki. He saw Julie Barr focused on the street and yelled to her, "Julie, I'll be the primary when they come out! Keep watching our backs. Watch the street and I'll put my rifle on the suspects when they come out."

Julie Barr got in the game and broadcasted, "35G13, drive-by shooting, officer hit. Attempt 187 of a police officer. Hispanic suspects in front and rear seats with handgun and shotgun, late eighties Camaro, silver in color, left northbound on Sepulveda. Attempt murder suspects. Two other armed suspects still inside the taco stand."

Detective McClain skidded to a stop and burst out of his police car, shotgun at port arms, completely blocking northbound Sepulveda Boulevard. As 9G27, the Van Nuys Gang unit, arrived, McClain ordered them to follow him into the taco stand to engage the suspects that had been seen walking in with a handgun. Lieutenant Adams had taught him that the longer you wait to engage suspects, the more dangerous it was.

Walking toward the front of the taco stand, McClain broadcasted, "35G11, give me a perimeter around this location, four full blocks." McClain couldn't bring the name of the streets to bear on his order, but he knew the responding Van Nuys Gang and Patrol units would fill the perimeter in.

"Rand, you take point. Take us in." McClain placed Mike Rand in front of him and the two Van Nuys Gang officers behind him. The team began pushing into the taco stand.

#

As Takster and his young accomplice, Calvin Velasquez, moved through the kitchen, the employees saw the gun Takster held and fell to the floor. One of the employees recognized them from the robbery two weeks ago.

Takster yelled at the employees to stay on the floor and felt the adrenaline rush through him as he waved the gun across the room. He thought about where he would put his new BP13 tattoo. Calvin Velasquez laughed as the employees cowered, feeling a sense of power that he had not experienced before. He was a gangster, a killer.

The back door of the small kitchen stood open to allow air to cool the business, while the barred security door remained closed. Takster made his way across the kitchen and looked into the alley, where he saw Felicia driving slowly toward them still a full block away. "Come on, bitch." Waving frantically for Felicia to speed up, he heard the gunshots from the drive-by shooting in front of the taco stand. A lot of shots.

Takster was sure that the two female officers were now dead. His vision of himself as a shot caller partnering with Mara Salvatruche flooded into his psyche. Brown Pride would now be BP13. He would finally get the respect he deserved.

Calvin Velasquez, only thirteen years old, had made a reputation as a talented Brown Pride tagger. His artwork adorned many alleys and building walls, although he was viewed as a plague in the neighborhood by the people who lived and worked there. Accompanying Takster into the taco stand as a decoy to draw officers into an ambush would change his life for the better—or so Takster told him. This was his next step to becoming a Brown Pride gangster.

Calvin Velasquez heard the gunshots as he waited at the rear door of the taco stand and long before he dove into the rear seat of the Chevrolet. All of a sudden, everything got real. He no longer felt like a gangster, like a killer. He lay on the floor behind Felicia and had very different thoughts than what was going through Takster's mind. All he wanted was to go home.

Opening the passenger car door, Takster yelled, "Fucking bitch, where were you?" Takster never heard her answer as he saw the Ford Crown Vic carrying 35G14, Torres and Halverson, accelerate into the mouth of the alley behind them.

Takster brought his gun up, fired at the police car, and saw the windshield crack. He heard Felicia yelling but didn't know what she was saying. The police car skidded to a stop three car lengths behind the black Chevrolet. The cops were scared—they were stopping.

Standing up and yelling, "Brown Pride!" Takster held his gun sideways in his hand like he saw on television and fired two more rounds as both officers exited the police car, the "coffin."

Both officers had shotguns as they stood up, and they hadn't even flinched at being shot at. Suddenly it registered to Takster that neither officer was ducking or hiding; they weren't backing up in their car like he saw on television. Both of these officers stepped out of the police car and were standing straight up, and they had shotguns.

Takster wondered why police were even behind the taco stand. The plan was for Felicia to drive them away without anyone even seeing them. Takster felt the right side of his face burn hot as a shotgun blast from Halverson grazed his head. He was barely able to dive into the front seat as Felicia began to drive away without him, dragging his legs on the roadway.

Felicia pressed hard on the accelerator and the back window of the Chevrolet shattered as a shotgun blast struck the rear of the car. As the glass showered down onto thirteen-year-old Calvin Velasquez, his thoughts were to bail out of the car and run. But as Felicia accelerated, Velasquez froze in place. He just couldn't move, and all he wanted was to go home.

Hearing multiple shots that sounded as if they had been fired inside the taco stand, Rand pushed into the kitchen with his rifle, scanning each of the persons inside. Three people he believed to be employees were huddled together, crouched low on the floor. Rand saw the rear door of the kitchen was open and slid along a commercial stove toward the door. He knew McClain would cover the three people on the ground as he stepped past them.

McClain and the two Van Nuys Gang officers slowly followed Rand into the location only to find three employees huddled on the ground. As they entered the small cluttered kitchen, two of the employees pointed out the back door. Suddenly the dispatcher spoke loudly over the police radio, "35G11, be advised Air 3 is en route and K9-7 is en route from Wilshire Division."

Rand heard Halverson broadcast over the radio, "35G14, officer needs help in the alley rear of the taco stand, Sepulveda and Nordhoff. Shots fired."

The radio dispatcher, as if on cue, immediately broadcasted the help call. "All units stand by. 35G14 is requesting help, shots fired—"

Halverson cut the dispatcher off and began broadcasting, "35G14, two suspects exited the rear of the taco stand and fired multiple rounds. Unknown if suspects were hit by return fire. Suspects loaded into a mid-seventies Chevrolet, four door, black, no plates, driven by female, possible Hispanic." Taking a deep breath, Halverson put his seat belt on. Torres hit the accelerator and Halverson calmly and slowly began to broadcast, "35G14 is in pursuit. Suspects are now eastbound on Nordhoff. Two male Hispanics with a female driver, possible Hispanic. Suspects are armed, shots fired. Attempted murder of a police officer."

As Los Angeles police officers responded to the location, searching for the silver Camaro that had fled the scene after the drive-by shooting, they now had a second car with attempted murder suspects to find.

Rand pushed forward toward the door to the alley just as Torres, driving the police car, slammed the gas pedal to the floor, intent on not losing the suspects. The Ford Crown Vic rose up off the ground, shaking off its layer of dust, and roared down the alley.

Rand and McClain watched as Torres and Halverson drove northbound in pursuit of a black Chevrolet.

Inside the police car, adrenaline was pumping in both officers who had been shot at. Training had taken over, and Torres had brought the car to an immediate stop with both officers exiting the coffin holding shotguns at port arms. They weren't someone to hide in a coffin, nor were they going to back out of the situation. They were not willing victims. They would fight.

As Takster fired multiple rounds at Halverson, the first officer to get out of the car on the passenger side, both officers held their ground and returned fire. The suspect's car was already moving when Takster dove into the front seat.

"I'm pretty sure I hit him, Mark. Bumper lock those assholes—don't you lose them for anything," Halverson ordered. Torres was the better driver and began gaining on the suspects as they fled. Both officers remained courageous and driven, intent on capturing all three suspects.

The dispatcher began to clear the frequency of other radio transmissions to broadcast the pursuit. "All units, all frequencies stand by. 35G14 is in pursuit of attempt homicide suspects in Van Nuys Division, Sepulveda and Nordhoff. 35G14, your location?"

"35G14, eastbound on Nordhoff. 35G14, now northbound on Noble . . . crossing Tupper and coming up to Black Oak."

CHAPTER EIGHTEEN
THE BEST LAID PLANS

Lieutenant Jack Adams was in his car, the Mustang GT, racing through the gears as he headed northbound to the far other side of Los Angeles. No one gets anywhere fast in Los Angeles, but Adams was giving it his best.

As the fire department paramedic unit stopped in the street next to the officers protecting Officer Aoki, the two paramedics bailed out without even considering their own safety. A full engine company followed, completely taking over Van Nuys Boulevard. As two firemen from the engine company secured the gurney from the rescue ambulance, the two paramedics moved Aoki into the street where they could assess her injuries and work on her.

Aoki had lost a lot of blood and transitioned into shock. The paramedics knew their job was now much harder as her vitals struggled. Cutting her pant legs, they saw two separate areas of trauma: an obvious shotgun injury to her left hip with massive blood loss and a single bullet wound at her left thigh. They would later discover two more bullets that had impacted into the back of her bulletproof vest.

Aoki was turned on her side then rolled onto the gurney that was immediately brought up into an extended position. As the two firemen pushed the gurney toward the rescue ambulance, her IV was already running.

The gurney was forcibly smashed against the rear of the ambulance where the legs folded up and launched Aoki into the treatment area. Julie Barr jumped into the back of the ambulance and helped to lock the gurney into place as the paramedics worked.

"You have to get out, Officer, she'll be fine. We'll meet you at the hospital." The paramedic never looked up from Aoki when he issued the order.

But neither did Barr when she replied, "Fuck you."

The fireman standing outside the ambulance immediately sensed what the outcome of this argument was going to be. He slammed the doors shut, and the rough ride to Northridge Community Hospital was expedited by the firemen who would stop at nothing to save the officer's life.

#

Felicia was so angry, she had no time for feelings of panic. "You said there wouldn't be any cops chasing us, T! You said the cops would be in front, not in back! What the fuck? You fucked us, *pendejo*! We were just supposed to drive away quietly. You fucked us, pendejo! *No mames.*" Felicia stayed on the gas pedal, all the while yelling at Takster, driving over curbs and through intersections without regard for anyone else. She was headed back for the west side of the 405 Freeway, back home.

As she slammed against the side of a parked car, thirteen-year-old Calvin Velasquez was violently thrown headfirst against the rear passenger door. He yelled, "Let me out!" but no one seemed to hear him.

Takster, holding the right side of his face that was bleeding profusely, hit against the passenger door with his body and his face slammed against the window, smearing it with blood.

Felicia yelled, "Fuck you, T! Bleed, pendejo. Fucking die, you motherfucker." Keeping her foot on the gas pedal, she bounced off the parked car and continued down the street.

Halverson, broadcasting the pursuit, tried to anticipate what the driver was going to do next. "35G14, westbound on Plummer. Suspects hit a parked car at Noble and Plummer, continuing on Plummer. They might be heading for the 405 Freeway. Advise Highway Patrol. Do we have the airship en route?"

"35G14, be advised, Air 3 is en route. Highway Patrol has been notified."

Immediately after the dispatcher broadcasted, a Van Nuys Division patrol sergeant joined the pursuit. "9L50 is with the pursuit, trying to catch up."

Halverson jumped back on the radio as Torres kept the black Chevrolet in sight. "35G14, passing Burnett. Making a northbound turn onto Columbus . . . 35G14, suspect hit two pedestrians, both are down. Request an RA unit and a traffic unit to this location. Have 9L50 respond to the pedestrians."

Felicia, driving to escape and seeing blood flowing heavily from Takster's face, began overdriving and never saw the woman and her teenage son in the crosswalk until she hit them with the right rear fender of the black Chevrolet. Leaving them down in the roadway, Felicia accelerated and yelled at Takster. "Pendejo, why are they chasing us? I'm just driving the fucking car! Motherfucker, you got me in shit."

Takster held his face and finally realized that the shotgun blasts had hit him, but not a solid hit, or he would be dead. The pain was excruciating as he held his hand on his face to stop the bleeding. He kept wondering what went wrong. *Why were the police behind the taco stand?*

"9X11, we're in the pursuit behind 35G14. Be advised, Columbus dead-ends. We'll check on the pedestrians." 9X11 was a Van Nuys patrol unit with two young officers, Herrera and Myers, working mid-PM Watch. This was the excitement they lived for, and they relished the opportunity to get involved.

Sergeant Williams, 9L50, the Van Nuys Patrol sergeant, thought the pursuit was becoming too dangerous. The suspects had hit a parked car and had now hit two pedestrians. "9L50, discontinue the pursuit. Have 35G14 discontinue the pursuit and have Air 3 take over. I'll be Code Six at Burnett and Columbus with the pedestrians." Code Six was merely an LAPD code meaning the sergeant would be at a certain location until further notice.

„35G14, we're westbound on Superior, missed the dead end. Headed back toward Sepulveda." Halverson told Torres, "Some Van Nuys sergeant wants us to discontinue the pursuit, Mark. He wants the airship to take over."

Torres, fully engaged with every fiber of his being, replied, "We don't work for that guy, and the airship isn't even here yet! I'm not giving up and letting this guy go after he shot Karen. Fuck that." It was still unclear to some of the officers what had happened to Officer Aoki and that there were actually two separate carloads of suspects.

Moments later, as the police airship arrived in the airspace over the pursuit, the Tactical Flight Officer, TFO, was able to immediately locate the suspect's car. "Air 3 is over the pursuit. Suspect vehicle, black Chevrolet, is westbound on Superior."

The pilot commented to the TFO, "I can't believe some patrol sergeant wants to discontinue the pursuit. We got it, but they can't let go of these guys. They shot a policeman! They're not stopping them for running a red light. What's that guy thinking? I hope they stay with it."

"35G14, suspects are now northbound on Langdon. Residential area." Halverson made no remark or response to the request of 9L50 to discontinue the pursuit.

The two young patrol officers from 9X11 stopped quickly at the scene of the two pedestrians who were knocked down. With a practiced quickness, they triaged the scene and pulled right back into the pursuit. They certainly didn't want to get stuck at the scene of a traffic accident taking reports when they could be pursuing armed suspects. "9X11, pedestrians are injured but okay. Request an RA unit and a traffic unit to Burnett and Columbus. 9L50 will be Code Six there—he's right behind us. We're back in the pursuit."

9L50, Sergeant Williams, pulled up to the scene of two persons sitting on the ground just as 9X11 pulled away. "9L50, have 35G14 and 9X11 discontinue the pursuit. I'll stand by at my Code Six location for the RA unit."

"35G14 and 9X11, be advised that 9L50 requests you terminate the pursuit."

"Just crossed Kinzie Street. 35G14, suspects are westbound on Lassen through Kinzie. Headed to the 405 Freeway." Torres had gained on the black

Chevrolet and was only half a block away.

"9X11, there's no freeway on-ramp on Lassen. It just goes under the freeway."

"35G14, roger that. We're continuing under the 405 and coming up to Aqueduct."

There was no response from either unit or from the airship concerning the request by 9L50 to discontinue the pursuit. Policemen from throughout the city were commenting and punching the dashboard about the attempts by 9L50 to discontinue the pursuit.

There was a lot of pressure on officers in pursuits due to accidents and injuries caused by the suspects who oftentimes crashed their cars. The political pressure always aimed at police officers was to blame, which is standard operating procedure for many of our politicians. The pressure for police officers to merely allow suspects to escape was intense. In this case, no one on the streets of Los Angeles, or in the air, was willing to let these suspects escape. Except for Sergeant Williams, that is.

"Air 3 to 35G14. Be advised you have an accident ahead on Lassen next to the Sepulveda Veterans Hospital, heavy traffic." As Air 3 flew overhead, Torres and Halverson observed that the roadway was completely blocked in both directions due to the traffic accident.

Halverson looked at Torres and said, "Mark, we need to get these guys quick. Don't lose them."

Watching the black Chevrolet approaching the heavy traffic at full throttle, Torres knew they would crash and told Halverson, "Get ready, Jim, they're going to crash and there's lots of people around. We need to watch our fire and isolate these assholes from all these people."

As if on cue, Felicia, driving the Chevrolet, swerved to the right and up onto the sidewalk, trying to pass the roadblock of cars involved in the accident in front of the hospital.

The Chevrolet smashed into a tree with the left bumper, while the right front tire was sheared completely off the car by one of Los Angeles's famous uneven sidewalk hazards. Sometimes the failures of Los Angeles politicians work out for the best.

Before the car even came to a rest, Felicia pushed the door open and bounded over a parked car seemingly in one leap, running southwest across Lassen toward the VA Hospital.

"35G14, suspect crashed. Driver bailed and running south . . . or west, I'm not sure, across Lassen toward the VA Hospital. Female Hispanic with dark clothing and red belt." Torres, holding the police car back a safe distance, considered chasing the driver but knew the two suspects from the taco stand robbery were in the car. "Jim, let the driver go. Let's take the two shooters in the car."

Halverson quickly transmitted over the radio to the Van Nuys patrol unit pulling in behind them. "35G14 to 9X11. Take the driver on foot across Lassen; we'll take the car."

"9X11, roger. 9X11 is in foot pursuit southbound across Lassen."

Breaking into a run, both Herrera and Myers began to discuss tactics as they assumed the role of pursuers. "Myers, don't take any chances with this bitch. Let's stay with her but keep a little distance. Let's don't separate. We're in Devonshire Division now and I don't know where the fuck we are. I'm lost over here."

Meyers yelled as he ran across Lassen and through the cars stranded by the traffic accident, "Got that! Let's keep eyes on her and wait for K9. The VA will have their own police. If this bitch runs into the VA, let's stand by for them. They know the location."

"9X11, requesting a perimeter. Lassen to Plummer and Woodley to Haskell. Air 3, can you direct units to fill in the perimeter?"

"Air 3, stand by on that. We're over the pursuit termination with 35G14." Hovering over the pursuit termination, the pilot and tactical field officer in Air 3 attempted to support the arrest of the two suspects in the car. The tactical flight officer aimed the downward-facing searchlight at the suspect's car, trying not to illuminate the officers.

Both Torres and Halverson assessed their background and the position of other persons nearby as they held their positions, standing behind the doors of the police car armed with shotguns. The group of people involved in the three-car traffic accident, along with the seven cars stopped in the roadway that was blocked by the accident, were no strangers to police pursuits in Los Angeles. The restrictive pursuit rules adopted by the LAPD had encouraged criminal suspects to flee, and the entire group knew immediately that the police sirens and the Chevrolet crashing into a tree meant another pursuit was terminating and everyone hit the ground.

The officers watched as a man exited the right front door of the car with a silver handgun in his left hand. They recognized him as the man who had shot at them behind the Mexican restaurant. The right side of his face was covered in blood. He raised the gun up and shakily pointed it at the officers. He fired two rounds at the officers, who simultaneously fired each of the two shotguns they held.

Takster's decision to engage Torres and Halverson in another gun battle was his last decision. Takster's bullets hit the headlight and passenger door of the police car while he was lifted off the ground and knocked backwards four feet when 12-gauge rounds from both officers' shotguns impacted on his chest. Halverson knew Takster's rounds were fired directly at him and he expected to feel the pain of the bullets, but the pain never came. The bullets lodged in the police car.

Torres had fired two rounds, one immediately after the other, then hit Takster with a third shotgun round before Takster ever hit the ground. KMA. Although neither officer was hit, Takster died immediately, still clutching his handgun. Four people in the nearby traffic accident scenario broke and ran toward the hospital while the others were frozen in place, lying or kneeling on the ground.

From his position, Halverson could see movement inside the car and then two hands pushed out of the left rear window of the black Chevrolet. Halverson told Torres, "Mark, I've got this asshole on the ground. You take the one in the car."

Ordering him from the car, Torres watched Calvin Velasquez crawl on hands and knees from the disabled car and walk back toward the police car, crying, "I just want to go home!" Just a boy. A very dangerous boy with his first personal taste of violence. Gang violence. Torres handcuffed and took the suspect into custody as Halverson covered both suspects.

While Torres held the handcuffed boy and covered his partner, Halverson moved forward and handcuffed the suspect lying on the ground. Takster appeared to be dead. The officers would allow rescue personnel to pronounce death, but until then, he was still a threat and got handcuffed.

After Halverson handcuffed the suspect and moved the suspect's gun away, he removed his radio from his belt and broadcasted, "35G14, one suspect down, one in custody. We need an RA unit and a supervisor. Driver, female Hispanic, running southbound across the baseball field. I need a perimeter. Show 9X11 in foot pursuit."

Torres searched the young boy a second time before he felt comfortable that they had the situation under control. Looking at Halverson, Torres said, "You good, Jim?"

"God was watching over us, Mark. Looks like the rounds hit my door. That was close."

"Damn, Jim, that happened so fast." Adrenaline was still pumping in both officers' bloodstreams as they took deep breaths and scanned the people in the street to guarantee no one had been injured in the pursuit termination.

Watching the two suspects get taken into custody, the Tactical Flight Officer on Air 3 extinguished the searchlight and the pilot turned the helicopter toward the VA Hospital in search of the fleeing driver. "Air 3 is clear from the pursuit termination and is now with the foot pursuit. Suspect is now running southbound through Mission Hills Golf Course next to the Sepulveda VA Hospital. Suspect dropped dark clothing, now wearing dark tank top."

As Air 3 moved away from the pursuit termination point, Torres and Halverson noticed a news helicopter hovering overhead.

The K9 officer had been driving northbound up the 405 Freeway toward the pursuit termination. "K9-7, northbound on the 405 Freeway at Devonshire Street, direct me in." K9-7, Officer John Sheffield, assigned to Metropolitan Division, raced toward the pursuit termination with his canine, Blue.

"Air 3 to K9-7. Drop down to Lassen and Haskell and stage up at the ball field. Be advised, you have Van Nuys and Devonshire units staging around the perimeter. Suspect is on FLIR and inside the perimeter."

"9X11, suspect was running across the golf course but we can't see her; we lost sight of her. Too dark and too many shadows. Air 3, direct us in."

"Air 3, stand by 9X11. K9 unit is staging with another search team."

The K9 unit was used to using air units to coordinate searches. Responding to situations in different parts of the city, and commonly with officers from various police divisions on scene, they often required the air unit to bring everyone together with the same game plan. "K9-7 to Air 3. On scene and I've got 9X17 with me and 9X11 staged on the golf course standing by for us. They can't see any movement."

Suddenly, 9L50, Sergeant Williams, who had cleared the scene of the pedestrians who were struck, came on the air. "9L50, have the K9 unit, 9X11, and 9X17 stand by for me."

The dispatcher broadcasted the request. "K9-7, 9X11, and 9X17, stand by for 9L50."

There was no response from the three units. K9-7, Officer Sheffield, advised the officers on 9X11 and 9X17, "We don't have time to wait for your sergeant. You're with me now on this search team, so follow my direction." The four officers from 9X11 and 9X17 were apprehensive about the situation but knew that their sergeant could yell at them later. Right now, it was time to do police work.

Looking across the field, the K9 officer could see the Veterans Affairs Hospital and two white police SUVs at the rear, who he believed were federal police officers for the VA. "K9-7, please contact Sepulveda VA and advise federal police of our actions on their property. Have them secure the rear of the hospital and disallow entrance by our suspect."

"Roger, K9-7. VA police have already been notified and they have initiated a lockdown."

"Air 3, suspect is on FLIR and providing a strong report. Suspect ran across the golf course and then headed west for the hospital. Suspect is hunkered down in bushes near a double tennis court. No other persons or animals visible near the location. Cross the baseball field, walk onto the golf course, and look to your right for the tennis courts. Your canine can start working from the edge of the tree line." The LAPD airships were equipped with a number of tactical tools, including FLIR, a thermal imaging system that can track a person's body heat.

"K9-7, roger that. Moving forward now. There's some light but lots of shadows."

Breaking into the search efforts at the pursuit termination, the dispatcher announced another emergency situation. "All units, be advised. California Highway Patrol is in pursuit northbound 405 Freeway of a silver Chevrolet Camaro refusing to yield. Northbound 405 merging onto I-5 northbound."

#

McClain, standing by at the first shooting location where Karen Aoki had been shot, was busy setting up a crime scene and making notifications. LA Fire Rescue was on scene with boots on the ground in only four minutes and was now transporting Aoki to Northridge Hospital.

Barr stayed at Aoki's side on her trip, while Rand and Andrews provided security for everyone at the crime scene. As much as they wanted to get to the pursuit, they knew their job now was to protect the officers and the crime scene operations.

McClain ordered a Van Nuys unit to survey the front and rear of the scene to guarantee there were no other victims of errant gunshot wounds. When McClain's phone rang, he already knew it was Lieutenant Adams. "Hey, Mac, it's Jack. Where are we with this?"

"Looks like an ambush, Lieutenant, or that's what I'm thinking. Julie and Karen identified two suspects walking into the taco stand with a handgun and put out a backup. They eased up to the location and were standing by for backup units a few doors down and got hit by a drive-by. I'm sure it's related. I think your concern over them only hitting on Wednesdays and Thursdays played out; it looks like a setup to me. Karen took two rounds to her left leg when she was standing in the street. Julie sent a handful of rounds into the car, but we don't know yet. I think Karen let some rounds go after she went down, but that's unclear. Andrews got pressure on Aoki's leg right away. There's damage, Jack, but she's alive.

"Halverson and Torres took the first two suspects out the back door of the taco stand to a waiting car with a female driver. They abandoned the car out front that they arrived in, so I think they planned to pull our officers in to set them up for the drive-by. They made their getaway in the car in the alley. They went through the kitchen and then capped multiple rounds at our boys out back, but no hits. Did hit their car, though. We returned fire but it's unknown if there were any hits. You probably heard the pursuit going over into Devonshire Division on the other side of the 405 Freeway. If our suspects are Brown Pride, looks like they're heading back to their stomping grounds. They crashed on Lassen just west of the 405. Sounds like 35G14 just dumped one of them at the pursuit termination where they crashed, one's in custody, and there's a foot pursuit on the third into the VA Hospital. Now, it just came on the radio that CHP has a silver Camaro northbound on the 405. Might be the shooters in our drive-by."

"Ok, Mac. I'm on my way from San Pedro. I should be able to fly up the 405 as long as it's not slammed past LAX, so it won't take too long in this Mustang. Mac, I'm sorry I'm not there."

"You can't be everywhere, Jack. Just get here safe. Don't over drive that car; I've got this for now. They're transporting Aoki to Northridge Hospital. I've got four Van Nuys detectives here, so I'm going to leave this crime scene to them and set up a command post in front of the VA Hospital."

"Roger that, Mac. Be sure to get a security detail on Karen right now." Pushing the Mustang up the HOV lane, Adams slammed the dashboard with his fist. Somehow it seemed to make the car go faster.

McClain ordered four officers to protect Karen Aoki at Northridge Community Hospital and then left for the pursuit termination.

"Air 3 to K9-7. Suspect is sixty yards directly in your path. Suspect's heat signature is strong, but broken up by the trees and brush. Hasn't moved, so I think she's hunkered down."

Officer Sheffield scanned the area with his flashlight. "K9-7, roger that. Is it this large brush area I'm lighting up?"

"Air 3, roger. Suspect hasn't moved; may even be in the tree. Ready for daylight?"

"K9-7, roger, light her up. My canine is off leash and I'm ready for the announcement to the suspect." Air 3 directed his searchlight into the brush area, bringing daylight to the area.

Air 3 announced that a canine was being deployed, encouraging the suspect to give up. With no response, K9-7, along with two officers from 9X11 and two officers from 9X17, both Van Nuys patrol units, moved cautiously toward the suspect's location with Blue tracking in front of them.

Felicia Marquez grew up in the LAPD's Devonshire Division, living there her whole life. Her family boasted three generations of Brown Pride membership, and she took the gang life in stride; she knew nothing else. Even so, she only became involved in criminal gang activity from a distance, as a helper. She had only expected to pick up Takster and Carlos behind the taco stand and drive them home.

Felicia was always fast, and she'd tossed her coat to lighten her weight and be more agile. She turned to look behind her but saw that no one was there. She had lost them, but she knew they would come looking. If she ran any farther, she would be in a well-lit area next to the veteran's hospital where two white police SUVs were parked. Then she saw two men and a woman in dark-blue uniforms standing at a double glass door into the hospital. Felicia knew the police officers would see her, so she found a dark spot in the brush and hunkered down on her stomach, lying with her face flat on the ground. She decided to play dead and hoped that the policemen would give up looking for her. She lay quietly, holding a handgun under her chest, and waited for the opportunity to get back home.

As the five officers approached, Sheffield held the lead. The four officers of 9X11 and 9X17 trailed behind so as not to interfere with the canine. "K9-7 to Air 3. My canine is on point; suspect is located." Blue, a large German shepherd, slowly moved closer to the suspect's hiding location and began barking.

Felicia held her face tight to the ground as she watched the large German shepherd barking at her, inching closer and closer. The dog jumped at her and she fired two times, panicked, scrambling back from the dog. Felicia hurried up to her knees and held the gun in both hands.

As the officers tightened upon her location, they heard two gunshots emanating from the brush.

The four Van Nuys officers crouched down and assumed lowered shooting positions to reduce their profile, but the canine officer, Sheffield, continued forward to recover his canine. "9X11, shots fired by suspect."

As Sheffield moved closer, he saw that Blue appeared to have been hit and was lying on her side. He scanned his flashlight left then right, revealing the suspect secreted within heavy brush on her knees with a handgun outstretched in front of her. Sheffield ordered for her to drop the gun, but when the suspect failed to comply and turned the gun toward Sheffield, he fired two rounds in rapid succession, striking the suspect in the upper body, then a third round that struck the suspect in the head. Simultaneously, Officer Meyer from 9X11 fired two rounds, one missing the suspect and one striking the suspect in the upper chest.

Air 3 extinguished the searchlight and veered off the scene.

Sheffield approached the downed suspect and observed her to be around twenty to twenty-five years old. She was armed with a 9-millimeter blue steel semiautomatic handgun, and Sheffield believed she was dead.

"K9-7, be advised, one suspect down. Request an RA unit for a gunshot wound and a Metro Division supervisor. Additionally, my canine is down. I'll notify canine rescue myself."

"9X11, requesting a supervisor to our location. Code Four at our location."

"9L50, show me Code Six at the VA Hospital with 9X11 and 9X17." Sergeant Williams had just arrived, and the scene at the pursuit termination began to wind down as the Code Four was broadcast.

CHAPTER NINETEEN
OUT OF THE CITY

Just as all of the LAPD units on the scene realized that all three suspects were now in custody, the dispatcher brought forth another emergency broadcast. "All units, be advised California Highway Patrol is northbound I-5 past the I-14 interchange with a silver Chevrolet Camaro. Vehicle comes back to a West Valley Division stolen vehicle. Code Six Charles, suspects armed and dangerous."

"Hey, Lieutenant, you almost here?" McClain pulled into the scene in front of the VA Hospital and began feeling the pressure of so much going on all at the same time. He was more than ready for Lieutenant Adams to arrive on scene. "K9-7 and two Van Nuys patrol units were shot at by the female runner. She hit the canine in the side, but the dog's still alive. I don't think the dog's going to make it, though. K9-7 and one of the Van Nuys officers returned fire and knocked her down. She's KMA at the scene."

"Just minutes away, Mac. Listen, get a couple of our Gang units on that CHP pursuit going northbound. It has to be our shooters, and I'm not letting them go. Not sure where they're headed—probably to Bakersfield. I remember something about Brown Pride connections out there. Tell our guys to stay with Highway Patrol clear to Bakersfield, then pull them back if it keeps going. They can gas up out there at the CHP station. I'm calling Chief Nelson to let him know we're northbound out of the city."

"Roger that, boss. I'm gonna send two units from Devonshire Division Gangs that are here now if that's okay with you. Their sergeant, Alvarado, is pulling in now so I'll send him, too. I need Van Nuys Gangs at this scene at the VA. I've also got Van Nuys patrol holding the scene at Sepulveda and Nordhoff."

"Sounds good, Mac. Get your hands on our shooters and get them transported to Van Nuys station, not Devonshire. Leave their cars where they are. Van Nuys has more room to host the officer-involved shooting investigation. Remind all the officers to stand by on any statements until they're represented."

Driving well over the speed limit as he crested the Sepulveda Pass past the Getty Museum, Adams was juggling radios and phones lying on the front passenger seat of the Mustang GT. As he looked at the screen of his ringing phone and saw it was Commander Stans Jelenick, Adams debated answering but finally picked it up. "Lieutenant, this is Commander Jelenick. What the hell's going on? Why haven't I been called?"

"We've been a little busy, Commander, but I'm starting to make notifications now. I was down in San Pedro but I'm almost to the scene. I was just calling Chief Nelson."

"I'm coming out now, Lieutenant, to take over. Why weren't you there when this happened? Why were you in San Pedro? I didn't know anything about you driving down there. Where's the crime scene?"

"Which one? We have multiple scenes with robberies, vehicle pursuits, pedestrians hit, car crashes, foot pursuits, four shooting locations—two down, by the way, and an officer hit—and a CHP pursuit of our shooters northbound right now, probably to Bakersfield. I sent a couple of our units out of the city with CHP but I'll pull them back at Bakersfield, if they get that far. We know that Brown Pride has alliances and family members out there. You can have whichever one you want, Commander. Force Investigation Division, the officer-involved shooting team, will be split between all the shooting scenes, along with the District Attorney's Office, the FBI, councilmen, and I'm sure the mayor will be here. Everyone will want a piece of the officers who dared to shoot criminals who tried to murder half a dozen of our officers. Commander, I'm actually thinking that it would probably be good if you took over the whole thing and coordinated all the different scenes and different investigations."

Jelenick barked, "Who gave you permission to send our officers out of the city?"

"I'm doing my job, Commander, I don't need permission. We're chasing murder suspects who shot one of our officers. I am notifying you, though, and I'll advise Deputy Chief Nelson when I talk to him."

After quite a long pause, Jelenick changed his plans a little bit. "Well, I'll come out to oversee things. Until then, you keep moving forward, but I want you to run everything past me. Where will you be?"

"I'll stop briefly at the command post at the VA, and then I'll be at the trauma center at Northridge Hospital with Officer Aoki, who was hit. There's a Devonshire field sergeant over there with her now and she's stable, I understand. But don't worry, I'll take care of her. No one will really care about the crime scene where our officer was shot. We have it buttoned down, but I'm guessing all the city brass and reporters will be going to the scene where we shot the bad guys. God knows we need to investigate what the police did, not what the suspects did."

"Lieutenant, you know why we do this. We're answerable to the public."

"Of course we are, Commander. Detective McClain will be at Lassen and Nordhoff, where he's setting up a command post. That's where the press and the mayor will be, so you might want to go there."

Jelenick felt a strong case of déjà vu as Lieutenant Adams dictated the course of LAPD actions in what sounded to Jelenick like an overly aggressive response. Adams hit the disconnect button and muttered, "Damn, must be a bad signal in the Sepulveda Pass."

The dispatcher at the Communications Division came over the radio with a follow-up broadcast about the CHP pursuit. "All units, California Highway Patrol advised suspects in excess of one hundred miles per hour at Calgrove Boulevard approaching the city of Valencia. Shots fired. Suspects fired a handgun at the pursuing CHP unit. A traffic break is being developed."

Adams sighed and went on to make his next call. "Chief Nelson, it's Lieutenant Adams. I wanted to brief you on some events that occurred tonight. I apologize for bothering you at home."

"Jack, everyone in the world has been calling me, even Chief Fuller. Guess I already have a pretty good picture of what's happening. How are you doing? What do you need from me?"

"I feel like crap because I was down in San Pedro when this happened, but I'm pulling in now and have control of things through Detective McClain. It's mostly out of our hands now, Chief, and Force Investigation Division will take over. They arrive quick, like you know. Aoki is off to Northridge Hospital with a leg wound. McClain told me it's a big hit and she'll be recovering long-term, but she's stable and she'll be okay. I'll meet briefly with McClain at the command post, then let him have it and I'll go to the hospital. There will be plenty of bosses at the scene and they won't need me, but I'll stay on top of everything through McClain. I could use your staff, though, to look at Aoki's emergency contacts and help to transport her family to the hospital. She's not married, but I think her parents live in Torrance. Maybe we could send a sergeant from one of the South Bureau Divisions to go and get them. This was an ambush, Chief."

"Okay, Jack, hang in there. Try to get some sleep somewhere down the road. Let me know whatever you need. I'm sure we'll cross paths somewhere tonight."

"Yeah, no sleep for a while, sir. CHP picked up who we think are our shooters and they're northbound on the I-5 Freeway. I'm sending two Devonshire Gang units and a sergeant behind them as far as Bakersfield, but if they keep going I'll pull them back. But thank God, Commander Jelenick is on his way out."

"He means well, Jack. He's just out of his element when he's in the field. I'm headed to Northridge Hospital first to see Officer Aoki and after that to the command post with the Valley Bureau Chief. I'm sure the chief of police will be showing up, but if I know Chief Fuller, he'll be going to the hospital first. This is getting a lot of attention, Jack. I know your details are squared away, but let's avoid any comments to the press. We'll save that for myself or Chief Fuller. I'll probably see you at the hospital in a bit."

#

"Roy, someone is at the door. A policeman." Nancy Aoki stood back, braced herself in another doorway, and covered her face with her hand. She didn't want to see anything or hear anything. She wanted this not to be real.

"Mr. Roy Aoki, I'm Sergeant Workman. I'm sorry to tell you that Karen has been injured at work. She's doing fine, I was told, and she was taken to Northridge Community Hospital in the San Fernando Valley for surgery. Lieutenant Adams is on his way to the hospital and he asked that I transport you and your wife there."

Roy Aoki, Karen's father, struggled comprehending what Sergeant Workman was saying. "She's injured? What happened to her? Surgery? Where is she? Where is Northridge Hospital?"

"Mr. Aoki, I'm here to drive you and your wife to Karen. I was told that she's going into surgery, but I don't have any other details. We should leave right now, sir."

Roy Aoki held his wife's arm and said, "Nancy, we must go. Let's go now." Sitting in the rear seat of the police car, Nancy Aoki continued to hold her face in her hands. The two were afraid to talk, afraid to look at each other or discuss what might have happened to their daughter. The young girl who had stood up to bullies, the soccer star. The young woman who had graduated from college with a 4.0 average and was supposed to be a nurse like her mother. Their only child.

#

"All units, Highway Patrol advised suspects in silver Camaro exited I-5 at Valencia Boulevard. Los Angeles County Sheriff's Department has joined the pursuit."

After shooting Gang officer Karen Aoki at the Mexican restaurant, Alley-Dog yelled for the driver, Tomas Perales, to get them to the freeway. "Move, motherfucker, move! Stay in front of the police!"

The plan: Takster would draw the officers in to the restaurant and then escape out the back door to a waiting car driven by Felicia, gone before anyone knew they abandoned the car parked in front. Out front, AlleyDog would drive by in the Camaro and shoot the officers as they get out of their police car, then escape to the freeway. They would drive the Camaro, which they had stolen, northbound out of Los Angeles to the small town of Castaic, a truck stop.

AlleyDog and his crew would get off the freeway before the police caught up to them and make their way to the two cars they had parked at a truck stop coffee shop, abandon the Camaro, and then split up into the two waiting cars. AlleyDog had laughed while making the plan that they would backtrack in the two cold cars and drive back home, probably passing the police chasing them who would be coming the other way.

The part of the plan that had amused Takster the most was that he would be out the back door and gone while AlleyDog lured the police away. Whether AlleyDog was caught or not didn't really matter, because Takster would still profit by his new liaison with DogDayz of Mara Salvatruche. Probably better for him, actually, if AlleyDog was taken out by the police.

But like all well-made plans, wrenches were commonly thrown into the system. Takster's belief that he would escape out the back without notice was upended when the two Gang officers had appeared in the alley before they even got into the black Chevrolet.

For AlleyDog, it was the dead body in the back seat of the Camaro and police cars behind them before they were able to change cars. That wasn't in the plan.

As they fled at high speeds, hitting one hundred miles per hour, AlleyDog yelled to the two other live persons in the car. "Get off the freeway somewhere! We'll lose them and hide around Magic Mountain somewhere. Then we'll go out to Castaic and get our cars."

After hearing the LAPD broadcast of the drive-by shooting, California Highway Patrol officer Lisa Doyle observed the Camaro with the back window shot out and occupants that matched the LAPD's description. The car was northbound onto the I-5 Freeway from the 405 Freeway just minutes from the shooting location.

CHP Officer Doyle requested a backup to assist her in stopping the suspects. Doyle's plan was to stay with the suspects and follow the car without taking any police action until a backup officer arrived. She hoped they would just keep heading northbound.

As they began climbing over the Newhall Pass, the secondary Highway Patrol unit driven by officer Steve Henson fell in immediately behind Doyle.

The suspect's car was traveling at seventy-five miles per hour and accelerated to ninety-five when Doyle brought her car closer. *Time to go to work.*

As Doyle followed the car over the crest of the Newhall Pass, she saw the muzzle flash from the broken back window of the Camaro and leaned over low in the seat of her police car. She tried to cover her face and her eyes as her windshield exploded. Officer Doyle had never been in a shooting before, and she had never been shot at. She took her foot off the gas pedal and the police car began to drift slower behind the suspects after her windshield shattered.

AlleyDog was using the handgun that had been dropped onto the floor of the car by Arturo Mejia after he was shot and killed by Julie Barr. AlleyDog was intent on hitting the police car behind them to make them stop chasing them, and he kept firing until the gun was empty.

While turned in the seat so he could fire at the police car behind them, AlleyDog rummaged through Arturo Mejia's pockets and retrieved two more fully loaded magazines. As he reloaded, he saw the California Highway Patrol police vehicle slowing and falling further behind them. The police were scared and were quitting. They would get away.

Tomas Perales turned off the headlights like he had seen on television and held his speed as he left the police car behind him, cruising over the Newhall Pass toward Valencia. When he saw the sign for the Valencia Boulevard offramp, AlleyDog yelled at him, "Little Clown, get off up there! Get off, get off the freeway. Lose them over by Magic Mountain and take side roads to Castaic."

As Little Clown swerved to the right and headed for the offramp of Valencia Boulevard, he was suddenly blinded by high beams behind him. Then came the flashing red and blue lights filling his mirrors.

Officer Doyle had brushed the glass from her face and the front of her uniform, paused to realize what had happened, and felt that her car was coasting. As she mashed the gas pedal back to the floor, she had almost lost sight of the suspect's car.

CHP officer Steve Henson pulled his car right behind Doyle and stayed with her. Only moments later, a Los Angeles County sheriff's unit, LASD, that had pulled in behind the two Highway Patrol units joined the pursuit.

As the silver Camaro crossed lanes toward Valencia Boulevard, Doyle knew they were headed for the off-ramp, and she pushed her car right up behind them. She hit her high beams, then lit up every single light on her police car. Tomas Perales yelled, "Fuck, they're going to hit us!"

Just after entering the first of two curves on the offramp, Doyle initiated a pit maneuver by pressing the right front fender of her Ford Explorer against the left rear fender of the Camaro. After the suspects shot at the pursuing

Highway Patrol unit, the decision had been quickly made to disallow the occupants of the Camaro from entering a heavily populated area.

The rear of the Camaro was forced to the right, pointing the car to the left. Little Clown overcompensated, pulling the steering wheel hard right, and immediately lost control. The car launched off the right side of the roadway and through a chain-link fence onto a grassy knoll next to College of the Canyons, a community college. A hiking and biking trail ran through the area directly next to the freeway that had only a few trees and bushes, mostly barren.

The Camaro traversed down the bank and struck a washed-out hard-packed area that caused the car to nosedive into the ground. The rear wheels slowly rose off the ground and the car tilted to the right side, falling onto its side, and slowly, as if in slow motion, continued to roll over onto the roof.

CHP Officers Doyle and Henson left their vehicles on the freeway off-ramp, following the suspect's car on foot. The two sheriff's deputies drove their car off the paved off-ramp and partially down the dirt embankment until it became stuck before exiting their car. A sheriff's helicopter appeared overhead within moments and, with a searchlight on, illuminated the suspect's car.

Inside the car, AlleyDog lay entangled with the dead body of Arturo Mejia. He couldn't see out of the car very well but knew they were under bright lights. The car spun out of control and turned over so fast that he wasn't sure where he was or what had happened. He looked out the back window of the car and saw two people approaching wearing tan pants with a dark stripe and knew they were police officers.

AlleyDog did not know where the shotgun was, but he realized the handgun he had taken from Arturo Mejia was next to him. AlleyDog tried to point the gun at one of the officer's legs, but everything was so tight he could barely move his arms. Adjusting his body and pulling his arms loose, he decided to shoot the two police officers, slide out of the car, and escape on foot. He was confident he could still get away.

As the two Highway Patrol officers approached on the north side of the suspect's car and the two sheriff's deputies covered the south side at a greater distance than the Highway Patrol officers, shots rang out from inside the Camaro.

The officer's vision of the event was compromised at best, as the Camaro had a low-profile top and small windows which were now partially caved in. The car was dark inside even though the helicopter had shown a bright light on the scene from above.

Officer Henson, an experienced officer with prior military experience, knew that he and the other officers were being fired at. He instinctively fired two rounds from his shotgun directly at the muzzle flash that emanated from the broken back window of the Camaro. Henson continued to aggressively approach the suspect's car with his shotgun pointed toward the rear window. Absent any cover or concealment and in a high-danger situation, he tried to protect the other three officers by covering the inside of the car.

AlleyDog felt the first shotgun blast hitting hard against his left shoulder, even though only part of the round struck him. Panicked, he tried to lift himself onto his hands and knees to shoot again so he could escape on foot. He was able to slide his left foot and leg out of the passenger window as he raised his gun up to fire again. He planned to fire the gun and cause the police officers to duck or to hide, then he could slip out of the side window and run.

Officer Doyle, holding a flashlight, lit up the inside of the car and observed through a side window a male on his hands and knees in the rear of the vehicle with a handgun pointed toward officer Henson. Believing the suspect, AlleyDog, was about to fire again, she fired two rounds from her handgun and observed the suspect, apparently hit by the gunfire, fully slump forward on his stomach with the gun falling to the ground. Officer Lisa Doyle was in her first gun fight, and AlleyDog was to die inside the car.

Simultaneously, Tomas Perales, aka Little Clown, crawled on hands and knees out of the front driver's side window and into the helicopter's bright light, dragging the shotgun with a pistol grip and a sawed-off barrel underneath his body. Little Clown had recovered the shotgun that AlleyDog dropped. His face was bleeding profusely after the impact with the windshield. Little Clown knew he had to get away from the vehicle and find a place to hide.

Sheriff's Deputies Brian Mays and Bill Scott both fired their handguns as the suspect slid the shotgun from underneath his body and pushed the barrel forward toward the deputies. The impact on the suspect's upper body was clearly visible under the bright light of the airship overhead. The suspect appeared to have been disabled and probably killed as he lay flat on top of the shotgun.

Both Highway Patrol officers stepped back to the cover of Doyle's Ford Explorer and requested additional units and a supervisor, along with a Fire Rescue unit. They advised the rescue unit to stage northbound on I-5 Freeway and south of the Valencia Boulevard off ramp until their safety could be guaranteed.

The two sheriff's deputies ordered the occupants out of the car, not knowing how many suspects may be in the car. When there was no response, the deputies requested their SWAT team to respond, with a plan to allow the SWAT team to approach and secure the occupants of the car. A good call. Approaching the car at this point was extremely dangerous.

As Lieutenant Adams arrived at the command post, throwing on an LAPD windbreaker over his T-shirt, he was met by Detective McClain. "Hey, Lieutenant, all kinds of shit happening. Got some follow-up for you. You know K9-7 and Van Nuys had an officer involved shooting out here and the female driver was shot. She's KMA. Of the other two who were in the car, Devonshire Gangs knows the one 35G12 shot. His name is Takster from Brown Pride. Got a big BP tattoo on his calf, so he may be the one described by wits last week. Devonshire says he's a new shot caller and he's probably the head guy in this. Trying to move up the career ladder." McClain was obviously thinking like the senior detective he was, trying to piece the case together in his mind.

"Now the new news. Sorry, LT, it just keeps on getting better. CHP took rounds from the Camaro they were pursuing while they were northbound on I-5. They pitted the Camaro out in Valencia somewhere and rolled them off of an off-ramp. They took rounds and returned fire and they think two are down in the car, but they don't know how many are in there. They're not able to approach the car safely, so they pulled back and they're waiting for sheriff's SWAT. I've got four Van Nuys officers with Karen, and I think our brass are headed her way."

"Okay, Mac. Get a Devonshire unit over to Northridge Hospital to replace Van Nuys. I want one patrol unit there and they're not to leave until relieved by the next watch. I want a security detail on Aoki twenty-four seven until she's released. The Captain III at Devonshire doesn't have a clue, and he's gonna balk at that, but the patrol captain will be okay with it. Tell them it's coming from Chief Nelson, and I'll let the chief know I'm speaking for him. If the chief disagrees, we'll pull the Devonshire officers out. You have everything you need at the command post, Mac?"

"Seems like. Force Investigation Division is just showing up and they'll be taking over to investigate the shootings. Won't be much for me to do in a few minutes, so I'll just keep the command post going. They'll want to interview me tonight sometime, but let me tell you, there's about a million people here. It's not like the old days when policemen were heroes. Everyone's out to get these officers, Jack. We're the new suspects."

"Yeah, things have changed somehow. I know I don't have to tell you, Mac, but our officers don't talk without an attorney. Is the Protective League on scene yet? And any word on the two we shot?"

The Los Angeles Police Department Protective League is the "employee union" for Los Angeles police officers that provides administrative and legal representation to officers involved in an officer-involved shooting. They are considered to be the premier organization of all such efforts in the country. The demands to "police the police" have grown to an unprecedented level over the last two decades, and police officers are often viewed as "suspects" by many involved in the investigation and review of the event.

"Yeah, the Protective League Rep was one of the first people here, and he immediately grabbed our officers and briefed them about waiting for an attorney. He told me he requested the full force of the Protective League to respond to the scene and he hasn't left their side since. Those guys don't drag their feet," McClain assured Lieutenant Adams.

McClain completed his breakdown of the events. "Apparently, when the vehicle pursuit terminated, Takster bailed out of the car and shot twice at Halverson and Torres. They both hit him and he's KMA. The other one gave up—really young, thirteen. His name's Calvin Velasquez and we have him in Cal Gang as a Brown Pride tagger. From a wallet on the ground, the driver appears to be a twenty-three-year-old female, Felicia Marquez, but we don't know her and she's not in Cal Gang. She dug down into some brush at the VA Hospital and the canine flushed her out. She shot the dog and put him down, then tried for K9-7. The canine officer and one of the Van Nuys guys dumped her ass."

"Listen, Mac. There's so much going on and investigations are going in all directions, so I need you to stay here at the CP as long as possible. They can interview you last. I'm going to meet with our officers here for a bit and then pull away and go see Karen. I should be there already."

"Jack, you know tomorrow's my anniversary. Andrea and I are going to Santa Barbara in the morning. We're staying at the Four Seasons for three nights. It costs a fortune, but gotta make Momma happy."

"Yeah, well, we're not doing that, Mac. You'll be here for at least a couple days. Tell Andrea it's my fault. I'm sorry, pal, but I'll buy you breakfast in the morning to celebrate your anniversary."

#

"Excuse me, Lieutenant Adams? I'm Shelley Givens. I'm an investigative reporter for the *Los Angeles Times*—here's my card. I've been assigned to write a piece on the heroic efforts of your Gang officers in reducing crime in Los Angeles. I understand the article is at the direction of Mayor Hernandez, and it's possible that my editor will expand it to a series. Everyone seems very excited about this. I'm hoping I can interview you about the events tonight. Maybe I can shadow you now and just watch. Would that work?"

Adams and McClain looked at each other before Adams responded. "You work for the *LA Times* and you're doing a piece on how heroic we are? A positive take on the LAPD?"

"Yes, Lieutenant. I'm really excited about getting to know you and the Gang officers. I'm hoping to go to your roll calls and even sit down with each of your officers to talk with them. Do you think we could work out a ride-along for me? I'd love to go out with you and your officers and see firsthand what you do out here. I just want to get to know everyone. This is so exciting."

"Yeah, well, I don't think so. You're being dishonest, Miss Givens, and burning your bridges. The *LA Times* has never made a positive comment about the LAPD. But I tell you what, you should talk to Commander Jelenick; he would be pleased to work with you. Hand me your notepad and I'll write down his cell phone number for you."

"Do you really think so? That would be so awesome."

#

Adams and McClain stepped under the yellow tape around the scene, just out of Shelley Givens's reach. "What do you think she's up to, LT?"

"Nothing that's good for us, Mac. Let's keep her away from us. I'll let Chief Nelson know that she's dropping the mayor's name."

The conversation was interrupted just as Detective McClain began to make his case for taking time off. "Who's in charge here?" Sergeant Williams, 9L50, had finally arrived at the pursuit termination.

"I'm Detective McClain. I guess I'm in charge for now. Unless you'd like to do it." McClain was actually hoping that someone else would take over for him. He wanted to leave for the Four Seasons with his wife.

"I ordered that pursuit to be discontinued, and I ordered my two Van Nuys units to stand by and not start the foot search for the suspect until I arrived. Now they've been involved in a shooting. There's going to be hell to pay."

McClain looked at Lieutenant Adams and knew immediately that this poor sergeant had no idea what the tornado looked like that was about to modify his outlook on life.

"Williams, is it?" Adams started calmly. "Sergeant Williams, we're the Los Angeles Police Department and we don't discontinue pursuits of attempted murder suspects, especially when police officers are the intended victims. And we don't wait for young, inexperienced sergeants in order to deploy a tactical event to engage those very same suspects—armed and dangerous suspects. What questions do you have about that?"

McClain was amazed at how calm Adams could be while shooting a verbal cannon in your direction.

"I just thought that the pursuit was out of control; people were in danger. People were getting hurt." Sergeant Williams began to sound a little less sure of himself as he spoke.

"Well, thank you for that observation, Sergeant. But now that you're coming to realize what a large mistake you made, and that you made it on the radio and the entire Los Angeles Police Department is now talking about the stupid and cowardly sergeant who tried to stop a pursuit of three suspects who tried to kill Los Angeles police officers, I'm wondering how you're going to find a big enough hole to hide in?" Adams let his words sink in.

"I just tried to do my job. We're supposed to monitor pursuits and stop them if they're dangerous." Williams just couldn't seem to score any points in his favor.

Somehow, Adams found it within himself to smile and place his hand on Williams's shoulder. "Sergeant Williams, it takes a big man to realize he's made an error in judgment, and I want you to be that man. I want you to rethink your responsibilities as a sergeant. I want you to consider that it's not your job to catch policemen doing something wrong. But it is your job to teach policemen, to support them, mentor them, and guide them. Stop being a sergeant and start being a leader. That's what leadership means. All toward making the streets of Los Angeles a safe place for the people who live here. If you can do that, I will support you tonight."

Williams wasn't sure what was happening, but he sensed that he should follow the lieutenant's lead. "Thank you, Lieutenant." And that was it. Sergeant Williams made an about face to find his police car and return to Van Nuys Division, where he was going to somehow figure out how to write an entry in his supervisor's log that he was teaching, supporting, mentoring, and guiding police officers.

CHAPTER TWENTY
AN ENVIRONMENT OF RISK AVERSION

"I think you got through to him, Lieutenant. Guys like that are usually so blinded by these crazy rules that they can't see anything else. It seems like no one's thinking for themselves anymore."

"Mac, law enforcement is all about risk aversion now. The LAPD and maybe police departments everywhere have changed; the concepts of courage and leadership have been replaced by all the rules and the red tape. We've created this environment of risk aversion, and everyone is afraid to lead and afraid to do their job. Policemen are just cruising and doing nothing. They're not protecting people because it's all about risk aversion now."

At Northridge Hospital, Lieutenant Adams pulled into a spot with a sign that read "Reserved Parking, Hospital Administrator." It was pretty conveniently placed near the emergency entrance, and Adams was sure that the hospital administrator would want him to park there. Pretty sure.

Adams had just finished a phone call with the emergency room staff and learned that Officer Aoki was still in surgery. He saw that a couple was just walking into the ER with a uniformed LAPD sergeant.

"Mr. and Mrs. Aoki? I'm Lieutenant Jack Adams. Karen works for me."

"Where is she? I need to see her! She's been shot—my daughter is shot! No one will tell me, but I know she's been shot." Mrs. Nancy Aoki was small in stature but spoke with a sense of authority, conveying a no-nonsense presence.

"She's in surgery, ma'am. I just arrived and we don't have much information yet. She was shot in the leg and the hip. I'm told that when she arrived here, she was stable."

Mr. Roy Aoki put his finger in Adams's chest, poking his badge. "I told her not to do this. She wanted to be a nurse. Now look what you've done to her."

"I'm sorry, sir. You know Karen better than I do, and not many people tell her what to do. She's the best of us. She was courageous, sir, and she was working on a very special detail to keep people safe from gang members."

Mrs. Aoki was very emotional now, crying, holding her husband's arm. "Why do you let her work with these gangs? With these monsters? This is your fault, Lieutenant Adams."

Adams wanted to say so much, but all he could muster was, "Yes, ma'am. I'm sorry."

With only a few minutes to himself, Adams sat on the bench just outside of the emergency room ambulance entrance. His head bowed and his eyes closed, Adams prayed for the recovery of Karen Aoki when he was suddenly interrupted. "Lieutenant Adams, I need you inside."

"I just need a minute, Commander. I'll be right in."

"There's no time right now, Lieutenant. Officer Aoki is out of surgery and the doctor wants to meet with her parents. He wants us to be there, and I'm not doing this by myself. I'm not good at this kind of stuff. Her mother was crying when I walked by. Chief Nelson and Chief Fuller are both here, but I'm not sure where they got off to."

"Yes, Commander. I'm ready."

The trauma surgeon was tall and lanky with a crew cut that made him look extremely young. He spoke really slow with a Midwestern accent with overtones from the South. "Y'all must be exhausted. Sorry it took so long, but Karen's doing fine. What we did tonight was to address the trauma and hemostasis, to stop the bleeding. Between myself and the vascular team, we have her breathing and all her vitals right where they should be. A CT angiography shows us that her blood supplies aren't creating an issue for us right now. She will still need some subsequent orthopedic surgery to her hip. The single bullet wound to her thigh was through and through, but the shotgun wound to her hip has caused numerous complications at the femoral head. Our most prominent concern right now will be infection, so we'll be watching that closely.

"Nerve damage is certainly an issue, but we won't know about that for a bit. I can tell you she'll be fine, and I know she'll be glad to see y'all. She's in recovery, so figure about two hours and she'll be able to see guests. She may not be fully awake for quite a while after that, though. Sometimes after an event like this, a patient just needs to sleep, so try to let her be; it's good for her. We'll bring her meals every few hours, but there's no medical need for her to eat right now, so if she's not interested, just give her time. She'll eat when she's hungry. I'll stay until morning, so I'll be checking on her all night. Neurology and Orthopedics will be in shortly."

As the doctor excused himself, he asked to meet privately with Adams. "Lieutenant, the patient was already receiving meds when I got to her, but I want you to know she said she wasn't scared. She's quite the young woman. Medically, there's nothing life-threatening, and all I really did was triage the wounds and guarantee we have sufficient blood flow. The round to her thigh shouldn't be too troubling for her and I think her hip will be fine over time, but Orthopedics will tell us more. Neurology will be part of the team because I'm confident that we'll find traumatic peripheral nerve damage. Figure the next surgery will be in the next two weeks, certainly no more than three weeks. We handled the immediate concerns, but she will need some more surgery. We just have to wait a bit to assess muscle and nerve damage, and we have to fight our asses off to ward off infection."

#

As Deputy Chief Nelson and Chief Fuller walked in, Commander Jelenick intercepted them to make sure he was the one to brief them. "Chiefs, I was here with the family for the doctor's briefing. Sounds like Officer Aoki is going to be fine. They're worried about nerve damage, but they won't know about that for a while."

Chief Fuller was all business. Silently looking at Commander Jelenick and Lieutenant Adams, he spoke slowly and clearly. "Jack, there is nothing the Los Angeles Police Department, the City of Los Angeles, and me personally won't do for Karen. You give her and her family whatever she needs. I'll be meeting with the officer-involved shooting team, then I'm coming back here to try and talk with her when she's awake." The chief of police of the Los Angeles Police Department garnered a lot of attention wherever he went, and the entire medical staff made note of his presence.

As Chiefs Fuller and Nelson left the hospital, Jelenick approached Adams. "Lieutenant, I want you to go home now and get some sleep. Take two days off, and then give me a call at my office to make an appointment for us to meet. I'll be looking at how you lost control of all this, and our conversations may be painful."

"Yeah, well, I'm not doing that, Commander. I have a couple days of work here, and when I'm not working I'll be here with Karen."

"Lieutenant, don't put me in a position that you're not going to like. I want you to go home, get some sleep, recuperate, and let the rest of us finish this cluster. You're not the only asset that the LAPD has. We at the management level have a lot of work in front of us to clean all this up."

"Yeah, well, again, I'm not doing that, Commander. I don't work for you. You heard what Chief Fuller just said. You'll need to go and talk to him about any orders you may have for me."

"I'm fed up with you, Adams. I'll be talking with both Chief Fuller and Deputy Chief Nelson to relieve you of duty. You're running out of control, and that can't happen. Now I'll probably get stuck with fixing everything that happened here tonight." Jelenick headed toward the hospital main entrance and to his car.

You would have thought that Jelenick would have noticed Adams giving him the finger as he walked toward the hospital entrance. *Guess he's just not very observant.*

\#

The sheriff's SWAT unit entered the area on a dirt access road from College of the Canyons next to the baseball field in an armored vehicle. They positioned the armored vehicle close to the suspect's car. Deploying an Andros robot to the car was difficult due to the uneven ground surface, but the SWAT members were able to ascertain that there were four occupants.

Arturo Mejia lay dead in the rear portion of the overturned vehicle, hit by one of Julie Barr's shots as the suspects fled the scene of the drive-by shooting. AlleyDog, who was still armed, appeared unresponsive and was probably dead. The driver, Little Clown, lay partially outside of the vehicle in clear view with the shotgun still visible under his body. Little Clown was not moving and was unresponsive, believed to be dead, while the fourth person in the car, Felix Olmos, appeared semiconscious with a visible head wound, probably from the car rolling over.

The robot was successfully used to collect the shotgun from under Little Clown, who had attempted to crawl out of the front driver's window. After that, a handgun was recovered from AlleyDog's hand as well as second handgun found by the robot loose in the rear of the vehicle.

The SWAT element members were able to approach the vehicle protected by handheld shields. Using an extendable arm, they were able to extract the four occupants and place them out in the open where they were more visible. Removing the suspects from the small windows proved to be impossible, but the task was finally accomplished by breaking the windshield out and using the larger opening. Three of the occupants were found to have expired, most probably from gunshot wounds, while the one injured suspect was transported for medical care to Henry Mayo Newhall Hospital. The SWAT leader brought the paramedics up to care for the four suspects as soon as they were extracted from the Camaro, searched, and handcuffed.

Lieutenant Adams made a beeline to Valencia to gain firsthand knowledge as to the identities of the four men in the Camaro. Communicating with the Los Angeles County Sheriff's shooting team was so much easier than talking to LAPD's team. The Sheriff's Department still retained some sense of sanity in investigating officer-involved shootings and maintaining an air of support for their deputies. Of the shooting event in Valencia, Adams was mostly interested in the connection between the four suspects in the Camaro and Brown

Pride. Adams wanted to know why they had been set up to be shot.

"Mac, I'm out here at the Santa Clarita Sheriff's Station. I'll pass the names of the four assholes in the Camaro to you as soon as we meet. We need to know everything we can about them. Brown Pride affiliations or connections, arrests, family, everything. The quicker we figure out whether we were targeted or whether it was just any policeman who showed up, the better. Before I forget, be sure to talk to each of our officers about using their personal medical insurance if they're planning on any therapy support after this event."

Adams knew that each officer involved in the use of deadly force would be ordered to a psychologist employed by Los Angeles. There was no choice in the matter. The officers would be told that the appointment with the psychologist was to assess what support they needed in the aftermath of a life-threatening event and then to receive counseling or other support efforts. Nonsense. The appointment with the psychologist was not a confidential patient-doctor conference; the psychologist then turned around and reported directly back to the Los Angeles Police Department as to whether the officer was a liability or not. Any officer who, under these circumstances, candidly discusses the facts of the event or the trauma they have experienced, including the impact on their psyche or life, is foolish. Tell the city psychologist you're fine and get out of that office as fast as you can.

As Adams walked through the lobby of the sheriff's station on his way out to his car, he was met with a familiar face. "Lieutenant Adams, we've been trying all night to contact you. Can you answer a few questions about last night's events?"

"Hello, Miss Morgan. Aren't you a little off your beat?" The last thing Adams needed was to deal with Candace Morgan or any of the media from Los Angeles right now.

"No, Lieutenant. We go wherever the story is, and the public is waiting to hear the real story behind last night's events. The LAPD Media Relations press release was a generic response that doesn't tell the public what really happened. We only want to get to the truth and tell the public what happened. Isn't that what you want, Lieutenant? Doesn't the LAPD want to give an honest response to the questions we all have? Can you just answer a few questions? Why were the officers at the restaurant where they were shot? The employees at the restaurant told us that the officers endangered their lives. They're afraid to go back to work now. Did the officers need to do that?"

Adams was out of patience and had to force a response. "I'm not able to answer any of your questions, Miss Morgan. But if you stay in touch with Media Relations, they will be able to help you."

"Lieutenant, your officers were in a pursuit in which people were run over. They shot people in front of a crowd and endangered their lives! There were children nearby, Lieutenant. Did the officers have to shoot those people with children nearby? Couldn't they wait until the children were taken away from the scene before they tried to arrest anyone? And why did a woman need to be shot when she was protecting herself from being attacked by a police dog biting her? Is it really necessary to have attack dogs on the Los Angeles Police Department attacking our citizens? It all looks bad, Lieutenant Adams, but I'm glad to print your version of what happened. I want to be fair, and I want the story to be accurate. If you could give me some of your time, I think I'd be able to report the events from your point of view. Is this a good time to sit and talk for a bit, Lieutenant? Maybe we could go and have something to eat. Over coffee, maybe? I'm hoping we can partner up and talk about getting some stronger gun laws in our city."

"You do know that a lot of our officers were shot at, don't you, Candace? One of our officers was shot, and she's in the hospital. Were you thinking about writing something about that? About the courageous and selfless acts of those officers to defend themselves and to keep the people who live in Los Angeles safe?"

As Adams continued to walk away, Candace Morgan tossed the last few bombs. "But they're police officers, Lieutenant. Weren't they doing their jobs? Don't they get paid to do dangerous things? Have your officers been relieved of duty, Lieutenant? Has the District Attorney's Office decided to file criminal charges on them? Is the FBI going to investigate your officers, Lieutenant? Maybe I can help with all that, Lieutenant. Will you give me a chance?"

As Adams walked away, he thought to himself, *Don't shoot her. We have enough going on right now. Remember, risk aversion.*

After a long couple of days and nights, Adams took McClain back to his police car at Van Nuys Division. "I'm headed home to sleep for a bit, Lieutenant, but I'll be back tonight. There's a lot I want to do in staying on top of this investigation. I still need to get the statements from the asshole in the Camaro when he comes around. I've already lined up Devonshire and Van Nuys Gang detectives to pitch in."

"Okay, Mac. Since we're this end of town, I'm going to grab a little sleep over at LA Fire's Station 88. It's over by Van Nuys Division on Sepulveda. It's one of their training stations, so they always have extra bunks. I'll try to grab a bite there tonight and then come and find you. I'm guessing you'll be here in the San Fernando Valley somewhere."

Adams pulled into Los Angeles Fire Station No. 88 and found a parking space for the black Mustang GT. He slid his business card onto the dashboard and headed for the station house. "Hey, Captain Jennings. I'm Lieutenant Jack Adams from Gangs. Wondering if I could bunk with you guys for a few hours."

"Sure, Lieutenant. LAPD kick you out?"

"Nah, just slumming."

CHAPTER TWENTY-ONE
THE THIN BLUE LINE

"Lieutenant, time to wake up. Dinner's almost ready. You can shower at the end of the hall and come downstairs. Twenty minutes—get moving."

"Thanks, Captain. I was wondering what you paid for that haircut."

Jennings looked at Adams peculiarly and wasn't sure what to answer. "I think about twenty bucks, why?"

"Damn. Well, if you want me to have one of my officers come over and take that robbery report for you, just let me know. It will only take them a couple of minutes."

Adams took Captain Jennings up on his offer and enjoyed a blazing hot shower. *Firemen are so spoiled.* Most LAPD locker rooms only had lukewarm water.

"Hey, Lieutenant. Welcome, find a seat. I'm Brandon. I do the cooking around here. Pot roast tonight, then white cake with coconut frosting or German chocolate."

Wow. Adams would have been satisfied with a Tommy's chili cheeseburger. "Hey, Brandon. Why did God make policemen?"

"I don't know, Lieutenant. But I'm sure you'll tell me."

"So firemen have something to aspire to." Adams had a really, really dry sense of humor. "So, Brandon, what was going on in Hollywood last week when that fireman evacuated four people out of that house before it even caught on fire? It didn't catch on fire for two more days?"

"What? I don't even know. I hadn't heard about that." Brandon struggled for an answer, but thankfully Adams had it for him.

"I'm thinking it must have been premature evacuation."

#

At Van Nuys Division, McClain was already at work coordinating with Devonshire and Van Nuys Gang detectives. District Attorney Beth Stevenson was also present, evaluating the prosecution of the case against the thirteen-year-old from the first pursuit along with the suspect arrested at the pursuit termination in Valencia.

After working through some of the issues with McClain, Adams headed back to Northridge Hospital to visit with Karen Aoki. The two officers posted outside her door were not friendly looking. When police officers protect their own, they're serious about it. The senior captain in Devonshire Division had already balked about having to send two officers to be there around the clock, but his calls to the Valley Bureau Chief had fallen on deaf ears. The word had already come from Chief Nelson, from downtown.

And Julie Barr? A human shield seated in the chair between Karen and the door. "Julie, have you even gone home?"

"Not yet, sir. I've been hanging out with Karen, but she's not very good company. She sleeps a lot. She's really boring."

"How you doing, Karen? You feel any pain?"

"Hi, LT. I'm fine. Julie's been hogging the remote control, though. What the hell is the Hallmark Channel? Some craziness about coffee shops and bakeries with the same actress on every show. They've got me hooked up to an IV and I just push this button for pain meds. The more Julie talks, the more I push the button. Life is the best."

Julie Barr was reluctant to leave even though she hadn't been home for three days. "I can stay awhile longer, LT. I'm still good to hang out here. Karen will just bore you, and I'm really interesting to talk to."

"Thanks, Julie, but I have a lot of work to catch up on and you'll talk my ear off. You better get home. Can you come back early and relieve me? I'd like to get home tomorrow for a little while and go to my kids' games. I haven't seen them for a few days."

Adams knew Aoki would be fine, but he also knew she may never return to street police work. Her heart was so big that she could never continue on in the police department sitting at one of those desks in the police headquarters building. He prayed for her.

It was still dark when Barr began shaking Adams's shoulder to wake him up, but he was on the freeway before the sun blinded him.

At the ballpark, Adams heard his phone ringing over the parents' cheers. "Hey, LT. Man, it's really loud there. It's Roger Leigh."

"Hey, Roger. I'm at my son's game. What's up, pal?"

"I have more scoop on the Portland jewelry store robbery. I think we need to meet, though."

"Ok, how about at my office in the Wilshire FBI building tomorrow? I'm going to take today off. I'll leave your name at the desk. I can get there by about 1800 hours."

"Sounds good, sir. See you there."

The next day, Adams rolled into the warehouse construction project off Benton Way and appreciated the new sign on the door, "Gold Rush, Gold and Jewelry, International." The roll-up door was open and John Andrews's massive four-wheel drive with comically large tires had been backed into the warehouse.

"What do those big tires cost, John?"

"Ah, Lieutenant, it doesn't really matter what they cost. You know what they say about the size of your tires."

The group spent the next few hours trying to get the two walls drywalled and even hung the door into the warehouse. *So far, so good.* Aoki's helpful YouTube videos were the best, even if she wasn't there. Dan McVay showed up to test the cameras and set up a folding table in the warehouse to set all his equipment on. Adams watched as the monitors revealed all the positions of the cameras. *Perfect.*

"Okay, you knuckleheads. I've gotta head over to FBI on Wilshire and meet with Detective Leigh. If you guys can finish hanging the drywall before you leave today, that would be great. Dan, what about the outside cameras?"

"I hope to get them installed tonight. I brought one to insert over the door to get a clear face shot of anyone coming in, and then I've got enough to cover the parking area and the street and alley. The alley won't be any problem because I can mount them to the building, but I haven't figured out where to mount the ones out front for the street. Because the building is set back from the street, I need a place out on the street. If not, I'll just do what I can in the parking lot."

#

The FBI building was so much like LAPD Headquarters. Pretty much empty after 5 p.m.

"Hey, Roger. Good to see you, but you're early. I'm never going to get my paperwork done. Sounds like your trip to Portland was interesting."

"Yes, sir. Couple things. First, got the results of the warrant on Thrifty Car Rental. You won't believe this, but it was rented by a female at LAPD Communications Division. I matched the in-store video of her to her DMV picture. This is bigger than we thought. Her name is Karen Jones and she's a dispatcher for us."

"You're kidding me. An LAPD civilian employee? We're too busy to have to deal with this, Roger. Why can't we just have a simple robbery?" Adams's mind began spinning up with who had to be notified and what administrative steps must be taken.

"There's more, sir. Thrifty gave me her rental record, and it's pretty big. She rents a lot of cars there, but two were at the same time as the two previous Wilshire Division robberies, and one at the same time as the Chula Vista robbery. And there's more." Detective Roger Leigh hadn't made it to Gangs by being lazy or by missing clues or evidence.

"How could there be more, Roger? People are so stupid, sometimes it just never stops amazing me. This is like the burglary suspect who leaves his wallet in the victim's house." Adams began seeing the bigger picture here.

"Each of the four 211's occurred while she was on a string of days off. And even more—I got a little help to look at her LAPD computer queries. After every robbery, she returned to work and the first thing she did walking in the door was run the license plates on the cars she rented." Leigh just let that information hang there.

It took Adams only seconds to put it together. "So, she rents a car. Her crew steals another car. They use the stolen to do the robbery and then drive it to the rental, where they dump the stolen and then go home in the rental. The rental becomes the getaway car. Then Jones goes to work where she sits at her computer and runs the car she rented to see if it's hot, to see if anyone saw it. To see if any wits saw the rental car."

"Yes, sir."

"Okay, Roger. Sit on this for a bit. I want to run it past Chief Nelson. In the meantime, find all the pawnshops around Lil Sweet's house and around this Jones's house. Meet with our Pawnshop Detail from Burglary, Auto Theft Division to hit all the pawnshops and see if you can find the jewelry from any of these robberies. I can't believe that low levels like this would have any kind of network to move jewelry, so they have to be pawning it for pennies. If you find anything, have the Pawnshop Detail photograph it and put a hold on it."

CHAPTER TWENTY-TWO
PLAYING FAIR WITH THE FBI

The new day was overcast and slow to clear. The marine layer crept inland for miles. Adams was compiling his list of supplies he needed to get repairs done on his Skipjack until the first call of the day came in.

"Hey, Lieutenant. It's Roger Leigh bothering you again. Hope you're having a good morning. I wanted to call you earlier but got hit with all kinds of crap already. Listen, we've been working our butt off and found a pawnshop over in Crenshaw with jewelry that our employee Karen Jones pawned just a day or so after each of the robberies. The Pawnshop Detail put a hold on everything, and I photographed every piece to show to the victims. They said they did it in such a way that if Jones goes in to get it, they'll tell her it's in a safe with a faulty lock and she'll have to come back some other time. So far, the Portland jewelry store has already identified some of their pieces."

"Good work, Roger. You're a good detective."

"Not really, you told me to do it! That was a great call to check pawnshops."

"I was just reading your mind, Roger. I knew you were already thinking it."

"One more thing, Lieutenant. I got a call from an FBI agent down in San Diego. He says he's working our jewelry store crew as an interstate crime investigation. He says they identified a robbery in Prescott, Arizona, that matches the two robberies here in LA along with the San Diego hit. He didn't say anything about our employee; I think they're not that far yet. I was going to tell him about Portland but he hung up too fast. He says he wants to meet with us to swap info. He said he can come today about two o'clock, 1400 hours. I was hoping you could be there."

"Ok, Roger. I have to be at City Council at 1530 hours anyway, so I'll come in early and meet with you and the FBI agents first. Tell FBI we'll meet at Headquarters downtown in Chief Nelson's office. We'll use one of the chief's conference rooms. Please do not meet with them or even talk to them about this case unless I'm with you. Let's get there early so we're together when they arrive. I'll meet you at Starbucks at 1st and LA Street about 13:00 hours. I'll buy."

#

Adams had enjoyed a rare night's sleep with no callouts, and spending the morning hours at home was awesome. The marine layer made the morning peaceful and calm and cut through the usual heat of Southern California. The drive into downtown Los Angeles was no more terrible than usual—bumper-to-bumper up the Harbor Freeway through Watts. Freeways lined with dead landscaping, piles of trash, graffiti, and a sense of dread.

Breaking down on the Harbor Freeway through Watts scared everyone to death. It always amused Adams how drivers could tell the moment they left Orange County and entered Los Angeles County. No one ever needed a sign to tell them they had crossed the boundary, only the conditions of the freeway and the bordering neighborhoods.

The Starbucks was packed from downtown workers, commuters, and guests of the Double Tree, but they were accustomed to the load and had a large staff. All in all, Adams's day was starting off quite nicely.

Adams didn't really like the bitterness of Starbucks coffee, but if you put enough cream and sugar in it, it was much better. "Well, Detective Leigh, good to see you. Sounds like you've been doing a lot of good work already today."

"Hey, Lieutenant. Sorry I'm a few minutes late; I wanted to gather up all my paperwork before I came. FBI sounded like they were really in a hurry to do this, or I would have put them off to another day." Detective Leigh looked like he had been running.

#

Lieutenant Kathy Moss greeted Adams and Detective Leigh as they walked into Chief Nelson's office carrying their coffee. "Good morning, Jack. Hi, Roger, long time. The FBI is in the conference room down the hall and on the left. They've been waiting about twenty minutes."

Adams smiled. "Well, they must have arrived early. Roger, leave your briefcase here with Kathy."

"But it has all the case packages for the four robberies. I made copies of everything for them." Detective Leigh was a very efficient man, but he didn't always consider the big picture.

"Yeah, I know. Let's leave it here for now. Kathy, can you watch this for us? What time does the chief come in today?"

"He went to the Police Academy to shoot on the combat range, then I think he's meeting someone for lunch in the cafe there. I know he's at City Council with you at 1530, then he's going home after that. He has something with his family."

"Perfect. If anyone from the FBI calls or comes in later on to ask for him, just tell them he's out until tomorrow and can't be reached. And Roger, let's hold off on saying anything about our employee, Karen Jones, unless I bring it up." Preplanning was Adams's forte.

#

"Good morning, Agents. Hope you had a nice drive. I bet you're already missing San Diego. I'm Lieutenant Jack Adams, LAPD Gangs. This is Detective Roger Leigh, Wilshire Division Gangs."

"Good morning, Lieutenant. I'm Special Agent Matt Kidder, and this is my partner Stephanie Wills."

"How can we help you, Agent Kidder?"

"Lieutenant, I understand we're overlapping on the same case: an interstate jewelry store robbery crew that comes back to your Gang unit. Apparently, they've hit at least twice here in LA, which is what you're working on, but we think the same crew has also hit once down in our neighborhood in Chula Vista and we just picked one up in Prescott, Arizona. Now that it's interstate, we've picked the case up. We would love to share our information with you so we can move forward with this case as quickly as possible. Hopefully before they hurt someone." Agent Kidder sat so straight in his chair, he moved like a robot. His complexion was terrible and his cheeks kind of sunk into his face. All business, and he appeared in a perpetual hurry.

Lieutenant Adams jumped right on the train. "Sounds great, Agent Kidder. What do you have to share with us?"

"I do have to apologize, though, Lieutenant. We were late leaving San Diego because of other issues, and in my haste I left my case package that I have for you on my desk. It has everything we know so far, and I wanted to get you a copy of everything. The quicker we can help you solve your robberies, the better. As soon as I get back, I'll have my staff courier it up to you."

Detective Leigh spoke up instinctively. "Don't worry about that, Agent Kidder. Here's my business card. Ship it to my office."

"Well, it's the damnedest thing," Lieutenant Adams broke in. "I was in such a hurry that I left the package we put together for you in my office on the other side of town. I'm afraid it would be impossible to get there this time of the day and I'm due in front of City Council in just a few minutes. But as soon as we get yours from the courier, we'll review it and send you whatever we have that you don't already have. We'll fill in the blanks." Lieutenant

Adams smiled as Agent Kidder scowled.

Detective Leigh looked very uncomfortable, confused as to whether he should remind Adams that the package was right down the hall in his briefcase at Moss's desk. Agent Kidder looked sternly at Adams, then at Leigh and back to Adams.

"I'll get back to you on this," Kidder remarked. He and his partner stood and left the room without any further conversation, leaving Adams and Leigh alone.

Detective Leigh looked as though he didn't have a clue about what just happened. "Roger, listen. The FBI are trained to take everything they can from you and give you nothing. It's not that they're bad guys; they're just trained not to share. Although we're supposed to be on the same page, you have to be careful or they'll steal your case and leave you hanging. But if they play fair, then you should play fair. Just be prepared for other contingencies, because today they showed up not planning to play fair. After you gave them a copy of your case, they would never have sent you anything."

One meeting done, Adams and Leigh walked down the hallway toward the elevator and stuck their heads into Chief Nelson's office to grab Leigh's briefcase. "The two FBI agents were just here," Lieutenant Moss commented. "They asked to see Chief Nelson, but I told them he's out until tomorrow. How did you know they were going to ask me, Jack?"

"Well, I just had a feeling. See you, Kathy. I'm going over to City Council. They want to know why Gang officers aren't writing traffic tickets."

"The rumor mill says that you told them not to write tickets," Moss added with obvious delight.

"Yeah, well, I don't recall that."

On the walk to the Council Chambers, Adams gave Detective Leigh his running orders. "Listen, Roger, I want to arrest our Communications Division employee, along with Lil Sweet, today. As quick as we can, before our two friends from the FBI get back to San Diego. But I need for you to get over to the district attorney's office to file the cases on the two LA robberies before they close up shop. While you're doing that, send a couple of your detectives over to Communications and arrest Jones, then get her city keys and identification card. Cut off all her access to our computer systems. After that, send a crew out to pick up Lil Sweet."

"Will do, LT. You want to call her commanding officer or should I?"

"I'll call him, Roger, and I'll notify Internal Affairs also. Or Professional Standards, whatever they call themselves now. I'll brief Chief Nelson over at Council Chambers. Your job is to get over to the DA's office and file the robbery cases before the day's over. You know I try to file all our cases Federally with a US attorney because our district attorney supports criminals more than he supports the people who live here. That being said, the four cases in LA can't go federal, so we're stuck with this DA until we get someone else. Take your filing package over there but be aware there's a new filing deputy, Troy Sears. Absolutely don't take the case to him; he's denying everything and doesn't know shit about gangs. We have no time to screw around with amateurs, so make sure you grab someone besides him."

Since the FBI agents had said nothing about where they were in their investigation or what their plans were, Adams felt confident about moving forward with the LAPD's case.

"Roger, after you file our cases and arrest Karen Jones, let's give Chula Vista and Portland everything they need to sew up their cases. Find the jewelry store the FBI talked about in Prescott and if it's our suspects, connect with them also and give them our suspect information. See if you can pair up the date of the Prescott 211 with Karen Jones's days off and car rentals. Tell them we're glad to help them with their prosecutions."

"So, LT, are we stepping on the FBI's toes?"

"Not that we know of, Roger. They seemed to be in a pretty big hurry to leave and they didn't tell us anything. Too bad for them. When they don't share, they lose. Sharing is caring. So, let's get Jones arrested and warrants served on her house, car, LAPD locker, bank accounts, phone records, and anything else you can find. I really want those pawn receipts and that shotgun she used—and warrants on Lil Sweet also. I'm off to City Council, and you're on the run all afternoon, Roger. Good luck."

Detective Leigh, knowing he had a long day's and possibly night's work still ahead, headed for the district attorney's office while dialing his phone to call his partner. Lieutenant Adams headed for City Council, he knew he was cutting it close. As he walked through the double doors he was met by Deputy Chief Nelson standing just inside Chambers and looking uncomfortable.

"Good afternoon, Chief."

"Hey, Jack. You're cutting it close, but the Council's running late anyway. There's an inquiry on the Council floor about the number of tickets our Gang officers are writing. Or aren't writing, I should say. Patrol tickets are way down, and it's hurting these City Council members' ability to spend everyone's money. Although, I'm sure the Council members will only talk about traffic safety issues, not money. Apparently they've noticed your Gang guys only write about one per month. One ticket a month, Jack?"

"Well, our guys are pretty busy, sir. They're arresting gang members and taking guns off the street for photo ops for the mayor. You know, all that stuff."

Nelson oftentimes wished that Adams would beg for forgiveness like most other subordinate supervisors. "Be cautious in your response to them, Jack. They want more money from us, and we don't need them pissed off."

Lieutenant Adams thought about that for a second, then responded, "Chief, the mayor and most of the City Council hate us. Most every one of them has a liberal, anti-police agenda. Why do we always need to cater to them?"

After Chief Nelson gave Adams the half turn and rolled his eyes, he replied, "Because they decide who the chief of police is and because they decide what our budget is. How did it go with the FBI?"

"Great, sir. We both agreed to share information on those jewelry store 211's. They're going to send us what they have and then we'll fill in some blanks for them. You know me, Mr. Cooperation. New scoop, though. I didn't share this with the FBI because it just came to my attention and I haven't run it past you yet, but one of our LAPD civilian employees in Communications Division is an active player. She rented cars for four of the robberies, maybe a fifth, and on her days off held a shotgun during the takeover robberies."

Chief Nelson stopped in his tracks, looked over his shoulder to see if anyone else was listening, and whispered, "Damn it, Jack. Are you sure about this? How do we keep this out of the press?" The poor chief already saw fires to put out with the press on the horizon.

Adams immediately seized on this new opportunity as another reason to get in front of Agent Kidder on the robbery investigation. Sometimes you just get a gift. "We won't be able to keep it away from the press, sir, so I'm moving on this right now to get in front of them."

Adams thought that went over perfect. Sometimes you just get lucky. "The FBI is just getting on board, but we can't wait for them. I've got Wilshire detectives taking her down today, along with one other gangster we identified. I'll notify Professional Standards after this Council meeting. I'm really concerned about her access to LAPD facilities and computers, so we'll cut off her access today and file the criminal case against her. I want to completely close her down. Hopefully, when we squeeze our employee, she'll give us the other players and the guns they used. I don't know yet if there are other city employees, so we really have to jump on this fast. We found the jewelry in pawnshops by her house over in Crenshaw and tied her to other robberies in San Diego and up in Portland. The FBI was nice enough to give us another possible lead in Arizona, so we're firming that up now. We'll get them all online and help them with their prosecutions. By the time the press gets wind of it, the case will be closed."

"Good work, Lieutenant. You always amaze me. How do you get so much done so fast? Let me know if you need anything from me. And if you're dropping my name, be sure to let me know." Nelson got involved just enough to help and not so much as to hinder. *Good man and good leader.* He was comfortable delegating to his staff and trusted them to do the right thing, but sometimes he suspected Adams used the weight of the chief's office to fudge a little bit.

Nelson kept telling himself to keep an eye on Adams, but he could never figure out how to do it. Even so, Nelson was sure the people who worked for him appreciated not being micromanaged. Competent people always work best with a free rein.

"Thanks, Chief. We really need to get the initial case filed before the end of the day, so if we have any problems I'll let the District Attorney's Office know we have your support as a priority case." *Boy, did that work out well.*

#

Councilwoman Connie Dixon did not seem to be buying Lieutenant Adams's response. "I understand you're busy, Lieutenant, as are the gang officers in your command. But in addition to policing gang crime, don't you also have a responsibility for traffic safety? Shouldn't all Los Angeles police officers be concerned with traffic safety for the citizens of our city?"

"No, ma'am, not necessarily. We have many specialized units throughout the Police Department that do not engage in traffic enforcement. However, Gang officers don't go out with blinders on, and when we see traffic violations that endanger public safety we do take the appropriate action. But our focus is on gang crime and making the streets safer by reducing violent crime. That focus doesn't allow us to spend much time with traffic enforcement. That being said, LAPD has a very specific and effective dedication to traffic safety. LAPD officers address traffic safety along with dedicated traffic enforcement officers. Those guys are the experts, and they're really good at their jobs."

"I see, Lieutenant. Do you provide performance expectations to your officers?"

"Yes, ma'am, but not in relation to writing tickets. That could only be presented in the form of a quota, which would be illegal."

Councilwoman Dixon shifted in her seat as she tried to develop the appropriate response to Adams. She wanted money, and there were no excuses that she would accept. Even so, this was a tough one for her to handle in a public setting with the press ever present.

"Lieutenant," Councilwoman Sharon Williams interrupted. "Of the citations your gang officers do seem to find the time to write, have you examined the racial balance in regard to the people receiving the citations?"

Wow. The level of political interference and ignorance thrown around Los Angeles never stopped surprising Adams. "No, Councilwoman, I never have. On most occasions, when police officers make a traffic stop, they don't see the driver until after the stop is made and the officers approach the car on foot to speak with the driver. Sometimes even then the officer can't see the driver until they roll their window down. Remember that the officers are behind the traffic violator, and most cars today have small and tinted windows. Our gang officers work after dark, making it even harder to see the driver or to know what the race of the driver is until after the stop is already made. That being said, it's usually impossible to assess that an officer harbored a racist intent for making a traffic stop because they don't know who the driver is until after the stop is already made. If we did, however, identify an officer that harbors racially biased attitudes, I'm confident that it would be displayed in many other ways in addition to citation issuance. That situation would most probably be rather apparent, and I would consider it a priority concern that I would investigate and share with Deputy Chief Nelson."

Adams paused and looked across the row of councilpersons to seek out any support from any of the members. "I'm also aware, Councilwoman, that Los Angeles Police officers have been provided audit forms that they must fill out after every stop in an attempt to identify whether police officers are discriminating against minority drivers. The time it takes to fill out those audit forms is unwieldy and takes them away from their duties protecting and serving the people of Los Angeles. More importantly, the audits present to the officers that they are being accused of being racists, which doesn't go over well."

Adams noticed the room was very quiet now. "I can tell you candidly, Councilwoman Williams, that police officers in Los Angeles today are always apprehensive in making traffic stops for a variety of reasons in addition to officer safety. As you know, many officers are injured or killed during traffic stops. But what we are talking about today has to do with the officers not being able to see the driver of a car who has committed a traffic violation and the officers being apprehensive about stopping that car for fear of being labeled as racist or discriminatory due to the political and media pressure concerning this topic. What we don't want, Councilwoman Williams, is for officers to discontinue traffic enforcement efforts because they fear being labeled as discriminatory or racist. There is a pathway, however, to achieve what you and Councilwoman Dixon are asking for. I believe that the best way we can encourage officers to be involved in traffic enforcement is to guarantee that our officers feel supported in their role of promoting traffic safety, and I'm sure you and each member of City Council supports that concept."

Adams got out in front of the response. "Councilwoman Williams, have you ever seen anyone driving the speed limit on our freeways through Los Angeles?"

"No one drives the speed limit, Lieutenant. Isn't that the point of these questions?"

"Councilwoman, when was the last time you saw a California Highway Patrol officer patrolling our freeways? Being even more specific, when was the last time you saw a California Highway Patrol officer writing a citation on the freeway for all of those people you see every day who violate the law? Do you ever wonder where they are?"

"Well, I'm not sure, Lieutenant, but I can't recall the last time I've even seen the Highway Patrol on the freeway unless they're at a traffic accident. And yes, I consistently ask myself why there is no law enforcement presence on our freeways. But that is the state, Lieutenant. We have no control over the California Governor or the California Highway Patrol management." Councilwoman Williams seemed confused.

"Exactly, Councilwoman. Here in Southern California and maybe other areas, there's a historical lack of visible California Highway Patrol enforcement, or even a presence on our freeways, and the result is a situation resembling the Wild West. No one obeys the traffic laws because the California Highway Patrol is never there anymore. Drivers have actually learned that they don't have to follow the speed limits. No one, Councilwoman, *no one* abides by traffic laws on our freeways anymore. This is the result of a lack of enforcement by the California Highway Patrol on Los Angeles freeways over a prolonged period of time. Years. What I'm going to say next is the really important part: because the California Highway Patrol has failed us, everyone has learned over time that they can get away with speeding on our freeways. The situation has evolved into everyone believing they have a right to speed. A right, Councilwoman. A right to break the law."

Councilwoman Williams struggled with her goal of keeping the discussion within her parameters. She wanted to be in control of the conversation. "Lieutenant, we don't have input into the California Highway Patrol. But we do have influence with the Los Angeles Police Department."

"That's exactly my point. We don't want to create a situation, a Wild West, on the streets of Los Angeles that starts to resemble the Southern California freeways. I agree with you that it's critical for our officers to be vigilant in enforcing traffic laws, and to do so, it's absolutely critical that they feel supported by the political body in Los Angeles and by the management of the LAPD. Councilwoman Williams and Council members, Los Angeles Police Officers have to feel comfortable enforcing traffic laws based upon law violations without being concerned about the sex, age, race, or ethnicity of the traffic violator. That being said, I would ask, Council members, that the Los Angeles City Council communicate to the officers of the Los Angeles Police Department your support for effective traffic enforcement efforts based solely upon law violations. If you agreed to provide your support to these officers, your interest in traffic safety could be enhanced by the partnership that each of you personally forge with street police officers."

Chief Nelson began squirming in his seat, hoping Adams would leave this conversation be. He was also hoping he personally would not get pulled into it; Nelson wanted nothing to do with these questions. He began to wonder whether he should have come to Council this morning at all. Adams could have handled this by himself.

Councilwoman Connie Dixon responded, "Lieutenant, that's certainly an issue that the Council will consider. Thank you for your time." Lieutenant Jack Adams had just been dismissed.

#

"Thanks, Jack. I thought I was going to be standing tall in front of City Council and immediately after that, right in front of Chief Fuller. Now, I can yell at you and I skate. Good job, Jack. Consider yourself yelled at."

"Yes, sir. I just don't have the patience I used to have. Policemen just want to do their job, sir. Anyway, I was hoping we could stop and get a bite on the way back. As much money as a deputy chief makes, you should probably buy, sir. You feel like a French dip sandwich at Coles over on 6th street?"

"I know you make more than me, Jack. I don't get overtime and you swim in it. But I'll buy so you don't cry and whine for the rest of the day. Crybabies really irritate me."

"Good call, sir. That's why you're a chief and I'm just a lieutenant."

CHAPTER TWENTY-THREE
GOLD RUSH BEGINS

Adams had a lot on his plate, and now his team was shorthanded with Karen Aoki out of play. Even though he was pulled in many different directions, he pushed forward as hard as he was able to stay in the game.

After a long and slow morning drive from Orange County to the warehouse in Rampart Division, Adams inspected the warehouse project with his crew and felt pretty amazed that it didn't look too terrible. The desks and chairs from Salvage were perfect, and the two safes looked amazing. Jon Moser had provided "Gold Rush" decals for the door of each safe and a couple posters for the wall. The business cards on the counter displayed the new phone number. "This looks great. Dan, how are the cameras working?"

"They're working good, Jack. I can only get the street a short distance out front, but enough to capture license plates of cars coming in and out of the parking lot and catch the direction they're traveling. I tested the audio in here this morning and it works good. I have microphones along the counter so pretty much wherever anyone stands, we'll get good audio."

"Thanks, Dan. The safes look great, and the counter is impressive. Where did you guys get this countertop? It's granite?" Adams thought it looked better than the counters in his own kitchen.

"Karen got it through her dad. She's lying in the hospital and still on the clock. Amazing," McClain offered. "We also got the sandbags through him from some plant out in Canyon Country north of Los Angeles. We got enough to stack against the entire inside of the counter and stacked the rest against the opposite wall to give us a safe background if we have to return fire. Then we got the computers from Salvage, and Julie loaded a few business forms for Gold Rush."

"Thank Karen for me, Mac. I actually heard she's going home this morning and staying at her parents' for a while. Mac and Julie, I need to pull someone in to replace her until she's good to go. I'd like the two of you to get together and select someone."

"I'm fine by myself, LT. I can wait for Karen to get better." Julie was obviously emotional about her partner being missing in action and not ready to replace her.

"Yeah, well, we're not doing that, Julie. Get her replaced right away, Mac. When Karen gets better, we'll bring her back, so tell the replacement what the situation is. It's temporary. Hey Torres, get off the safe!"

"Jack, we're ready to get to work," McClain interceded. "I've got the paperwork in the city files, construction is done, signs are up, the place is staged, and the burglar alarm works. It's patched into Rampart Division desk. I've got enough fake stuff in the safe so it shows well when we open the door. The cameras and audio are working, and we have tactical plans in place if we get hit. Once we have cash on hand, I say we open for business."

"Okay, Mac. I have the commitment from Narcotics Division to fund us, at least for a while. I'll give you the contact info for Detective Thompson and you can go get cash today. Guess we'll keep it in the safe. Tomorrow morning, Gold Rush opens. Excuse me, Mac, I need to answer this call."

"Good morning, Lieutenant, it's Roger Leigh. Well, we've been working our butts off and worked most of the night. I already sent everything off to Chula Vista and Portland and to the jewelry store we identified in Prescott, Arizona. They're all working on filing their cases and I have one of our detectives assigned as a liaison to help them. I'm pushing forward as quick as I could for you, LT; we don't usually work at this pace. But now, as an afterthought, I'm wondering if I should have called you prior to sending everything to Chula Vista and Portland. And should I call the FBI?"

"No, I'll do that, Roger. Good work, pal. Just keep moving forward and let me know if you need anything."

#

"FBI, Special Agent Kidder. Can I help you?"

"Good morning, Agent. Lieutenant Jack Adams from LAPD here."

"Good morning, Lieutenant, I expected your call today. As you probably know by now, we found that due to some sensitive issues that arose here at the Bureau, we're not able to release our files to you on the interstate jewelry store robbery case. We have, though, submitted a request through your chief of police and through Mayor Hernandez to have access to your investigation. I apologize that this is one-sided, Lieutenant, and that I had to go over your head to your command staff; that wasn't my decision. But there's some issues involved that we can't ignore, and I'm not at liberty to release the info to you at this time. If it's convenient, I'll have a courier come by your office this morning to pick it up."

"Yeah, well, we're not doing that, Agent Kidder. Due to some sensitive issues that arose here at LAPD that *I'm* not at liberty to discuss with *you*, we're not able to release our files to you. Deputy Chief Nelson is scheduled to brief the chief of police today and I'm sure he'll brief the mayor's office. After that, I'm guessing the chief's office will probably reach out to your SAC to give the FBI our decision."

Since there was silence on the other end of the line, Adams figured he would lay out the entire scene for Agent Kidder, who seemed to be slow getting up to speed. "In the meantime, we've identified who we believe are the entire robbery crew. My staff is filing felony charges on the Los Angeles robberies as we speak. We've assisted Chula Vista, Portland, and Prescott to identify their suspects and they should be filing their charges this morning also. I'm guessing they've already dispatched their investigators to LA to tie up their cases."

More silence on the phone. When Kidder finally started talking, it was low and slow. "You've interfered in a federal investigation, Lieutenant."

The tense tone in Kidder's voice was obvious, but Adams didn't react well to being threatened. He was not one to be victimized by others. "Really? What investigation is that, Kidder? The investigation that the LAPD has already solved and cleared? I'll warn you that the LAPD would not take lightly a federal agent with the FBI interfering in an ongoing investigation and prosecution, Agent Kidder."

"I'll be in touch, Lieutenant."

"Yeah, well, I doubt it." New friendships were not developing today.

McClain, overhearing the conversation, guessed what had happened. "Man, you would think the feds would learn their lessons. But I guess they get away with that shit so much that they think they can push their weight around and screw everyone else."

"Yeah, well, I wish they'd play nicely, Mac. We'd get a lot more done."

After stewing for a good five minutes at Agent Kidder's nonsense, Adams figured he had better get the rest of LAPD in the loop. "Good morning, Chief Nelson. Wanted to get you up to date on a couple things. I've got an FBI agent calling me for a copy of our jewelry store robbery investigation involving our LAPD employee, but I'm reluctant to release that without your guidance. Because we have an LAPD employee involved who used secure government databases to support her criminal actions, along with all the subsequent legal personnel confidentiality issues and possible city liability, I'm reluctant to release anything to them without a court-issued discovery order served on the department. I'm probably not the best person to make a decision as to releasing information to the FBI in this case. This is a serious legal situation and way over my head. I'm sure the chief of police, the custodian of records, and the City Attorney's Office will want to be involved in that. All that being said, I'm pretty much cutting this loose now and letting Detective Leigh from Wilshire Division run with the prosecution. What do you think about the FBI request?"

"Interestingly enough, Jack, I have a message on my desk to call Chief Fuller about providing the FBI with investigative documents. I'll let him know where we are with this and you're right, Jack. At this point, it's not your place to release anything, so we'll let the legal process come into play here. I'm sure the FBI are interested in the interstate aspect of this, but sounds like the case is already wrapped up and they're late to the game. How's Karen doing?"

"She's going home this morning, Chief, thanks for asking. I'm going to replace her, temporarily, until she's good to go. I'll pick someone to come over on a loan and when Karen gets back, I'll send the officer back to their division."

Chief Nelson's pause started to make Adams uncomfortable. "I'm good with that. But Jack, there's no guarantee Karen will be coming back in the near future. There's no guarantee she'll make it back at all—her injuries are really serious. We'll do everything we can for her, but I want you to be prepared for that."

Sometimes it's better not to say things out loud. "I got it, Chief. Heads up, my crew is in business starting tomorrow, so they'll be out of play for anything else for a while. We're calling this 'Gold Rush.' I've told them not to go to any police facility while they're doing this, so I'll shuttle their paperwork from the department to and from Gold Rush for them. I'm also working hard through Detective McClain to limit any court appearances they may have coming up. I'll try and get continuances on their cases. I don't want them exposed."

"Sounds good, Jack, makes sense. Do you need anything from me?"

"Not today, but I'm sure I'll be asking in the future. Right now, we'll be focused on marketing and getting the word out to draw some gangsters in. That's where we're going to succeed or fail, so we'll have to be very imaginative. McClain will be there full-time, so my plate is going to be fuller than usual without him helping me. I'll get the word out that I might not be rolling on all the gang shootings for a while, unless there's something interesting involved. I did hear that El Salvador is requesting me to visit their fine country to consult on gangs, MS13, but I'm hoping your office could respond with a respectful refusal. It's not a good time for me. Although, if they're ever in town, I'd be glad to discuss the issues they have. Maggie has everything, so if Lieutenant Moss could reach out to her for the contact information, that would be great."

"I'm on it, Jack. Anything else you want to assign me to do, just let me know. Pick your uniforms up at the cleaners? I'm only a deputy chief of the Goddamned Los Angeles Police Department! Be safe, Jack."

"Be safe, Chief."

Adams felt pretty comfortable that he was on top of most of the important issues and believed his crew was ready to begin the Gold Rush operation. "Okay, Mac, you're in business tomorrow morning. You've got the lead on this, and I'll be in and out. I don't need constant updates; I don't micromanage, but keep me in the loop. I'm okay with Andrews's suggestion of using prostitutes to help get the word out, but you'll need to keep really tight controls on that. Don't let it go sideways, Mac, and you're personally carrying that responsibility. Consider having Torres be the front man at the counter; no one will take him for being the police. Most of the time, *I* don't even believe he's the police. How are we doing on a US attorney?"

"Damn, I forgot to tell you—Dan McVay at ATF set us up with Roger Gibson. I met with him and it's what we thought. He wants multiple gun buys—actually he wants three gun buys, for what he calls a 'pattern and practice' before he files a gun sales case, and yep, he wants everything recorded. He'll consider a single buy if the gun comes back to a homicide and the cases can be combined. He says that, but I'm sure he'd deal the gun case away for an admission on the homicide."

"Okay. Be safe on this, Mac. Our crew will get fire from a lot of different angles, some we don't even know of yet. Keep their heads in the game and keep everyone safe. That's your primary job. Before anything goes sideways, I'll pull everyone out and screw the mayor. I've got a call coming in, Mac. Get to work."

"Roger that, LT."

"Lieutenant Adams. Can I help you?"

"Hey, Lieutenant, this is Southwest Gangs. I wanted to let you know that we had a shooting with one down, KMA at the scene, and two in custody."

"Thanks, pal, who are the players?" Adams consistently attempted to keep a running tally of who was fighting with whom at any given moment.

"LT, the dead guy is a Rollin' 30s Crip and the two shooters are West Side Rollin' 20s Bloods. We also took a possible Black P. Stone juvenile in. He was two blocks away walking away from the scene and we initially thought he was probably uninvolved, but when we jacked him, he had a nine millimeter missing seven rounds from the magazine. One of our gang units was right on top of it when it happened and put a perimeter around the two shooters, who gave up when they were surrounded by a group of Hispanics in their backyard just four doors down. Looks like the two Rollin' 20s ran through the backyards after the shooting, but their escape got derailed when the group of Hispanics apparently didn't appreciate them climbing their fence. Then the juvenile was walking out of the perimeter when our Gang guys decided to take a moment of his time."

Adams was mostly interested in the connection of the juvenile. "Were the two shooters armed when they were arrested?"

"No, sir. They had already dumped the guns. But I'm thinking they may have handed off to the juvenile. West Side Rollin' 20s have been cliqued up with Black P. Stones in the past, so I think it's worth looking at."

Adams was certain the connection was there. "Great work. Please try and connect that nine millimeter to the shooting as quickly as you're able. Keep that juvenile buttoned down but don't interview him yet. I'll work my way down to you; I'm up in Rampart Division right now. Listen, better yet, I'm going to send Detective Roger Leigh from Wilshire Gangs down to you. I want him to sit in on the interviews with the juvenile. He may be interested in info for a robbery case he's working on."

Going directly to the next call, Adams attempts to connect the dots. "Hey, Roger, sorry to bother you. I know you're head over heels with your 211 case, but Southwest Division Gangs has a juvenile Black P. Stone in custody on a homicide case. He may have received the handoff of the gun and got popped leaving the perimeter. I'd like you to drop down and sit in on their interview of this kid. With that much pressure on his ass, let's see if he has any info on the Black P. Stones you have in custody for the jewelry store robberies."

"On my way, boss. I'll go straight to Southwest and stand by until they're ready for me."

#

Arriving at the scene of the shooting at 39th Street and Dalton, Adams was met with the familiar sight of yellow tape, streets blocked off, and press unloading from their vans. Leaving his car outside the tape and walking in, he was intercepted by a familiar face. "Miss Morgan, how's the news business today?"

"Hello, Lieutenant Adams. I was hoping to get an official comment about the shooting. If you're here, it must involve gangs. Which gangs are involved, Lieutenant? How many victims are there? A bystander told me there were two people shot. Are any of them juveniles? Do you have anyone in custody, Lieutenant?"

"How do you get here even before I do, Miss Morgan?"

"You can call me Candace, Lieutenant. We are friends, aren't we? We want the same thing—to report the facts and get to the bottom of things."

"I'm sure that's the case, Miss Morgan. Excuse me, I need to get a briefing on this situation from the detectives on scene."

"Lieutenant, can I listen in on the briefing with you?"

"Not this time, but maybe next time. Excuse me."

"Lieutenant, would you be willing to go on camera once you're done to discuss what happened here and to comment on the need for more effective gun legislation?"

"That won't work for me today, Miss Morgan. Maybe another time."

"Lieutenant? On a personal note, I have tickets to the Dodgers and Padres game Saturday and I was wondering if you'd like to go with me? I noticed you always wear a San Diego Padres ball cap and figured they were your team. First base field box over the dugout. I'll even buy hot dogs."

"That's tempting, Miss Morgan, but I'll be attending my kids' games on Saturday. They'll get a lot more runs than the Padres, and the hot dogs are cheaper." Smiling, Adams waved over his shoulder as he walked under the yellow tape.

Turning to face the camera as Lieutenant Adams disappeared under the yellow tape, Candace Morgan straightened her jacket, composed herself, and began her presentation. She needed to get to Adams and her editor, Dolinski, was putting heavy pressure on her.

"That was Lieutenant Jack Adams, head of Gang units for the Los Angeles Police Department. Lieutenant Adams has refused our request to be interviewed about the violent events here this evening. To date, the Los Angeles Police Department has yet to comment on the rising number of deaths of our young people in Los Angeles. We need answers, and without effective gun legislation, these deaths will continue. There is fear for our children on the streets of Los Angeles. This is Candace Morgan."

Within the perimeter, Adams met with the Gang sergeant on scene. "How are things going, Sergeant Miller?"

"Well, we have five nine-millimeter casings on the ground here with the victim. Still looking for more. Looks like my hunch was right in that the juvenile was sneaking the gun out for the shooters. The victim is a Rollin' 20, but he's Belizean. His name's Dion Price. Not really common, but we're seeing a few Belizeans in the 20s. I think they've been in the neighborhood so long that some of them have slid in. We've been seeing some Rollin' 20s tagging crossed out by Rollin' 30s in the alley between Denker and LaSalle, just north of 39th. Something's going on between them, and we have some rumors to follow up on."

"All right, Sergeant. Detective Leigh will sit in on the interview of the kid, but he won't be involved until you're done. I don't want him to interfere with your case, but as a long shot, I want him to ask a couple questions about the Black P. Stones involved in a 211 in Wilshire."

"I think tonight may be the night for long shots. Let's hope we all get lucky. Hey, LT, I'm pretty swamped here. Could you make the death notification on your way to the station? I'm told Price's parents both work at the Belizean restaurant over on Western."

A few paces away, the white sheet covering the body of Dion Price on the sidewalk on Dalton Street was an island in a blur of activity. The focal point that everyone seemed to ignore.

Detectives were searching the brush for shell casings or other evidence, taking preliminary interviews, and recording their notes. Photographers diligently recorded each detail. Uniformed officers surrounded the scene. Fire Rescue personnel stood by after announcing death, cleaning up, and repacking their gear. All the while, a neighborhood full of people in their front yards crowded along the yellow tape. The white sheet in the middle of all the commotion was ignored. The elephant in the room.

#

Parking on Western in front of the restaurant drew a lot of attention to Adams. This was not a place that police officers ate at. As Adams walked through the front swinging screen door, the ancient wood frame banged loudly as Adams let it go. There was immediate silence in the small crowded and usually loud restaurant.

Adams noted colorful tablecloths on each table, along with mismatched plates and glasses. The aroma from the kitchen was strong and heavy in the air. As an overweight middle-aged woman in a bright full-length dress approached, she stopped in her tracks and stared at the policeman standing in the doorway in a police uniform. She seemed to sense that Adams was not a customer, while Adams sensed that she was the mother of Dion Price. They both stared at each other. The atmosphere turned dark.

"Miss Price?" That was all it took.

Falling to her knees, sobbing, a man came from the kitchen to kneel next to her. The man looked up at Adams and said, "Not today—it's his birthday. We have a party today." Both parents spoke English, as it was the native language in Belize, but they didn't need to understand English when Adams walked into the restaurant and asked for them by name. They already knew why he was there.

There was no place to talk in private. There was no way to ease their suffering. In that moment, on that spot, their lives changed. Adams knelt down in front of the two parents. "I'm sorry. Your son, Dion, has been killed."

Adams directed the parents to Southwest Division police station to meet with Sergeant Dana Miller. Adams had tried so many times to explain to people what it's like to tell a family member that someone was killed. Violently, criminally, unnecessarily. He's never been able to find the right words. Even when the victim is a criminal, a gang member, the approach to the family is stifling. Parking the police car out front with neighbors watching. The slow walk up the walkway and knocking on the door. Those long, deep breaths before the door opens. There's no easy way.

Stepping out of the restaurant, taking a deep breath and feeling pain for the family, Adams watched as the news van carrying reporter Candace Morgan stopped at the curb behind the police car. A second news van hurried behind them, and people from both vans raced to the restaurant door, trying to get there first. *Criminal bastards.*

CHAPTER TWENTY-FOUR
BUSINESS PLANS AND MARKETING

"Hey, cutie. Need a ride?" John Andrews was making his first undercover approach to a prostitute since he had worked the Prostitution Enforcement Detail in Hollywood Division over nine years ago.

The young woman looked into Andrews's car and replied, "Are you looking for a date? If you're not the police, that is." Her dyed red hair caused her to stick out as she walked north on Alvarado Boulevard crossing 6th Street. But it was the attention she paid to passing motorists that grabbed Andrews's attention. From his experience at Hollywood Vice, Andrews knew that it was the eye contact he needed to watch for. Prostitutes always made eye contact.

Andrews's smile was contagious. "Sure am. I got a place over off Wilshire. You game?"

"Well, what do you want, honey?" She really was very pretty with an outgoing personality.

"Hot sex for hot money. Isn't that what everyone wants?" Andrews wasn't interested in a prosecutable case of prostitution, so he was much more free in the verbiage he could use. The object of Andrews's desires loaded up in his Toyota 4Runner and off they went toward Gold Rush.

"Mind if I make a quick stop at a pawnshop? I need to get a little more money. I think you're more expensive than what I thought. Those legs are incredible, and I love red heels. Do you wear them when you're naked?"

"Is there any other way to be naked, lover? I don't mind stopping. Load up, honey, because we're gonna be doing this all day, I think." Such a big smile.

One of the surveillance units, 5K3, followed Andrews and his newly made friend from the pickup location to Gold Rush. Detective McClain had ordered that other officers consistently have "eyes on" whenever a female was picked up.

McClain received the radio message from 5K3 indicating Andrews was bringing someone in. He stood in the warehouse on the other side of the walls he and his team had built for Gold Rush and watched the monitors. The black Toyota 4Runner pulled into the parking lot and McClain was relieved that the license plate was clear on the screen. Andrews got out and opened the car door for his passenger. What a gentleman.

At 11 o'clock a.m., 1100 hours, the first customers walked through the door of Gold Rush, the camera over the door clearly displaying the faces of two really happy people. Inside the office, four cameras picked the couple up and the audio microphones placed along the edge of the counter did a good job recording the conversation.

Torres was the first one to get up from his desk, swinging the door to the safe closed and turning the dial locking the safe. Theatrics. Looking at Andrews, Torres began the conversation. "I remember you. What can I help you with today?"

"I'd like to sell one more, the one I told you about last time." Andrews held the woman's hand as he talked to Torres. The smile on her face revealed that she probably wasn't used to someone being so nice to her. Julie Barr sat at her desk, uninterested and putting polish on her fingernails with two stacks of papers and forms in front of her. Out of sight, Mike Rand practiced positioning himself behind the side door to the warehouse, his familiar AR15 rifle held at port arms. Jim Halverson continued eating his turkey sandwich as he watched the monitors with McClain.

"Oh yeah, the Glock. Okay, let's take a look. Unloaded, right?" Torres laid a felt cloth on the granite countertop.

"Yeah, it's unloaded." Andrews let go of his friend's hand and withdrew a blue steel Glock 9 millimeter, his personal gun, from his waistband. Dropping the empty magazine and pulling the slide back to a locked position, he laid it on the counter.

Barr noticed that the woman with Andrews stiffened up, and her eyes widened as she took two steps back from the counter and one step toward the door. Thinking that she may break and run, Barr interrupted, "Can I get you something to drink, honey? We have water and coffee."

"Uh, no. I'm okay, I guess." She stopped her movement toward the door but still lingered slightly behind Andrews.

"You said eight hundred, right? It's like brand-new, just like I said."

Torres examined the gun, worked the slide back and forth, and then looked at the serial number on the frame. "Yeah, I can do eight hundred. It's not stolen, right?"

"No way. It was my brother's but he passed away. I'm just getting rid of it because guns scare me."

Torres walked to the safe and manipulated the dial, opening the door. Blocking the contents with his body, he placed the gun in the safe and removed a stack of money. He stepped back and relocked the door. At the counter, he placed one-hundred-dollar bills on the counter one at a time, eight of them. "There you go. Are we good?"

"Yeah, we're good." Andrews slid the bills into his pocket and turned for the door, grabbing the woman's hand again and guiding her as he whispered, "We're going to have a great day."

"By the way, if you refer anyone else to us, I'll give you a finder's fee," Torres added. "I'm trying to fill a box for our next shipment out through customs. It costs us money to ship half-empty boxes." Torres played his role so nonchalantly and so perfectly that even Barr was impressed.

"Ummm, what kind of finder's fee?" The red-headed woman finally entered the game.

"Something good like this? A hundred bucks."

Looking more interested, she asked, "Where do you send them?" And just like that she was on the hook.

"Usually to Africa with our jewelry shipments. But it just depends what country we're trading with that day." Torres hit the mark.

John Andrews and his new friend loaded back up into the Toyota 4Runner. "For eight hundred dollars, you're gonna get anything you want, anywhere you want." The redhead was already making plans for spending the money that she expected John Andrews to gladly give her for the best afternoon of his life.

Andrews steered the Toyota away from Gold Rush. Barr gave him the predetermined three minutes, then called his phone. "Damn, let me answer that phone. Hello? Hi, Chrissie. No, I'm in Hollywood. What? Now? Where did they take her? Okay, I'm on my way." Andrews's conversation with Barr was, naturally, pre-rehearsed.

"I'm so sorry, but our mom had a stroke—I have to go right now. I'll drop you off at the park but I've gotta run. Can I call you later?"

"Can I go with you?" The woman didn't want to let the money walk.

"No way, this is my family! Can I call you later? Or meet you?" Andrews tried his best to make the situation appear urgent.

"Sure, here's my number. But don't give it to anyone else. I get lots of bad calls."

With a surveillance unit set up on both ends of Benton Way, 5K3 to the north and 5K5 to the south, they were able to take the Toyota in either direction. For practice, they followed the two occupants in the undercover police car to 7th Street and Grand View, where they observed the female with red hair exit the Toyota and walk eastbound on the sidewalk.

5K3 took the Toyota back to Gold Rush, communicating their movements and teamwork for the surveillance. 5K5 stayed with the redhead in an attempt to identify her, but as she disappeared into the crowded park, they broke off and returned to Gold Rush. They would show her pictures to Vice and get a name on her. The telephone number would be a dead end, a burner.

After dropping his date off at MacArthur Park, Andrews made his way back to Gold Rush. "Give me my gun back, Torres. Here's your money." McClain came through the door into the warehouse with a smile on his face.

"Okay," McClain beamed. "Everything worked! Now go get another one."

Picking up his phone, he called Adams. "Hey, Lieutenant, it's McClain. Andrews met his next ex-wife and sold a Glock in front of her. Seemed like it went well, so we'll stay on track with this for a bit and see if anything pans out. One more thing: I'd like to pick up Jennifer Thomas from Newton Division to fill Karen's spot. Hate to do it, but we need staff now. Only problem is she has lots of beefs in her package. Nothing terrible, but a lot of false arrests and excessive force. None of them were sustained, though. Do you want some input on this, or do you have another idea?"

"No, Mac. I know who Thomas is and she's a great choice as long as Julie bought off on her. Pull her in now, and let's get her in to Gold Rush tomorrow."

"You're okay with her beefs, Jack?"

"We all get beefs, Mac. Every gangster we arrest makes a beef against us. It's standard procedure for them. As long as it's not 'rape, pillage, and burn,' she's good to go on our detail. Call the Newton Division captain and tell him Chief Nelson ordered her loan to us. I already cleared it with Nelson. She starts tomorrow."

The personnel complaint structure within LAPD was difficult to understand and made it impossible to compare one officer against another based upon the documented complaints against them. Police officers in the active divisions, primarily in South Central Los Angeles, had many complaints in their personnel file because they're more active and made more arrests than officers in slower parts of the city.

Not surprisingly, Gang Detail officers had the most complaints of any police officers because gang members have been schooled for many years to complain about every officer who arrests them, every time they get arrested, and oftentimes even if they're stopped but not arrested. On top of that, every altercation and every shooting an LAPD officer is forced into results in a personnel complaint and a lawsuit against the officer, the LAPD, and the city. There are attorneys who specialize in suing police departments, and their "Open for Business" signs are always swinging in the wind.

Jack Adams, a realist, was concerned about complaints that had merit but ignored the rest. It wasn't surprising that the bulk of those promoting up the chain of command had no, or very few, personnel complaints. The promotional system in the LAPD commonly favored those in administrative assignments instead of field assignments and they rarely, if ever, got complaints while they sat behind those desks.

Meanwhile, smooth-talking John Andrews was able to coax two other females he met to visit Gold Rush with him. Each time, they appeared interested in the gun sale they witnessed and the promise of a finder's fee. Andrews worked in different parts of the city, knowing that prostitutes talk to each other.

Feeling they had been successful on the first day and finding other prospects difficult, Andrews picked Barr up at Gold Rush and they made their way to the Original Tommy's on Beverly Boulevard to order some food. Sitting at one of the concrete tables near two questionable-looking groups of people, they loudly discussed Andrews selling two guns to "Gold Rush on Benton Way" and the high prices he got for the guns, then they made their to-go order to take back to the others. Like always, it was chili cheeseburgers, chili fries, and Cokes. Good thing everyone liked chili.

Although the sign on the door said Gold Rush closed at 6:00 p.m., McClain ordered the group to hang around another hour. The first day seemed to be going great. At 6:40, McClain saw on the monitor that a car was pulling into the parking lot with a young Hispanic man driving and a woman with bright-red hair sitting in the passenger seat.

"Showtime, everyone! We have our first customer. Looks like it's Andrews's redhead." Torres jumped down off the one safe and everyone made a point to appear busy.

Torres smiled at the redhead as she walked through the door. Walking directly to her and ignoring the young man, Torres engaged her with a large smile. "Hey, I remember you. Couldn't stay away from me, huh?"

Barr, also standing at the counter, rolled her eyes at Torres. Jim Halverson stood behind the file cabinet filing a stack of papers. Mumbling to himself just for effect, his Smith and Wesson .45 lay in the drawer. Mike Rand, with his AR15 at port arms across his chest, stood at the door with his left knee braced against it. The doorknob had been taped open with duct tape from the warehouse side, and a simple push on the door would reveal the barrel of Rand's rifle.

"Hi, I was here a few hours ago. This is a friend of mine, Miguel." The woman with the red hair acted as if the two of them were old friends. Doubtful.

Torres jumped right on the bandwagon, wanting to make his first purchase. He had already been warned to avoid speaking Spanish so that the other officers could follow the conversation. A tactical decision more than a prosecution decision. Torres slapped his hand hard on the countertop and barked,

"Miguel, I'm Mark. We're not usually open this late, but let's do business."

"Sissy told me you buy stuff, you buy guns."

Sissy? Really? "Sure do, and you caught us at a good time—for you, anyway. I've got a shipment going out to Africa and I need to finish filling a crate. We don't make any money if the crate's not full. I'll give you the best deal in town. What do you have?"

McClain stood in the warehouse watching the monitors while Mike Rand was all business standing at the door into the office. From the outside cameras, McClain recorded the license plate of Miguel's car and called the description in to the two surveillance units on scene, 5K3 and 5K5. Miguel was much shorter than the female, only four inches over the sixty-inch mark scratched on the door jamb used to gauge people as they walked in. With a shaved head and a thin build, he appeared to be only a boy at first glance. But the tattoo on the front of his neck under his chin, MS13, and the absolute lack of compassion in his demeanor told the policemen looking at him that he was dangerous. Boy or man, he was a killer.

"A Glock. I only carry Glocks. It's a nine," Miguel bragged.

"Okay, let's take a look. It's not loaded, right?"

"It's in my car. I'll get it."

Guess Miguel didn't trust Sissy to not rip him off. "Hey, Miguel. Unload it outside for me before you bring it in. I might shoot my own foot. I don't know much about guns." Torres had a reputation for goofing off a bit, but he was a great tactician and really quick on his feet.

As Miguel walked out through the glass door, Sissy remarked, "I get a finder's fee, right?"

"You sure do, Sissy. If it's a Glock, that's good for a hundred bucks. My name's Mark, by the way. I'm sure you couldn't forget." Sissy smiled like she'd won the lottery.

McClain watched on the monitor as Miguel sat in the front seat of his car. He seemed to linger in the car, but Miguel finally walked back in through the glass doors carrying a blue steel semiautomatic handgun. "Here it is. Cleaned it this morning. How does this work?"

Rand pressed his AR15 tight against his shoulder and pushed his knee against the door.

Torres smiled at Miguel in approval. "Well, if it's not stolen, I take the gun and you take some money. If it's stolen, I don't want it."

Miguel, displaying his incredibly high level of intelligence, said, "It's not stolen. It's mine. How would I steal my own gun?"

Torres, displaying his own incredibly high level of intelligence, replied, "Good point. I never thought of that." Torres inspected the gun and commented, "This is sweet. I can go up to eight hundred dollars for it. You game?"

After placing the gun in the safe and paying Miguel, Torres smiled and handed Sissy a crisp new one-hundred-dollar bill. Barr thought she was going to hug Torres; good thing the granite countertop was so wide. As they walked out the door together, Sissy turned, smiled, and said, "Bye, Mark. Don't forget my name."

As the door closed behind Sissy, Julie Barr remarked, " 'Bye, Mark. Don't forget my name.' You make me sick, Torres."

The surveillance units took the car away from the location and back toward MacArthur Park. They would stay with the suspect until they found a way to identify him.

McClain walked through the warehouse door with a smile on his face and everyone immediately relaxed, even Mike Rand. "Congratulations, we did it! Our first gun buy, and on the first day . . . and to MS13. Even the LT wouldn't expect this. Julie, let's have you take the gun and book it into evidence and request forensics. Let's do everything through Central Division because it's harder for anyone to see you coming and going. You'll always be the evidence person, Julie, because the lieutenant wants us to minimize our exposure at police facilities, so we'll just use one person and the guns will always go to Central. Let's stay uniform in what we do. Call McVay at ATF and give him the particulars of the gun.

"Let's give LT the good news . . . Hey, LT, it's Mac. Bought our first gun today from an MS13 gangster right when we were getting ready to close up shop! One of Andrew's girlfriends from this morning brought the guy in, so maybe this prostitute angle will bear fruit. The ball's still on the top of the mountain, Jack, but at least we just gave it a little kick."

"Good job, Detective McClain. I'm very proud of you and of your team. Keep pushing forward and make this happen. Hey, Mac . . . keep everybody safe. Don't let your guard down."

"Roger that, LT. I've got Jennifer Thomas showing up here tomorrow morning teamed up with Julie. The Newton Division captain wasn't real pleased with giving her up with only one day's notice, but he's a really squared-away guy and rolled with it. I think we have enough at the counter with Julie, Torres, and Halverson, so I'm going to use her with me doing detective work on all the follow-up we have. See ya soon."

Near the park, Paul Stanford on 5K3 saw his opportunity to identify the suspect he was following who was now standing with three juveniles at the taco stand on Lake Street just off of 6th Street. The three juveniles also appeared to be gang members. Stanford requested two Rampart Division Gang units to detain the group and identify each of the players. Miguel's tattoo of

"Cuto" on the left side of his chest helped to identify him as Miguel Aguilar, listed in the Cal Gang database under the gang moniker "Cuto" of Mara Salvatruche—MS13.

CHAPTER TWENTY-FIVE
SELLING THE INTEL ANGLE

Adams made a beeline back to downtown Los Angeles to support Detective Leigh's efforts to file the robbery charges on the LAPD employee and stay in front of the FBI.

"We got the case filed, Lieutenant, but I have a long list of work to do that the DA's office asked for. We're walking over now to Communications Division to arrest Jones. I've got my other detectives looking for Lil Sweet, and hopefully we'll grab him tonight also."

"Okay, Roger. I talked to the captain and he's standing by in his office. I'll meet you over there, but the plan will be to have the captain call her into his office and we'll take her down there."

Adams pulled in to the employee parking lot off of Los Angeles Street and met Detective Roger Leigh and three other detectives in the lobby of the Metropolitan Communications Dispatch Center. "Hey, LT, perfect timing. Karen Jones has been on duty for a few hours. I've got a couple teams out picking up Lil Sweet while we're doing Jones. My plan is to get her arrested and then straight into an interview room. Does that work for you?"

"Well, think about waiting to interview her until you have Lil Sweet in custody also. Put them in interview rooms right next to each other and make sure they see each other. If you want to make it fun, put Jones in the interview room with the door open and keep her handcuffed. Get Lil Sweet a bag of McDonald's and walk him past the open door without handcuffs on carrying the McDonald's. Let Jones know that he's getting preferential treatment because he already rolled on her and the whole crew."

Captain Steve Kessinger sat uncomfortably at his desk as Adams and the group of Gang detectives walked into his office. "Captain Kessinger, I'm Lieutenant Adams. Thank you for meeting us here tonight."

"What kind of heat am I in, Lieutenant?"

"Excuse me, sir?"

"What kind of heat am I in? How did she do this shit?"

"No, sir, there's no blowback to you as far as I can see. And if something comes up, I'll meet with you personally so we can work through it. Deputy Chief Nelson truly appreciates what you're doing here, sir, and I'm sure he would want me to keep an eye on that issue. I only asked you to be here so that we can take her into custody without any incident and hopefully out of the view of others. Do you mind calling her in to your office for us?"

Only a few moments went by before a uniformed sergeant assigned to the Communications Center not wearing a gun belt walked into the captain's office with Police Service Representative Karen Jones. Roger Leigh stepped up to face her. "Karen Jones, you're under arrest."

#

"Chief Nelson, I wanted you to know that our employee, Karen Jones, is in custody. We're on the line to taking down the whole crew now. Chula Vista, Portland, and Prescott are working with us and they're filing their cases, probably today or tomorrow. All three cities offer their thanks to the LAPD for our support in solving their cases. While I have a few moments, has Commander Jelenick briefed you on the assignment he gave me?"

"Excuse me, Lieutenant? What assignment? You work through me now. You know that."

"The commander ordered me to work with the LA archbishop to assist the Catholic Church in setting up a program to work with at-risk youth in all their schools and then follow up on their efforts. About three hundred schools and over seventy thousand kids. I wanted to make sure you knew that it's a pretty massive undertaking and would take most all of my time for the next couple years or so. I'd have to kick loose my responsibilities in the LAPD Gang world. It would also create an environment of high liability for the LAPD and the City of Los Angeles, so I knew you would want to be briefed in on this. Working with at-risk youth, vulnerable youth, is really sensitive, Chief, and the Catholic Church is still battling some pretty serious allegations along those lines. This assignment may not be in line with what the LAPD stands for and is certainly not something I could personally morally support. I'm not sure we would want to become involved in this effort without a lot of LAPD management and legal oversight. But I'm ready to move forward with that if it has your support."

Chief Nelson didn't need to think about his answer very long. "We'll pass on that, Lieutenant. Anything else?"

Adams's tension immediately eased as he escaped from this no-win situation. He respected the deputy chief's ability to make a decision and move on. "Nothing else, sir. I'm back to work."

"You're doing a good job, Jack. Be safe out there."

"Be safe, Chief." Just as Adams finished his call, his phone rang again.

"Commander, how can I help you?"

"Lieutenant, I've got this reporter from the *LA Times* camped on my doorstep because someone told her I'd be glad to work with her on the article she's writing about gangs. Someone gave her my cell phone number, and I'm pissed. Apparently, it sounds like the *Times* is willing to do a piece on our Gang details and that would benefit all of us, Lieutenant. She tells me that you gave her the cold shoulder and that you're the one who told her to call me. Did you give the press my cell phone number, Adams?"

"I did, Commander. I know how busy Chief Nelson is at the moment and I thought you may be a good alternative for her. I hope I haven't made a mistake, Commander." Ahh, that dry sense of humor.

"Her name's Shelley Givens and I'm approving a ride-along for her so she can glean what she needs while riding in the car with you. I want you to call her and make the arrangements. I told her I'll give her the next month to ride with you, and then when she's done I'll personally meet with her to give her an overview of our efforts from a management level perspective. Are you ready for her number?"

"Yeah, that won't work for me, Commander. My schedule is all over the map, and I don't think the chief's office or the City Attorney's Office would want to address the liability and personal safety of someone being in my car while I'm at work. Remember, I'm mostly at the scene of gang shootings and other tactical events that provide a high level of liability for the City of Los Angeles, along with the confidential personnel issues. We have undercover operations, surveillances, informants, all of which could not be revealed to the press. Man, would that be dangerous."

Commander Jelenick felt the shot of anger go through him. "You just do what I tell you, Lieutenant! We have an opportunity to strengthen our relationship with the *LA Times* and it could result in positive press for us. Deputy Mayor Sarah Holly called me and said the mayor himself asked us to work with this reporter."

"I'll run it past Chief Nelson, Commander. If he approves it, I'll get on it right away."

"Lieutenant, there is absolutely no need to bother Chief Nelson. I want you to call this reporter and get this done. Do you understand me, Lieutenant?"

"I certainly do, Commander. I understand that I work for Deputy Chief Nelson and that if any other person on the Los Angeles Police Department gives me orders, I'm going to run it past Chief Nelson. I also don't work for Deputy Mayor Sarah Holly or Mayor Hernandez. I won't violate the chain of command, and I won't be disloyal. I'll get back to you as soon as I get the chief's approval, Commander."

Adams saw that the call disconnected. He hated to call Chief Nelson again so soon but thought he should address this issue with the *LA Times* before it got out of hand.

"Lieutenant? Didn't I just hang up with you? I know I did, Lieutenant, because I was eating the enchiladas my wife made, and here I am still eating those same enchiladas."

"I'm sorry to bother you again, Chief Nelson. Commander Jelenick just called and gave me another assignment that you should know about."

"What? I'm still angry about this LA Archdiocese issue. I thought I was clear with the commander as to who you work for."

"Well, I met an investigative reporter from the *LA Times* the other day and she said she was doing an article about the courageous and positive work our gang officers are doing."

"What? The *LA Times*? They're not going to do an article on LAPD that's positive. What are you talking about, Lieutenant?"

"Exactly, Chief. She's just lying to me, and she wants information to screw us somehow on the front page of the *LA Times* so I kissed her off. So now, apparently Deputy Mayor Sarah Holly called Commander Jelenick and asked him to cooperate with this reporter. She said it was coming straight from the mayor. Jelenick just called me and said he approved a ride-along for this reporter with me for the next month."

Deputy Chief Nelson laughed out loud. "We both know that won't work. I have a million thoughts going through my brain as to why that won't work."

"I told the commander that I'd run it past you, that whole chain of command thing. I did give him some of the most obvious reasons that we wouldn't want her in the car with me, her personal safety being the paramount one. But revealing our task forces, surveillances, informants, or any gang intel I work with would be disastrous, potentially life endangering. How about the confidential information from shooting scenes? On top of the whole mess it would create, we have no idea how the *LA Times* would spin it. Whatever ends up on that front page would have no resemblance to the facts. We don't even know what their real motive is. What do you think they're up to, sir?"

"If it's coming from the mayor's office, it's certainly suspect. I'll make sure the chief of police is aware of the request, Jack, and I'll talk to Commander Jelenick about it. Again. For now, that's not something we're going to entertain."

"Sorry to call you again, Chief Nelson. I'll get back to work, sir."

"Well, it's about time you did some work, Lieutenant. And it's about time I ate my enchiladas. Be safe out there."

CHAPTER TWENTY-SIX
GOLD RUSH PANS OUT

The month went by fast, and word seemed to have gotten out quickly about Gold Rush. Most of the customers interested in selling guns walked in on their own and when Torres asked how they heard about Gold Rush, the answer was always the same: "From a friend of mine." Although not all customers showed up with guns to sell, McClain and Adams agreed to buy other items if it appeared it may benefit the detail somehow.

William Garcia, a Fresno Bulldogs gang member, had recently been incarcerated in Los Angeles County Jail for stealing cars and did two stints of harder time at Solano State Prison. Driving from Fresno to Los Angeles to visit his mother a handful of times each year, William Garcia had picked Sissy up on one of his visits and taken her to his mother's house while she was in the hospital. After that trip, William made it a point to drive on Alvarado, looking for Sissy, on each of his trips.

"Hey, Sissy, you out here looking for me?"

Sissy stepped down off the curb into the street and looked into the familiar tan Chrysler, considering whether to get in. She had been hurt the last time and was afraid of William Garcia. She was also afraid to say no. "Hi, William. Yep, you're reading my mind."

Garcia took Sissy to the Holiday Inn Express north of Beverly Boulevard. Placing a semiautomatic handgun in the drawer of the dresser, Garcia told Sissy not to go near it. The sex was violent again; Garcia hit her and knocked her onto the floor. Only moments after walking into the hotel room, Sissy's nose was already bleeding. When Garcia grabbed her hair and pulled her on to the bed, he told her to clean up. "What the fuck? I'm not doing you with blood all over your face! You think I paid for that shit? Go clean that shit up and get your ass back in here."

Within the hour, Sissy was covered in bruises given to her by Garcia. Once their business had been completed and Garcia retrieved his gun from the dresser drawer, sliding it into the back of his waistband, Sissy told him about Gold Rush. She wanted to divert from the beating she expected after having sex with Garcia and thought the story about Gold Rush may gain her a free ride.

Luckily for Sissy, Garcia seemed really interested and asked her a lot of questions about Gold Rush. What did the store look like, how many employees were there, was there a security guard? Garcia told Sissy to take him to Gold Rush, but it took her quite some time to fix her hair and apply makeup to hide her injuries. Garcia followed Sissy's directions and drove to Gold Rush with her still in his car.

Garcia liked the idea that Gold Rush was in an industrial area and there weren't many people nearby. When he parked in the small parking lot, he saw a camera over the door that looked pretty small and noticed that there was hardly any traffic on the street. There were no pedestrians anywhere near the business.

Garcia entered the doors of Gold Rush behind his date and saw two men and a female behind the counter. The office was small but held two large metal safes, and he didn't see any security cameras inside. He noted that there were no security guards, and the three employees did not seem to be armed. They didn't even seem to pay much attention when he walked in.

"Hey, Sissy, good to see ya. Have you brought us another customer?" Mark Torres greeted Sissy like an old friend. The plan to use street prostitution as an avenue to advertise Gold Rush appeared to be at least partially successful, with several prostitutes bringing in customers and receiving their commission.

"I sure have. You should give me a bigger commission now—I think I'm your best customer! This is my friend William. He's from Fresno, but we're really old friends. Like, really old. He comes down to LA just to visit me." Sissy was dressed to the hilt in a summer dress and heels. Her red hair looks professionally done today. Most of her bruising was hidden by her makeup, but both Torres and Julie Barr noticed that she had recent injuries on her face.

"You look gorgeous. Are you doing something different, Sissy?"

"Sure am. I found a stylist in Beverly Hills that works with movie stars, and she did a makeover on me. Am I irresistible, Mark?"

"Totally. You know you're smoking hot; you don't have to ask me. Look at William, he's staring at you. Hey, William, nice to meet you. What kind of business can we do today?"

William Garcia stepped up to the counter and pushed Sissy aside with his body. *Hmm, maybe he's not as good of a friend as Sissy thinks.* A Hispanic man with braided hair, he had an "FBD" tattoo on his chin and "F14" tattoos under each of his eyes. William was dressed in red pants cut short just above his ankles with high-top red tennis shoes and a red Fresno Bulldogs sweatshirt. *Come to think of it, he looks a lot like a cartoon character.*

"I'm interested in selling a gun my grandfather left me, but I don't think it's registered. I don't have any papers on it."

Torres smiled and leaned forward over the counter to whisper, "It's okay, William. As long as it's not stolen, we don't need any paperwork on it. If Sissy knows you, that's good enough. My little brother lived in Fresno for a while, on Mayfair, before he went in the army."

Torres knew he had to try and get more information, but William didn't take the bait. He ignored Torres's comment about his brother. "Yeah, so what? My gun's in the car. I'll go get it."

When Garcia went outside to retrieve the gun from his car, he sat in the front seat and considered robbing the business right then. He was sure he would be in and out and then on the road back to Fresno.

Garcia felt the 9mm semiautomatic in his waistband in the small of his back as he recovered a second gun, a Taurus TX22 .22 caliber handgun, from under the front seat. He had stolen the gun when he burglarized his neighbor's house two years ago. He decided to try and see what they had in the safe before he decided to rob them or not. He placed the Taurus handgun in a green plastic Sprouts bag.

As he walked back into the business, Garcia noticed the female employee was tense and that the other male employee was still standing behind a file cabinet. He noticed the file cabinet was turned facing the back wall instead of facing the workspace like most offices. Not very convenient for the employees. He felt like something was wrong and decided to wait on the robbery. He could always come back.

"We don't see Tauruses too much. This is a .22—that's really cool. I could do about five hundred dollars for it. Are you game?"

"I was hoping to get a little more." William stepped back from the counter and straightened up. Halverson, positioned in his favorite barricaded position behind the file cabinet, tightened his grip on his handgun in the drawer of the cabinet. He thought to himself that he could hit each of the F14 tattoos.

"Sorry, William, that's all I can do on a .22." Torres knew that was probably more than the gun sold for new.

Garcia watched Torres open the safe, but his view of the inside was blocked by Torres's body. He could see that a number of items and bags filled the safe, and Torres seemed to be counting bills when he retrieved the money to pay for the .22 caliber Taurus.

After Torres paid William, Sissy told him she'd meet him outside. After he stepped out, Torres laid one hundred and fifty dollars in her hand. "You're right, Sissy, you deserve a little more."

"Sissy, that guy's really scary looking. You know him well?" Julie Barr joined the conversation. Believing William was from Fresno, the team knew they had to try and get more information to identify him before he left the location. His car and his license plate were already being investigated by McClain and the new addition, Jennifer Thomas, in the warehouse.

"Yeah, he's weird looking but he's really nice. See ya." And with that, she was out the door.

After selling his .22 caliber handgun and dropping Sissy off on Alvarado near MacArthur Park, Garcia picked up his phone and dialed while he drove. "Homes, I found a place and it's ripe. They got a safe and it's open. Got gold, jewelry, cash, and guns. I think they might have lots of guns. You game?"

Jorge Mendez receiving the unexpected call responded, "I'm always game. Where you been? Thought you were coming this morning?"

"Drove into LA to see Moms. She's out of the hospital. I was gonna call you but I got sidelined. Little tail wagged at me while I was driving. Found this spot to hit down here, but not today. I was just in there. Next time I come down, maybe in a few days. I'll let you know. Strap up and mask up, homes. I'm sure they got a camera in there somewhere. We can hit it and be back home before dark." Garcia sold his idea to Mendez and then went to visit his mom.

Back at Gold Rush, McClain entered the front office from the warehouse and advised the crew that the car William was driving was registered to William Garcia in Bakersfield. "The FBD tattoo is from Fresno Bulldogs—not sure about the F14. Surveillance is on them, but I think we already have him. He's in Cal Gang with a photo and he's pulling a long arrest record behind him. He's on parole for 211 right now, so this gun buy will violate his ass right back to prison. Your girlfriend hangs out with the best class of people, Torres."

McClain's phone started ringing and he went back inside the warehouse. "Detective McClain, this is Bowler at Scientific Investigation Division. I have some results on one of the guns we have for you, a nine-millimeter Glock. Looks like it's the shooter in a double homicide in Northeast Division that occurred four days before you took it into custody."

Scientific Investigation Division always had a large backlog of cases, but they had been notified by Lieutenant Adams that Chief Nelson ordered testing for all guns submitted by Detective McClain to be expedited.

"We gave you that gun a month ago, Bowler. Why is the delay so long?" McClain knew that Lieutenant Adams's first question would be why they didn't know this earlier.

"A month is fast, Detective. The mayor doesn't give us enough people to do the job. We prioritized your testing because Lieutenant Adams said it was direct from the chief of police. Anyway, Adams scares me. That guy's intense."

Dialing Adams's number with a sigh, McClain knew he'd be hot about this. "Hey, Lieutenant, it's McClain. Remember the MS13 gangster who came in on day one? He sold us a Glock and SID just gave us the scoop that it's good for a double homicide in Northeast Division. This is the exact gun you started this whole thing for. The hot shooter."

"Damn, Mac, why are we just getting this? I expedited SID on all our guns!"

"I know, sir, but they said this *is* expedited. I'm sorry about that. I'll get to work on the homicide case in Northeast Division and we'll see if we can pair this guy up to it. He sold it to us only four days after the shooting; it's got to be him."

Calling Northeast Division Homicide, McClain was anxious to get the information on the murder tied to the gun Gold Rush now had in custody. "This is Detective Scott. I understand you're interested in one of our shootings, Mac."

"Yeah, Dave, the double from up in the Avenues on Isabel Street. We may have a lead, but I'd like to know what the scoop is on the case."

A smile immediately hit Dave Scott's face. His clearance rate on solving murders had been lagging this year and he really needed a break. This could clear two murders and get him out of the penalty box. "Sure, Mac. Guessing you big boys wouldn't be calling unless you had something solid. Let's see, I've got the murder book just over here. Suspect is reportedly a young Hispanic guy with MS13 on the front of his neck. Short, maybe five foot three and skinny, bald head. No one was willing to roll on him, but we got the picture."

McClain was thrilled that the description matched the person who had sold them the gun.

"So, looked like the Avenues had a get-together to celebrate one of their low-hanging fruit beating a case at 210 Temple. This guy shows up at the party with Shirley Garcia, a little thirteen-year-old who lives there. Of course, she told us she doesn't know him. She said she just met him out front and invited him in."

Mac cut in to fill in the blanks. "You weren't able to roll her for his name?"

"Nope. She played stupid, but she lives in a house full of assholes and she's well schooled. We did a warrant on her phone and got what we think was the shooter's phone, but it's a throwaway. Anyway, at the party one of the Avenues rubbed her butt, allegedly, and this little guy started a fight with a bruiser twice his size. He poked his chest out in front of his little girlfriend and then got the shit kicked out of him for his effort. I think he had a little man complex that the Avenues didn't appreciate, and they had a field day on his head. He slid out the front door and less than five minutes later walks back up the driveway and shoots the first two guys he sees. He runs down the sidewalk never to be seen again."

Detective McClain was pretty sure they had the shooter, but he knew better than to commit to that fact without Lieutenant Adams's input. "Okay, Dave. I'll run it past the lieutenant and then get back to you. I might need some more detail from you after I talk to Lieutenant Adams. See ya soon."

"Thanks, McClain. Anything you have will help. You'd think this would be easy to close, but no willing wits. I'm not having any luck this year except bad luck."

McClain got Adams on the phone again immediately. "Hey, LT. Talked to Dave Scott over at Northeast and his double 187 fits our suspect, Miguel Aguilar. He goes by Cuto. I'm guessing he dumped a couple gangsters and then wanted to get rid of the gun as quick as he could. He sold it to us four days after the murders. I haven't let anything out to Northeast until I talked to you. Should we move forward in helping them solve it? They have no willing wits and nothing to file the case with."

Adams suddenly saw the first opportunity to fulfill his vision of an intelligence-based investigation to use as a model for future gang enforcement efforts. His frustration with traditional gang enforcement efforts by uniformed Gang officers had peaked out long ago, and he knew there was a lot on the line in leading the way toward a new model to police gangs.

"Hold off on that, Mac. If they don't have any corroborating wits and no one who will identify him, his selling the gun to us is probably not enough to do the 187 case on him. Let's continue on our path to move it into a phone tap and see if we can come up with more evidence for them. Get the case package and all the details and tell Northeast we'll keep them in the loop as we move forward. Don't leak anything about Gold Rush or phone taps, though. Come time to file on Cuto, we'll let Northeast file the case so they get the credit on paper and we'll walk it through with them."

CHAPTER TWENTY-SEVEN
MARA SALVATRUCHE

Miguel Aguilar, Cuto, emigrated to the Unites States from El Salvador when he was thirteen years old. His parents had abandoned him in the custody of the National Civil Police after he was arrested for violent assault against a twelve-year-old classmate. After escaping custody, he found his way to the United States in the company of an elderly man who agreed to accept a fee to guide him.

As an adult, Miguel remembered very little of the trip except for the long hours waiting and of being hungry and thirsty. He tried never to think about the sexual assaults he endured.

Living in the MacArthur Park area of Los Angeles where there was a heavy population of other émigrés from El Salvador, Miguel was immediately recruited into the arms of Mara Salvatruche. Only a boy still, Miguel became a pawn in the game of selling false identification papers to illegal immigrants.

A few years later, he was deported back to El Salvador after being arrested for assault with a deadly weapon. By that time, the Los Angeles Police Department had already encountered Miguel during multiple gang investigations and entered him into the Cal Gang database, identifying him as a member of Mara Salvatruche, MS13, known as "Cuto."

In an effort to return to the United States, Miguel crossed through Mexico with two of his older brothers. During their travels across the state of Durango, all three brothers were recruited by the Sinaloa Cartel as enforcers and protectors against rival drug cartels. Many of those traveling through Mexico toward the United States only became tools for the drug cartels to use.

Although all three brothers had lived a life indoctrinated with violence, only Miguel survived the two years in Mexico and found his way back to the United States, crossing the border at Tecate, California.

Miguel found his way to distant relatives working a cattle feed production company in Brawley, California, and quickly made a name as a violent predator. He knew no other way and resorted to preying upon illegal immigrants in the area. Thefts, robberies, and assaults earned Miguel the attention of the United States Border Patrol.

The El Centro Sector Border Patrol agents chased him along the shore of the Salton Sea and through the Anza Borrego Desert State Park. Miguel escaped when he broke into an unoccupied mobile home in Borrego Springs and hid there for over two months, as it was common for people to only use the properties there as winter homes as they fled from the extreme winters in the Midwest.

When the couple from Indiana who owned the home returned and found the house literally destroyed and disgustingly filthy, they were killed within moments of walking through the door.

Miguel Aguilar took their Jeep Cherokee and made his way on back roads to Escondido, about an hour north of San Diego. From there, he returned to the area of his home in MacArthur Park before officers of the Los Angeles Police Department pulled up behind the Jeep and turned on the red lights.

The Indiana license plates did not fit in MacArthur Park, and when the officers ran the plates over their computer, they received a response of Code 6 Charles—suspect armed and dangerous connected to a double homicide.

Before the officers could gain more information, Miguel pulled hard on the steering wheel, pulling the car into the alley next to the El Guanaco Salvadoran restaurant. Miguel knew it well. Stopping the car outside a metal gate at the mouth of the alley, Miguel fled on foot to the rear parking lot. He scaled a tall fence topped by vegetation, one he had climbed over many times, and ran through the so-called "Art Park" developed by well-meaning but ignorant Los Angeles politicians.

The Art Park, a vacant lot populated with canopies for local artists to display their work, had become one of the focal points for sales of fraudulent immigration documents. Situated just off the roadway and out of sight of passing cars, local residents were afraid to go there and MS13 controlled the location. The gang members were very appreciative of the Los Angeles city councilman responsible for providing taxpayers' money to build it with the stated goal of bringing art to an underserved community.

When the police are chasing you, Miguel knew not to stop moving, a technique he had used successfully many times. He covered two blocks to the Universal Church on Bonnie Brae, where he was able to shed his black sweatshirt and steal a gray jacket lying on the steps next to an elderly couple. By then, the information of a double homicide connected with the Jeep Cherokee had hit the LAPD airwaves and a full-scale tactical operation was underway to capture the driver who had fled on foot. Miguel knew he had to make his way out of the perimeter being set up by the police officers and find a spot to weather the storm.

He headed north to the Guatemalan street food market on 6th Street, then west on 6th Street to the Quetzaltenango Restaurant. He could see down the street that the police were focusing heavily on MacArthur Park, obviously believing that would be where the murder suspect would flee. Miguel hit the alley and ran northbound clear to 3rd Street. He had an idea and headed down Ocean View toward Park View and to the Mexican Consulate.

He was sweating and breathing heavily. Inside the doors of the consulate, he was stopped by physical barriers and security guards. He cried that he was from Mexico and sought asylum in America. It would be five hours before the Mexican Consulate realized he was not a Mexican citizen and expelled him from their building. Miguel Aguilar had extended his ability to hide far beyond the will of the Los Angeles Police Department to continue searching, and after those five hours he walked down the street without a police officer in sight.

While standing in front of the old Swap Meet building on Alvarado across from the park, Miguel observed a group of six youths standing in the middle of the block in front of the money transfer business. Defiantly continuing his life in America as a predator, he flashed the "devil's head," a hand sign resembling the letter *M*. Mara Salvatruche.

The group of El Salvadoran youth with Mara Salvatruche tattoos pulled him into the depths of Los Angeles, out of the view of the Los Angeles Police Department.

#

Miguel Aguilar, known by his moniker "Cuto," met thirteen-year-old Shirley Garcia in MacArthur Park on the banks of the lake. Cuto appeared much younger than his age, as he was only five foot three inches tall and exceptionally skinny. He persuaded Shirley Garcia to give him her phone number, which he diligently called every day for over two weeks.

Upon being invited to a party at Shirley's home, Cuto ventured away from the small neighborhood in Los Angeles where he felt safe and headed for a working-class residential area not too far away north of the I-5 Freeway in LAPD's Northeast Division.

When Cuto walked into the house, a run-down single story with a garage that had been converted into a bedroom, he immediately felt the tension. The room full of gang members from the Avenues made it abundantly clear that Shirley Garcia should not have invited him.

When Shirley's uncle, Luis Sanchez, wrapped his arms around her and whispered in her ear, Cuto accused him of rubbing her butt.

Cuto had spent many years standing in front of men and scaring them with his fierce bravado. In reality, the tattoo on his neck displaying that he was a member of Mara Salvatruche carried much more weight than Cuto's slight 130 pounds.

Luis Sanchez straightened up and laughed, just before Cuto swung his fist up at his face. That turned out to be a painful mistake. Everyone in the room seemed to be taking turns hitting Cuto, who ended up curling up on the floor trying to protect his head.

Shirley began crying and pulling at Cuto's arms, telling him to get out. Somehow, probably in deference to Shirley, the group allowed him to crawl out of the front door.

After being brutally beaten in the fight at the party, Cuto fled the house. He had learned to be evil during the course of his life, and he wasn't ready to change that part of his character. He retrieved a 9mm handgun from his car and returned to the party with the intent to shoot everyone. As he walked back up that very same driveway, his path was blocked by two of the men who had enjoyed beating him. They were both immediately shot and killed. Miguel fired nine more rounds into the two front windows of the house, then calmly walked back to his car, out of bullets. That would have to do for tonight.

Cuto knew he had to get rid of the gun he'd used to kill two men that night. He didn't know if anyone else inside the house had been killed, and he certainly never read the article in the *Los Angeles Times* about the shooting which reported that luckily, no one in the house was hit.

Los Angeles is a violent city and people who live there are well trained for this sort of thing, so at the sound of the very first gunshots, everyone fell to the floor where they would be safer.

Cuto had intended to hand the gun off to one of the younger El Salvadoran gang members but changed his mind when he met what he considered to be a very cute young woman he picked up for sex on Alvarado Boulevard just blocks east of MacArthur Park. She had beautiful red hair. The prostitute who sat in the seat next to him talked about a pawn shop that bought guns for cash, and with no paperwork. She said she would get a commission if she brought people in to sell guns.

CHAPTER TWENTY-EIGHT
DEPUTY CHIEF STEVE NELSON

Deputy Chief Steve Nelson felt grateful every single day for his job and his career. Moving up the ladder had been relatively easy for him. He didn't seem to have all the drama most others endured at the hands of the Los Angeles Police Department.

Nelson had also been lucky in life. He'd married his college sweetheart, had great kids, and lived in a nice house in Huntington Beach. It was an older craftsman-style house, only 1,300 square feet, that he had purchased as a young policeman when houses were much cheaper. The house was small, but it sat on a large lot only five blocks from the beach. It was now surrounded by the larger houses that had replaced the old neighborhood; he wouldn't have been able to afford it today.

Deputy Chief Nelson was having a good day. "So, Jack, you've successfully got Gold Rush off the ground, and you've made good progress. What kind of predictions do you have as to the length of time you'll need to bring it to an end?"

"Were doing pretty good, Chief. Like you know, we tagged Cuto from MS13 on day one and linked the Glock he sold us to a double 187 in Northeast Division. That's the exact gun we were looking for. That's what the Gold Rush plan was all about! Two of the Avenues got dumped in their front yard during a birthday party. The evidence against him is sketchy, and the fact that he sold us the gun isn't enough to guarantee a prosecution against him, but I'm ready to phone tap his ass and I'm sure we'll put it all together. But I'll fill you in on that in a moment."

"You know I'm uneasy about this phone tap aspect, Jack, so help me understand where we're going here." Chief Nelson was not avoiding the investigation, but he wanted to fully understand situations before he made decisions. Although Adams scared him sometimes with the curves he tossed in, Nelson was proving to be supportive and pretty savvy.

"Okay, Chief. In the last month, we've bought seventeen guns. So far, four have been ballistically matched to Los Angeles shootings and a little .22 to a Fresno shooting by one of their local gangsters who frequented Gold Rush. I'm really happy about this so far. We're also buying cell phones, laptops, and even two catalytic converters."

"What? I thought we were buying guns? Why are we buying all that junk? Catalytic converters?" Nelson's desire for a clear picture just got clouded. His good day was on shaky ground.

"Well, I'd hoped to keep you out of the weeds, Chief, but I made the call to buy pretty much whatever people brought in. I leave it up to McClain in the moment; it's just a judgement call. If he thinks it's a criminal or the property is stolen, he buys it. And then he lays the story on them that we pay almost nothing for that stuff but we pay a lot for guns. You never know. It may be a small investment that leads to more guns coming in. If he gets the feeling that the person standing at the counter is a nobody, though, he sends 'em walking."

"What are we doing with that stuff? Are we investigating them for burglaries or car burglaries?" Chief Nelson's analytic mind began to cloud the big picture with more questions.

"Nothing really, Chief. Again, it's a judgement call I made. That's not our goal, and I want to keep us in the elephant hunting business. Ignore the small stuff. Right now it's scattered around Gold Rush as props, but eventually I'll have McClain book it all as recovered property. It's just not worth our time, Chief. Kind of like writing tickets. We have elephants to hunt."

"Oh, boy. Yeah, I'm still suffering this ticket issue. Well, you make the call, Jack. This is your detail. Now what about wiretaps?"

"I'm ready on Cuto from MS13 for the double 187, and I'm really close on two of the other three guns tied to Los Angeles murders. On the Fresno case, I'll liaison with Fresno police and give them the suspect who sold the gun. It's up to them to put the rest of it together. But I have to figure out when and how to do that so as not to jeopardize Gold Rush. We need money to run the wiretaps, so I've been really busy trying to identify sources for the cash. I just firmed up a money commitment from the Bureau of Justice Assistance. They have a Firearms Trafficking Program that's funded really well. I'm in for one hundred and fifty thousand dollars, but I'm told that depending on the results of our efforts, there may be more available."

"You have a hundred and fifty grand right now? How did you do that?" Chief Nelson's excitement level, or irritation level, tended to peak rather quickly when confronted with situations that were uncomfortable for him.

"I'm not sure, boss, but we have it. I also tapped two different branches in ATF for a total commitment of two hundred thousand dollars from them, with a similar promise of more if we find a successful path to gun crimes. Dan McVay helped me navigate to the right people for that. Through the US attorney's office, I found forty thousand dollars, the FBI Los Angeles Metro Task

Force on Violent Gangs is giving me eighty thousand, and DEA is giving me a hundred thousand. So we're good for up to about six hundred grand."

"Are you crazy, Jack? Who authorized you to do this? They can't just write you a check! Can they just write you a check? They can't just write you a check. Six hundred grand—are you crazy, Jack? Where does that money go? Do we have to pay this back? Are you crazy, Jack?"

"You sort of authorized me, sir. But each agency will give us a written contract that goes to Chief of Police Fuller and the city attorney for signature. The money goes to LAPD as a line item on our budget only accessible by me, or whoever the chief assigns. Basically, when we spend money, we get an invoice and the money is drawn off that line item."

"Let's meet with Chief Fuller. I can't believe there's really going to be a line item on the LAPD budget that says 'Lieutenant Jack Adams.' I want to make sure we're not going out of bounds. This is a lot of money, Jack. I have to see him tomorrow at eleven; meet me at his office."

"Will do, sir. See you then."

"Six hundred thousand dollars . . . are you crazy, Jack?"

As Lieutenant Adams walked out of the headquarters building, Deputy Chief Nelson wondered how it would feel to make things happen. To take charge, make decisions on his own and engineer situations. He found he was admiring the work Adams was doing. At first, he saw Adams as someone he needed to watch closely and keep a tight rein on, but now that they were in the thick of it he found himself admiring the courage to make decisions and make things happen.

He wondered if Adams ever struggled with the fear that he might be wrong or might make a mistake, like he did. He wondered if Adams ever played it safe. *Probably not.*

#

Preparing for the meeting with Chief of Police Fuller found Adams deep in thought with the details he believed the chief would need to know. Everything seemed clear to Adams. His path continued to be straight: help those who needed care and arrest those who broke the law. But he knew from experience that the checks and balances of leadership rarely exposed a linear path to the final decision. So many different perspectives, competing goals, and ulterior motives. And in Los Angeles, the poison of politics and the ensuing corruption.

Damn. Walking through those double doors again, Adams felt like everyone was staring at him like he's the only man in Victoria's Secret. The elevator ride to the tenth floor felt like it took a month. Adams knew everyone was wondering why he was there. *Probably in trouble. Might get fired.* If nothing else, he was going to walk out with only half his ass intact.

Adams walked into the outer office of the chief of police and saw the chief's door was closed, but the chief's adjutant, Lieutenant Jim Dawson, was there to greet him. "Hi, Jack. Chief Fuller and Chief Nelson are both here and waiting for you. Think you stirred something up. Go on in, the door's not locked."

"Shit."

"What was that, Jack?"

"Ah, nothing. Just another day."

"Hey, Jack, come on in," Chief Nelson welcomed him. "Chief Fuller and I were just talking about you."

That's exactly what I was afraid of.

Chief of Police Fuller looked comfortable sitting behind his desk, his ever-present cup of coffee in front of him. "Lieutenant, Chief Nelson was briefing me on your efforts to raise money to support wiretaps. I understand you've raised six hundred thousand dollars. Is that right?"

"Yes, Chief."

"Well, that's quite an accomplishment, Lieutenant. I remember our talking about that, but I didn't realize we were moving forward with that just now."

"Right now I just have commitments, sir. In order to finalize and move the money, the paperwork will come to you for your approval and your signature, and we will probably need the city attorney's signature. You're the boss and you have to give the ultimate authorization." As soon as Adams said that, he thought it sounded good. Like he didn't really do it—like he was just thinking about it.

The ensuing silence in the room, however, made Adams uncomfortable, so he finished his presentation. "I have a US attorney on board and I'm able to pull one of the FBI agents, Bill O'Reilly, from one of our Gang task forces to oversee the wiretap process. He has a lot of experience with pen registers and wiretaps and works with the federal monitoring centers. He was stationed overseas and is pretty comfortable crossing jurisdictional boundaries. He already has contacts with the security departments of the major phone carriers."

Chief of Police Fuller mulled that over for a second. "So, Jack . . . I'm constantly over at City Hall begging for money. I can barely keep this place running, and you drop a few dimes and voila—six hundred grand. Is that about right?"

"I want to make you proud, Chief. And Chief Nelson told me not to ask you for money."

"I see. Well, keep up the good work, Lieutenant."

"That's it?" Adams was confused.

"Yeah, that's it. Did you need anything else, Lieutenant?"

"No, sir. I have a lot to do today, so I better get to it." Adams couldn't get out of Chief Fuller's office fast enough.

Fuller sighed and leaned back on the back legs of his chair as he smiled at Deputy Chief Nelson. "Steve, your lieutenant's a good man. He just gets out in front of things a little before we're comfortable. The guy has a good heart, and he means well. He just irritates people sometimes. Well, maybe all the time. But I gotta tell ya, I've never seen anyone get things done the way he does. Wish we had a bunch of those."

"I get it, George, and I do support him. I'm wondering if I should pull the reins a little and have him brief me daily."

"Man, I doubt it. I don't want to tell you what to do, Steve, but with a guy like that, I'd let him run full speed. We can always do damage control later. So far, I've never seen that we have a need to clean anything up. He's opinionated, but aren't we all? He just makes other people, like us, feel anxious because we're not used to moving at that pace. For a lieutenant, he just doesn't see all the block walls other people see. He just knocks stuff down and moves on."

#

As the chief's door closed behind him, Adams stopped and took a deep breath. Lieutenant Jim Dawson looked up from his paperwork and asked, "How'd it go, Jack? Looks like you still got most of your butt."

"Not sure, Dawson. In and out, but not sure if I'm in trouble or not."

"If you were in trouble, you'd know it. Chief Fuller doesn't pull any punches. From what I heard, they're just trying to figure out how you're getting so much done in such a short time. And doing stuff no one else even knows how to do. Then there's something about you raising money to finance one of your operations—never heard of such a thing. You're financing your own operations? Who are you, anyway?"

"Yeah, right. I'm a nobody and you'll be a chief before you know it, Jim. And when you're sitting in that big office, I'll still be pounding the pavement and eating barbecue off the trunk of my car. Be safe, Jim."

"Be safe, Jack."

Adams stopped at the door. "Hey, Jim? You're a good guy. You're ugly, but you're a good guy. You ever need anything out in the the streets, drop a dime and I'll take care of you."

"Ditto, Jack. And Jack, I don't think you're supposed to call people ugly—political correctness and all." Dawson had a big smile on his face, teasing and hoping to ease up Adams's mood.

Jack thought about that and responded, "I'm thinking you're probably right, Jim. From now on I'll call you 'facially challenged.' "

Adams was out the door in a second, double-timed it to the elevator, and flew out of the double glass doors of the building. He turned to look over his shoulder to make sure no one was chasing him as he left the golden tower.

"Hey, Mac, it's Jack. Just wanted to give you a call. Somehow I survived the chief of police and Chief Nelson and I'm out the door and escaping. I think I got away."

"Damn, Jack, you're not afraid of anything. I've seen you! Why does that building scare you so much?"

"You don't understand, Mac. Facing someone in an alley with a gun is nothing like walking in that building. By the way, I'm bringing Bill O'Reilly over from the FBI. He's the new addition to Gold Rush. He'll be our wiretap expert."

#

Adams parked his Mustang GT in front of Gold Rush and hoped they had donuts inside. "Mac, and the rest of you Gold Rush knuckleheads, this is Bill O'Reilly of the infamous FBI. He's going to be helping us with the pen registers and wiretaps. Mac, I'd like you to sit down with Bill and lay out everything you have with Cuto and the Northeast Division double homicide. I'd like that to be our first incursion into wiretaps, because it's our strongest case and we have the most background on it. Then lay out the other homicides we have and move forward with those as soon as you're able. Don't worry about moving slowly, Mac, or one at a time. Push forward hard and get taps on everything if you're able. I'll do my best to keep the money rolling in."

Adams turned to Agent O'Reilly. "Bill, try and work through Roger Gibson, the US attorney we have on board. If you need to shop attorneys, please let me know. We'll do what we need to do, but I don't want to alienate Gibson. We're already walking on eggshells."

O'Reilly had a pleasant and easygoing personality that meant he didn't seem fazed by challenges or hard work. He played some semipro baseball after college, one of those guys that was comfortable in any setting and immediately fit in. He just seemed to take everything in stride like it was no big deal. He also gave the impression of an incredibly confident and capable man, and he knew a lot about baseball. Best of all, Adams seemed to like him.

FBI Agent Bill O'Reilly stepped right up to assume his position with the team. "I know Gibson and he's a good guy. He's not afraid to extend a single into a double, and if he sees you're good rounding the bases, he'll send you to third. I think we're fine with him. Don't take this wrong, but I think he's more comfortable working with the FBI at the federal level than with the LAPD. That means I might be able to help you get your prosecution filings, also."

O'Reilly had hit a sensitive issue but presented it tactfully. Adams believed he was going to fit in just fine. "I don't think Agent Matt Kidder down in San Diego has gotten to all the US attorneys to bad-mouth you yet, so Gibson may still think kindly of you. I think Kidder is still busy reaching out to every FBI agent in the world telling them how you kicked him to the curb and stole his robbery case."

Perfect. O'Reilly has a sense of humor.

With that, O'Reilly jumped right in and started to make things happen. "Detective McClain, I'm going to reach out and start reserving some computer stations at one of the federal monitoring centers. Sometimes these warrants come in hot and heavy, and the monitoring centers can be pretty short on space sometimes. I'm not sure which center will be available, but I'll work on setting it up in LA or as close to LA as I can. As soon as we have a phone tap online, we'll need some detectives to assign there to work with the monitors, so you may need to add another couple people to your staff. After that, I know you have surveillance assets to move on hot information as it comes in, but you'll need a pretty strong investigative staff to follow up on any clues and info that come out of the taps."

"My mom is the only one who calls me Detective McClain. For you, Bill, of the infamous FBI, call me Mac." McClain just realized that Gold Rush was beginning to grow by leaps and bounds. *This ain't Kansas anymore.*

Lieutenant Adams was just handed an expansion of the Gold Rush plan. "Mac, I didn't really want to make our team bigger, but Bill's right. I'm thinking about pulling Dave Decker and Maddie Hill over from 77th Gangs to run with the monitor spots. That's going to end up being the key position for us moving forward and we need sharp, aggressive people there. It's going to hurt them at 77th because their caseload is so big, and losing two detectives will be tough, but they have to come from somewhere and I need the best. See if you can find a couple Gang cops to loan to 77th Gang Homicide to at least give them a hand, even if they're just gophers. Also, give some thought on expanding your crew here with an investigative arm to follow up on info coming from the taps. Surveillance should be able to help a lot, but you'll need more support staff, more detectives. I'm betting it's going to get pretty overwhelming pretty fast. I'm thinking you should pull in four more detectives for now, but obviously no more from 77th. We can go up or down later. Decide where you want to house them, because I'd like them to all be together in the same place. Like all your other jobs, you'll run them also."

"Got it, Jack. I'll give you four names as quick as I can, but as to finding workspace for them, that's gonna be tough. Agent O'Reilly, if you've got some time now, we can sit down and start going through the cases."

"That's good, but I think we'd better use my office on Wilshire. In order to do this, we need a lot of room to plot and chart information. I have two agents who have worked with me in the past that I think I can pull in. This is a lot more work than what you might think. With your permission, Lieutenant, I'll tap them as a resource. Also, I can make room there for your new investigative team."

Adams wanted to move fast but was cautious about overstaffing. "Why don't we hold off until we get something on the board that I can see? I'm not averse to bringing in your two agents, Bill, but I want to wait until it's necessary. I do think the FBI building would be great for the new office space. If you can firm that up, that would be great."

"I'll keep Gold Rush until we close tonight, Mac. You and Bill head to his office and set up a new home for us. That will be headquarters for Gold Rush from now on. Although you oversee everything, you run the op center here at Gold Rush, have Dave Decker run the federal monitor center, and put one of the four new detectives in charge at Gold Rush Headquarters. Once you pick the four new detectives, house them there from now on."

"Roger that, Lieutenant. I'll work with O'Reilly today and then get four new detectives to our new headquarters ASAP. Do I have permission to pull them out of their divisions?"

"Yep, and lay Chief Nelson's name on their captains. Apologize to the captains but get them over there within the next few days." Adams was sure Chief Nelson would want him to expand the detail in order to get the guns on the table for the mayor's photo op as quick as possible. *Pretty* sure.

„Okay, Lieutenant. I'll be back here at Gold Rush early tomorrow."

CHAPTER TWENTY-NINE
THE RUSSIAN CONNECTION

The next day started slowly. Gloomy and cool, the sky looked like rain, which was always a welcome sight. Rain in Los Angeles washed down the streets, the sidewalks, and all the homeless encampments, which the city politicians failed to do. The smell of urine washed down the street with the rain. It even washed the police cars for a nice change.

Detective McClain and Julie Barr had teamed up in the same car today and were the first to get to Gold Rush. It was 9 o'clock in the morning, the time marked on the glass door for Gold Rush to open, but no customer had ever been there before eleven or so. Halverson and Rand were en route in the van and Torres was only minutes away. Andrews was a couple hours behind everyone else because he had to take care of personal business. Working so many hours day and night, policemen often find it hard to get personal business like banking done. Every now and then, you have to take the time to take care of your responsibilities.

A black Mercedes-Benz sedan with dealer plates and tinted windows was already in the parking lot. As McClain and Barr approached the door, the driver of the Mercedes left his car and followed them to the glass door. A female passenger remained in the car.

Julie Barr found the grip of her Glock .45 caliber handgun in her waistband and gripped it tightly as she walked through the door. McClain and Barr walked through the narrow gate at the end of the counter, then closed the gate. "Good morning, can I help you?" McClain offered.

The customer who followed them in was young, maybe twenty-five, with jet-black hair and striking features. He was dressed in black shirt and slacks and presented a cocky smile.

Barr felt apprehensive and sat at her desk, sliding her handgun from under her jacket and holding it in her lap. She had learned long ago to trust her instincts when it came to her safety. "Good morning. I have something to sell. You buy shit, right?" The customer seemed to have a Russian accent, although neither McClain nor Barr were experts in this. McClain hoped all the cameras were running. They didn't usually turn them off when they left for the night, but you never know.

"Yes, sir. We buy and sell gold and jewelry. How can I help you?" McClain wasn't ready to be the front man for the business, but sometimes you just have to step up and do the job at hand.

"I have a gun to sell. You buy guns, right?"

"Not usually, sir. But sometimes we make exceptions."

McClain remembered that Halverson and Rand were en route in the van and he didn't want to burn them. "Julie, would you call Jim and Mike and let them know I can't meet with them right now? Ask them to come by in about twenty minutes."

Picking up the phone and dialing, Barr hoped they would get the right message. "Hi, Mike, it's Julie. Mac said not to come over right now. He's busy with a customer and can't see you for about twenty minutes."

"Are you in danger, Julie?" In his mind, Rand was already spooling up a rescue operation and hit the gas pedal of the van, racing toward Gold Rush. Rand spun his finger in the air to signal Halverson to gear up.

"Oh, my God, you just never know. We just have an early customer that Mac wants to work with. His girlfriend's a little shy, though; she's waiting in his car out front. I guess we're all a little late getting here today. Our bad."

"We're going to stand by on the street with eyes on you. We'll be careful not to get burned by the female in the car. Does that work?"

"Sure does. I know I can always count on you. See you in a bit. Would you let the other guys know also?"

"You mean surveillance?"

"Yeah. Tell those bastards not to be bothering me this morning. I'll call them when I'm ready. I'm sick of them staring at my ass. Although, you can't blame them."

"Damn it!" Rand yelled to Halverson. "Gold Rush has a customer and Julie told us to stand by until he leaves. They don't want to burn us, but something's wrong. Julie's on edge. Get geared up in case we have to engage."

Rand parked the van one building away from Gold Rush on the opposite side of the street. He reached out and adjusted the side mirror so he could see the front of Gold Rush. Halverson fell into the rear of the van and pulled a tactical vest over his head. He slid his radio into the vest pocket and placed the earpiece into his ear. After he slung a 12-gauge shotgun over his shoulder and pulled on loose-fitting tan gloves, he yelled up to Rand, "I'm staying back here, Mike, and I'll go out the rear doors. You take either front door you want."

Halverson placed Rand's tactical vest on the front passenger seat and laid his Colt AR15 rifle on the floor between the front seats. Rand's vest was already equipped with extra magazines for his rifle and for his .45 caliber handgun.

Rand got on the radio to the surveillance units. "35G12 to 5K3 and 5K5."

"5K3, go ahead."

"35G12, there's an early customer inside with a female passenger seated in their car in the parking lot. We're just arriving and Mac and Julie are inside alone. Something's up and we're playing this careful, so be geared up if it hits the fan. If it does, we'll bring the van in first and block the driveway. You lay back a second then come in behind us. We'll do this in the parking lot."

"5K3, roger. We're on scene now and we're suiting up. We see a black sedan, a Mercedes, I think, in the lot. Can't see inside the car—it's all blacked out. He must have pulled in before we even got here. I'll pull 5K5 in to cover the rear and we'll both bring long guns in. I have 5K8 out here today and I'll send him out on countersurveillance to see if there's anyone else laying back."

The office door unexpectedly opened, and Torres stepped in to see the customer at the counter. He suspected someone may be inside when he saw the Mercedes in the lot. What a terrible day to be late. "Hi, guys, sorry I'm late. Don't tell Jack; he'll fire me this time." Torres worked his way through the gate then closed it behind him.

The customer revealed a brushed stainless-steel Smith and Wesson semi-automatic handgun that he placed on the counter. It was loaded with a full magazine. McClain wanted to take control of the gun and immediately picked it up off the counter, pulling it out of the customer's reach.

"Do you mind if I unload it and look at it?" Dropping the fully loaded magazine from the gun and locking the slide back, he extracted the round that was loaded into the barrel. The gun was hot.

McClain began his inspection. "What do you want for the gun? It's not stolen, right?"

"No, it's not stolen. One thousand dollars."

Torres picked up on the tension in the room and saw that Barr was sitting at her desk with both her hands in her lap. There was only one reason for that; he knew her hands must be wrapped around her handgun. Torres walked around to the filing cabinet purposely placed to provide a shield from customers who were standing on the other side of the counter. The drawers were placed on the opposite side, allowing Torres to step behind the file cabinet and open a drawer. Drawing his handgun out of the customer's sight, he held his position while pretending to go through the files. His shooting position would be over the top of the cabinet. "Anyone see that bill of lading from the Concorde? Greek Customs is looking for it and I can't find it."

Barr helped to keep the tactical odds in their favor. "No, but you stay in that file cabinet until you find it. We need it this morning."

McClain didn't really care what he paid for the gun but had to play the part. "Yeah, I can give you a good price, but not that much. I can do seven hundred. Does that work for you?"

"If you pay in cash, I will take eight hundred." This guy seemed really intense, really serious.

McClain examined the gun again. "Well, I can't do that much. These Smith .45s have such a big grip that most people don't like them. Hell, most people can't wrap their hands around them. But I'll do seven fifty. I'll meet you in the middle."

Barr became more nervous as each minute passed. Concealing her handgun, she stood up from her desk and positioned herself next to the counter closer to McClain, being careful not to block Torres. She wanted to take the advantage away from the person on the other side of the counter who could use the counter as a shield if he stooped down. Without Rand in the warehouse, there was no one else to help. Holding her gun in her right hand below the counter, she pretended to be admiring the gun McClain was holding.

After the customer agreed on the price, McClain opened the safe while blocking it with his body. He placed the gun in the safe and removed seven hundred and fifty dollars. "Okay, here's your money. Nice doing business with you. We're interested in purchasing more guns for our next shipment to Africa, so if you have any more, let me know."

"No paperwork, no problems?" The customer seemed to be testing McClain.

"No, we're good. Hope to see you again."

As the customer walked out, Barr picked up her cell phone and called Rand. "Mike, the guy's leaving now. Is surveillance out there?"

"Yeah, they're already set up on Benton Way."

"Okay, let me get on the radio."

"35G13 to surveillance units, black Mercedes leaving now. Take it away and stay with it until further. We need this guy."

"5K3 and 5K5 are on the Mercedes, northbound on Benton Way. 5K8 will stay on scene."

Rand and Halverson opened the roll-up door and brought the van into the warehouse. Both officers exited the van fully suited up for battle with grave expressions.

McClain knew this was his responsibility and his failure not to maintain stronger discipline. He had just let the lieutenant down and jeopardized everyone's safety. "We all fucked up. The lieutenant's going to kill us. Listen, you guys, we can't roll in here at 0900. We need to be inside and set up by 0800. We never know when a random person will wander in, and we have to be more prepared than this. We would've been screwed if shit happened. We had no backup. Rand and Halverson were still outside."

"I don't know what it is, but that guy scared the shit out of me," Barr added.

"I had him, Julie. I would have saved your life." Torres was taking the situation too lightly for McClain, who was still shaken. Not by what happened—no, he was shaken by his leadership failure. The lieutenant had left him responsible for the officer's safety and he'd screwed up. He had endangered the other officers.

Taking deep breaths and feeling terrible, McClain was gratefully distracted by his phone ringing. "Detective McClain, it's Paul Stanford on 5K3. We've got the black Mercedes. He's northbound and we just got on the Glendale freeway into Glendale."

"Roger that, Paul. Stay with this car as long as necessary. He's a player, and there's no plates on that car. Let's ID everywhere he goes and everyone he sees. Just leave one of your units here. If we need you back, I'll call you."

Knowing he couldn't avoid the inevitable, McClain opened his phone and swiped to the Favorites page. Sliding his finger over Lieutenant Adams's name was painful. As the phone rang, McClain took a deep breath.

"Lieutenant, it's McClain. Sorry if I woke you up. Wanted to brief you on a gun buy today. Nothing out of the ordinary, I guess, except this young guy shows up in a black Mercedes wearing a black suit. Some kind of European nationality, I think. Maybe even Russian. I don't know how he came on us, but we'll figure that out. We bought a Smith forty-five from him, but this guy's a player, Jack. I'm working up a profile on him and I'll let you know if anything pans out."

"Good work, Mac. Wonder how he came upon us? I'm proud of everything you're doing, Mac. Keep it up."

"Well, don't be too proud, Lieutenant. I screwed things up this morning and I need to beg forgiveness—"

Adams cut McClain off mid-sentence. "Yeah, well, you're forgiven. But do it better next time. Get back to work, Mac. I can't be talking to you all day. I have other things to do, you know."

"Be safe, Lieutenant. I'm going over to Karen's in Torrance tonight. She said you were there yesterday. Her dad really likes you."

"Hard to blame the guy. Tell her I said hi."

#

Putting the whole team to work on the background investigation revealed a Russian Mafia connection that got everyone's attention. "Lieutenant, it's McClain. Sorry to bother you again. We got some results already from the black Mercedes. It had dealer plates that came back as invalid. Guessing the plate is bogus. Dealer plates are just paper plates and probably pretty easy to make. Surveillance took the guy home and we crossed his name to DMV and got a driver's license. We think this guy's name is Aleks Antonov, twenty-six-year-old Russian national connected to the Russian Mafia here in the US. His residence comes back to the apartment building in Glendale. We ran the building address for other names and it looks like everyone in the whole building has Russian names, like they've taken over the building. It's tough to track a lot of the connections with these people because we don't track them like we do street gangsters. Can you press your FBI contacts in Organized Crime to give us a hand? Or should we pull O'Reilly on this? The gun he sold us is listed as a 'lost or stolen' from two years ago. Possibly taken during a burglary in Burbank. Nothing else attached to it."

"Okay, Mac. Let's hold off a little on tapping FBI sources until we know a little more. Let's see if we cross paths with him again. I don't want to put them in play unless it's really necessary. If anything else develops with this guy, we'll look at it again and talk to Agent O'Reilly. He's a good man and we can trust him. Does that hold okay with you?"

"Sure, LT. I just know this guy's a player. I wish you had been here when this went down to get a feel for him. Who knows if he'll even cross our path again, though. I think you're right in not putting in a lot of work until we see more reason. But the undercurrent is, I don't want to cut this guy loose."

CHAPTER THIRTY
TURNING THE CORNER

Adams had set up a meeting at his office in the FBI building on Wilshire with Detective McClain, US Attorney Roger Gibson, ATF Agent Dan McVay, and FBI Agent Bill O'Reilly. "Okay, Bill. I'm anxious to move forward with this 'Cuto' from MS13, Miguel Aguilar, and get on his phone. "

"There shouldn't be too much of a problem, Lieutenant Adams," Agent O'Reilly offered. "I've got space reserved at one of our phone monitoring centers just outside of the city on the east side of LA, so now I'd better request to schedule at least one of our federal monitors. Your funding is in place, right?"

Adams was happy that O'Reilly was pressing forward on his own. "Yeah, Bill, we're ready to go. Mac, you have the lead, so review the case with O'Reilly and let's get moving on this. I'd like to get a tap on Cuto's phone as quick as we can, so I'll start pulling more people in for you. Bill, if you set up the federal monitor, I'll set up two detectives to work split shifts."

McClain was quickly becoming overwhelmed in the back of the warehouse trying to follow up on the leads generated from Gold Rush. He wanted to make sure Adams was ready for building the team larger. "Lieutenant, we talked about growing our base of detectives here at Gold Rush and possibly housing them at the FBI Wilshire building. O'Reilly has committed four agents now, two for Gold Rush follow-ups and two to work wiretap follow-ups. I'm working with him on when we think we need them in place. Right now they're on hold. I'm pulling in the four LAPD detectives, two from West LA and two from Rampart Division in Central Bureau. Dan McVay is giving us two ATF agents, so they'll be doing the legwork on the guns wherever they come into play. We'll be housing everyone here at the Wilshire Boulevard FBI building. O'Reilly has two conference rooms assigned to us for this. I'll have to be at Gold Rush most of the time, but I can see the need to split my time between there and here at FBI."

Adams appreciated the plan being set in place. "That sounds good, Mac. I want everything we need without overstaffing. People sitting around are no value to us."

"Wow, this is moving really fast now, LT. There's not going to be any jurisdictional issues, is there?" McClain preferred things very clean.

"No, Mac. O'Reilly and I have hashed through this as much as we can. I'll continue to be the leader and we'll call it a federal task force. With my federal status, everyone will work under me. You will have investigative lead on everything Gold Rush, but I want you to focus on the big picture, like making sure we're keeping our ears open for the connection between MS13 working as enforcers and tax collectors for the Mexican Mafia. O'Reilly will manage the wiretaps and follow-up investigations for you. Dan McVay will manage gun investigations for you. I'll be talking to LA County sheriffs to grease the skids in case we need to partner with them also. We're all going to cross paths, but I think we can work together when that happens. Your biggest job, Mac, is to have an eye on everything. I don't want you to try and do everything yourself, but I do want you to have an eye on everything. I will try and remain the big picture guy, but if I start getting in the weeds and stepping on your toes, you need to tell me, Mac."

When Adams finished his call, Agent O'Reilly stepped up to the plate to take control of the wiretap side of the investigation. "Detective McClain, I get that you linked Miguel Aguilar, Cuto, of MS13 to the double homicide over in your LAPD's Northeast Division. Although we only have the one gun buy for him, with the 187 connection I can move forward with that wiretap right now. Attorney Gibson and I have discussed the case and he's ready to approve it. Keep in mind that in every case, one wiretap always expands into others, so you'll need to be ready to expand operations at a moment's notice."

Lieutenant Adams was eager to set things into motion. "Roger, if we're good to go on this case, I would like to move forward now. There's no reason to ease into this."

US Attorney Roger Gibson was all business and appreciated someone with the courage to make decisions. "Sounds good, Lieutenant. I have the affidavits ready for Detective McClain and we can hit the ground running."

Gold Rush thus moved forward to hit its next milestone: a tap on the phone of an MS13 gang member involved in a double homicide in Los Angeles with the gun in custody. This was the exact situation that Gold Rush had been designed for.

Adams saddled up in the Ford Explorer parked in the FBI's lot. He felt confident the team was moving forward as he headed to the LAPD's 77th Street Division to meet with Gang Detective Dave Decker.

"Good to see you, Decker. How's your brown-on-Black effort going?"

"Hey, Lieutenant. So far, at least a handful of these murders look like brown-on-Black, so it feels like I'm pushing a heavy weight up the mountain. I'm sure we won't be able to prosecute them as a racial crime."

Detective Dave Decker already knew in his mind what the Big Hazard gangsters were up to, but he believed it wouldn't go anywhere in the current political climate. Everyone knew that Big Hazard was making racial hits; it was just that no one was talking about it because of Los Angeles politicians.

"Let me run some preliminary info past Chief Nelson. I'd like to move forward with an expanded investigation into Big Hazard, some kind of federal or civil rights case that we can use as an umbrella over all the shootings we're looking at. But that's a big wish in Los Angeles. I'm really doubting the mayor and City Council will allow it. But I still have to do my job and present it. But before you go any further, let me hit Nelson up. This isn't the best time for me to be standing in front of his desk talking about this, but I'll figure something out."

"Lieutenant, you already know they don't allow anything in the press about brown-on-Black or Black-on-brown. Only white guys are allowed to be racists in this city. You really think this will go anywhere?"

"I don't, Dave. But I'm going to do my job anyway. Stand by until you hear from me. And Dave, I've got a new job for you and Maddie. It's going to take pretty much all your time, so I want you to begin preparing to hand off all your cases. I'll be meeting with our bosses to arrange it. And don't take on any new 187s. You're off the rotation until further notice."

"Uh, Lieutenant? You know I'm holding about a hundred homicides, right?"

"I do, Dave. But something is on the horizon, and as soon as it blossoms I'll hook you up. Probably within the week. In the meantime, I just want to give you a heads-up that I'll be pulling you and Maddie for a special detail in the very near future, so start developing a plan to hand all your cases off."

"Wow, that's a big one. But okay, sir, you're the boss. I'll tell Maddie."

With an ever-growing amount of things on his plate, Adams needed to connect with Detective McClain to delegate more tasks to his team. "Mac, I'm driving over to Gold Rush. I'll be driving the FBI surf wagon. Can we meet there in about thirty minutes?"

"I just pulled in, Jack, so I'll wait for you. Busy here right now. We bought two guns within forty minutes of each other already today."

Driving toward Gold Rush, Adams set his phone on the console and used the quiet time to catch up on his briefings with Deputy Chief Nelson. "Good afternoon, Chief Nelson, it's Adams. I have something to run past you."

"Good to hear from you, Jack. Will we be meeting with the chief of police today?"

"No, sir. The US attorney, Roger Gibson, is preparing the affidavits to get up and running on our first wiretap. The MS13 gangster we got for the double homicide in Northeast Division. The gun he sold us is good for the shootings, and even though we're not ready to move forward with an arrest, we're confident he's good for it. This is exactly the situation we built this effort for. I'm pulling two gang detectives from 77th to staff the federal monitoring center so that they can work on real-time information. They'll be deploying surveillance units and whatever investigative staff they need to work on information as it comes in over the wiretaps. I'm also going to pull two from West LA and two from Rampart Division to staff the FBI office for follow-up investigations. The FBI is giving us Agent O'Reilly plus four others, and ATF is giving us Agent McVay plus two. I dropped a dime to my counterpart in the LA Sheriff's Department to let him know I may be asking them for support resources in the future. I can see needing some of their surveillance assets, but I already know not to commit to LASD without Chief Fuller's say so. This is a really big step toward the endgame of guns on the table for the mayor's press conference. The difference is that the guns we're going to put on this particular table are ones that will really make a difference. I know the mayor only cares about the picture of the guns on the table to get him votes, but to us, we're turning it into something that actually makes Los Angeles safer."

"Okay, Jack. I want you to hear me really clear on this: I trust you to do your job, but I want you constantly on top of everything we're doing. I know you delegate this stuff, but you stay on top of everything, Jack."

"That goes without saying, sir."

"And with LASD, I know you have a good relationship with them but when it comes to partnering on this with the sheriffs, there's more to it than you may know. There's long-standing block walls between the Los Angeles City Council and the Los Angeles County Board of Supervisors, and with that comes questions about who pays for what. It's not set up like you're doing with the feds. The mayor and City Council would have to be read in, along with the County Board of Supervisors. That means two separate Los Angeles political bodies with competing interests and no love for each other coming together to agree on you and the Sheriff's Department working together. Give that some thought before you rely on that resource."

"Hmmm, will do, sir. Not sure I have that kind of time, and I certainly would have to give a lot of thought to the safety of bringing the city and county politicians into our efforts. I'm certainly not ready to brief them on what we're doing. My goal is to wait until we're done, then brief them and let them take credit for it. Let them stand in front of the cameras and tell everyone what a great job they did."

The tactics involved in working around Los Angeles politicians become frustratingly hazy at times. Adams believed that all of law enforcement should be free from political interference, but he knew he had to be very careful even in voicing that opinion. Things had changed and policemen now worked for politicians, not the public.

Even with a history of political and criminal corruption, Los Angeles city councilmen carried a lot of weight in the city, even after the recent arrests of several councilmen for corruption. The courage and leadership skills of those few in law enforcement who stand up to politicians for what is right is always reflected in high morale on the part of the officers in their organization, along with much higher levels of success in reducing crime and serving the public. But sooner or later, the wrath of the politicians will land squarely on their heads, and Adams knew his day was coming. By keeping his command staff in the loop, he hoped to temper how hard he would get hit.

"One more thing, Chief. I'd like to brief you on an issue that keeps rearing its ugly head. The brown-on-Black issue with Big Hazard. We've been looking at Big Hazard a lot lately and it's clear that the situation exists. If we had the opportunity to address some of these crimes for what they really are, racial attacks, it would sure make it easier to identify the suspects and to prosecute them. Right now, we're constantly battling the issue of proving intent and motive because we're not allowed to present it accurately as racially motivated crimes. I know it's not popular, sir, but I gotta believe we should just be laying the facts out for what they are."

Adams could hear the large sigh on the phone and felt uncomfortable with the silence that ensued before Deputy Chief Nelson responded. "Jack, I get it. But we are in Los Angeles. This is a very specific political environment, and this issue is one that is just not tenable. Speaking of brown-on-Black or vice versa is just not a tenable subject."

"Yes, sir. I understand. We're not necessarily lying for our politicians, but we're not telling the truth, either. That situation is hard to explain in court when we are under oath, so we pretty commonly lose cases and let criminals walk instead of being forthcoming with our testimony. You know I support your decision, but I'm guessing there will come a time when we're backed into a corner and the truth will have to be spoken."

"Okay Jack, I get it. But let's kick that can down the road a bit and wait until it's unavoidable. Keep your eyes on this, Jack, and be prepared to address it in the future. I know it's important to you. Not because of the prosecution problems, but because your character balks at someone not allowing you to do the right thing. For now, put it to the side until we're in a better position to address it. When that happens, you'll have my support."

"Thanks, Chief."

"Be safe, Jack."

A moment later, Adams was back on the phone that was consistently glued to his ear. "Hey, Mac, I'm going to pass on coming by Gold Rush. I'm going to swing by to see Karen Aoki at her folks' house, but I need you to do a couple things. Call the area captains at West LA and Rampart Divisions and pull the two Gang detectives you chose from each one. Assign them to our new conference rooms at the FBI building—let's call it Gold Rush North—beginning Monday morning at 0900. Call Agent O'Reilly and have him get clearance and parking for them. They'll be briefed Monday—need to know. They don't need to bring anything, just show up. Attire will continue to be suits while they're in the FBI building unless we decide differently in the future. Tell the captains the order comes from Deputy Chief Nelson and that they'll be gone for an unknown period. Unfortunately, we can't brief the captains on what they'll be doing."

"Okay, got it, Lieutenant. Me, being a nothing detective, I'm to tell these two captains that we're taking two of their senior Gang detectives without telling them why and without telling them for how long. I'm getting a lot of the dirty work lately, I see! These captains are going to be really pissed. Especially the need-to-know part."

"I'm teaching you to be a lieutenant, Mac. You're doing a great job. By the way, while you're giving all these captains the good news, also call the 77th Division captain and pull Detectives Dave Decker and Maddie Hill. For now, have them show up at FBI Wilshire Boulevard, Gold Rush North, but they'll be staffing the federal monitoring center listening to wiretaps as soon as Agent O'Reilly gets it set up. Don't tell the captain that, of course. And let's see if we can find some Gang officers to replace the six detectives and help out a little bit."

"Of course. Why would I tell the captains anything? I'm only stripping them of their resources that they can't do without. And after I do that, they know they're still going to be held accountable for clearing cases, even without their detectives. I'm sure the captains will have no problems with this at all! Hell, they'll probably want to take me out to lunch. I'm getting really good at taking stuff from these captains without telling them why or for how long. If this is what a lieutenant does, Jack, not sure I want your job."

#

"Mrs. Aoki, nice to see you. How is Karen?"

"Come in, Lieutenant Adams. Karen is Karen—never stops moving and eating all my food. We love having her at home, but it's not quiet here anymore. Lots of activity, lots of people coming and going. Firemen were here all day yesterday, police are everywhere. All I do is cook."

As Adams walked into the Aoki home, Karen was lying on the living room floor with an enormous smile. "LT! Hey, good to see you. You ready for me to come back to work? Is everything a mess without me there? Does Julie cry every single day? How are you guys even getting anything done?"

"Hi, Karen. Are you supposed to be doing sit-ups?"

"Of course, LT. You don't want me getting soft, do you? UCLA scheduled my ortho surgery on my hip, so I want to be in good shape for it. After surgery, I plan on kicking the physical therapist's butt when they send me to rehab. I'm going to make him cry like Julie always does trying to keep up with me."

Adams felt absolutely sure Aoki could come back to work today. "Well, we all look forward to getting you back. Just concentrate on your next surgery and then getting stronger. And Karen . . . just between you and me, everything *is* all screwed up without you. You need to get back as quick as you can."

"I knew it!" Aoki had a large smile on her face as Adams walked out of the house.

CHAPTER THIRTY-ONE
THE RUSSIAN GOES INTERNATIONAL

Each day that went by, the crew at Gold Rush learned to work better as a team. When the surveillance units saw the black Mercedes-Benz headed toward Gold Rush, they went on alert and started the wheels turning.

"5K3 to 35G11."

"35G11, go."

"5K3, the black Mercedes is back southbound on Benton Way approaching Gold Rush. Same driver. Looks like he's alone this time."

"35G11, roger that."

"Okay, you guys, that black Mercedes from last week is headed our way. Heads up." McClain walked back into the warehouse and closed the door to the outer office.

Torres took his position at the counter and Barr moved to his side. Halverson went back to his spot behind the file cabinet with his handgun at the ready, this time pissed off and slamming drawers trying to find an elusive file. Rand and Andrews positioned themselves behind the door to the warehouse while McClain manned the monitors, donning headphones to listen to the conversation.

"Hey, welcome back. Good to see you again." Torres appeared calm and welcoming while Barr did her best to appear busy reading a contract on the counter. Barr saw that the customer was carrying a backpack this time.

"Thank you. I have more to sell." Setting his backpack on the counter, Aleks Antonov removed a Sig Sauer P220 10mm in blue steel and laid it on the felt cloth Torres had spread out. This time, the slide was locked back and the emptied magazine had been removed from the gun.

Torres examined the handgun and asked the usual question, "Is it stolen?"

"No, not stolen. I don't bring you stolen guns. How much for this one?"

"It's a nice gun . . . what did you say your name was? Mine is Mark."

"My name is Anthony. How much for this one?" Torres did a great job soliciting a name from the customer, which reflected on the suspect's real name. Another step forward.

"I can do eight hundred. Are we good?"

Antonov considered for a moment, then replied, "Yeah, we are good, Mark."

They completed the exchange and Antonov asked, "How do you send these to Africa?"

Unexpectedly and without planning for this new situation, Torres unknowingly opened the door to a higher level of criminality. "We have our own containers. Forty-foot-high cubes. That just means they're a little bigger inside; they're a foot taller. The owner has another business where he owns a bunch of containers and leases them out of the Port of Los Angeles and we can always use whatever's available. We don't use the whole thing, of course, so the boss leases the container out but saves a little room for our stuff. Customs only inspects about five percent of containers, and we're already cleared through Homeland Security, so we never get inspected."

Torres used to work stacking shipping containers in the Port of Los Angeles prior to his time in the LAPD. A real job. Sometimes, a previous life helps out later.

McClain, watching the monitors from the warehouse and listening to the audio, was afraid Torres was revealing too much too fast. Someone illegally smuggling guns out of the country probably wouldn't be so open about the methods they used to do it. When Antonov didn't reply, McClain whispered, "Damn it. We're blown."

"Do you ever ship cars, Mark?" Antonov challenged Torres, who was now tap dancing around this whole situation.

"We haven't, but we could, I guess. If it fits in the container, we can ship it. I think probably two cars per container. I know we've shipped all kinds of stuff. But I don't think cars." Torres's answer seemed safe enough, and McClain felt a sense of relief that maybe everything was going to be okay.

"What is your name, beautiful?" Antonov showed an interest in Barr, who had been purposely ignoring him.

"My name's Julie."

"I own a business, Julie, and I'm always looking for beautiful women to work there. If you get tired of working here, let me know. Much more money. Much more fun."

Julie was already offended by Aleks before he ever opened his mouth. "I don't think so. I'm having all the fun I can stand right here."

Aleks came right back without missing a beat. "How much to ship cars, Julie? To Russia, to St. Petersburg?"

Wow, what a curve ball. "I just work here. You need to ask Mark." Ah, the cold shoulder. And Barr was really good at it.

"I'll find out for you, Anthony. I'll call the owner and get his input. Can I call you?" With a telephone number, they'd be able to further identify and connect to the suspect standing at the counter. McClain smiled at the effort and vowed to say something nice to Torres for a change.

"No, but I'll come back. Thank you."

And just like that, Aleks Antonov was out the door with his eight hundred dollars and down the street with the two surveillance units in tow. The second gun buy. One more to go.

"So, love blossoms," Torres rubbed it in with Barr.

"Blow me, Torres."

Only a policewoman could have such a sense of humor, until Torres responded, "You're such a dick."

McClain walked into the office from the warehouse. "I'm not sure what's happening, but we're not shipping cars, Torres. Do you remember we're supposed to buy guns? LT said he already got heat for the cell phones and other shit we bought."

"Just trying to make conversation with him, boss. As long as he's bringing in guns, what the hell? That's our second buy in to him."

"Well, be prepared to keep the conversation going. Call some shipping company and get some quotes to ship cars to Russia. If he comes in again, give him a price but drag him out. Tell him there's no containers available right now, that they're all leased out. We got two buys into him now; let's get the third for a federal filing." McClain immediately fell back on his job: get guns off the streets of Los Angeles and get Federal filings. Oh yeah, and the mayor's photo op. *Can't forget about that.*

The following morning, Gold Rush was once again visited by what they were calling the "Russian Connection."

"Hello, Mark, my friend. The cost of shipping cars to St. Petersburg?"

"Hey, Anthony. I've got a price sheet for you. It varies a little by weight and cargo line, but these figures are really close. It's the insurance that really costs us, and believe it or not, the weather and the time of year can push the price up. Then I learned that it may change a little day-to-day on the other end of the line. The docking prices in St. Petersburg seems to fluctuate for no reason. When it comes time, we'll get exact prices, but these are ballpark." Torres handed Antonov a billing form with "Gold Rush" heading upon which he had handwritten a group of figures he had obtained from Pacific Global Cargo. "How many cars do you need to ship, Anthony?"

"Twenty right now, but more in the future. Mercedes-Benzes, all new cars."

In the warehouse, McClain watched the interaction and began coloring outside the lines. Whispering to John Andrews, he said, "Let's see. An obvious player. Russian national, Russian Mafia. Selling guns. And now he's interested in shipping cars, new cars. Mercedes. Shipping them to Russia. What do you bet these are stolen cars?"

"You're probably right, sir. What should we do?"

"John, call Burglary Auto Theft and ask them if they have any scoop on stolen Mercedes, new ones, and if they have any scoop on Russians. Oh yeah, maybe something having to do with dealer plates on the cars, or bogus dealer plates."

Torres focused and got back in the game. "I still need to pick up some guns, Anthony. I have a shipment going out on Thursday to Durban Harbour in Africa and I have room in a container. What do you have for me?"

"I brought this one gun to sell. It is my brother's, and he no longer wants it. He has children in his house and it's not safe." From his backpack, Antonov withdrew a Sig Sauer P225 9mm. "Russians do not like German guns, anyway."

"This works perfect for us, Anthony. Eight hundred?" Torres was about to make the first case, the first federal case on three gun buys. A major milestone that Lieutenant Adams could use as ammunition to keep the effort moving forward, and keep funding coming in.

After exchanging the gun for the money, Antonov returned to the conversations about shipping cars. "How many cars can you ship at same time, Mark?"

"Well, it depends on how many containers we have available. I talked to the owner and he said he would rather send a large group all at once so he could maximize on his profit on the containers. I think the twenty you have now would qualify, so we can see how that goes and modify the plan in the future if we need to. So, figure at least ten containers." Torres followed through with McClain's instructions to stall the car shipping idea. "Here's my cell, Anthony. Call me tonight and I'll firm that up." Torres, the devious little genius with a cold cell phone, kept working toward capturing a phone number for Antonov.

John Andrews hung the phone up and approached McClain with a sly smile. "Detective McClain, Burglary Auto Theft says Mercedes are being stolen from car lots after they close and sometimes during test drives. In the test drives, the salesmen are robbed and pushed out of the car, but there's also been one rape of a female saleswoman in the car before they tossed her out and took the car. BAD said it's been going on for almost two years. The dealerships always require the prospective buyer to leave a copy of their driver's license, but in every case the license comes back bogus. These guys have some resources at the DMV. The highlight of the story is that none of the stolens have ever been recovered. That's got everyone confused. At first they thought it was an insurance scam, but it involves too many different car lots. They've hit car lots all over LA and Orange County. A whole bunch of different suspect descriptions. They have a lot of video from the car lots, but the suspects are always different and some of them are female. Some are listed as white, some Middle Eastern, some Hispanic. Kind of all over the map."

McClain saw where they had to go even before they got there. "Okay, John. When you can slip out of here, head over to BAD and see if you can look through the crime reports. I want you to watch every video they have. Look for our guy, Antonov, and tell me if the suspects fit any kind of pattern. If you're able, print out a still photo from each of the security videos and let's see if we come across any of them in the future. You may be there awhile, so don't be in a hurry. Be thorough and find the needle in the haystack. We just don't know what the needle is yet."

"Got it, sir. I'll take my lunch with me."

"Hey, John, one more thing. When you get outside, connect with the surveillance team. Tell them after they take this guy home, I want them to search the area around his apartment building. We're looking for any new Mercedes-Benzes with dealer plates. They could be on the street, but most likely in parking lots, on private property where they wouldn't accumulate parking tickets."

"Got it, boss."

McClain then realized that Gold Rush was getting off track with the stolen car case. He called up Adams for direction, thinking they might turn the case over to Burglary, Auto Theft and keep Gold Rush in the gun-buying business.

"Lieutenant, I need to brief you on something that's coming on our radar. It's not really clear, but I have a pretty good feel for it. We got this Russian guy—think I told you about him, the Russian Mafia guy. He sold us his third gun today, so that's our first federal case on three buys. Congratulations to us."

"Wow, great job, Mac! We really needed that. The pressure is building for us to make something happen or get off the pot."

"Well, we need to figure out how to file on this guy for the gun buys but not burn Gold Rush. I'm guessing you're not ready to close up shop yet. But there's another twist: he's asking questions about shipping cars to Russia. Torres laid some line on him that we get our guns out because we own containers to ship jewelry and gold to Africa and this guy jumped on that like crazy. He said he's got twenty new Mercedes to ship to Russia, but Torres was trying to stall him for a while. Surprisingly, the Russian stayed on the hook. We called BAD and they laid out a pattern of new Mercedes being stolen from dealer lots all over Southern Cal. Some a straight auto theft off the lot after hours, and some by carjacking the salesmen during a test drive. I tell ya, I think this guy is part of that crew. I can't connect him right now, but I think he's a player in this."

"Well, that's a new twist for us, Mac. We're supposed to be buying guns." Adams had started to sound a lot like Deputy Chief Nelson.

"Yeah, I got that, Jack. But I'm just feeling this is big stuff. I think we should keep this guy on the hook and see what develops. It's a Russian Mafia case; that falls under us in Gangs."

"Okay, Mac. Where does he have the twenty cars?"

"Not sure on that, but on a hunch I've got surveillance checking the area around that apartment building in Glendale where he lives. Maybe they jack the cars and park them near their house until they're ready to ship them. It would be pretty dangerous to group them in a warehouse. He told Torres they have twenty cars, though. It's doubtful they can hide twenty stolen Mercedes in plain sight surrounding where they live."

"Mac, for now let's try this: Tell your little buddy that we have a warehouse where we store containers down in Long Beach at the Port of Los Angeles. Let's keep this on the Long Beach side of the Vincent Thomas Bridge. Tell him we can store his cars for him until they're ready to ship. If they've been doing this awhile, they're probably already shipping cars but need a better shipper, so they're shopping. Maybe if we can store their cars for them in addition to shipping them, it would sway them to move over to us. Tell them to drop the cars off at Gold Rush and we'll take them from there. If it plays out, we'll store them until we're ready, then load them in cargo containers and ship them."

"This is crazy, Jack. How much should we tell them we're charging them?"

"Get a quote from another shipping company to make sure it's in line with what we already have, then triple the amount. That's what we charge. They know we're storing them and taking all the risk shipping them. They'll jump at the price."

"Okay, Lieutenant. We already have one quote and I'll get another, so come time to wrangle with this guy, we'll triple everything and say our costs have gone up."

#

The two surveillance units took their target back to Glendale, where they sat on the location for an hour to wait for any activity. With nothing happening, they begin their search of the area for Mercedes-Benz sedans with dealer plates.

"Detective McClain, this is Paul Stanford on 5K3. We got four new Mercedes with paper dealer plates up here in Glendale, all within three blocks of the Russian apartment complex. Every one of them is black. Should we call Glendale police?"

McClain thought about building the case that Lieutenant Adams had laid out. "No, let them sit, Paul. I need to talk to Lieutenant Adams. Take a photo of the VIN numbers on the dash, but try not to get caught. I don't want to get burned on this. Then let them go and pull out of the area."

After receiving the VIN numbers on the four cars, McClain discovered each car had previously been reported stolen by car dealerships. After a couple busy signals, McClain finally got through to Adams's cell phone. "Lieutenant, surveillance picked up four Mercedes with paper plates surrounding the Russian apartment complex. The VINs all come back to stolens. They match the reports of three after-hours stolens off car lots in LA County and one carjacking during a test drive out in Riverside. Apparently, they think the stolens are taken with some type of electronic device to override the computer. Mercedes can't be hardwired like old Chevys."

Adams saw more work about to fall onto his plate. "Wow. Well, let's just sit on this, Mac, until this guy comes back to Gold Rush. That's the only way to work this. Let them come to us and tell Torres not to be too anxious. We've already got the three gun buys into him, so I want to continue to play hard to get on the Mercedes. I'll grease the skids to store the cars in one of our parking structures, and I'll see if I can find a connection to obtaining cargo containers. My old partner at Harbor Division retired from LAPD and now he's a lieutenant at Port Police. Maybe he can help us. On the guns, let's move forward now with Agent O'Reilly and a wiretap—if you ever get a phone number, that is. In the meantime, it's time for me to brief Chief Nelson on the stolen car angle. That's gonna be fun. Are you busy, Mac? How about you brief Chief Nelson so I can finally go get something to eat?"

"I doubt that will fly, sir. I don't think deputy chiefs talk to detectives. I'm surprised he even talks to you. And you're the one getting lieutenant pay, anyway"

#

"Hey, Lieutenant Moss, how're the promotions going? You make captain yet?"

"Jack, when I am a captain, I'm going to fire you."

"It's good to have goals, Lieutenant Moss."

Stepping into Chief Nelson's office, Adams tried to persuade himself to be calm. Walking dark alleys was much easier than this. "Hi, Chief. You're working late again."

"Damn it, Jack, I always work late. I've told you that a hundred times. You think no one above lieutenant does any work around here? It's a lot of work trying to cover your butt all the time, and I don't get paid for overtime like you do."

"Well, there's a new spin on Gold Rush. We did get our first trifecta with three gun buys, which means we're now on track for federal filings, not including the ones we're tying to homicides."

"Good news, Jack. About time. You been dragging your feet?"

"Probably, sir. I'm slowing down as I get older. So, the spin is that I want to start taking in stolen cars."

"Excuse me? No. You buy guns, Jack. Remember the mayor? The photo op for him to drum up votes? He calls about twice a day asking when we're going to be ready to set up a table full of guns and call the press so he can be a hero on our dime. When are we going to be ready to do that, Jack?"

"Yeah, well, something has come up, sir. We got a Russian national attached to the Russian Mafia living in Glendale. He's the one who came in with the three gun sales. One of our officers, while shooting the shit with him in Gold Rush, told him we have our own containers to ship our guns to Africa. This guy jumped all over that and asked about shipping new Mercedes-Benzes to Russia, to St. Petersburg."

"Jack, are you not hearing me? We buy *guns*."

"Yeah, well, we may want to consider this, Chief. Burglary Auto Theft is on top of this case because this crew is hitting dealerships all over Southern Cal. This is a big deal, Chief Nelson. Sometimes they rip the cars off the lots after hours and sometimes they carjack a salesman during a test ride. One female saleswoman was raped during one of the jacks. These are Russian Mafia, sir. Organized crime. They're boosting cars and assaulting people, then shipping the vehicles to Russia. How can we look the other way? We'll still work guns, Chief. We'll just work this also. I can walk and chew gum at the same time."

"Goddamn it, Jack. I'll have to brief Chief Fuller on this. You think he wants me in his office every two seconds? You think he has nothing else to do but listen to me? And what do you think his first question is going to be, Jack?"

Adams already knew the answer. "I know this one: When are we going to give him a table full of guns so the mayor can show up in front of the cameras and take credit for it and lie to the press and be a hero?"

"Exactly, Lieutenant Adams. Now get out of here so I can figure out how to drop on the chief of police that we're doing the exact opposite of what he asked us to do."

Walking into the outer office, Adams had the distinct feeling his luck was running out. "See ya, Lieutenant Moss. Hey, I think I saw a sale at Macy's on really thick pads for that desk chair of yours."

"You're getting on my nerves, Jack."

"Yeah, other people have said that. I don't get it."

"Well, you're going to get it if you don't get out of here!"

#

Getting the call from Deputy Chief Nelson to meet him in the office of the chief of police didn't surprise Adams. He just didn't think it was going to be only fifteen minutes later. He had stopped to have an iced coffee at Starbucks after leaving Nelson's office and the call came before he even finished his drink.

Every meeting with Chief of Police Fuller seemed much more tense than the last. Adams started to wonder if Fuller was ready to send him back to Patrol where he could supervise officers writing traffic tickets. Walking into the chief's outer office, Adams found Lieutenant Jim Dawson greeting him with a big smile and shaking his head. "Hey, Jim, how you doing?"

"Fine, Jack. Heard you have another meeting with Chief Fuller. You're getting to know each other pretty well. It's like you're hanging out together."

"Yeah, well, don't be jealous."

"Jack, get in here. I have a lot to get done today." Chief Nelson, standing in the doorway of Chief Fuller's office, looked a little upset today. Adams wondered how bad the chief of police had been yelling at him.

"Good morning, Lieutenant Adams. Sit down." Chief Fuller was in the middle of laughing at the *Los Angeles Times*. "Where do they get this stuff, Steve? Do people really believe this? Remember when the press reported the facts, the news? Now the entire news industry is a big opinion page. They're all editorialists. They spin everything, facts be damned. Maybe we should let them police the streets, and then they can report on themselves. I'm sure they'd make themselves look a lot better than they make us look. Do you think there's even one of those bastards that has the courage to do what our officers do every day?"

Deputy Chief Nelson didn't appear to be listening but responded, "I don't have faith in the press to do anything, sir, especially what our officers do every day."

Adams wasn't comfortable with small talk at the moment. He would rather receive the brunt end of the boom being lowered and then get on with the day. "I'm sorry to take your time, Chief Fuller. I know you're busy, sir."

"No problem, Lieutenant, that's what I'm paid for. I hear you want to buy stolen cars? A lot of them. And from Russians who don't even live in the city. I don't remember that being part of our plan to develop a press conference for Mayor Hernandez."

"Well, I don't exactly want to buy them, sir. I actually want to take twenty stolen cars for free from the Russian Mafia who live over in Glendale. They want to ship a bunch of new Mercedes-Benzes that they've stolen to Russia. My crew at Gold Rush told them we have our own shipping containers and that we could ship the cars for them. With your permission, I plan to store them in one of our secret LAPD warehouses with all the seized cars and then work up some kind of federal RICO organized crime case. These are Russian Mafia gangsters, Chief Fuller, so I want to do a federal racketeering case against them here in Los Angeles for stealing cars, carjacking, assault, and rape. Then I want to add some kind of international charge for shipping them out of the country. I'm not real clear on that part of it yet. I've never done that before."

"Is that all, Lieutenant?"

"Not exactly, Chief Fuller. I'd like to ship them in cargo containers to Russia. I want to find some free cargo containers somewhere and then arrest the people over there who show up to receive them."

Chief Nelson's eyes opened wide as his jaw dropped. "Are you crazy, Jack? Chief Fuller, I don't know anything about all of this. Are you crazy, Jack? You're supposed to be buying guns for the mayor's photo op with the press! You work in Los Angeles, Lieutenant Adams. You don't work in Glendale, and you don't work in Russia. Are you crazy, Jack? We are the Los Angeles Police Department. We don't ship cargo containers to Russia."

Chief Nelson was a little louder today than usual. Nelson was a really good guy in Adams's opinion. He just sometimes got, well, excitable.

Lieutenant Dawson rose from his desk in the outer office and quietly closed the heavy wooden door to Chief Fuller's office. The two captains sitting in the outer office waiting for each of their appointments with the chief of police were silently thanking Lieutenant Adams, in their own way, of course, for stirring things up and making people mad. They really appreciated Adams putting the chief of police in such a good mood.

Dawson still wore that stupid smile on his face, shaking his head as he closed the door. Adams knew he'd never get out of the headquarters building in one piece this time. Unless he got thrown off of the chief's balcony, that is.

Chief of Police Fuller leaned back in his chair again on the back two legs. Adams hoped he wouldn't fall backwards because he knew he'd get blamed for it. "That sounds pretty fun, Lieutenant. Like in a movie. But I'm the chief of police of Los Angeles, Lieutenant, not Glendale and not Russia. We were supposed to be buying guns for the mayor's photo op. Does it sound to you like we might be getting a little off track? Because I've gotta tell ya, Lieutenant, it sounds to me like we're drifting off track a little bit."

Man, Chief Fuller could be the calmest guy you ever met. "It sure does, sir. But these are Russian nationals involved in organized crime in our city. See that American flag over there in the corner, Chief? We can't look the other way. It won't affect our ability to continue to buy guns; that will stay on track, and we'll file federal criminal charges on this Russian guy selling us guns. But on these stolen Mercedes, I'll liaison with Burglary Auto Theft to clear their cases with the Russians, too. I'll make sure they keep the lead on the prosecution; I'll just lend a little assistance. I'll be their liaison to the FBI and US attorneys, and I'll RICO these bastards here in the United States of America. Where we don't allow Russian nationals to move in and commit these kinds of crimes where we live. Then I'll work with Interpol to arrest these bastards in Russia."

Silence in the room. *Oh no, Chief Fuller is headed for the terrace again.*

"Steve, Jack, care to join me?"

Chief Fuller and Deputy Chief Nelson found their way to the balcony, but Adams stopped short. Chief Fuller turned and asked, "Jack, you coming?"

"Are you going to throw me off the balcony, sir?" Adams appreciated clearly understanding the situation he was in at any given moment.

Chief Fuller smiled. "It's tempting, but I'm not throwing anyone off the balcony, Jack. I delegate that kind of work."

The view from the chief's terrace was pretty impressive. Adams felt the overwhelming urge to give the finger to the mayor's office, but he decided that might be pushing the envelope a bit too far. *Maybe another day.*

"Jack, you're doing great things in the world, and I appreciate that. I know that we at the management level oftentimes display frustration with those in operations. We have competing interests sometimes. But we support you, Jack, both Chief Nelson and I. It takes a moment, sometimes, to get over the terrifying shock of what you're telling us. But then we remember when we were real policeman, arresting people and solving crimes instead of managing things and worrying about politics. I apologize that we come off as if we're reluctant to your ideas sometimes, but you're a pretty challenging piece of work, Jack. What do you need from us to make this happen?"

"First, I need a place to store twenty or so stolen Mercedes. I'm thinking the parking structure over on the east side where we store seized cars and stuff."

"You're not supposed to know about that parking structure, Jack. It's secret. Do you know what secret means, Jack?" Chief Fuller smiled at the supposed secret.

"I don't really *know* about it, sir. I just want to use it. I also need permission to work with Interpol through my FBI contacts and I'll need some political cover when I go to Russia."

"Excuse me? *Go* to Russia? Are you crazy, Jack?" Chief Nelson just couldn't stay quiet a second longer.

"Probably, sir. I'm guessing I'll have to transcribe our case into Russian and then transport a copy of it to their prosecutors, whoever that is, then make myself available to lay the case out to them and support their prosecution when they arrest the people over there who show up to pick up the Mercedes from the containers."

"I'm doubting we're going to Russia, Lieutenant, but I'll give that some thought," Chief Fuller smiled and calmly responded. "What else?"

"I don't want to notify the insurance companies of the recovered vehicles when the Russians give the stolen Mercedes to us, so I want to call the State Department of Insurance and work through them. Maybe they can slow down the insurance companies paying claims on the stolen vehicles until we close our case and return them."

Chief Fuller responded while looking out across the city. "That makes sense. I hadn't considered that. Okay. Steve, take your eager lieutenant and release him on his unsuspecting prey. God help them. And Jack . . . I want guns to keep coming in."

"Yes, sir."

"See you tomorrow, Jack?" Chief Fuller joked.

"God, I hope not, sir."

As Adams headed for Gold Rush, McClain told the team to clean the warehouse up. It was starting to look like one of the police stations. Mike Rand had just walked into the warehouse side of Gold Rush to see the new member of the team, Jennifer Thomas, seated at the control table with all the monitors. "Hey, Jennifer, welcome aboard. What are you doing?"

"Just shining my badge. I want to look good for the lieutenant because Detective McClain said he's coming today." Thomas was intent on making a good impression not only for the lieutenant but for the whole Gold Rush detail. She couldn't believe her good fortune in getting this assignment. Then, her day suddenly turned for the worse as Mike Rand pushed his face only inches from hers.

"You better knock that shit off, Thomas. Are you hearing me? If the lieutenant sees you doing that shit, you'll be back in Patrol." Rand wasn't someone who pulled punches.

"Why? I'm just shining my stupid badge." Confused, Thomas didn't know if she was being yelled at or if this was just an initiation joke, but Rand looked serious. Really serious.

"The lieutenant is a ghetto gunfighter, an OG from South Central. We're only out there at night, Thomas, when the monsters are out there, and he doesn't want anything shining and giving our position away. When your badge shines, it's a target, and that means the guy standing next to you is a target also. You want to shine your badge, Thomas, go work in West LA with the yuppie crowd. Oh, yeah. Don't be spit shining your shoes, either. We work in the ghetto, Thomas, in the alleys. We get dirty and we never, ever fucking shine."

"Wow, this is like *real* police stuff." Thomas started to like the feel of this.

Rand hoped she would catch on fast. "Yeah, well, the lieutenant is a street policeman. Not a pretty boy, and not a climber. He gets the job done. You're in the trenches now, Thomas, so remember one thing: the fight is never over. Welcome aboard and try to keep up, Thomas. We don't have time to babysit anybody."

Jennifer would never again, through the rest of her career, shine her badge.

CHAPTER THIRTY-TWO
CONTAINERS

Adams made his first call to figure out how to get ten free cargo containers to ship to Russia, for free. Jess Gile had retired ten years prior and was comfortable in his new position as a lieutenant with the Port Police. "Hey, Jess, it's Jack Adams. What's happening down in the Port these days?"

"Jack, how the hell are you? Same stuff down here. Not like your job. What's up, brother?"

"Jess, listen. I'm working an angle on something and I need your help, but it's sensitive and for your ears only."

Jess Gile was used to keeping secrets. He found that situation popped up more frequently in his job at the Port Police than it did while at LAPD. "No problem, brother. Shoot."

"Okay. I've got criminals shipping stolen stuff out of country. I have a storefront going and I want my crew to be able to ship it for them and then arrest them on both ends. We've told them that we have containers and we can ship it. My goal is to take possession of the property, load it into containers, and then, when it arrives in the other country, arrest the people receiving it. That way we arrest the criminals on both ends. I need a source for about ten free containers I can use, and some way to grease the skids for these containers to be shipped."

Jess Gile loved the idea. "No problem. I don't think you really need to ship containers, though. You can ship virtual containers."

"What? How does that work, Jess?" Adams felt like he was missing something.

"Well, we can put the paperwork in place to ship containers but not really ship them. We don't need the containers and the property to show up in the other country for a criminal violation. We only need someone to sign the paperwork to receive the containers. That's probably all you need to make an arrest."

"Man, I hadn't thought about that. The only thing is that we're talking cars here. Containers with stolen cars. I was thinking that once the container shows up, we arrest the guy accepting them and then all the people driving the cars away, people changing VIN numbers, people selling them. The whole chain."

"You can do that, Jack. But you have no control over what the police do on that other end. Consider which country you'll be dealing with and whether the politicians or the police are corrupt. What you're considering sounds pretty involved, and I'd suggest you just target the guy signing for them and be happy with that. If the police on that end want more, let them squeeze that guy or keep investigating. That eliminates the need for actual containers or the actual shipping of cars." Jess Gile, an unlikely hero, was the perfect source for what Adams needed.

"Got it, Jess. That's the plan." Adams was satisfied.

"One more thing, Jack. Instead of working with the police in this other country, we work through Interpol on cases like this and let them be the middleman between us and whoever the local law enforcement is. I have that contact at Interpol for you. If you want to meet me at my office tomorrow around 1500, I can introduce you."

With one call, Lieutenant Adams had the plan he believed he could convincingly sell to Nelson and Fuller. Next he needed to bring the rest of his team up to speed.

"Hey, Mac, it's Jack. How fast do you think we can take possession of the twenty Mercedes? I have a plan that I'll firm up tomorrow afternoon, but we need to have the cars in our possession quickly. I don't want to put the plan into motion and find that there's a wrench in the system as to our actually getting the cars. Once we get them, we can sit on them as long as we want to put the plan into motion."

McClain's new plan was starting to take shape. "The little Russian guy says he has twenty cars right now, so it sounds like we can move on it pretty quick. He's supposed to call Torres tonight, so we can work the angle that we have containers available now but don't know when we'll have them available in the future. Once we get the cars, we can play the delay game until we're ready to make arrests."

Adams was short and sweet. "Sounds good, Mac. Make it happen."

McClain's first step was to prime Torres. "Torres, when the Russian calls, tell him that you checked with the owner and we have containers available now. Tell him that our shipping company is working through our shipping agent to plug ten containers on the next cargo line to St. Petersburg. Make it clear that this is time sensitive and he has to move on it *right now*, but I want you to sound bored with this—keep playing hard to get. Don't sell him on the idea. Let him sell you. One more thing: have them bring the cars here to Gold Rush. We'll figure out what to do with them."

Sure enough, at 6 p.m., 1800 hours, Torres's burner phone rang. "This is Mark. Can I help you?"

The voice of Aleks Antonov was easily distinguished. "Mark, this is Anthony. Do you have news about shipping for me?"

"Hey, Anthony. Yeah, I've got some notes here, hold on . . . okay, let's see. I called the owner's secretary and she referred me to our shipping company. Apparently, we have the ten containers available, but the shipping agent hasn't got back to me yet on a shipping date. He said we also have quite a few LCL containers, the ones that aren't completely full, but that won't work for us because their destinations are already chartered and none are headed to St. Petersburg. They did say scheduling on new containers would more likely be sooner than later. Apparently, there's spaces they're trying to fill now, but I expect that won't be the case starting the first of the month when the shipping volume starts to peak because the weather is better."

"That is good, Mark. We are ready with twenty vehicles, so a short time frame is of no consequence. Mark, the paperwork on our vehicles to be shipped may not all be in order." A sly way of saying they were stolen vehicles.

Torres jumped right on the opportunity. "Yeah, well, we can deal with that; it just costs a bit more. The problem is getting them to the terminal and loaded in the containers without inspections. I think it's best if you bring them to our office at Gold Rush and let us deal with the transportation and loading. We have our own staff already online."

"This is good, Mark. Tell me the price and we will continue."

"Hey, Anthony. I don't mean to be forward, but for this kind of situation, you would need to pay in full before we load the containers. Can you pay in cash when you drop the cars off?" Torres thought he was doing a remarkable job not being anxious.

"Yes, we pay in cash. I will bring cash when I bring the cars."

After they agreed on the price—three times the amount to actually ship vehicles to St. Petersburg—an agreement was made for Aleks to bring the twenty vehicles to Gold Rush.

Aleks Antonov's call to Torres allowed the team to capture his cell phone number. Finally the last piece of the puzzle in bringing Antonov up on a wiretap was to identify the phone he used. Torres's continued efforts to get access to the phone had finally paid off.

McClain called Agent O'Reilly to give him the heads-up. "O'Reilly, this is McClain. I've got some positive scoop for you. We finally got a phone for our little Russian Mafia kid. We already have three gun buys into him, but the forensics on the three guns he sold us don't come back to anything. They're all reported lost or stolen. We're also working another angle on him that I'll brief you on later, but apparently, they're stealing new cars off dealer lots and shipping them to Russia. I think his status as a Russian national and ties to the

Russian Mafia should solidly open the door to warrants on his phone."

Agent O'Reilly took the information in stride and followed Lieutenant Adams's orders to push forward. "I'll take it in under the umbrella of organized crime and we should get the warrant with no problem. Let's just include the gun sales for now, because that's all we really need for the paper. We can work the stolen car angle later on as it pans out. I'm going to start writing the warrant today, so I'll need some info to fill in the blanks. If you'll keep an eye on your phone, I'll call you on and off as I need follow-up information. Are you ready to expand your ranks at the monitoring center?"

"I'm sure we are, and Lieutenant Adams said to push forward hard, so let's make this happen. I'll let the lieutenant know."

CHAPTER THIRTY-THREE
A BRIEFCASE FULL OF CASH

Stans Jelenick woke up every day angry about the situation of his new assignment at Detective Bureau. He should be in charge of both the Gang and Narcotics Detail and Robbery Homicide Division—one of the most premier assignments on the LAPD. This was to be his step up to deputy chief, and he'd been sidelined. He'd complained about it nearly every day to his wife, Elana, but decided to give her a break today. Stans Jelenick had always told Elana everything—at least everything that made him look good in her eyes. But today, no complaining.

Jelenick parked his car in the parking lot of Farmer's Market at 3rd St. and Fairfax, not far from his home. Sitting behind a plate of chicken shawarma in the Mediterranean restaurant, he stared across the room trying to figure out what had gone wrong and, more importantly, how to fix it. He believed that somehow, Lieutenant Adams had stabbed him in the back, and now his whole career was in jeopardy. Lieutenant Adams was out to get him and was orchestrating this entire attack on him. Jelenick had heard about policemen from South Central Los Angeles and knew they were rebellious, that they didn't like authority.

The only answer he saw was to eliminate Adams from the picture and move back to his dedicated role in Detective Bureau. For some reason, Deputy Chief Nelson was protecting Adams, so he would have to be careful.

Jelenick flourished in the current state of affairs in which policemen displayed an unwillingness to enforce the law. He knew everyone in law enforcement across the United States was holding back. They feared being condemned by the media as much as they feared being disciplined by the police departments they worked for who no longer supported their personnel. Many corrupt and unethical politicians made sure of that. The last straw that had finally eliminated police officer's willingness to arrest criminals was the current stance of many district attorneys and federal prosecutors to seek out opportunities to prosecute police officers. Even as they refused to prosecute many criminals and released criminals from jail, when it came to police officers, they put a camera on their chest and a target on their back.

The current situation meant that Jelenick was able to avoid controversial situations caused by police officers in his command. If they did nothing, he could do nothing. He could sit behind his desk, invisible, and continue to silently move up the ranks. Except for one person who had derailed his ambitions: Jack Adams.

Jelenick drank his tea and finished his dinner, then made a decision. He committed right then and there to seek out every opportunity to regain control over Adams and resume his role in Detective Bureau. He now saw his true mission; he only had to find the pathway to get there. Jelenick smiled to himself and believed he would be promoted to deputy chief in no time at all. *It's just a matter of putting your mind to it.*

#

Adams spent the day with McClain strategizing the new twist on the Russian, Aleks Antonov. They needed to develop a solid plan to present to Deputy Chief Nelson. Adams was scheduled to meet with Chief Nelson tonight after discussing the case with Interpol at the Port Police Headquarters.

Special Agent Bill O'Reilly, on the other hand, spent the day with US Attorney Roger Gibson in federal court obtaining the warrant for the phone number provided by Aleks Antonov.

The plan was in place, funding would start moving, the federal monitoring center was being staffed, and captains throughout the Los Angeles Police Department were fuming about losing their homicide detectives for some unknown job at an unknown location and for an undetermined period of time. All thanks to Lieutenant Jack Adams.

At the Port Police Headquarters on Centre Street in San Pedro, Adams met with Erick Young of Interpol. "We can help with this, Lieutenant Adams, but understand that we will not be taking an active role in the operation. We will, instead, act as a liaison between you and the appropriate law enforcement or investigative bodies in Russia. That being said, we will be on the scene when possession of the virtual containers is transferred to the importer. That will allow us to clearly communicate your case and your desires to the local authorities. We will also communicate to you the official actions against those persons you are targeting in Russia in support of your case against criminals here in Los Angeles.

"Keep in mind, we have no control over the Russian authorities, so there are no guarantees as to the actions they will take. We will be the ones to provide you the official documentation of governmental actions against persons in Russia for inclusion in your prosecution file against co-suspects or co-conspirators in your local case."

Adams thought that Interpol's support was invaluable; it sounded like they eliminated the need for him to travel to Russia entirely. "Thanks, Erick. Detective McClain from my staff will be your contact person. Same for you, Jess—he'll team up with you as soon as possible to work out the details of documenting the virtual containers."

Leaving San Pedro, Adams headed for the briefing with Deputy Chief Nelson. "Good evening, Chief. I've cleaned up the plan for the stolen Mercedes and it's actually a little cleaner and a little easier than I originally envisioned it."

"Well, that's great, Lieutenant. Being that we're not supposed to be doing this in the first place."

Deputy Chief Nelson had a smile on his face. Surprising, considering that Adams was bothering him yet again with things he wasn't supposed to be doing. "Go ahead and lay it on me, Jack."

"Yes, sir. We're arranging for the Russian kid to drop off all twenty of the stolen Mercedes-Benz to Gold Rush in the evening hours when the street is pretty clear. They'll lay the cash on the counter, so we'll seize it and then address with Asset Forfeiture how to deal with the money. We're just going to stack the cars up at the curb. We'll have surveillance on-site to photograph all the players and the cars that return them home. After that, we'll get to work on identifying each person and tying them in to the Russian Mafia. Detective McClain liaisoned with Burglary, Auto Theft Division to use their resources to transfer all the cars to one of our secure holding lots in East Los Angeles. I'm told that a vehicle transfer company that partners with LAPD will be picking them up on flatbeds that carry multiple vehicles. There's no signage or plates on the trucks.

"Due to the counterintelligence that I fear the Russians may be running, I interceded with a plan the Port Police designed for us to have the trucks enter a secure gate in the Port on the Long Beach side. We'll scan each of the Mercedes for electronics and make sure there's no tracking devices. They'll stand by for three hours inside the port and then head out, crossing the Vincent Thomas Bridge to the San Pedro side, and take different routes. If we do have a tail, I want them to see the trucks going into the Port and that should satisfy them. Once they leave, I've got Surveillance units set to tail each truck and somewhere along the route, they'll set up a traffic break to cut off any countersurveillance. Right after the traffic break, obviously, the trucks will be instructed to change direction and travel on a different route to the Long Beach Airport. One of my old assistant Watch commanders is a pilot and he set up hangar space to pull the trucks into where we'll hold them for a week. The airport detour will stop any drones from tracking us. At the end of the week, we'll go get them and put them in our lot in East LA."

Deputy Chief Nelson was actually enjoying this plan. "Sounds like you're planning to win, Lieutenant. Let's talk about containers, ships, and takedowns."

"We always plan to win, sir. With the help of Lieutenant Jess Gile of the Port Police, ex-LAPD, we won't be using any containers. We're going to send virtual containers. In other words, even though we'll have the paperwork identifying that ten containers each loaded with vehicles are on the ship, they won't really be there. I learned that all we need is for the importer, or his agent, to just sign for the shipment, even though it's not really on the boat. That satisfies as a crime. I partnered with Erick Young from Interpol who will coordinate that side of things. An Interpol agent will be there to coordinate when they sign for the shipment, but the Russian authorities will be taking the actions against the criminals. Then Interpol will send us a copy of all the paperwork so we can attach it to our case."

Nelson felt much more comfortable with the plan now. "So the LAPD won't be going to Russia?"

"No, Chief. Unless you think I should go just to keep an eye on things."

Nelson smirked. "I think they'll do just fine without you being there, Lieutenant. Anyway, the food is terrible—you'd hate it."

"Yes, sir. Truth be known, I don't like to fly, anyway. We'll coordinate the takedown in Russia with the takedown here. That will put a little pressure on our Gold Rush timeline, but we'll figure it out. Once we have the cars, we have our primary Russian suspect, so there's no hurry. When it's convenient for us, we'll look at shipping schedules and find a cargo ship stopping in St. Petersburg that we can use as the decoy vessel."

"Okay, Jack. I'll brief the chief of police. Get the cars, store them, and after that, guess what I think you should be doing?"

Another softball question. "Getting guns to put on the table for the mayor's press conference?"

"You read my mind, Lieutenant. You must be psychic. Now get back to work."

"Yes, sir, Chief, sir."

#

Two days later, Aleks Antonov showed up at Gold Rush with a brushed aluminum briefcase filled with the cash to store and ship twenty Mercedes-Benz sedans to St. Petersburg, Russia. He strode into Gold Rush with two very beautiful women, not knowing that the criminal case against him had just been satisfied.

As the twenty cars were parked in the parking lot and at the curb, three white vans picked up the drivers and returned them to the apartment building in Glendale with surveillance units in tow. They worked through the night identifying the personal vehicles they got into and the addresses where they arrived.

#

"Hey, Mac, it's Paul Stanford on 5K3. We've got our entire team still working each of the players, but there's another issue. For the last two days, we've had a couple prostitutes we haven't seen before walking the street in front of Gold Rush, but neither one has gotten in anyone's car. They smile and wave them away, but they're only walking in this block. Today we're trying to find the car they showed up in; I'm sure they're together. You think this Russian guy has eyes on us?"

McClain had expected this. "It's possible—no, it's probable. Lieutenant Adams said he was planning for someone to be looking at us sooner or later, and he's made some moves to make us look legit. Expand your duties to watch for countersurveillance from now on, Paul, and I'll let the lieutenant know."

He immediately dialed Adams after hanging up. "Hey, Lieutenant, it's McClain. We ran the VIN numbers on the twenty cars from the Russians. Anyway, all come back boosted from new car lots and they're all carrying invalid DMV dealer plates. No trackers on any of the cars. I'm trying to figure out if there's a way to trace the dealer plates to a certain DMV office or person, but as far as we know they're printing them in someone's living room. I'm betting, though, that they have someone inside DMV, so I'm going to be working that on the side."

Adams was relieved to get this part of the plan off to a start. "Good work, Mac. I agree it's good to reach out to DMV for help on this, but not yet. They're outside the yellow tape, so that part of our investigation goes on ice for now. Keep our focus on guns, pal, but make sure we don't sacrifice our safety over these cars. This part of the plan is still a work in progress. Now that we're playing the game, I'll start working with my friend in the State Insurance Office over the recoveries and see how long we can stretch this out without insurance companies addressing the payouts. When we get together next time, let's talk about what the endgame will look like, and after that we should be able to fill in the middle. We have a lot of guns for your buddy the mayor, and some pretty strong cases are coming together. My hope is that what we're doing will get the attention of law enforcement everywhere so that we can start modifying the way we police gangs. I'm feeling good that LAPD has the lead on this, just like we did with RICO prosecutions, but if we lose Chief Nelson and Chief Fuller, God knows what will happen. We could get shut down in the blink of an eye."

McClain was comfortable with how the Mercedes operation was going and knew that they would massage it as time went on. "One other thing, Lieutenant. Stanford identified two pro females walking the street on our block but not getting in anyone's car. They're only walking and waving in the block in front of Gold Rush."

"Okay, Mac, we expected that, just not under these circumstances. Our paperwork is good, and as long as you guys are smart coming and going, we should be okay. I'm sure you have Stanford working up some countersurveillance moves to identify who's watching us, so let me know how that pans out. I'm pretty sure it's our friend, Aleks, and not the local gangbangers."

#

Segei Antonov met with Kostya Sokoloff at Kalinka Restaurant on Victory Boulevard near Western Avenue. "Kostya, my friend, my advisor. My son, Aleks, has successfully fulfilled his promise to repair this element of our business. As I said, he is young and will make mistakes, but the promise he shows is impressive. He will surpass our successes, my friend. We will be old and enjoying the fruits of our lives, and Aleks will be accomplishing things we did not imagine."

Kostya was contemplative in his demeanor. "Yes, Segei, he does show much promise. But this thing is not yet done. This is the first step. Let's wait to celebrate success until success is achieved. I am your attorney and your advisor. More importantly, I am your friend, Segei. That being spoken, enjoy your son, Segei. Enjoy your family and your blessings. Your friends celebrate your successes."

CHAPTER THIRTY-FOUR
THE MEDIA SPIN

William Garcia had spent the last few days at home in Fresno considering the pawn shop he had sold the gun to and what he would do with the money after he robbed them. He'd probably even get his gun back; it had to be in the safe. The only wrench in the system was Sissy. If he robbed the place, she knew enough about him to help the police identify him. Garcia knew he had to scare her so much that she would never roll on him, that she would leave town.

Gold Rush was quiet all morning, and McClain had agreed to a food run. He was getting tired of the same eating spots and persuaded the team to share pizzas. He knew sending someone up to his favorite spot on Rampart Boulevard above MacArthur Park would take a bit, but he ordered the pizzas ahead so they would be ready for pickup. He thought it would be best to send John Andrews and Jennifer Thomas, who were typically assigned to the back room inside the warehouse. That left McClain and Mike Rand to provide security for the team in the front office. Andrews drove his undercover Toyota 4Runner, which he loved, and admonished Thomas not to get pizza on the seats.

Up in Fresno, Jorge Mendez saw the tan Chrysler pull up in front of his house and he knew it was William Garcia. Garcia looked intimidating, but Mendez was tired of him. Both men were Fresno Bulldogs, but Mendez saw himself as being the tougher of the two. He wasn't impressed with Garcia.

As soon as Mendez got into the passenger seat, William Garcia felt the need to take charge. "This is my thing, homes, and it's easy. Two or three pushovers inside with the safe standing open. They got jewelry and gold in there, so we'll take it all. Take all the money and all the guns. You go over the counter and get them on the floor. I'll watch those fuckers while you fill the bags. We good?"

"As long as they do what I say. What does the woman look like?" Mendez loved watching movies and perpetually tried to sound as if he was in the big scene. A drama queen that talked with his hands.

William Garcia leaned closer to Mendez, their faces almost touching. "No shooting, homes, and leave the woman alone. We got no time for fucking around. I swapped plates, but this is still my car and I've gotta get it back to

Fresno. Just do what I said and they'll be scared shitless. Just get the shit and let's get out. I'll change the plates over in Hollywood, and then we're on the 170 and outta town before the police even know who to look for."

"I got it, I got it." Mendez was awash in his own thoughts as to how this was going to go down. He had a lot of experience with robberies and brutalizing people, and he wasn't going to let Garcia tell him what to do. The woman would only take a few minutes.

After the four-hour drive south from Fresno, William Garcia dropped Mendez off at Starbucks on the corner of 3rd Street and Alvarado. "You stay here, homes. I'll pick Sissy up and bring her back. We gotta scare her enough that she won't roll on us. She already knows I'm a killer and she's afraid of me. Everybody's afraid of me, but we gotta make it real to her. You know what I'm saying?"

At MacArthur Park, Garcia found Sissy without any trouble hanging out at her usual spot. "Hey, Sissy, I been looking for you. Jump in."

Sissy had decided to never again endure William Garcia. "Hi William. I have a date and I'm on my way there now. I'm so sorry, sweets. Maybe we can meet later?"

Garcia was playing a game he wasn't willing to lose. He laid his gun on the seat next to him. "Get in, Sissy. Don't make me mad. I got something to talk to you about. Something where we can make big money."

Sissy reluctantly opened the door and sat down but couldn't bring herself to close the door. William hit the gas pedal and accelerated into traffic on Alvarado as the door slammed shut, along with Sissy's fate.

Garcia pulled into the run-down hotel at 3rd Street and Alvarado tucked in between all the medical offices, one of those places that no one likes to stay at because it's worn out and only minimally clean. But in a place like Los Angeles, there's enough people willing to stay there that management doesn't really care. They can cut all the corners they want and still make money.

Garcia handed her a stack of seven twenty-dollar bills. "Here, Sissy. Take this into the office and pay cash for tonight." As Sissy walked to the office, Garcia called Mendez and told him to walk over to the hotel. Garcia said he would stand at the room door so Mendez could find them.

Sissy and Garcia found the room she had rented on the second floor. Garcia stood outside the open door leaning against the rail, smoking a cigarette, while Sissy sat on the bed. The flowered bedspread and stained carpet were not inviting.

When Garcia walked back through the hotel room door and Mendez followed him in, Sissy immediately knew she was in terrible danger. Mendez grabbed Sissy's hair and roughly pulled her head back. "Yeah, we gonna play for a while, bitch. We gonna have fun, aren't we?"

Sissy tore herself loose, shoved her backpack at Mendez's face, and broke past him as she sprinted toward the door. She knew she had to get out of the room—it was now or never as she lowered her head and rushed forward. Sissy extended both her arms at Garcia, who was blocking the door, and knew she only had to slide past him, just get out the door, and someone would see her. Someone would help her.

Garcia grabbed Sissy's right arm as she tried to slide past him. He swung her body and hit her face solidly against the doorjamb. Sissy was dazed and only saw blackness as blood ran from her nose. Garcia punched her viciously in the stomach, knocking her to the ground, and she gasped to regain her breath. Mendez kicked with all his strength and Sissy folded over his boot.

Sissy never noticed the door closing as she lay prone on the floor with her face pinned against the stained carpet by Mendez's boot.

Most of what happened after that was only a blur to Sissy. The sexual and violent assaults left her helpless, and she knew she would never make it out of the hotel room. She knew she would never see that door open again.

Three hours went by. Sissy stopped breathing as Mendez choked her. "Fuck, man, I didn't do anything! The bitch is dead. She just fucking died, and I didn't even do anything."

William Garcia was angry. "Fuck that, I said scare her! Fuck no. This is bullshit. Fuck no. Motherfucker, now what do we do with her? Well . . . fuck her. I gave her cash to pay for the room and I stayed in the car. I'm clean. It's her fucking room. She's on camera. Her name's on it." Garcia hadn't intended for her to die, but he didn't really care one way or the other.

#

William Garcia pulled into the small lot in front of Gold Rush and backed into the parking space so he could make a quick escape. The surveillance units stationed outside the warehouse called it in to McClain: a tan Chrysler that may have been there before. McClain recognized the car on the monitor and slightly cracked the door to the warehouse, announcing, "Heads up. Looks like someone coming in. Sounds like that Fresno Bulldog cartoon that Sissy brought in."

McClain watched the security camera in the parking lot and wrote down the license plate on the Chrysler. As Garcia and Mendez got out of the car, he noticed that the license plate was different from last time. A red flag.

When the two men got out of the car, Garcia pulled a red bandana up around his face and Mendez pulled a skull cap down over his face as a mask with eye holes cut out. Stanford in 5K3 got on the air. "5K3 to 35G11. Heads up, suspects are in masks. Looks like a 211."

McClain acknowledged and saw the front glass door opening as he announced, "We're getting hit, it's a 211!"

Paul Stanford coordinated with the other surveillance unit, 5K5. "5K3 to 5K5. We're moving in close and we'll take them at their car. Let's block the driveway." Stanford changed his radio to the Rampart Division frequency. "5K3, officer needs help. 211 in progress. Suspects are two possible Hispanics in masks, tan Chrysler. Have units stand by at the end of the street until we call them in. Have them close the street down both directions and then get a two-block perimeter going. Advise all units that plainclothes officers are on scene. Get us an airship."

After putting the address out, a Rampart Division Patrol unit broadcasted that they were responding and requested a perimeter around the location. The two surveillance units moved closer to the location, covering both north and south escape routes. 5K3, Stanford, blocked the parking lot exit with his car headed south, then bailed out and positioned himself to engage the two suspects when they exited Gold Rush. 5K5 positioned his car just south of Gold Rush and blocking the northbound lane, causing any northbound traffic to drive around them to pass and creating a buffer for the tactical event at Gold Rush.

It happened fast. The two men entered through the front door wearing masks, both armed with semiautomatic handguns. Both men held their guns out in front of them and yelled, "Get on the floor!" Not one of the undercover police officers lay on the floor.

As Torres bent lower behind the barricaded counter, it registered in Garcia's mind that Torres was going down to the floor as he was told. But instead of getting on the floor, Torres brought his handgun up to his chest, preparing to engage Garcia standing right in front of him on the other side of the counter. Halverson continued his movement to the file cabinet, where he unholstered his handgun and began to push it upwards over the top of the cabinet.

Julie Barr placed her left hand on the edge of her desk and aggressively pushed her chair back and out of the way as she knelt on one knee behind her desk. The chair made a lot of noise as it crashed backwards into one of the safes. She drew her handgun and brought it up over the desk just as Mendez jumped to the top of the countertop with his handgun in his left hand.

Mendez saw that the three "employees" were responding to his order to lie on the ground. They were all dropping down. He knew they were scared of him—he was a killer. People feared him.

As he bounded on top of the countertop, Jorge Mendez yelled again, "Get on the floor!" Already on the countertop now and pushing off to jump down to the other side of the counter, Mendez knew this would be easy. He'd have plenty of time to sexually assault the woman he saw when he came through the door. He'd take her in the bathroom or some back room.

William Garcia stood in the lobby on his side of the counter but immediately lost sight of Torres and Barr as they fell below the counter, obviously scared to death. Then he saw Halverson turn and hide behind a file cabinet. Garcia was satisfied that Mendez was already on top of the counter and jumping down to the other side, grateful that Mendez was doing as he was told for once. He knew the employees at Gold Rush would be scared and do everything they were told to do, but this was even easier than he'd thought.

Garcia thought about filling his pockets with money, gold, and guns. His plan was working perfectly, and he intended to keep most of the profits for himself. This was his caper and Mendez was just there as a helper. *Fuck Mendez.*

Garcia stepped back away from the counter and decided to allow Mendez to do all the work while he covered everyone and kept his eye on the front door for any other customers who might come in. He looked back at the front door, then stepped toward it to turn the lock and solve the problem of anyone coming in.

Mendez was surprised when he saw the inner door to the warehouse swing open out of the corner of his eye.

The report from Mike Rand's Colt AR15 rifle filled the room. As Rand sent three Remington .223 caliber high-velocity rounds through Mendez's chest as he jumped down from the counter, Julie Barr fired two .45 caliber rounds that also struck Mendez in the chest. Mendez fell forward over the counter as Torres fired two .45 caliber rounds upward, adding to the trauma in Mendez's chest, who then fell on to the floor next to Torres. It all happened in less than six seconds.

Garcia had entered Gold Rush first and pushed farther into the room as Mendez jumped onto the counter. As he turned to lock the door, Garcia's bandana came dislodged and fell down around his neck. Torres and Barr were low in their positions below the level of the countertop and Halverson stood barricaded behind the metal file cabinet. McClain, frustrated, stood behind Rand who was blocking the inner door to the warehouse. Lucky for McClain.

After Rand fired a three-round burst at Mendez, he stood in his practiced barricaded shooting position at the door to the warehouse and traced his barrel toward Garcia.

As Garcia moved toward the front door, he was surprised by Rand and brought his gun up, firing twice at Rand and striking the wall and door but not hitting the officer. The rounds struck where McClain would most probably have been standing in the doorway had he been able to get past Rand.

Halverson fired two rounds at the F14 tattoo under Garcia's left eye, with only one round finding its mark on the rapidly moving target. The impact glanced off and fractured Garcia's zygomatic bone underneath his eye, not a lethal contact.

As Garcia held his gun pointed at both Halverson and Rand, Halverson fired again over the counter, shattering Garcia's clavicle. Garcia fell below the counter a fraction of a second before Rand's next two rounds flew just over his head. Garcia scrambled to the door and, partially blinded, reached up and searched for the lock.

When Rand lost sight of the suspect, he quickly moved forward and brought the barrel of his AR15 down over the counter, searching for Garcia, when suddenly the glass door opened and Garcia was out and on the run. Just that fast.

McClain stepped into the room, frustrated. "Hold your position at the counter, Rand. If he comes back through the door, dump his ass. Surveillance will hit him outside. Is anybody hit?"

Torres began to climb the counter. "I'll lock the door and keep him outside."

McClain immediately saw the danger. "Hold it, Mark. Stay on this side of the counter; rounds might come through the glass. Is anybody hit?"

Barr roughly turned Mendez onto his stomach and handcuffed him. Searching him for other weapons and finding none, Barr put her foot on the back of Mendez's right shoulder to hold him down. Mendez displayed no signs of life.

Garcia fell face-first into the parking lot as he bolted out of the glass door. The pain in his chest was searing hot, and he knew he had been shot. He had blood in his left eye and couldn't see clearly. He had been able to maintain his grip on his gun and scrambled to get to his feet. He had to get to his car and get someplace where he could change the license plates. Maybe to his mother's house.

Fumbling to get his car keys from his pocket, Garcia crashed against his driver's door. He panicked as he saw the two cars parked in the middle of the roadway blocking the parking lot. His car was blocked. Then he saw two men at the mouth of the driveway armed with a handgun and a shotgun. Cops. *Undercover cops . . . where did they come from?* Then the sirens. *More cops. How did they get there so fast?*

Garcia abandoned his car as he dropped his keys and bounded over the three-foot block wall surrounding the parking lot separating each of the businesses. He ran northbound through the neighboring parking lots, narrowly avoiding the line of fire of the two surveillance units.

Paul Stanford was still on the Rampart Division radio frequency. "5K3, officer needs help, shots fired. Suspect is male Hispanic in red clothing with a bandana armed with a handgun. Suspect is running northbound from the location."

#

John Andrews and Jennifer Thomas were on their way back to Gold Rush with pizza when they heard 5K3 broadcast over the tactical frequency that masked suspects were entering Gold Rush. Only moments later, they saw down the street that the two surveillance cars were abandoned in the roadway in front of Gold Rush and traffic was stopping behind them.

Andrews maneuvered his Toyota 4Runner to the left and onto the sidewalk north of Gold Rush in an effort to get closer. They were not on the Rampart Division radio frequency and failed to hear the help call or the suspect description. They never heard that the suspect was running northbound right toward them.

Finding a tree and a large commercial trash can blocking his path and still three buildings away, Andrews turned in his seat, looking over his right shoulder, put the car in reverse, and tried to back out of the dead end. Thomas threw the pizzas into the back seat, which really made Andrews mad.

As Andrews blurted out, "I told you, don't get the pizza on the seats!" he was suddenly surprised by his driver's door opening. Andrews looked to his left and saw a man dressed in all red and bleeding profusely. The man was holding a gun and standing in the void.

It flashed in Andrews's mind that he recognized Garcia from his first visit to Gold Rush. Blood covered Garcia's face and neck as he pointed his handgun at Andrews and yelled, "Get out! Get out, motherfucker!"

Garcia grabbed Andrews's left shoulder and held his gun to the back of Andrews's head as he pulled him from the car, pushing him to the ground. Andrews looked for the opportunity to draw his handgun or engage the suspect to disarm him, but Garcia pushed him forward out of the driver's seat and away from the car, causing him to fall forward on his hands and knees onto the street. The car was still in reverse and slowly moving backwards as Garcia sat in the driver's seat. Right next to Jennifer Thomas.

Andrews rose to his knees and tactically positioned himself in front of the Toyota 4Runner so that Thomas was not in his line of fire. Even so, he knew that shooting into the windshield was not an exact science as to the trajectory of the bullets breaking through the sloped glass, which meant that there was a chance, however slight, that Thomas could get hit or even injured by the broken glass.

Lieutenant Adams had taught his crew to never give up, and in a hostage situation where an officer's life was in jeopardy, it was better that the officer be killed or injured by the rescuing officer trying to save their life than by the suspect murdering them. This was one of those very rare events that Lieutenant Adams had warned them about. Shit really does happen in the field, and it happens fast.

Jennifer Thomas was surprised by Andrews suddenly being pulled out of the 4Runner. As quickly as Andrews was pulled out, Garcia sat in the driver's seat next to her. She didn't recognize the suspect but immediately recognized the grave danger she was in. The suspect, dressed in red, was covered in blood and holding a semiautomatic handgun.

Thomas instinctively opened her passenger door and had one foot on the ground as Garcia, who did not know that these were undercover police officers, sat in the car with a gun held in his right hand, yelling, "Get out, bitch!" Garcia held his gun out, pointed at Thomas's face. With one foot on the ground and one foot still in the car, Thomas knew she would be shot at point-blank range.

While looking at the barrel of the gun only inches from her face, Jennifer Thomas would not give up. Her father's face flashed in her mind and gave her a sense of calm as time seemed to slow down.

Life was in slow motion now. In that fraction of a second that seemed like she would never get to the end of it, Jennifer Thomas chose not to be a willing victim. Never again. Jennifer Thomas was a Los Angeles Police officer, and she would fight.

Facing Garcia's gun and knowing she was going to be shot, Thomas pushed her right hand down the side of her body and tightened her fingers around the grip of her handgun in the holster on her right hip. She pulled the gun straight up along her rib cage and thrust it out in front of her. Thomas's gun collided with the gun Garcia was holding, and she immediately fired two rounds in rapid succession into Garcia's torso. Garcia flinched and drew both his arms over his chest, firing one round into the dashboard of the 4Runner. Thomas raised her gun up to eye level and found the front sight, pulled the trigger back, and fired a third considered round into Garcia's right temple.

Andrews regained his balance and got to his feet, knowing the danger his partner was in. He followed the Toyota 4Runner as it reversed and fired three rounds through the windshield, purposely firing low through the bottom of the glass. He knew the bullet trajectory would be sent slightly upwards after they hit the windshield.

As Thomas's last round hit Garcia, the windshield shattered and the rounds fired by John Andrews struck Garcia in the chest and neck. Thomas slowly squeezed on the trigger again, applying slight pressure but not enough to fire the gun. She watched as Garcia lowered his gun to the seat and slumped forward against the steering wheel. Thomas slid her finger off the trigger and stepped completely free from the car. She watched it slowly roll backwards into another car, where it stopped. Where Garcia died in the front seat of the undercover police car.

Andrews scanned the area for additional suspects, then ran to Thomas, grabbed her arm, and pulled her to cover behind another car stopped in the roadway. Jennifer Thomas yelled, "I'm okay, I'm okay! The dumb idiot carjacked us."

Andrews gave her arm a shake. "Jennifer, he's dead, forget him. Watch our backs. Find the rest of them."

Thomas paused and realized the fight wasn't over. The fight is never over. Physically pushing their backs together, the two officers began searching for the other suspects. Suspects who never came.

#

At the scene, Lieutenant Adams briefed Commander Jelenick and Deputy Chief Nelson, who had arrived in the same car. Jelenick was the first to interrupt. "This is the end of this, Lieutenant. I should have been brought in to manage this effort from the beginning. This is way too much for a lieutenant to handle."

Adams looked to Chief Nelson for an answer as to why and how Jelenick came to be on scene; he was not in the loop on this effort. Chief Nelson saw the problem but could not alienate the commander. "Jack, Commander Jelenick is now briefed in on what we're doing here. Should I become unavailable, you will answer to him. Until then, he will receive general briefings so he gets kept up to speed."

Adams responded with a slow and considered response. "Chief Nelson, our effort here was designed to pull in the worst of the worst. Killers. Monsters. We have preplanned tactical responses to violent assaults during this effort, and our planning and teamwork caused us to survive this deadly attack on our officers. Our mission is to remove guns from violent criminals. This event today was not our doing; we only responded to what the monsters did. And we did, in fact, draw monsters in and remove them from the street. The only obstacle I see is how we continue to move forward with our operation with the press we're going to receive from this. This could burn our operation, and I'm not ready to close up shop yet."

Jelenick jumped right back in. "Didn't you hear me, Lieutenant? This is over. You're already burned. The press is going to burn you and you're done. Don't you get it?"

"Commander, respectfully I disagree. Chief Nelson, I believe there is a way to maintain the integrity of our operation and move forward and continue to do the incredibly valuable job that we're doing. Chief, with your permission, I'd like to personally give the press release and keep our command staff at a distance. I can bear the burden of any future heat we may get. I can play it off as a Major Crimes surveillance of known criminals who robbed a pawnshop. Plainclothes detectives from Major Crimes, SIS, were surveilling these two known criminals with prior knowledge that they planned to commit a robbery. During the robbery, SIS attempted to arrest them and encountered a violent assault resulting in an officer-involved shooting. As soon as I mention SIS, the *LA Times* will jump all over it. They've been trying to burn SIS for years and won't even question it. They'll be on this like hounds on a rabbit. I think I can sell it and our operation will end up being an invisible part of it. I won't even mention Gold Rush in the press release. It's irrelevant."

Deputy Chief Nelson spoke softly. "Jack, we'll give it a shot, but releasing a veiled story to the press carries a lot of hazards with it. In the interest of public safety and maintaining the safety of our officers, I'll okay it. We can release the actual facts later with an explanation as to why it was not possible to do so now, for the safety of many people. I'm not sure how Chief Fuller is going to feel, but I agree that it's the only real option. The big picture supports unusual actions on our part. How are you and your guys doing, Jack?"

Jelenick's face flushed red, his anger clearly wanting to break through the surface. He was being sidelined by Lieutenant Adams again. "Chief Nelson, I have to disagree. This will take us down a path in which we lose the faith of the media. We need to close this down and cut our losses. I'll give the press release myself."

Lieutenant Adams was visibly affected by the shooting and by the incredible heroism displayed by the Los Angeles Police officers in his unit. Ignoring Jelenick's comments, Adams replied to Chief Nelson, "We're all doing our jobs, Chief. A lot of heroic actions on the part of these officers today, but I wouldn't expect anything less of them. These are the heroes of our society. These officers are the best of us. Whatever we need to do to support them, we have a responsibility to do just that."

Jelenick began walking in place as he talked. "Didn't you hear me, Lieutenant? I'll give the press release. We're not embellishing the story on this."

Chief Nelson sensed the pressure on the lieutenant's shoulders and felt the pressure on his own. He knew Jelenick could become a real problem for him personally now. "Okay, Jack. This is going to be tough for you, for us. Keep the operation under wraps and try to give the minimal amount of information to the press that you can. I'll call the commanding officer at Major Crimes and let her know we're going to be pawning responsibility for this off on her. They've already got so much bad press from some of their shootings that this is not going to make them happy. You guys will be tied up all night for the officer-involved shooting investigation. The usual time off, interviews by the LAPD psychologist, and then get them back to work, Jack. Come in and see me in a few days when you're back up and running. We'll both have some things to think about between now and then."

"Chief Nelson," Jelenick interrupted. "I'd like to recommend I take over management of this operation going forward. The lieutenant has completed the task of setting this operation into motion, although in a questionable format. Certainly not something that I would have ever approved of. It has reached a point where a higher level of constant review is necessary. We're now in a terrible position and hanging out with the press. I can step in and take over as of tomorrow morning. We can give Lieutenant Adams an opportunity to clean his mess up today, and then we can start fresh tomorrow with me in charge." Commander Jelenick was fighting hard to regain his position in charge of Gangs and Narcotics.

Chief Nelson took a breath and began to speak but was again interrupted by Commander Jelenick, who this time directed his remarks to Adams. "Lieutenant Adams, tomorrow morning at 1000 hours report to my office, where I will expect a full briefing on every aspect of this operation. Henceforth, I will expect you in my office every day at 1000 hours for a follow-up briefing to discuss current efforts, future planned efforts, and expected outcomes. I will expect a written report to accompany your daily briefings and we will begin a paper trail to detail your efforts."

"Yeah, well, I don't work for you, Commander. I take orders from Deputy Chief Nelson." Adams responded as calm as you please. It was his way.

Deputy Chief Nelson looked at both players, then responded, "I think we'll hold off on that, at least for today, Commander. We'll continue on our current course, but I will give this some thought. Right now I'd better give the Commanding Officer of SIS a call and warn her that she's going to take some heat for this. This should be fun."

Walking away from Nelson and Jelenick, Adams saw his opportunity to give the press everything they wanted. "Good evening, Miss Morgan. It's Candace, isn't it?" Just call him Mr. Cooperation.

"Yes, Lieutenant Adams. Jack. It seems we're always bumping into each other. Any way I could get an exclusive on what happened here? You know you owe me, Jack."

Adams took a deep breath and stepped a little closer to the reporter, whispering, "I guess I do owe you, Candace. I put you off a few times, and that's not very fair to you."

The exclusive press release Lieutenant Adams provided to Candace Morgan, what would be a prime-time news lead, identified a preplanned surveillance of William Garcia and Jorge Mendez by LAPD Major Crimes Surveillance, known to most as SIS, Special Investigation Section. An anonymous informant had reported that Garcia and Mendez were headed to Los Angeles from Fresno to commit a violent crime. SIS plainclothes detectives followed Garcia to a pawn shop where he and his accomplice, Jorge Mendez, armed themselves and wore masks to commit an armed robbery. After the robbery was committed, the suspects shot at the surveillance officers when they identified themselves as police officers in an attempt to make an arrest. Mendez was immediately shot and killed. William Garcia fled on foot, after which he carjacked a passing vehicle. As officers approached to arrest, Garcia threatened the officers with a handgun. Garcia was shot and killed. The passing motorists, the victims of the carjacking, were unharmed.

#

The office of Senior Editor Kevin Dolinski was buzzing with excitement. "Forget the gang angle, Candace. This is SIS, and we have an exclusive! We'll put it on tonight. Finish your filming, then get in here. We'll edit it now, pull research on SIS, and make it our lead. We'll filter gun control into the details. Good job, Candace, you finally got him. You got Lieutenant Adams! Now hold on to him."

Hours later, Lieutenant Adams watched the nightly news from his desk. "Controversial LAPD Surveillance Unit Shoots Two." The lead breaking news report by Candace Morgan was not a positive take on the Los Angeles Police Department, to say the least.

Captain Paula Broadhurst, Commanding Officer of Major Crimes, threw her shot glass of Patron Silver onto the floor of the restaurant and loudly yelled, "Damn it!" The other patrons at McCormick & Schmick's gave her a wide berth. She was steaming mad, mostly at Lieutenant Jack Adams.

CHAPTER THIRTY-FIVE
THE DOMINOES BEGIN TO FALL

Rand, Torres, Barr, Halverson, Andrews, and Thomas were assigned two days off connected to their regular days off. That gave them a four-day stretch. The sign on Gold Rush read "Closed for Repairs." Lieutenant Adams and Detective McClain teamed up to address the issues of the robbery and keep things moving forward.

As the team returned to Gold Rush, McClain decided they would ease back in to work. John Andrews slid in to work late, as expected, and then went on his usual rounds to look for street prostitutes that he had not already contacted. He had not seen Sissy in over a week, which was strange, as she was always very visible in the area. Andrews knew she wasn't involved in the robbery but needed to stay in touch with her in case they needed more information about Garcia. She was also a witness to the gun buy from Garcia.

Rampart Division Vice had previously identified Sissy as twenty-eight-year-old Carolyn Mays from Iowa City, Iowa. She had once been a waitress at the Texas Roadhouse on Corridor Way in Coralville and walked out mid-shift, never to be seen again. One customer too many had irritated her, so she packed up and left.

Her parents had made a missing persons report with no results for months, until Rampart Division Vice stopped her in Los Angeles to conduct a prostitution investigation. She had apparently come to Los Angeles seeking her fortune and warm weather. No more snow.

Contacting Rampart Division Vice to see if they had any contact with her this week, Andrews found some shocking news. Carolyn Mays from Iowa City had been found two days ago choked and bludgeoned to death in a hotel room off 3rd Street.

"Hey, Lieutenant, it's McClain. Listen, I've got some bad news. Sissy was found KMA in a shithole hotel off 3rd Street. It's a murder case. Coroner puts the time of death around the same time as our robbery. I'm guessing Garcia took out one of the loose ends who could roll on him before he hit us. I've got Rampart Homicide comparing their forensics against Garcia and Mendez."

"Okay, Mac. I feel bad for her . . . that's not what she deserved. Why do people ever come here? Everyone thinks it's better here because we have good weather. Damn it."

"My thought exactly, LT. I'm going to reach out to Iowa City Police Department and have them notify the family. I remember Andrews saying they made a missing report before she turned up here in LA."

#

The federal monitoring center east of downtown Los Angeles looked like any other business office, like an insurance office. A guarded reception desk blocked a hallway that led to a very secure section of the building. Individual workstations were equipped with multiple computer screens manned by federal monitors wearing noise-eliminating headphones, each one monitoring intercepted telephone calls supported by federal warrants. The calls were all recorded and transcribed.

Agent O'Reilly felt at home at the federal monitoring center. O'Reilly had spent hundreds of hours in this setting and loved the excitement and the adrenaline. Agent Bill O'Reilly was one of those guys that loved his job, had fun every day, and sported a contagious positive attitude. "Okay, Decker, you and Maddie have a big job here. This is an around-the-clock gig and things tend to move really fast, so you have to be on your game. But you'll get the hang of it really fast. Your job is to figure out what these guys are saying and then try to tie them in to past crimes. Then you need to make decisions about intervening in crimes they're planning in real time without burning your investigation. A lot of pressure is going to be on your shoulders, but I'm sure you're up for it."

Detectives Dave Decker and Maddie Hill stood behind the monitor assigned to the cellular telephone of Miguel Aguilar, Cuto of MS13. The monitor wore headsets as she listened to telephone calls and transcribed the verbiage as it occurred. The ability to listen to both English and Spanish intermixed, understand what is being said, and continuously advise Decker and Hill of the events, while at the same time transcribing the conversations on the computer in front of her, was nothing less than astounding.

Agent O'Reilly continued to support their efforts. "You guys are now live on Cuto's phone. The assigned monitors all speak Spanish, and they'll start feeding you real-time information as they're listening and typing the conversations on the screen. We keep the same monitors on the case so they can get to know the person they're listening to. That helps them to understand what's happening. They'll be typing in English and translating as they go. Most of the time, it will be difficult for them to have conversations with you, to answer your questions. They just have too much going on at the same time.

You need to just listen and watch what is being typed on the screen."

Detective Decker seemed less than confident about the whole process, but Maddie Hill was ready for the challenge. "Decker and I will be together today, but after this we'll split up on two shifts. One of us will be here all the time, and we'll bring someone in to help us during the evening hours."

CHAPTER THIRTY-SIX
ON THE WIRE

Maddie Hill was stationed behind the federal monitor tonight. Miguel Aguilar, "Cuto," made a lot of telephone calls, and most of the detective's time was spent charting out who each of the calls were made to or received from.

Detective Hill knew after only her second day on the wiretap that the support detectives stationed at Gold Rush North would be extremely busy. She and Detective Decker relayed everything to Gold Rush North, where the detectives investigated each involved person, phone number, and address. The amount of information at their disposal mounted quickly.

At 8 o'clock that night, 2000 hours, Miguel Aguilar called a new phone number. Aguilar's conversation was clearly Salvadoran Spanish and initially discussed "solving the issue." But when Aguilar used the phrase "Lay the bitch out," Detective Hill started seeing red flags.

Hill and the federal monitor listened as a plan was developed by Aguilar and the person on the other end to meet at King Taco on Roseview and Cypress Avenue at 10 o'clock, 2200 hours. Detective Hill knew it was a long shot, but that was really close to the home of Shirley Garcia on Isabel Street. The young girl who had invited Aguilar to the party, and the best witness against him to the double homicide.

"Detective McClain, it's Maddie Hill. Listen, we're moving on something that's happening right now. Miguel Aguilar is talking to someone we don't know, but I'm guessing it's someone he knows from El Salvador, so MS13. Aguilar's planning to meet him over in Northeast Division at 2200 hours. That's over where the double 187 occurred—that's where the little wit Shirley Garcia lives. During the call, they talked about solving some issue and then Aguilar talked about 'laying the bitch out.' I think they're going to kill the young girl, Shirley Garcia. She's the best wit against him."

McClain knew to trust the instincts of experienced police officers. "Okay, Maddie. Where are you going with this?"

"Mac, I'd like to get surveillance set up at Roseview and Cypress Avenue to watch the meet and identify who this other guy is. At the same time, I want to set surveillance up on Shirley Garcia's house, which is only a handful of blocks away. We have to roll people right now, though. We need to get everyone in place in less than an hour to get set up before Aguilar arrives." Confident people have no problem voicing their opinion and making decisions.

"Sounds good, Maddie. Good job on catching this. This is exactly why Lieutenant Adams built the detail this way. Call Surveillance now and get them rolling. I'll call the lieutenant and tell him what you've got."

McClain hung up and dialed Adams. "Hey, Lieutenant, it's Mac. Detective Hill is at the monitoring center and they overheard Miguel Aguilar, Cuto, making what sounds like plans to dump that thirteen-year-old wit from the Northeast Area double homicide. He's meeting someone at the King Taco on Cypress at 2200 tonight. That's really close to her house where the double occurred. I was going to meet with the Surveillance team when they get on scene." McClain knew to take charge until he was told differently.

"Okay, Mac, I'll meet you there. Let's don't involve your crew from Gold Rush, because Aguilar saw them when he sold us his gun. We'll just use the Surveillance guys. Let's try and have Stanford on 5K3 pull in his entire team if there's time."

In less than one hour, Paul Stanford cruised past the King Taco while his team of seven units sat up on Cypress and on Roseview. "5K3, the suspect is not in the lot. We're standing by."

At 2215 hours, Miguel Aguilar pulled into King Taco in a yellow Honda Accord and met up with two men in a white Toyota Tacoma truck. All three men sat in the Honda Accord. The King Taco was closing, the doors were locked, and most employees were leaving. Only two persons remained inside, a cleaning crew.

"5K3, suspect pulled into the lot in a yellow Honda, no one else in his car. He's talking to two men in the white Toyota Tacoma truck. They're all getting in the Honda now. Suspects are still stationary in the lot."

Aguilar, sitting in the driver's seat, looked taller than he really was. "I'll pick her up and bring her to you. Just do it and let's get out. I'll get her out of my car and that's when you do it."

The man sitting in the front seat next to Miguel Aguilar was Danny Silva, and he didn't seem to like the plan. "Cuto, she's not enough. Let's just go to the house and do it there. Everybody. We gotta do everybody."

The younger brother, Horace Silva, was eager to become involved in the violence. The parents of Daniel and Horace Silva had been killed in El Salvador by military troops, and the future of the two boys became set in concrete. "Let's go kill everybody. Fuck this."

Miguel Aguilar was more of a planner, and he knew that Shirley Garcia provided the most jeopardy to him. "I get it, but not yet. Let's get this little bitch out and kill her. Then we can go to the house if we need to. We don't even know who's there."

"5K7, I'm in the lot but I have to pull out. King Taco is closing and I'm the only car left besides the suspects. Be advised, I just got a clear visual on the passenger and I know this guy. Daniel Silva, MS13. We have a 187 warrant on him for a murder in Hollenbeck Division. I think the warrant is about three years old. I can't see the guy in the back seat, but male Hispanic about twenty-five, average everything."

With the Surveillance team set up in the four winds to cover both of the suspects' cars if they left the parking lot, the suspects stayed in the Honda Accord with no significant movement visible to the team.

At 11 o'clock p.m., 2300 hours, Detective Maddie hill listened at the federal monitoring center as Miguel Aguilar called a familiar telephone number. The cell phone number of thirteen-year-old Shirley Garcia.

During the call, Shirley Garcia assured Aguilar that after he had shot the two men and the police had come, she had not told the police who he was. She sounded like she was starting to cry. "I told them you shot them, but I didn't know you. I just invited you to the party when you walked by. I said I don't know shit."

Aguilar replied, quickly cutting her off. "I did that shit because I love you, because we're together! I killed those motherfuckers because they disrespected you."

Detective Maddie Hill listened to the recorded conversation and remarked out loud, "We've got you, motherfucker."

Shirley was thirteen years old and didn't really understand the concept of a real family or loyalty, and she was confused by Aguilar's stated admiration for her. She did believe, however, that being a witness was never a good thing. A product of being raised in a gang family, a family of criminals. Never be a witness against anyone.

During the phone call, Shirley Garcia sounded very much like Aguilar's "girlfriend." It came from youthful inexperience, hope, and from fear. Aguilar, on the other hand, had already decided that Shirley Garcia must be killed. "Come and pick me up at my house. I'll meet you out front," Shirley said. She wanted to rebel against her family. Thirteen-year-old Shirley Garcia wanted to be in love.

Aguilar began setting the plan into motion to remove Garcia from her home and take her to an isolated location where he would leave her for Daniel and Horace Silva to kill. "That's crazy, everybody knows me at your house. Walk down the street and I'll pick you up. Meet me down the street on Future."

Without wasting any time, Hill made a call. "Hey, Detective McClain, it's Maddie Hill. Miguel Aguilar is on the phone with Shirley Garcia. He's telling her he loves her and that he shot her two cousins because they disrespected her. He's planning to pick her up on the corner of Isabel and Future. She's the best wit we have against him; I'd hate to lose her."

"Okay, Maddie. It's going to be tough protecting her, but let's see where this goes. I'm thinking we should not let her in the car with him. Keep feeding me whatever info you hear."

Sitting in the driver's seat of his car, Aguilar put the plan to murder Shirley Garcia in place. "You guys pull into the park where Future Street dead-ends at San Fernando Road. There's a circle thing when you go in the park—just go to the right and pass the soccer fields. There's a maintenance yard right there and I already cut the lock off and opened the gate. Pull your truck in there and stay out of sight. I'll bring her and park by the kid's playground next to the soccer field. They got swings there. When I walk her past the gate, pull her ass in. Then she's yours, and I'm out. Do whatever you want with her, but she better be dead. And be careful, because there's a bunch of homeless tents out in the field behind the maintenance yard."

"5K3, Danny Silva and the other guy he showed up with just got out of the Honda. Everyone is back in their own cars. Both cars are exiting the lot onto Cypress."

Four Surveillance units followed Miguel Aguilar in the Honda Accord to Isabel and Future Street, where he parked at the curb. The two Surveillance units sitting on Shirley Garcia's house on Isabel watched her leave her house and begin walking south toward Aguilar. She passed Silver Street, then Frederick Street.

„5K7, we've got the two guys in the Toyota Tacoma driving into . . . let me see the sign. Rio de Los Angeles State Park. It's at the end of Future; it dead-ends into a park. I need someone on foot in the park. We can't follow in cars."

"5K8, I'm getting on foot now and working in to the park."

Detective Maddie Hill listened to the next call between Miguel Aguilar and Daniel Silva. Aguilar was parked, waiting for Shirley Garcia. "Okay, I see her walking. Get set up in the park and stay out of sight until I walk her past you. I don't want her to see you until you grab her."

She called McClain to give an update. "Detective McClain, Cuto just got off the phone with a male. I think Cuto's picking her up on foot and then driving her down the street and into the park where the Toyota Tacoma is. Cuto told them to stay out of sight until they're ready to grab her. It sounds like they're going to kill her in the park."

The LAPD air unit dedicated to surveillance operations was not available on such short notice. Air 3, already on duty, arrived on scene and maintained a high altitude to help obscure its presence. The airship observer located the white Toyota Tacoma inside the park, inside a maintenance yard. "Air 3, be advised we have the Tacoma inside a fenced maintenance yard with the gate standing open. The truck is hidden behind a yellow tractor and next to two portable offices. Looks like two occupants."

"5K3 to 5K5. Let's intercept her before she gets to the car. As much as we should play this out, I don't want her in the car."

"5K5, roger. I'll move closer and intercept her while you do the takedown of the Honda."

"5K3, let's have K9, 5K11, and 5K12 do the takedown of the Honda with me."

Shirley Garcia wore a black-and-white striped tank top and jeans with black tennis shoes. As she headed toward the Honda Accord, 5K5 moved closer to cut her off and intercept her while the other three units with 5K3 assembled in a caravan and traveled southbound on Isabel toward Future.

Detective McClain thought the plan for 5K5 to intercept Shirley Garcia while 5K3 and three other units arrested Aguilar seemed sound. It would keep Aguilar from having any personal contact with Garcia. The two men in the Tacoma who hid their vehicle in the park would then be taken down by the other Surveillance units as soon as Shirley Garcia was safe.

5K5 pulled his Volkswagen sedan into a driveway and blocked the sidewalk in front of Shirley Garcia. He would drive her out of the area to keep her safe. As he opened his car door, Shirley Garcia was immediately afraid and turned to look behind her to see the caravan of four tightly grouped undercover surveillance cars driving up behind her. Garcia believed they were after her. A drive-by!

Garcia broke into a run, bolting around the surveillance officer and his car. The plan was going sideways. "Shit! 5K5, the kid got around me! She made us! She's running to the Honda. We have to jam him, don't let him drive away with her."

Shirley was sprinting towards Miguel Aguilar in the yellow Honda. As 5K3 and the four other Surveillance units approached to arrest Miguel Aguilar, they watched Shirley Garcia jump into the passenger door of the yellow Honda Accord. The driver, Aguilar, was surprised by the frantic actions of Garcia when she jumped in the car and yelled, "Go, go, go! They're after me!"

Aguilar saw the four cars tightly grouped bearing down on him. Suddenly, it registered that these must be Shirley Garcia's family members from her house. *They're coming for me!*

Aguilar pushed down on the gas pedal and accelerated from the curb southbound on Isabel and turned the steering wheel hard to the right as he slid around the corner onto Future Street.

"5K3, the girl got in the Honda. They're westbound on Future Street toward the park. Airship, you have them?"

"Air 3, be advised the yellow Honda is westbound on Future headed toward the entrance to the park where the Tacoma is parked with the two occupants."

Paul Stanford switched frequencies. "5K3, plainclothes officers requesting help in Northeast Division. 187 suspect westbound on Future Street toward San Fernando Road. Possible kidnap victim, female Hispanic, thirteen years old, in the vehicle."

Miguel Aguilar accelerated over the short distance on Future through San Fernando Road and into the park. He needed to get to the Silva brothers who could help to protect him from Shirley Gonzales's relatives. He tried to grab his phone from the center console to call Daniel Silva but knocked the phone to the floor as he drove into the park.

Aguilar veered to the right as he entered the roundabout, causing the Honda to lose traction and slide sideways. Aguilar kept on the accelerator. He realized that the person who could identify him as the shooter of her two relatives, sat in the front seat of his car. They had to kill her right now and still fight the people in the cars chasing him at the same time. If he could get her to the Silva brothers, he could keep going and lead them away. That was his new plan. Get to the Silva brothers, throw Garcia out of the car, then drive away with the four cars following him. He was sure he could lose them, and the Silva brothers would still kill Shirley Garcia. Then they'd come back, shoot their house up, and kill everyone.

Aguilar held the accelerator down to get to the maintenance yard and throw Garcia to the Silva brothers before the people chasing him could see her. They would think she was still in the car, and they would chase him away from the park. As he accelerated, the car did not make the turn and slid broadside into the large rocks lining the road that were apparently placed there to keep people from driving into the field.

Aguilar didn't care about the car and mashed the accelerator harder. Shirley Garcia pushed her hands forward onto the dashboard and began yelling. The car hit the rocks hard and the back end came up off the ground, causing the car to roll over the large boulders and land on its top. Garcia screamed in fear as the car rolled. Neither of them wore a seat belt and they violently bounced around the interior of the car.

The dust cloud engulfed the car, and both Aguilar and Garcia were badly injured. Paul Stanford and the other detectives carefully approached on foot. The officers were intent on arresting Aguilar and rescuing Shirley Garcia, but the first mission was to rescue both of them from the wreckage of the car. The threat of fire or explosion was high.

Aguilar appeared semiconscious as he was pulled from the wreckage and immediately disarmed and handcuffed. The handgun in his waistband had not been dislodged during the crash. Aguilar's visible injuries were minimal, but he was not fully conscious.

Shirley Garcia was disoriented and dazed. She was pulled from the passenger window with obvious injuries to her right arm and face. Her arm was bleeding profusely. Two detectives helped her away from the wreckage and the danger of an explosion, then waited with her for LA Fire rescue to arrive.

The incident was just slightly out of the view of Daniel and Horace Silva in the maintenance yard, but the two brothers saw the police helicopter at it descended over the park and heard the loud commotion of the car hitting the boulders and rolling over.

"Air 3, the two occupants of the Tacoma are out and on foot. Correct that—back in the vehicle and moving, driving out of the maintenance yard. Suspects will be northbound through the park." On the Northeast Division frequency, Air 3 broadcasted the suspects' direction of travel.

Detective McClain and Lieutenant Adams, each in their own cars, followed the Surveillance units into the park. Hearing the broadcast of Air 3, McClain and Adams drove past the wreckage and into the park. As the Tacoma drove northbound, they both accelerated and pulled behind the suspects.

Daniel Silva drove the Tacoma headed for the north entrance on Macon Street. He didn't know what had happened but was sure the incident was related to them. Daniel Silva yelled to his brother, Horace, "We haven't done shit, they got nothing on us! If they stop us, we were just sitting in the park and we left because of all the police shit. We were just scared and we left. We don't know shit!"

11A37, a Patrol unit from Northeast Division, raced into the park on Macon Street from San Fernando Road. The road into the park was divided by a landscaped area scattered with large boulders. The two officers saw the Tacoma approaching on the other side of the divided road. Finding a break between the boulders, the officers drove directly into the path of the approaching Toyota Tacoma.

5K7 and 5K8 were on foot in the park. They ran to intercept the Tacoma as it traveled northbound toward the park exit. As the Tacoma stopped, facing the LAPD black-and-white police car with its red lights flashing, the two plainclothes detectives approached from the passenger side of the Tacoma.

Both detectives held their badges up for the uniformed officers from Northeast Division.

Detective McClain pulled his car slightly to the right of the suspect's car, while Lieutenant Adams pulled to the left and drove on the other side of the divided road. The suspects were boxed in.

As he stopped in front of the police vehicle, Daniel Silva saw the plainclothes officers on foot approaching from the passenger side. Then the two Ford Crown Vics pulled alongside both sides of the Tacoma. The odds were not in their favor. Daniel told his brother, "Don't fight—put the guns behind the seat. Just do what they say."

Daniel and Horace Silva were not aware that the LAPD detectives had monitored their conversation with Miguel Aguilar. They were convinced that they had not broken any laws, but they would be released.

#

To their dismay, both men were arrested for conspiracy to murder Shirley Garcia. Daniel Silva was also finally arrested on the warrant for murder from three years prior.

The arrests and the rescue of Shirley Garcia just seconds before her murder in Northeast Division was nothing short of miraculous. The wiretap had proven its worth, and a new tool to fight gang crime was sold to the command staff of the Los Angeles Police Department. A tool to support a new tactic: intelligence-based investigations to fight gangs. Lieutenant Jack Adams sat in front of Deputy Chief Nelson to discuss the takedown of Miguel Aguilar.

"You did a hell of job, Lieutenant. Shirley Garcia owes her life to you and your crew. Chief Fuller sends his commendation. I can't even tell you how pleased he is."

"Thank you, Chief Nelson. Detective Maggie Hill at the federal monitoring center was responsible. She's proving to be an incredible asset to us. And the important thing is that we got three more guns for the mayor's photo op."

Nelson wasn't even sure how to respond. "Yeah, well, I'm not too concerned about the mayor right now. You know I was uncomfortable with this whole issue on wiretaps, but I've learned to trust what you tell me, Jack. Not only did you make a gang member from MS13 on the double homicide up in Northeast Division and recovered the gun he used—you saved the wit's life. Then the icing on the cake was you pulled in this Silva guy, another MS13, for the murder warrant. His brother goes, too. Good job, Jack."

Jack Adams dropped the famous *Seinfeld* line, "I'm just trying to get ahead, sir."

CHAPTER THIRTY-SEVEN
PILLOW TALK

Commander Stans Jelenick and his wife, Elana, were attending the highly anticipated annual gala event at the Knupp Gallery that allowed her to display her painting efforts. Her opportunity to display her paintings at a dedicated Czech event found her and Stans surrounded by their friends and associates. They both seemed to fit in comfortably, but Elana felt weak as she attempted to fulfill her dreams of being one of the insiders, one of the wealthy and influential.

Stans was doing his best to play the role his wife demanded as the Czech, Slovak, and Russian attendees enjoyed the taste of European culture in Los Angeles.

Three years ago, during a Czech and Slovak Republics camping trip at Hurkey Creek campground at Hume Lake, Elana had made what she believed to be a lifelong best friend. Elana Jelenick and Yvonne Sokoloff, an accomplished Russian artist creating glass sculptures, immediately bonded and had been friends ever since. They were inseparable at the gallery.

"Yvonne, I have been so worried about Stans. He is so courageous and so smart keeping America safe, but I worry. They are investigating a dangerous man in the Russian Mafia. He is from Glendale, and we know so many people there." Elana displayed as much drama as she could muster in her efforts to exaggerate her husband's importance. To this group, being a policeman in Los Angeles was looked down upon.

Yvonne Sokoloff appeared interested and genuinely concerned about Elana. "Honey, you keep yourself safe, and don't let Stans get involved in these things. This is not his place; we do not persecute our own. Who is this man in the Mafia, as you say?"

Elana was now the focus of attention, and she glowed in the spotlight. "A young man from Glendale who is selling guns and stolen Mercedes-Benzes. Stans is undercover, Yvonne. A spy. It is so dangerous, but I can't tell you any more. I swore to Stans I wouldn't tell anyone."

Yvonne placed both her arms around Elana's shoulders. "Don't you say one word, Elana, my best friend. We all love you and appreciate Stans's work as a policeman. You made a promise, Elana. Don't you tell anyone. You tell Stans to quit that police department and come to work for my husband, Kostya. His law firm has many Czech and Russian clients, and he could use a good man like Stans. He could investigate."

Kostya Sokoloff did, in fact, represent many Czech and Russian clients. As it so happened, Kostya Sokoloff, a Russian national and corporate attorney, represented various members of the Russian Mafia in expanding their business enterprises in America.

#

Aleks Antonov had moved to the United States when he was fifteen years old. Living with his parents and two older brothers, he struggled to fit in with his schoolmates who were largely Armenian. Although Russian and Armenian relations are usually positive, Aleks did not find many allies in America. Many of his relatives and friends of his parents lived in the same apartment building in Glendale, so at least he could always find a sense of comfort and sanctuary when he went home.

During high school, Aleks's father, Segei, bestowed him with many expensive gifts, including expensive clothes and luxury cars, believing that it would help his son to be popular in school. It also maintained an appearance of wealth and power for the family as a whole.

Segei Antonov, sensitive to his image, served as a Brigadier in the Russian Mafia on his way up the ladder and hoped to be named Pakhan—boss.

Segei watched his son, Aleks, progress into manhood as he completed many tasks for the family. Now in his mid-twenties, Segei was ready to bestow Aleks with his next and very expected place in the family business: the business of making money. Aleks was provided with the position of manager of one of the family-owned businesses, a laundry service on Brand Boulevard not far from where they lived. What Aleks wasn't initially told was that the mostly all-cash business performed a very special function, that of laundering cash from criminal gains. The other financial enterprises the Russian Mafia engaged in could not be successful without an avenue to launder the illegal gains, and Aleks now sat in a key position.

As Aleks began the process of taking over the business, he wasn't happy about the image it gave him. The women he dated would not be impressed by a laundry service; his friends would make fun of him. He saw himself as a member of the Russian Mafia, the Bratva, and he worked hard to convince everyone around him that he actually was. He longed to have the influence his father had and, most of all, he longed to be feared.

Aleks was eager to gain the status of Vor, a made man in Bratva, and desired a much higher profile position than managing a laundry. Aleks was committed to placing himself on a fast track to Vor but didn't know he already was, and sitting on a gold mine at that.

Aleks began his life as a business manager, hiring only the best-looking females for the laundry service, always Russians and Armenians. Through his combination of being a suave, handsome young man and his ability to give people a false sense that he was a powerful and dangerous member of the Russian Mafia, Aleks quickly transitioned some of his attractive female employees into the business of prostitution.

One of these prostitutes, Kira, told Aleks about an import and export company named Gold Rush. She had met another woman, another prostitute, who had told her about an import and export company that bought guns. There was no paperwork. She heard they simply purchased guns and sent them out of the country.

Prior to hearing of Gold Rush from Kira, Aleks had made three successful purchases of small quantities of guns that he then turned around for a good profit as another self-starting business enterprise, one that would impress people. He never told his father, Segei.

Aleks wanted to expand upon his gun dealing efforts but struggled with a plan to sell large quantities of guns while staying under the radar of local law enforcement. Thus, Aleks decided to investigate Gold Rush and possibly attempt to sell a single gun to see how it went. If it went like Kira had told him it would, this had the potential to place Aleks into a whole new role as an arms dealer. Gold Rush sends the guns out of the country—that would make him an *international* arms dealer. That would impress people. That would impress women. That would impress his father.

As Aleks endeavored to develop his career as an international arms dealer, he stumbled upon another opportunity. Another in which he may be able to impress his father, Segei. Aleks was aware that his father was struggling with the ability to move stolen cars to Russia. His father's former business partner had met an untimely death for his failures to establish this part of their plan, and now Segei was under a lot of pressure to make the plan work.

At Gold Rush, Aleks was unexpectedly introduced to the opportunity to solve his father's logistics problem. Gold Rush was buying guns under the radar of law enforcement and had the ability to ship containers around the world. Containers they owned and controlled. Containers that could be filled with cars—*stolen* cars.

After dropping off the twenty Mercedes-Benz sedans to Gold Rush, Segei and the rest of the family treated Aleks differently. They showed him more respect.

The cars were equipped with California dealer paper plates that Aleks had obtained from the Department of Motor Vehicles thanks to one of the file clerks assigned to the Glendale branch that had fallen head over heels for the Russian who had stood at her window two years prior. Aleks's ability to obtain the DMV documentation solved many of the problems that Segei had faced earlier.

Now, Aleks had resolved the serious situation Segei had found himself in after his efforts to ship cars to Russia had been interrupted. It had taken a lot of effort to convince his father that he had developed an alternate plan to ship cars to St. Petersburg. Segei, understanding the serious situation he was personally in and wanting for his son to be successful, allowed Aleks twenty cars to trial the new opportunity. So far, the operation was proving to be successful. Segei was amazed at his son's abilities.

Aleks Antonov was now on the fast track to achieve the status of Vor. He decided not to tell his father about his gun dealing just yet. Even so, Aleks believed he was now indestructible.

Segei Antonov sat with his friends, his advisors, to brief them on his son's new enterprise. "My son has not yet considered the possibilities of success and advancement in his role with the laundry business. A cash business such as this can largely benefit us, and Aleks can become an integral part of our growth here in America. But he is young and enterprising, and he is a romantic. He watches many movies. I know of his business efforts with beautiful young women, but he has not spoken to me of it yet. He thinks his father is not as smart as him, as young people do. You will all keep an eye on him and advise me if he finds himself on ice he may fall through.

"If the transfer of cars is successful, it will solve many problems. As you know, there is much pressure to make these things happen quickly. We must move with great haste and that requires a higher level of risk. We have looked at this business in Los Angeles, and so far it appears to not be a problem for us. We are attempting to identify who owns the business but that information is unclear. Many businesses here hide many things through channels to avoid taxes and fees, which is why we are able to take advantage as well. The taxes and fees here are such that you are forced to break these laws to just survive. I have asked for the business to be watched and we continue to look at their business records.

"We will now begin to identify those who work inside. People we know are people we can control. Aleks also has a friend in the Department of Motor Vehicles who is proving to be invaluable in many ways, and I think she can help us with this task also. So far, nothing has been a concern to us, so we will allow Aleks to move forward on a small and tempered scale."

CHAPTER THIRTY-EIGHT
BURNED BY THE RUSSIANS

US Attorney Roger Gibson had successfully acquired the federal warrant for the phone of Aleks Antonov. The facts of the case did not require a sense of urgency. Once the twenty stolen cars were received directly from Aleks along with a payment and agreement to ship them to Russia, the Gang detectives could take their time in partnering with Burglary, Auto Theft Division to conduct a thorough investigation. The foundation of the crime had already occurred. Similarly, after Aleks committed three separate crimes of selling guns to Gold Rush, he was bought and paid for. Federal prison. The phone tap was expected to be icing on the cake to strengthen both cases against Aleks, seek additional evidence, and identify co-conspirators.

At the federal monitoring center, the case against Miguel Aguilar, Cuto, had been discontinued. Detectives Decker and Hill were able to transition directly into the wiretap on Aleks.

Now that the phone of Aleks Antonov had been brought into play, the federal monitor made herself comfortable and spread her personal things out across her workstation. She had done this before and was setting in for the long term. Detective Hill had instructed the federal monitor that they would "ease" into this part of the investigation and that they were looking for facts that strengthened the criminal investigation of Aleks Antonov and identified other crimes and co-conspirators. After a few minutes of orientation with Detective Hill, who played out the basis of the investigation, the wiretap was initiated.

At three o'clock in the afternoon, 1500 hours, forty-eight minutes into the phone line going live, the Russian-speaking monitor turned to Maddie Hill. "Detective Hill, you should review this. There's a conversation about an LAPD commander."

"What is it? What are they saying?" Detective Hill's immediate concern was warranted.

"Aleks is talking to an unknown male. There has been no name or reference, but he sounds older. The older man is telling Aleks that the LAPD commander discussed an undercover—although the word is different—an undercover operation by LAPD to arrest him and his father. A jewelry store?

A gold store? Policemen are in the gold store and undercover planning to arresting Aleks. They're going to fire—no, torch the building and teach a lesson. Aleks is being told not to go to the gold store by his father's order."

Hill began to raise the red flag. "Stay on it. Every word counts, and take really detailed notes." She grabbed her phone and made her first call. "Special Agent O'Reilly, this is Maddie Hill. I'm on the Russian and I need you here. I'll call you back in a few with details, but get in your car and get here as fast as you can."

After hanging up, Agent O'Reilly stood up from his desk, grabbed his coat, and headed for the door. It was a long drive from West Los Angeles to the east side of the city, especially during the afternoon hours, but he was intent on making every minute count. The tone of Detective Hill's voice told him that he had to move fast.

Hill made her next call as fast as she was able. "Lieutenant, this is Maddie Hill. I need you right now—"

Lieutenant Adams, stopping at Chief Nelson's door to answer his phone, hoped to get on the issue, whatever it was, right after this meeting. He only needed a moment to update Chief Nelson on the new wiretap that was now up and running. "I just need a minute, Hill. Can I call you back?"

"I don't think so. Officer needs help and I need you now, I think right now." The tone and the urgency in Detective Hill's voice turned Adams away from the deputy chief's door. "Go ahead, Hill. What do we have?"

"I'm on the Russian's wire. We just got on him. He's talking in Russian to someone we don't know who laid out an LAPD commander who rolled on Gold Rush. They know, LT. They know we're running Gold Rush. The Russian is talking about torching the building, although they're using a different phrase for 'fire.' The translation isn't really clear, but I get the meaning."

"Torching Gold Rush? Damn it. Stay on that wire, Maddie. Don't move one inch and feed me everything you hear. Get O'Reilly in there with you Code 3."

Code 3 is the LAPD radio code for driving with lights and siren on. Universally, in every situation, it means "move your butt as fast as humanly possible."

Chief Nelson appeared in the doorway of his office, wondering what had sidetracked Adams. "Lieutenant, I've only got a couple minutes for you. I have a meeting with the LA Business Networking Group."

"Pass on the meeting, Chief. I need to make a couple calls, but I need you here, sir." Dialing Detective McClain's number, Adams stepped into Nelson's office. "Mac, listen up fast. You're going to get hit. I don't know when; it may be any second. The Russian made us somehow and he's talking about torching Gold Rush. Not sure what that means—the translation could be off. Lock the front door and put everyone in the van, now. Light up Mike Rand and get him ready for anything. Trojan horse out of there right now. Everyone in the van and out. Once you're out, call me."

"Got it, LT, we're moving."

Detective McClain hung up and turned to Rand and said, "Mike, we're going to be hit. Suit up and be prepared for anything."

While Rand pulled a tactical vest over his head and picked up his rifle, McClain pushed the office door open. "Drop everything. Lock the door and everyone in the van, now! Do it! Halverson, open the roll-up and Andrews, get the van started."

Adams got back on the phone to call 5K3, the Surveillance unit assigned to Gold Rush. "Stanford, listen. I've got word Gold Rush is going to be hit by the Russian in the black Mercedes—we're burned. I'm pulling everyone out in the van. You guys stay put and keep eyes on the front and rear and see where this goes, but be sharp with counterintelligence and watch your backs. Suit up and be ready for anything. You stay on scene, and you've got the ball in requesting whatever resources you need. Beef up your Surveillance guys if anyone else is available this early in the day, but hold off on requesting uniformed resources until you see what goes down. Let me know everything you see."

"Got it, LT. There's only two units out here right now, but I'll pull some more in from home. These Russians are scary, so I'm going to build a full team out here. Is Metro around?"

Adams was spinning multiple plans and scenarios as he talked. "I'll get on the phone with them next. Don't confront anyone, just keep eyes on if you can. As you build your team, get a couple units over on their apartment building in Glendale. I don't know how we'll use them over there, but just have them stand by."

Adams's next call was to Metropolitan Division. "Officer Blaha, this is Jack Adams. Gangs is working an undercover storefront over in Rampart Division and we have word that we're burned and bad guys are going to hit the location. You have any troops on the street?"

"Nope. Everybody's working later tonight, Lieutenant. I can get the on-call SWAT team, R50David, on the road and moving in your direction from home. I've got the callout roster sitting in front of me. What do you think?"

"Get it done. Have them stage at your office in Rampart and stand by there for now. I'll get back to you. Thanks, pal." Adams kept spinning the situation in his mind. *Get everyone out of Gold Rush, then go find the suspects. Take the fight to them.*

"Chief Nelson, I apologize, sir. Detective Hill is on the wire listening to the young Russian. He's talking to someone we don't know. We got burned and it sounds like they plan to hit Gold Rush. They're talking about torching it. Chief, the Russian is saying something about an LAPD commander who rolled. Someone inside rolled on us, sir."

Adams's phone rang and startled him. "Lieutenant, it's Mac. We're clear of Gold Rush. Everyone's in the van and Rand is in the front passenger seat with all his gear. Halverson is in full gear in the rear and we're all ready. Where do you want us?"

Adams felt some pressure ease up, but the problem was not over. "Go to Metro Division over on Temple and stand by there. I initiated a SWAT callout and they'll be staging there also. When you get to Metro, see if you can arrange a clear area to set up a command post. I need a small command post there, Mac. You take charge of it until I get there. Our immediate plan is to clear out of Gold Rush and then find the Russian, Aleks. Surveillance is holding on Gold Rush and calling in troops from home. I'm trying to get some of them on the Russian's apartment in Glendale until we figure this out."

"Will do, Lieutenant. What happened? How did we get burned by the Russians?" McClain began asking the questions that many people would be asking over the next few hours.

"Mac, I can't talk about that right now. It's information for face-to-face, but not right now. Trust me on this and keep everyone safe. I don't know where we're going with this yet, but stand by at Metro until I call for you. Be on alert while you're driving, watch for a tail. Keep Rand and Halverson lit up. The cat's out of the bag, and we don't need to stay invisible any longer."

"Will do, Lieutenant. This is some bad shit." McClain knew this was big.

#

As the events progressed, Segei Antonov was concerned, and his face displayed the pressure he was now under. "Kostya, this new information is troubling. It may lead to many roads in which we are all in grave danger. I can handle these situations, but I must keep my son safe. In all good intention, Aleks did this thing for us and it was promising. We looked at this thing—even I looked at this thing, and it was promising. I will pay a price, but I fear it is Aleks who will carry the weight. I can't have that."

"Segei, we discussed these things, and I have to confide that we were somewhat blinded by the promise of success and the promise of your son. We should not have moved so quickly. But that has passed, and now we must survive all of the roads you have mentioned. I understand your fear for Aleks and agree that we must take unusual actions."

"Kostya, he is my son. I cannot allow these things to harm him. American policemen pose little threat to us, but a threat from our own is certain. I will send Aleks to Russia, to safety away from American policemen, and I will stay and answer for a failure that is mine, not his. Is that what you advise?"

"No Segei. International travel is risky at this point. I advise that we move Aleks immediately but stay within the confines of the United States so he may travel unnoticed. To Alaska, Segei, to Sitka. Our friends and family have a strong presence and a long reach there and we have many safe harbors that we have placed people before, when they should be away from prying eyes. Alaskan law enforcement is unaware of our presence and Aleks can be integrated into the community and St. Michael's without notice."

#

Detective Hill was glued to the screen of the federal monitor, watching her type as the woman verbally relayed what she was hearing on Aleks's cell phone. "Detective Hill, Aleks is saying he sent someone to the jewelry store to light it on fire. He talks with a lot of slang, but I'm getting most of it. Then someone who is shooting policemen as they run from the fire. He talks with so much slang that young people use today."

Hill got a busy signal from Lieutenant Adams's phone. The monitor raised her voice. "Detective, Aleks says they don't know who the policemen are, but it doesn't matter because they are all inside the jewelry store. The older man is saying something about . . . something of a boss. Something about the policemen's boss. The older man knows who the policemen's boss is and that he is always in the news."

Maddie Hill displayed her character in her response. "That son of a bitch. He's lucky I'm not standing in front of him. Keep on it, keep on the call. Can you tell who he's talking to yet?"

"I have the phone number and I'm seeking a subscriber, but no information is available. It's a non-assigned phone, so probably one of those throwaways. Aleks is not calling him by name, but he sounds older and talks with authority to Aleks. Not his father, I don't think. Someone else. Aleks says he is to protect his father. He talks about his father's wishes. Maybe this is ordered by his father—I'm just guessing on that. Now he's saying something about the person in charge again. He says the boss of gangs will be a trophy. I'm not sure what that means, but it sounds bad. They might be after that person, whoever the boss is of the policemen."

Detective Maddie Hill called McClain's cell phone number. "We're out of Gold Rush, Maddie. Are you still on the wire?"

Maddie Hill exploded into the phone, "Mac, they're going to hit the lieutenant! I can't get him on his phone."

"Okay, Maddie. He's with Chief Nelson at Headquarters—he'll be okay. Just stay on that wire and feed everything directly to the lieutenant. He'll relay to me. Got it?"

"I got it, Mac, I just can't get through to him. I'll keep trying." Hill took a few deep breaths then dialed again.

Adams's phone was ringing with multiple calls, and he chose to answer the call from Maddie Hill. "Lieutenant, this is terrible. Listen, what we're getting is sketchy, but I'm trying to fill in the blanks. This little Aleks bastard is setting into motion someone who's going to Gold Rush to torch it and then hit our officers as they bail out of the building. Lieutenant, the conversation is something about the fact that they don't know who the officers are, but they know who is in charge of Gangs. They're planning to hit the person in charge of Gangs. I think that means you, Lieutenant!"

In conservative Orange County, in Rossmoor, school was out and Adams's son and daughter were at home. That thought immediately consumed Adams.

CHAPTER THIRTY-NINE
MAKING A STATEMENT

Segei Antonov met again with his friends and advisors in the way that business is conducted in the Russian Mafia. "Unexpected information has come to us, and apparently a problem has occurred resulting from Aleks's efforts to strengthen our place in America. A police lieutenant in Los Angeles, the LAPD, has chosen to target each of us and our families. He has developed an undercover operation to trap Aleks and, in so doing, each of us. Do not be concerned, as I will step in to correct this problem. This lieutenant and myself, we have similar roles of leadership and planning but we have competing interests. He is insignificant, yet he is in the way. He has decided to interfere not only with our business, but with our families. With my son. So, I will have to show this lieutenant a hard lesson, one which will extend to the rest of law enforcement in America. We will take from him what he loves, and then we will remove him from interfering."

Russian organized crime is institutionalized in the political and economic foundations of Russia. Segei Antonov became involved in Russian organized crime at an early age as a thief, a violent thug and enforcer.

The criminal organization was structured such that those at the bottom of the organization committing crimes had no contact with the leaders. It was common that those at the bottom did not even know who was at the top of the organization giving orders.

Russian organized crime is not based upon ethnicity or other such structures as we see in the United States. Rather, the members are merely brought together based upon their complicity in criminal activity and many, if not most, bonds are formed in Russian prisons. The initial connection is based upon illegal gains.

By the time the Soviet Union fell on our Christmas Day, 1991, Segei had moved up a very convoluted ladder and oversaw the illegal trading and smuggling of rare metals in Russia. Immediately thereafter in 1992, Russian public property began to be sold to private investors and the system heavily favored those in organized crime. Years later, following the enormous profits that Russian organized crime realized from these purchases and investments, Segei Antonov was sent to the United States with the intent of investing and laundering the illegal gains in America. In turn, those investments were intended to expand the criminality and access to illegal gains of the Russian Mafia around the globe.

In 1995, Segei emigrated from Yekaterinburg in the Ural region, one of Russia's most violent cities. He was involved in the trading and smuggling of rare metals, along with the corruption, extortion, and violence that accompanied such an effort.

Although heavily involved in Russian organized crime, Segei seized the opportunity to move his family to the United States, along with many of his friends and associates, due to lax immigration standards and investigations in the United States. The immigration system was also hamstrung by Russia's refusal to cooperate with American authorities in identifying those with criminal backgrounds attempting to migrate to the United States. The separation of Russian politics, economics, and organized crime was not to be achieved.

Although Segei never admitted it, his fortune of moving to the United States was a welcome situation for him. He had been to the United States before and found it to have much more comfortable living accommodations. Segei found immediate success moving cash from Russia to America and investing in commercial real estate and existing businesses, then turning the businesses he bought into avenues to launder monies.

After arriving in America, Segei led a very successful operation and built a war chest from monies illegally gained through extortion based on the threats of arson. The extortions occurred in the Russian Jewish communities, primarily in West Hollywood. Over time, Segei expanded his criminal actions to include credit card and health care fraud, real estate investment fraud, interstate transportation of stolen car parts, and the theft of high-end cars. Violence, or threats of violence, accompanied each of Segei Antonov's efforts.

The National Insurance Crime Bureau indicates a nationwide stolen vehicle recovery rate of only 60 percent, indicating many stolen vehicles are broken down for parts or exported to other countries. The percentages are highest in those areas that host border crossings or international ports—areas such as Los Angeles. These numbers directly relate to the presence of organized national and international crime groups.

The FBI coined the term "transnational organized crime" while working cases of immigrants who brought organized crime from their countries to the United States. Transnational organized crime exploded during the 1990s, primarily as a result of the influx of Russian nationals. The term has also been applied to the influx of Mara Salvatruche gang members, MS13, from El Salvador.

Segei Antonov sat in the law office of Kostya Sokoloff with Kostya and three other men Segei had emigrated to the United States with. "My friends, we followed Yaponchik, Vyacheslav Ivankov, to America and found this ripe ground for our families to profit. My son, he is enthusiastic, but he is young. We can weather this and make a statement. Although we strive to live quietly and privately, it is a time to announce our presence and display our strength to assure no further interference by American law enforcement."

Kostya Sokoloff, long having represented Russian and Czech "Tovarisch" in their business enterprises, was uncomfortable in this setting. He had never represented those arrested and prosecuted for criminal actions. "Segei Konstantinovich Antonov, your son, Aleks, has played his cards openly on the table. American police are naive to our presence, but they are not stupid. They will come for him no matter what. This thing you're planning, this intervention with the police lieutenant, it will not dismiss this thing. They will still come."

"Kostya, my friend. Even if they know Aleks's true identity, he will be gone by the time the mess is cleaned up. Most importantly, we will send a message. I understand this is not Mother Russia, but we can begin teaching them. American policemen are difficult to purchase. Policemen in America are idealists. They believe in right and wrong, as if there is such a thing. But those in leadership positions are more vulnerable, more accessible. They have a sense of greed for the positions they wish to hold or wish to obtain. We now have such a friend on the police department, and he will continue, I am sure, to be our friend. At my urging, he will slow the investigation and give us the time we need so that Aleks will be returned to Russia far in front of their investigation. I have arranged for the transportation. The policemen will be left with nothing but death, and they will fear us." Segei Antonov spoke with the patience of a man used to giving orders and having them followed. A man used to imparting violence to others to control them, or eliminate them.

Kostya, largely a corporate attorney and one not used to being pulled into a possible criminal defense, just had to respond, "Segei, how can you be sure about this friend to us? He has only given us this bit of information."

With a slight smile, Segei Antonov responded slowly. "Surely, Kostya, your loving wife, Yvonne, would not want to lose her friend in art. This policeman, this commander, is now our friend. As is his wife. And they both will continue to be so, or they will not continue to be at all."

Kostya remained concerned. "Where do we go with this?"

"Kostya, we need to convince Commander Jelenick that, as his friend, we are more valuable to him than this police department he works for. We must convince him that we are more valuable to him than even his wife. When that is done, he will do as we command."

#

Lieutenant Jack Adams had made a command decision: take the fight to the criminals, and never be a willing victim. It was time to introduce the LAPD to the Russian Mafia.

Segei Antonov was seated in the rear seat of a black Mercedes-Benz when he arrived at the Glendale apartment building and Adams gave the order to arrest him. Segei wasn't concerned when the plainclothes police cars pulled to the front and rear of his car, forcing his driver to stop and capturing him inside a trap, boxing him in. In Russia Segei would have already been dead, but he knew that in America police officers had many rules and were micromanaged by many watchful eyes. Segei instructed his driver to follow the directions of the plainclothes police officers. Once the cars stopped, Segei was immediately taken into custody without incident. Segei only smiled.

Deputy Chief of Police Steve Nelson ordered that Segei be taken to the LAPD headquarters building, where he was placed into a large conference room at a table seating twelve people. Arrestees were usually taken to one of the police stations, not headquarters, but Nelson wanted Segei close. It was not long before Segei's attorney, Kostya Sokoloff, arrived.

Segei uttered his first words since being arrested. "Kostya, my friend. I am in no jeopardy; do not be concerned. Aleks may have ended his stay here in America, though. I still need a short period to arrange for his return to Russia, so a stalling of events may be in order. I have a jet being prepared."

When Detective Decker walked into the room, Sokoloff asked to speak with him in the hallway. "Officer, my client Segei Antonov wishes to cooperate with you in any way he can. He does not know why he is here. Can you help me, his attorney, to understand that?"

Decker had no patience for this. There was a lot going on all at the same time, and he needed to get down to it. He needed to know what Segei Antonov knew about the threats heard on the wire. "Your client was brought in due to threats made against police officers. I'm not quite ready to interview him yet. I'm waiting for an investigator from Immigration to get here to determine the status of your client in this country."

Sokoloff wasn't impressed with the veiled threat. "Officer, I assure you that Mr. Antonov's status in America is supported by legal process. He is a father and a businessman and lends much to the community he lives in. That being said, Mr. Antonov wishes to speak to a Commander Stans Jelenick. If this can be accommodated, I assure you that Mr. Antonov will comply with all requests for information."

#

Commander Stans Jelenick seemed taller after the request was communicated to him. "Why does he want to talk with me?"

"Can't answer that, Commander. Says he'll spill the beans if he can talk to you." Decker was immediately irritated by Jelenick. One of those brass who had been promoted to his level of incompetence.

On his way to the conference room where Segei Antonov was being held, Jelenick just had to stop by Deputy Chief Nelson's office. "I don't know why the Russian is asking for me, Chief, or how he even knows me. I'm guessing his attorney knows of me through another case. Either way, once I figure this out and we see why this is happening, I'll brief you and the chief of police. I'm thinking I should take this over for Lieutenant Adams. This is way over a lieutenant's head."

As Commander Jelenick sat at the conference table across from the two Russians, Kostya Sokoloff initiated the conversation. "Commander, I represent Segei Antonov. My client wishes to speak with you, but confidentially. Without recordings and without pictures. Can you assure us that this is the situation?"

"Yes, I'm sure it is. This is not an interview room, and we do not have recording capabilities here. You can be comfortable talking to me. I'm here to help clear this situation up while I take over this investigation. I will be in charge from now on."

Inside the large conference room, Kostya Sokoloff nodded to Segei, then sat back in chair with his hands in his lap. Segei pulled his chair closer to the table and placed both his hands, now out of handcuffs, on the table. Segei began the conversation as Sokoloff sat silently. "It was you, my friend, Commander Jelenick, that provided us with the information about your undercover police operation. Your wife is a friend to us, as you are. The chess pieces of this game have been put into place, and many are falling as we speak. You and I are Tovarisch. You know this word? Tovarisch? We are comrades, partners in this thing."

Jelenick's face was blank. "What are you talking about, Mr. Antonov?" Jelenick had no idea what this conversation was about or where it was going.

"Call me Segei, please. Your wife, Elana, who is our friend, has provided us with the information you possess about this undercover police operation, and we are indebted to you. And to Elana, a fine woman. Unfortunately, your police operation has pulled in my son, Aleks, who should not be involved."

Jelenick immediately grew angry and shocked at the mention of his wife's name. "How do you know Elana?"

"She is well-known to us, Commander Jelenick. She is a close friend, and she is currently in the possession of my comrades. You understand Tovarisch now, yes?"

"What are you talking about? Where is Elana?" Jelenick immediately slid his phone from his front pants pocket and dialed his wife's number, but there was no answer. The call went to voicemail. "Elana, call me right away."

"Commander, I assure you that Elana is fine for the moment. She is in our possession as a guest but not free to return home, if you understand. You are Tovarisch, Commander. We are indebted to you, and now you to us. We are bound together. It is best this conversation not leave this room, or I'm afraid your standing with the police department will be jeopardized. As will the safety of your beautiful Elana. But not to worry, we can assist each other in many ways in the future now."

Jelenick, for once, was speechless, trying to figure out what Segei Antonov was talking about.

"You wish to become deputy chief, maybe chief of police, as Elana tells us. That is an admirable ambition, Commander Jelenick. One in which your friends can assist you. Have you considered City Council or the mayor's office? With many friends, these things are achievable."

"If you hurt my wife—"

"Let me interrupt you, Commander Jelenick. These things should be unspoken. Clearly, your dear and lovely Elana could be brutally introduced to many men and endure many trials, but as friends, we would never allow something of this nature to occur to a member of our family. As friends, we protect each other, yes?"

"What are you asking of me?" Jelenick felt lightheaded. *What has happened?* He had talked about Gold Rush to Elana, but she would never mention it to anyone else.

Segei Antonov not aware of the wiretap on his son's phone or of Aleks's efforts in selling guns. He believed the foundation of this investigation he had been drawn into was the undercover operation in which Aleks agreed to use Gold Rush to transport stolen cars to Russia.

"Only that you address the well-being of your family, Commander, of your friends. That you oversee this thing the police department is doing and divert those priorities to things that matter more. This issue of Aleks with a stolen car, it is nothing, is it not? A police department should not focus on poor immigrants. We wish to live quietly and without notice. We take care of our own and police our own. I, Aleks's father, will address this thing and hold Aleks accountable for his actions. He is young and easily influenced by his youthful dreams and his friends, who are sometimes wild in their actions. It is an easy thing, is it not, to show such young persons their mistakes, and then they are remorseful? There is no need for police involvement in our lives. We only wish to be good neighbors and grateful for our blessings."

Jelenick sat silently, his head spinning. "You are Roman Catholic, are you not, Commander? A man of faith and compassion. That is all we ask of our friendship. That we show faith, compassion, and support for one another. Friendships go both ways. We help you and protect you, as you do us."

Jelenick continued to sit silently, incredulous at what he was hearing. *Is Elana truly in danger?*

"Commander, you are silent, which I understand. There is much to consider, but accept my word as to the possession of your wife, Elana. But, if we are in agreement, if we shake hands, your dear Elana will be free to return home after her pleasant visit with my many friends and family. She will have no knowledge of our conversation or even of the danger she has unfortunately entered into. But if all is agreed to by you and I, she will be welcomed into our friendship just as you are. She will be protected, and her dreams of fame in art will be assisted by her new friends. That must make you feel relieved in this violent place, the City of Los Angeles. And I'm sure she will be proud of all of your future accomplishments that are now sure to come."

Jelenick faced Segei in a fog. Calling his wife's cell phone again and getting no answer, he asked, "You will not hurt my wife?"

"Of course not. This is how things are accomplished, Commander. Friendships are made and relationships are developed. It is a very common thing in many places, including Los Angeles. We have made many friends here, Commander. Politicians are greedy for money and for power. Do not feel as if our relationship is one of novelty. As a matter of fact, it is one of commonality." Segei Antonov had a knack for speaking in a matter-of-fact manner that made it easy for people to believe him.

"One last thing, Commander. As I've said of the game of chess, certain pieces on the table have been set in motion and they cannot be recalled. You will hear of these things, and know it is us doing these things that we do not wish to do. Know that this is a message, nothing more, and that we wish to be left in peace and in anonymity. We will now appreciate your efforts to guarantee we live our lives in this manner. Your control of this thing can slow things down, Commander. Slow the investigation down—that is all I ask. You can redirect the police efforts away from my son and focus on those criminals involved in violence who are deserving of your attention, and no further messages will need to be sent. Are we in agreement?"

Jelenick stood up while looking blankly at his phone. There was no answer as the call to Elana transferred to voicemail again. *Elana always answers her phone.*

As Segei Antonov extended his hand over the top of the metal table, Stans Jelenick found himself at a crossroads that he had never asked for. *How did this happen? How did Elana become involved with the Russian Mafia, with criminals? Where is she now?* Looking across the table at Segei Antonov and then at Kostya Sokoloff, who stood silently blocking the door, Jelenick knew that what Segei was telling him was true.

In his heart, Stans Jelenick was a weak man. A climber, an administrator. Someone who was adept at hiding and being invisible. Another man may have turned this situation in a different direction, but Jelenick did not have that kind of courage.

With great reservation, Jelenick took the hand that was offered to him and shook it slowly. The Russian's grip was like a vise. An omen, Jelenick was sure, that the agreement was permanent.

"One last thing, Commander. We have a need to give information to your Gang lieutenant, the person in charge of the undercover police effort. But we must meet him casually. We need to know his whereabouts."

"Lieutenant Adams is here in the building. In the chief's office. Should I call him in?"

"No, Commander Jelenick. We will meet him under other circumstances. Less formal, I think. Thank you, Stans. We are friends now, and I am Segei to you. I welcome our new friendship, as I'm sure you will also."

CHAPTER FORTY
RESCUE OPERATION

Chief Nelson grabbed Lieutenant Adams at the elbow and walked with him to the office of the chief of police. Nelson briefed Chief of Police Fuller as Adams called home and found there was nothing out of order. His children were safe, for the moment. Adams knew he had to move fast, but Chief Fuller stepped in with the weight of the Los Angeles Police Department.

People in the Rossmoor neighborhood where Adams lived were eager to know why the sirens of three police cars terminated at Adams's house. Most people in the immediate neighborhood knew a policemen lived there with his children. The policeman was always pleasant but quiet, while the family kept mostly to themselves.

Four minutes later, a helicopter from the Orange County Sheriff's Department hovered directly over Adams's house, close enough that the downdraft was felt by the neighbors standing on their front porches. Two men in tactical gear stood outside of the helicopter on the skids, something Adams's neighbors had only seen in movies.

As the officers on the ground entered Adams's house and verified to the airship that the children were safe, the helicopter landed in the intersection of the small community—something else that had never before happened. Something that rarely happens in any residential area. Two Orange County SWAT officers with full tactical gear and automatic long guns jumped from the helicopter skids and made their way three houses down and into Adams's front door. In only moments, Adams's son and daughter were in the helicopter and gone. As it landed on the roof of the sheriff's headquarters building in Santa Ana, a full team of SWAT officers gathered to protect the children of one of their own. Every single officer was willing to give their life to protect these two precious children. The building was locked down, and visible security was placed around the perimeter.

This happening early in the afternoon meant that a lot of people were home and ended up standing on their porches and in their yards to observe the police presence. And as quickly as the commotion erupted, it was over and all was quiet. At least to the untrained eye.

Adams was conflicted as he stood in Chief Fuller's office. Have an LAPD airship fly him home to his son and daughter, or trust others to protect them and lead the tactical event forming in Los Angeles?

Chief Fuller was talking on the phone during the rescue operation in Rossmoor, getting moment-by-moment updates. He then handed the phone to Adams. Sheriff Bob Christie spoke calmly and supportively, "Lieutenant, this is Bob Christie. I'm the sheriff of Orange County. We have your son and daughter and will protect them here in our facility once the airship sets down. My SWAT team is guaranteeing the safety of the entire building. I have two female officers standing by to be with them, and they won't leave their sight. We can care for them as long as necessary inside our facility. As soon as they arrive, I'll give them a cell phone with your number programmed into it so you can contact each other as needed."

Adams closed his eyes and wondered if this was the dread that he had been feeling lately. His intuition was strong, and he relied on it heavily. Sheriff Christie interrupted his thoughts. "Lieutenant, we made a rather large statement at your residence, but we pulled out as quickly as we came in. We are making absolutely no response to requests by the public or the press. I have an initial Surveillance unit with eyes on the front of your house, and I have a full team en route there. I plan to covertly cover all four sides of your house and then throughout your neighborhood. Rossmoor only has a few ways in and out, so it's relatively easy for us to monitor vehicle traffic and most pedestrians. It's your call to make whether we stay or pull out. Element members of our SWAT unit have formed up and are staging nearby at the Los Alamitos Medical Center and are ready to respond should our Surveillance units see anything of concern. We're staying in place until you and Chief Fuller make a decision."

After thanking Sheriff Christie, Adams decided to get to work and find the Russian—just as Commander Jelenick stepped into the office. "Chief Fuller, Chief Nelson. I just finished with Segei Antonov. Lieutenant Adams, you may want to wait in the outer officer for a moment."

"That won't be necessary, Commander. How did it go with the Russian?" Chief of Police Fuller wasn't someone to be pushed.

Jelenick knew he had to take control of this situation without revealing his conversation with Segei Antonov. "Pretty well. His name is Segei Antonov and he's concerned about his son, Aleks. Before we start, with the information we have, I think it's imperative that I take over this situation from Lieutenant Adams. We are so far out of control now that I'm not even sure we can recover from this. I can't even understand why Mr. Antonov was arrested, and I'm sure his attorney is going to address this whole situation with litigation against us."

"Tell me about the interview with Antonov, Commander." Chief of Police Fuller was clearly impatient.

"He's been told that Aleks is the subject of an auto theft investigation, but I don't think Segei has any knowledge of it. I suggest we slow things down until we understand what is happening at Gold Rush and who is involved, if anything at all is happening. I understand the information coming in over the wiretap was pretty sketchy and hard to understand. In my opinion, we are really on thin ice with this wiretap issue, and right now we're just assuming a danger exists. I decided to release Mr. Antonov in the interim. I see no legal foundation to keep him."

Adams saw a blanket of red. "What? You let him go?" Adams was immediately out of the office and headed for the elevator. He planned to intercept Segei Antonov before he even left the building.

In the lobby of LAPD Headquarters, the uniformed officer at the reception desk verified that the man matching the description of Segei Antonov had left the building ten minutes prior, along with another man.

As Adams walked back into the office of the chief of police, Jelenick was not there. He had been dismissed by Chief Fuller. Both Chief Fuller and Deputy Chief Nelson saw in the lieutenant's eyes the level of jeopardy Commander Jelenick had placed himself in.

Chief of Police Fuller was the first to speak. "Lieutenant, what happened here was inappropriate, at least for the time being. I agree that we probably have no legal justification to keep Mr. Antonov, but I would have liked to stretch it out a bit longer. I've addressed this with Commander Jelenick and it's something we will be discussing later at our level."

#

Segei Antonov continued to call his son, Aleks, to no avail. Aleks was embarrassed and disappointed in himself. His dreams of success and power were being derailed by an undercover police operation. He had been fooled, made to look stupid, and now he must make it right before he talked with his father. Someone must pay.

Aleks had decided to merely assume his role in the Russian Mafia. He didn't need the blessings of all of those who decided such things. In America, Aleks learned to take what you want, to make your own path. He would speak to his father once the feat was accomplished, once the example had been made. Only then would his father believe that he was destined for power, for leadership.

Aleks met with those persons who he believed could help him the most.

The people his father used to extort Russian Jewish businesspersons, among others, under the threat of violence and arson.

As Aleks addressed the team of Russian enforcers, he presented his orders to them as originating from his father, Segei. The incendiary devices were readily available, and the enforcers were used to imparting violence on those unwilling to succumb to the threats imposed on them.

There were two parts of Alex Antonov's plan. First, flush police officers out of Gold Rush, where they would be immediately shot and killed as they escaped and fled in panic. It would take law enforcement many hours before they gained an understanding of the events, and almost certainly it would be after all the evidence was destroyed in the fire and the shooters had fled the scene, becoming untraceable.

But it was the second part of the plan that required more resources and more coordination. It was this effort that would provide the larger lesson that needed to be experienced and learned by American law enforcement. Lieutenant Jack Adams, the source of the law enforcement effort to wage war on the Russian community, would lose what he loved most, and then he would lose his own life.

CHAPTER FORTY-ONE
THE ATTACK ON GOLD RUSH

Upon arriving in Glendale, the Surveillance officers observed cars coming and going from the apartment building at a hectic pace, so much so that a decision to follow any single one was mired in confusion. These were all new players. Adams made the decision to focus on Segei and Aleks Antonov and issued an order to take them into custody.

What was not known was that Segei Antonov had no intent to return to the apartment building. However, the initial plan to move Aleks out of the state and to Sitka, Alaska, under the radar of law enforcement had been modified under the new advice of Kostya Sokoloff. Segei was told that due to the unfolding events, he and Aleks should return to Russia as quickly as possible where their safety could be assured. They could return to the United States as the situation allowed.

Kostya Sokoloff had become alarmed at the scale and scope of the developing situation and feared he would be held accountable for numerous failures along with Segei and Aleks Antonov. His phone call to St. Petersburg was to a confidant who slowly strolled along the short stretch of the Griboyedov Canal. Kostya received instruction that both Segei and Aleks should be returned to Russia immediately by private jet using the luxury jet broker in Los Angeles. The phone call was then abruptly terminated.

The unusually tall man walking along the canal in a long coat, followed closely by two other men, paused to look out over the canal. He was one of the privileged few to possess a cell phone during the nationwide shortage of devices caused by controversial political decisions. He put his cell phone to his ear and spoke softly, communicating the foundation of the Los Angeles Police Department investigation in America.

Hastily arranging the travel plans for the private jet sitting in a hangar at the Van Nuys Airport took far less time than commercial air travel and allowed Segei to be hidden within the jet until takeoff. The cost of the trip was high, but Kostya told Segei that he believed it was a worthy investment to guarantee the safety of his son.

After leaving the LAPD Headquarters, Kostya Sokoloff ordered the Mercedes-Benz limousine to head straight for Van Nuys Airport. Now that Segei sat in the luxurious environment of the private jet secured inside a hangar, it was time to set the plan into motion to get Aleks to the jet before takeoff. Segei decided to stop calling Aleks, who was not answering anyway. Aleks's phone could be compromised. Segei sent the limousine driver to find Aleks and personally bring him to the airport. It was time for Segei and his son to return to Russia and sort things out from a safe distance.

#

Lieutenant Adams sent Major Crimes SIS, Special Investigations Section, to the Glendale apartment building to liaison with the Gang Detail surveillance units already on scene. After that, he requested a Major Crimes SIS surveillance team be sent to his home in Rossmoor to liaison with Orange County sheriffs at the Los Alamitos Medical Center.

The commanding officer at Major Crimes was not all that fond of Adams at the moment, not after being elected to shoulder the brunt of the bad press from the Gold Rush shooting scene to maintain the secrecy of the operation. Now, Adams's requests for resources had literally drained her command. She made a mental note to have a conversation with Lieutenant Adams.

Adams's cell wouldn't stop ringing, but he picked up the call from Paul Stanford. "Hey, LT, it's Stanford on 5K3. I've got most of my full team en route to Gold Rush. I've got five units on scene now and five en route. We're covering the front and back but can't do much more until we get more units on-site."

"Thanks, Paul. You know what Detective Hill relayed to us, so stay on your toes, but we're not sure what the timeline is. It sounded like it's happening right now, but who knows. I asked Major Crimes to send you additional surveillance resources, so you can rely on them and their capabilities if you need them. Listen, I have to answer Hill's call. Stay in touch." He hung up and accepted the next call.

"Lieutenant, it's Maddie Hill. Aleks hasn't come back up on the phone—what do I need to know about what's happening out there?"

"Okay, Maddie. We don't really know yet where this will go, but I have my family with the OC Sheriff's Department for safekeeping. They put a surveillance in place on my house to see if anything plays, so I'm sending a team from Major Crimes out there to liaison with them. Metro is setting up R100 security details at the homes of each of the Gold Rush crew, so they'll be contacting you to brief you and get info. We had the father, Segei, here at Headquarters being interviewed but someone let him walk without my knowledge. Right now, we're looking for Segei and Aleks, so if anything comes up on the wire that lets us know where either one is, get to me Code Three. That's our priority right now, find those two bastards, so I want you to try and find them for us. We've got eyes on the Glendale location and on Gold Rush but we're still building our surveillance capabilities. SWAT is standing by at their office in Rampart."

Meanwhile, in the alley to the rear of Gold Rush, one of the Surveillance units observed a lone male on the roof of an adjoining building. "5K9 to 5K3. Paul, I just lost sight of a lone male on an adjoining rooftop but I've lost sight of him. I never saw anyone climbing up, and I don't know if there's access to the roof from inside any of these buildings."

It became immediately clear to Detective Paul Stanford that they were still under-deployed for the task at hand, and he really wished his additional five units would arrive on scene.

Stanford immediately got back on the phone to Lieutenant Adams. "Hey, LT. One of my guys observed someone on a rooftop but lost sight of him. All the rooftops are connected, but I don't know if there's access from the interiors of the building. I know Gold Rush doesn't have roof access. I was just thinking that we could use that Surveillance airship overhead. I apologize for not being more on top of this, but I've only got the handful of units here while we wait for more to arrive."

"I understand, Paul. We're midday and not fully staffed; we're used to working after dark. I've got the Surveillance airship over Glendale looking for our primaries. As to your location, I'm thinking it's probably not out of the ordinary for someone to be on the roof in the afternoons, but we can pull the airship if anything looks sideways. There's roof leaks, air conditioners, electrical, all kinds of stuff up there that needs maintenance. Even so, I don't like it. Connect with SWAT and brief them real-time on everything you see. Let's help them to be engaged."

"5K3 to R50David." After hanging up with Adams, Stanford reached out to the SWAT supervisor responding from home.

"Go for 50David."

"5K3, we have a lone male on an adjoining rooftop. Lost sight of him. Be advised."

"R50David, roger. We're on scene at the command post in ten. I can send one team over to you now so we have someone closer. I'm sending Klatt and Dave Scott on R53David."

The lone detective assigned as 5K9, Tommy Thompson, continued to change his position to get a visual on the male he had observed on the rooftop. An experienced Surveillance operative and an expert at blending in to most every environment, Thompson worked the alley, digging in trash and collecting plastic and glass bottles while wearing a beat-up rain jacket. Suddenly, he observed the same male walking northbound along the roof edge just one building north of Gold Rush.

"5K9, lone male walking northbound on the rooftop at the east side of the building along the alley. One building north of Gold Rush, but unknown if he came from Gold Rush."

Walking northbound the course of three buildings and stepping over the parapets that divided each rooftop, the lone male grabbed onto a ladder handhold and swung his leg down to the first rung of the ladder. Taking the steps of the ladder, he dropped down the wall and slipped behind a metal dumpster as a white van entered the north end of the alley heading southbound.

5K9, Thompson, observed the van stop next to the dumpster and saw the lone male getting in the passenger door. "5K9, the guy on the roof slid down a wall ladder and got in a white Ford van that pulled into the alley. They're southbound in the alley."

Adams saw his phone light up with a call from Orange County Sheriff Bob Christie. „Lieutenant Adams, we've picked up a Mercedes with no plates tracking up and down the streets of Rossmoor. Four males. The car has no plates, so I'm guessing we're hot. I've got Surveillance holding on them and it looks like they're scoping out the neighborhood. I know we may have competing interests here, Lieutenant, but if they leave the neighborhood without approaching your house, I've told my guys to stop them. Just a heads-up."

"Thanks, sir, it's your call. I appreciate everything you're doing for my family. I'll pay you back someday." Adams couldn't quite get the words out that he really wanted to use, but he felt sure Sheriff Christie understood.

A harsh explosion suddenly erupted as chunks of rooftop flew up and away from Gold Rush. Thompson looked up and saw the smoke and a flash of fire as debris floated down. Only seconds later came a second explosion, this one larger, and Thompson felt the repercussion.

The white van stopped in the alley near the rear door of Gold Rush and two men quickly got out. Thompson could see that they both had shotguns and were staged behind the open doors of the van. The unmistakable barrels of shotguns were visible in the air while the men appeared to be waiting. Still on the tactical frequency, Thompson began whispering into his radio as he worked down the alley toward the van. "5K9, officer needs help, alley rear. Explosions on the roof and two armed suspects with the van, shotguns, staged at rear door of Gold Rush. Both suspects are masked."

Smoke erupted from the roof of Gold Rush, followed by visible flames. With fire alarms blaring, people in neighboring businesses began emptying out of their respective buildings and flooding into the alley.

Paul Stanford, on the street in front of Gold Rush, saw multiple problems developing. "5K3, advise Fire to stand by on the alarm at our location. Possible armed suspects on scene. Stage them one block away and we'll escort them in."

Another white van pulled into the parking lot in front of Gold Rush, right in front of the glass front door. "5K3 to all units, we have another white van blocking Gold Rush's front doors. Repeating, van to the front door. 5K3, multiple suspects, armed and masked, to the front of Gold Rush."

As Paul Stanford on 5K3 watched the two armed men emptying from the front doors of the van at the front of Gold Rush, he realized they were waiting for the officers to abandon the warehouse that was now on fire. Officers who were no longer there. "5K3, officer needs help to the front of the building. Armed suspects."

At the rear of Gold Rush, Thompson worked down the alley toward the van. The other people that had flooded into the alley had created more tactical problems. Using large metal trash bins for cover, he approached the rear driver's side of the white van, thinking, *Too bad he's not watching his back.* Thompson chose to engage the driver first to hopefully disable the van.

The man standing at the driver's door of the van, a past operative with the Federal Security Service of the Russian Federation, the successor agency of the Soviet Union's KGB, suddenly surprised Thompson as he spun around, shouldering the shotgun and leveling it at the disheveled person he saw walking toward him.

Thompson sighted his .45 caliber handgun just over the top of the suspect's shotgun and hit him twice in the forehead, then once in the shoulder. Thompson's fourth round missed the suspect and lodged into the door of the van as the driver of the van fell to the ground, the shotgun loudly bouncing into the middle of the alley.

Just seconds later, R53David, SWAT, driving an unmarked car, entered the alley following the path of the van. Detective Thompson had no time to broadcast that a shooting had occurred, and the two SWAT officers of R53David were surprised when they saw Thompson standing in the alley with an apparent suspect down on the ground next to the van. Knowing that undercover Surveillance officers were on scene, they were relieved to see Thompson holding his badge up.

Officers pulling in to a dangerous tactical situation commonly only have seconds to figure out what is happening and who the players are—an oftentimes impossible task.

Holding back from the van, not knowing if additional suspects were inside the van or if the back doors of the van would open, SWAT Officer Dave Scott stepped out from the passenger side of the unmarked police car and assumed cover along the building wall behind a metal dumpster with his Colt M4 rifle. SWAT officer Klatt held a position behind the driver side door to cover the rear of the van until he could understand the situation.

The second man standing at the passenger door of the van, the man who was seen on top of the building—the arsonist—heard the gunshots behind him. He was startled at the sound and immediately began moving down the side of the van, unaware that his partner had been shot. He moved to the rear of the van, holding his shotgun low next to his right leg.

The man saw the unmarked police car and a uniformed police officer, Klatt, standing on the driver's side of the car with the car door standing open. With a sudden fast movement, the man pulled his shotgun forward and fired, skipping shotgun pellets over the top of the police car at Officer Klatt.

As he fired the shotgun, SWAT Officer Dave Scott standing behind the metal trash bin found the red dot from the AimPoint scope on his M4 rifle and traced a line of three rounds through the suspect's chest, knocking the shotgun from his hands and forcing the suspect down onto the ground.

As the man was knocked backwards by Officer Scott's rounds, Officer Klatt recovered from the burning sensation on his right bicep from the shotgun pellets and fired two rounds that flew just over the man's head as he fell. "R53David, two suspects down. We're Code Six with plainclothes officer, alley rear of the location. Supervisor and RA unit please."

At the front of Gold Rush, 5K3, Paul Stanford, brought his undercover police car to a stop just south of the driveway entrance. His plan was to block the driveway but as he approached, he realized the danger was too high; he would be too close. 5K5, Jay Mark, stopped his undercover police car to the rear of Stanford's car and the two plainclothes officers took barricaded positions behind the engine block of Stanford's car. The two officers heard the report of distant gunfire possibly to the rear of Gold Rush.

Out of his peripheral vision, Jay Mark observed two females walking northbound on the sidewalk toward Gold Rush. He waved for them to stop but they seemed to ignore him. Holding hands, the two females continued walking on the sidewalk. They would pass right between the officers and the suspects in the van.

Detective Mark left the protection of the police car to send the female pedestrians the other way. As he spoke, the female closest to him raised a small revolver and shot him three times. Detective Jay Mark fell to the street, dead. Twenty-three years on the Los Angeles Police Department, a wife and twin daughters, both in college. Detective Jay Mark would not go home to his family today. He had failed in his promise.

Paul Stanford rose from his protected position behind his car to engage the two women but was left with the vision of the two females running away southbound and out of his sight. "5K3, officer needs help, officer down. Suspects are two females, dark hair, short dresses and heels running southbound."

Stanford's attention was drawn to the front of Gold Rush where he saw the white van now backing out of the parking lot. The two men had loaded back up in the van and were leaving. They had heard the shots being fired to the rear of Gold Rush and believed the employees inside had run out of the rear door, where they were shot.

When they saw Detective Mark fall to the sidewalk as the two women ran, they knew they were policemen.

Stanford wanted to run to his partner but as the van backed out into the street, it collided with the front of a police car that was screaming into the location. Officers Henderson and Wills, SWAT officers assigned to R56David, were prepared for the collision as they blocked the path of the white van.

The collision was harsh. The passenger in the van, a young Russian man who had emigrated from Russia only twelve days prior, was pushed back against the seat and then knocked against the dashboard. He fell downwards onto the floor of the van. The young man was considered Shestyorka, an errand boy earning his place in the organization.

The driver, a Russian enforcer who had fled Brighton Beach when the FBI pressure on underground gambling became too intense, jumped out of the front door of the van. As if out of a movie, he strode to the rear of the van holding a shotgun at port arms across his chest.

Apparently, SWAT officers Henderson and Wills had already seen that movie, because both officers immediately hit him in the chest with .45-caliber handgun rounds from their Kimber sidearms. Both guns had the SWAT emblem engraved on the frame.

As the passenger bailed out of the passenger door, leaving the handgun he carried on the floor of the van where it was lost during the collision, he looked frightened and confused. Blood streamed down his face from the cut over his left eye. With both eyes open, SWAT officer Wills placed the sights of his handgun on the young man's forehead and eased pressure onto the trigger.

Wills immediately realized the young man was not visibly armed as he froze in place. Wills ordered him to walk back to the police car, where he was handcuffed and arrested. His first introduction to American law enforcement, and his first step on the path toward incarceration in an American federal prison.

By the time Stanford got back to his partner, Detective Jay Mark displayed no signs of life. Stanford yelled to the two SWAT officers, "Two females, I've seen them before! They've been walking the street in front of Gold Rush the last couple days. We think they're with the Russians." Stanford repeated the broadcast, giving a more detailed description of the two females.

The fire was visible now on the roof of Gold Rush, and the smoke was visible for miles. Stanford heard the sirens of the fire department and saw them stopping two blocks away from Gold Rush, waiting to be directed in by law enforcement.

"5K3, bring the fire department in. Officer down, get the Rescue ambulance here now."

As Rampart Division patrol officers Wilson and Herrera responded to Gold Rush, they observed the two females running in short dresses and high heels crossing the street in front of the fire department caravan. When the "officer needs help" call was broadcasted over their radio and the description of the two females was broadcasted by Paul Stanford, Wilson guided the police car up onto the sidewalk to block the females' path. Both females stopped more than fifty feet from the police car and placed their hands on the brick wall of the aerospace machine shop. They knew the drill. Neither female was armed with a handgun when they were arrested for the murder of Los Angeles Police Detective Jay Mark. The handgun was later recovered in the bushes lining the sidewalk, but no fingerprints were on the gun.

#

Down in Orange County in Rossmoor, the LAPD Major Crimes surveillance officers spread out throughout Adams's neighborhood walking dogs and riding bikes. As one officer sat on the tailgate of his Ford truck and played with a toy remote control car in the cul-de-sac, his partner sat next to him and sent a drone up to scan the neighborhood.

When the black Mercedes-Benz with no plates was seen driving northbound on Seal Beach Boulevard with four males, everyone went on alert as the drone captured the car turning westbound on Orangewood Drive into the small community.

The Mercedes-Benz was finally parked directly across the street from Adams's house. Not very smart tactically, as the men in the car would have to cross the street on foot. Three men exited the car while the driver stayed in the driver's seat, waiting.

As the three men walked up the driveway to the front door, a white van with a "Prime" sticker in the back window backed into the driveway and stopped. The van had paper dealer plates. The driver of the van stayed seated with the engine idling, but the passenger disappeared into the rear of the van and pushed both rear doors open.

There was a loud noise when the front door of Adams's house was broken open, then all three men disappeared through the door, largely hidden by the van in the driveway.

It was decided that the Orange County sheriff's SWAT team would confront the suspects. Although the LAPD Major Crimes surveillance team was in full force and geared up for a tactical confrontation, the Sheriff's Department had access to greater resources and were more familiar with the terrain. LAPD would provide surveillance intelligence and be available to assist.

The Orange County SWAT supervisor decided not to engage the suspects at Adams's residence, where they would have the opportunity to barricade inside Adams's house. The decision was made to allow both vehicles to leave, if they did, and then initiate a traffic stop on each one outside of the residential area on the major boulevard. If they didn't leave, the decision would be reconsidered.

After the Russians forcibly entered Adams's house, they moved throughout the rooms and found no one at home. The three temporary cameras left by the Orange County SWAT team members recorded their presence and their movement through the house. The microphones recorded their conversations.

The three Russian men discussed a plan to remain inside until family members returned home, but a phone call to Segei changed that plan. Segei directed the van to park on the street and observe the residence, while the four men in the Mercedes-Benz would leave the neighborhood but stay nearby. Once the family returned home, the plan to kidnap the two children and kill everyone else who was present could be completed. The conversation was forwarded to Sheriff Bob Christie and Chief of Police George Fuller.

As the driver of the van pulled out of the driveway, uniformed members of the SWAT team sat up on Los Alamitos Boulevard with the intent of stopping both vehicles before they got onto one of the two freeways, the 405 or 605. The driver of the van, however, merely pulled three houses down and stopped at the curb. It appeared as if they were watching Adams's house.

The three men who had forcibly entered Adams's house crossed the street and returned to the Mercedes-Benz, and the drone took the car out of the neighborhood on Rossmoor Way. LAPD Surveillance units followed north on Los Alamitos Boulevard and then south on Katella Avenue. The driver soon pulled into a Starbucks parking lot.

Orange County Sheriff Bob Christie personally made the call to immediately apprehend the suspects in both vehicles. Deputies from the Orange County Sheriff's Department began pulling into Rossmoor and set up a perimeter in Adams's neighborhood around the white van. Being careful not to be seen by the two men in the van, deputies set up a two-block perimeter.

When the caravan of three SWAT vehicles and an armored BearCat G2 pulled onto the street and approached the van from the rear, sheriff's deputies blocked off both ends of the street. The two SWAT officers who had parked one street south had worked their way on foot between the houses and positioned themselves secreted to the side of the white van on the passenger side. They would disallow the suspects from exiting the van and approaching the houses.

The BearCat G2 was positioned in the middle of the street, blocking the roadway and controlling the driver's side of the van, along with the rear doors. The next SWAT vehicle pulled partially onto the sidewalk and covered the passenger side of the van. The last two SWAT vehicles stopped directly behind the BearCat G2.

Each of the SWAT officers were attired in full tactical gear and armed with either automatic or semiautomatic rifles. It was time to go to work. It was time to protect the family of one of their own. You never threaten a policeman's family.

The black Mercedes-Benz was parked next to an enclosed trash bin in the Starbucks parking lot. Sheriff's units built a perimeter around the block to contain any possible situation and prevent the escape of the four men. As all four men left the Mercedes-Benz and went into the Starbucks, the SWAT team set up to confront them in the parking lot before they could get back in the car.

After standing in line and ordering their drinks, all four men exited through the swinging glass door of Starbucks carrying coffee cups in their hands, a tactical advantage for the police officers. The four men seemed to be in no hurry and lingered on the small patio separated from the parking lot by a low hedge of bushes.

Additional sheriff's units were directed to shut down all traffic on Los Alamitos Boulevard, Katella Avenue, and Pine, the three streets bordering the Starbucks. Four SWAT officers abandoned their vehicles on the northwest corner of Katella Avenue and Pine and walked up the sidewalk alongside the Starbucks. The officers were assigned to disallow the four men from returning inside the Starbucks.

Minutes later when the four men walked toward the Mercedes-Benz, a BearCat G3, an enhanced armored vehicle built for rural or off-road areas, entered the connected parking lot from Los Alamitos Boulevard. The BearCat G3 traveled eastbound before making an abrupt right turn into the Starbucks lot. The four men were startled by the large tactical vehicle as it came to a stop pointed directly at the Mercedes-Benz, blocking any forward motion of the car.

A SWAT SUV carrying two SWAT officers followed the BearCat G3 from Los Alamitos Boulevard and blocked the north end of the lot. A second SWAT SUV stopped on Pine Street, blocking the south parking lot exit.

The four men holding coffee cups realized this was all for them and that they were immediately trapped in a deadly situation—deadly for them. Although these officers were used to confronting dangerous people and dangerous situations, preplanning to put the odds in your favor is always wise. As the four men considered their options, the sight of a small army in full tactical gear carrying formidable armament seemed to make their decision for them.

One of the officers in the BearCat G3 announced over the amplified system his orders for the four men, then repeated the orders one more time. While not responding to the orders, the men looked in all directions and then talked among themselves. They would fight if they could see a way out. Then, the standoff was silent for two minutes.

The Russians' vehicle had been blocked in. Each of the SWAT officers were in barricaded positions and focused their attention, and their formidable weapons, on the four men. Support members of the SWAT team supported the encounter by controlling the surrounding area, allowing the initial SWAT officers to focus on the four men and not have to watch their backs. The outcome of a violent engagement was obvious.

For many years, the management of the Los Angeles Police Department had supported the concept that police officers should not present an aggressive appearance during the onset of tactical situations, particularly when mass demonstrations or rioting were expected. Police officers were ordered not to wear helmets or carry batons for fear of offending someone, for fear that the optic may be negative. An ineffective deployment of law enforcement resources.

The idea that police officers should not present a professional and aggressive appearance because of a fear of the optics and, in so doing, endanger their personal safety in a tactical situation is a failed concept that has actually spurred on violence and crime. This has proven to be a terrible management mistake after countless situations that have resulted in failure.

The Orange County sheriff's SWAT team confronting this particular tactical situation did not buy into that failed and cowardly philosophy, and it certainly paid dividends in the minds of the four men evaluating their options. The four violent and dangerous men who had decided to fight if they saw an escape route were overwhelmed by the force surrounding them.

Each of the four men surrendered, and their weapons loosely secured in their waistbands were taken from them. Two shotguns were recovered from the back seat of the Mercedes-Benz. The eldest of the Russians claimed, "A mistake has been made. We have done nothing." After that, each of the four men only spoke in Russian and claimed not to speak English. The element members of the SWAT team secured the safeties on their rifles and the very visible tactical event in Orange County came to a decisive conclusion.

Parked near Adams's house, the two young men in the van believed that they played a small and peripheral part in this operation. Two children would be secured with ropes or plastic ties and concealed in the rear of the van as they drove to Glendale.

The driver of the white van saw the police car stop in the intersection in front of him. Something then caught his eye and he looked into his mirror to see it was filled by a large armored vehicle approaching from the rear. The caravan of the three additional police SUVs approaching aggressively from behind him seemed to seal his fate.

The driver felt defeat and panic. He immediately left his seat and crawled into the back of the van. "Police! There are police! A lot of police behind us and a policeman in front of us. There's a tank!"

It all happened quickly. The passenger opened the door of the van and stepped out with a shotgun. He looked down the street, saw the police behind them, and decided to escape on foot. He was just supposed to transport people from the house in Rossmoor to the little house in Glendale where Aleks was. He didn't want any part of all of this; he just wanted to get away.

The passenger in the van ran across the front lawn of the house they were parked in front of. One of Adams's neighbors who had retired from teaching at California State University at Long Beach lived alone in the house. Adams paid him to tutor both his son and his daughter with their homework. Best to start early.

The passenger in the van saw the concrete block wall separating the two houses and ran for it, speeding up to help him scale the wall. He thought that if he could get in the backyards and out of the view of the police officers, he could find his way into an unlocked back door to one of the houses and hide. He could wait this out and find his way home tomorrow.

As he ran and only a few yards away, he was surprised by a man dressed in all black who suddenly stood before him. It took only a fraction of a second to register that the man was a policeman, but he had to break through—he had to get over the wall.

As he raised the barrel of his shotgun toward the policeman, his pace stopped when two 9mm rounds from a Heckler & Koch MP5 struck his chest. His plan to flee through the backyards of the Orange County neighborhood and steal away inside someone's home wouldn't pan out.

The BearCat G2 and the three SWAT SUVs came to a stop behind the white van. The young man who had secreted himself in the rear of the van heard the two gunshots after his partner had stepped from the passenger door. The young man decided in a split second to take advantage of what he believed could be a diversion and escape out of the back of the van while the police officers engaged the other man.

He opened one of the doors and burst out the back of the van. All he saw was the large black BearCat blocking his path. If he could break to his right and run, he could get away. No one would even know who he was.

He shot a 9mm handgun at the armored vehicle blocking his path, hoping that any policemen would duck and hide just long enough for him to cross the street and disappear. Hoping to escape while the police were distracted chasing his partner, the driver of the van was only able to get one foot on the ground before he was struck with seven bullets. The policemen staged next to and behind the BearCat had not ducked when they were shot at.

The young Russian, only twenty-three years old, fell back into the van on top of a bag of plastic ties and rolls of duct tape, knocking over a plastic jug containing a liquid with a heavy chemical smell. The chemical that was dedicated to disabling the two children and keeping them quiet during the long drive to Glendale. Even criminals had to endure the infamous Los Angeles traffic.

Suddenly, it was quiet. The police officers were still as they watched the two suspects for signs of life. They watched for signs of danger, for threats. But it remained quiet, and the two young Russians did not move.

The tires of the Rescue ambulance moving down the street made an ominous sound. A humming sound, no siren. The paramedics were out of the truck and moving toward the two young men just as the SWAT officers had moved forward to clear the inside of the van for more suspects. The guns were separated from the two men, and they were handcuffed while covering officers looked on.

The police action and gunfire again brought most of the residents of Rossmoor out to their porches. The subsequent investigation would last far into the night. This was a day everyone would remember, and as quickly as it had come together the second major tactical event in Orange County came to an end.

CHAPTER FORTY-TWO
POKING THE BEAR

"Lieutenant, it's McClain. All our officers are accounted for. Not sure what all is happening, but all kinds of shit broke loose at Gold Rush. Just trying to get the scoop on it. I heard the 'officer down' call."

Jack Adams was being pulled in every direction. "I got it, Mac. Listen, Jay Mark got hit at Gold Rush. He didn't make it, Mac. We have the scene now, but Jay didn't make it. Looks like they lit off an explosive on the roof to start a fire and scare our guys, then they set up to kill our cops when they bailed out of the building. The building went up really quick. I'm told that the roofs on warehouses are the most vulnerable to fire, and right now they're fighting the fire across four warehouses."

Adams thought about having to call Jesse Levin and tell him that his warehouse was burning down to the ground. Not only that, but Levin's second warehouse attached to Gold Rush was also burning down to the ground. *Damn.*

"Mac, right now we're focused on finding that little Russian. Like you know, we had his father in custody here at headquarters but he was mistakenly released before we could really interview him."

"Released? The only wit we have in custody, and he got released? He's probably in charge of the whole Mafia! What happened, Lieutenant?"

"Well, it was a call from management level, Mac. It was a mistake, but we'll work with it. I've got Surveillance teams with eyes on the apartment building in Glendale trying to rearrest him and Aleks, but so far nothing has panned out. Listen, Mac, OC sheriffs moved my kids, but after that one of their crews just hit my house. Orange County took some in custody and dumped a couple more out in front of my house. I've got Metro units headed to each of our houses to provide security for the time being, but it sounds like they only know who I am. Give Andrea a call and let her know that the cavalry will be setting up on your house within the next few minutes."

McClain's anger flared fast. "What? Those motherfuckers."

"Mac, I get it, but I need you to stay calm. Stay at the command post and keep our Gold Rush guys there. Our focus right now is to take the fight to them. Like I said, Orange County SWAT arrested a handful of the assholes at my house and dumped two of them. Major Crimes will be interrogating them, but I'll probably bring FBI in on that. We're looking for the two Russians, Aleks and his father, Segei. We have eyes on the Glendale apartment building and we're working with Glendale PD and Orange County sheriffs. I want you to talk to Agent O'Reilly and pull in their resources on this. I want to find the two Russians."

"He's already doing it, Lieutenant. He called someone at FBI and they're sending out a whole squad of people. I think it's their Organized Crime unit, but they're sending tactical teams also."

"Good job, Mac. Have O'Reilly get someone rolling to liaison with OC Sheriff's and then have him pull all travel authorities for both of the Russians. Put a hold on their passports; I don't want them leaving the country. I'm going to head down to the sheriff's headquarters in Santa Ana and check on my son and daughter, then I'll be back. Call me if anything comes up between now and then. When we find the Russians, I'll have one of our airships pick me up and bring me back. I want to be there for any takedown if possible."

#

Segei Antonov sat in the luxury plane as the engines started and preflight activities became apparent. The stewardess sat a glass of Ararat, Armenian brandy, on the side table. Segei felt more comfortable knowing he and Aleks would be in the air soon. After that, they would be safely on their trip back home. The message he was sending to law enforcement would be harsh, but it was necessary.

Segei had already planned an expanded role for Commander Jelenick. He was going to be useful in many ways. Once Jelenick was placed in a position of greater authority in the management of Los Angeles, Segei's successes in America would be greatly enhanced.

Segei was looking forward to briefing his comrades in Russia as to his plans and knew that his status would be greatly elevated because of it. Great work was always rewarded. He would live as a rich and powerful man when he returned to America.

The team of Russians on foot and in cars outside LAPD Headquarters were assigned to observe Lieutenant Adams leaving the building. Two different ambush points were set up: one to engage Adams if he drove northbound toward Gold Rush, and one to engage him if he drove southbound to his home. Segei had ordered those involved in the surveillance and in the ambush points not to fail. Adams was to be taken alive and driven to the safe house in Glendale. As a failsafe, Segei ordered two vans with gunmen to stand by and randomly attack Adams as a last resort.

The doors to the hangar remained closed by Segei's orders. After Segei gave the orders to bring Lieutenant Jack Adams and his family to the house in Glendale, he expected Aleks to meet him at the hangar for the flight to Russia. The events set in motion would be unfolding as they flew home together. Jack Adams and his family would be left in a location easily discovered by the Los Angeles Police Department.

The death of Lieutenant Adams would be a lesson to the police in America and a feather in his cap in Russia. Although he conceded that Aleks should have been more diligent in protecting the family's affairs, it would ultimately result in strengthening their position in America. Aleks would learn a valuable lesson and move forward with his very impressive capabilities.

Segei knew that their ability to return to America would probably be delayed, but the events he'd ordered would be for the good of all Russians in America. Segei realized how beneficial and far-reaching his plan was, and he looked forward to being greeted as a hero as he walked on the ground of his native country.

#

When the limousine driver who functioned as one of Segei's bodyguards arrived at the apartment building in Glendale, there was chaos. He was not able to find Aleks but received information that he may have gone to the house near the college.

The limousine driver arrived at the house near Glendale Community College and found Aleks inside berating members of their group. Aleks was angry and pacing as he yelled orders. He was not receptive to his father's order to leave at once for the Van Nuys Airport and meet him for the flight to Russia. When he was told that his father did not want him involved in the engagement with the policeman, Lieutenant Adams, Aleks became angry and ordered the limousine driver, the bodyguard, to leave the house and wait for him outside until he was ready to travel to the airport.

Wanting to be part of the solution for the situation he had initiated, Aleks decided to manage the events personally and delay his arrival at the airport. The policemen had tricked him, and he was too important to be tricked. Aleks went to the Glendale house to wait for Adams and his family. Only after personally dealing with this issue would he leave to meet his father.

The limousine driver shook his head, knowing Segei would be angry. He returned to the comfortable limousine and parked it two blocks away, not willing to be involved in the stupidity of Aleks's actions. He would wait until Aleks was done with his tasks, then drive him to the airport.

In truth, Aleks had no intention to travel to Russia, but only to meet with his father to advise him that the problem had been dealt with. To display his ability to resolve these problems. His life was in America. He had power here; he had beautiful women.

#

Adams left LAPD Headquarters literally racing to the Los Angeles County Sheriff's Department headquarters in Santa Ana. To his son and his daughter.

Adams left eastbound on 1st Street with blinders on. He was confident that other leaders were addressing the assaults on the officers at Gold Rush, and as much as he wanted to be involved, he needed to get to the sheriff's station first. After that, he would deal with the Russians.

Adams was always aware of his surroundings, always aware of who was standing in front of him and who lurked behind him. But today, he somehow never noticed when the gray car parked at the curb on Main Street pulled in behind him as he drove through the intersection. Nor did he see the white Mercedes-Benz Sprinter van with dealer plates pull away from the Russian-owned business on Main Street and pull in behind the gray car.

Driving through Little Tokyo, Adams turned his dark-blue Ford Crown Vic onto San Pedro Street headed for the I-10 Freeway. He had already picked his route across the I-10 to the I-5 Freeway and south to the sheriff's station in Santa Ana.

As Adams raced southbound through the Fashion District, a small yellow bus marked with the Los Angeles Unified School District identifiers pulled out from the Metro Bus Maintenance Yard on 15th Street. Adams drove through the intersection at Pico Boulevard, frustrated with the heavy traffic, and the Mercedes-Benz Sprinter van that had passed him was now blocking his path, slowing his travel down to a crawl.

15th Street intersected San Pedro in an offset format, essentially providing for two T-intersections. As he crossed the first T-intersection at 15th Street, the white van came to a stop, completely blocking his path. Adams looked for a path around the van and found himself captured between the van and the line of cars now stopped behind him. Yellow school buses lined most of the curbside parking north and south throughout the area, except for the red curb next to Adams's unmarked police car. Adams could see the green traffic sign mounted on two poles on the sidewalk, which everyone hit their heads on, announcing the on-ramp to the I-10 Freeway but just couldn't seem to get there.

Adams had nowhere to go and only seconds of warning before the small yellow LAUSD school bus from the maintenance yard barreled westbound into the T-intersection directly at Adams's car. Adams looked to his left and saw a blur of yellow, then fell into the chaos of the impact.

Without braking, the bus hit the driver's door of Adams's Ford Crown Vic with such force that it pushed his car sideways onto the sidewalk and wedged against a telephone pole, shearing off a water hydrant. Adams wasn't aware of the downpour of water landing on his car or of the line of yellow school buses parked behind the chain-link fence. Those in the homeless encampment that lined the fence and blocked the sidewalk erupted in an angry response to the inconvenience of their homes and belongings being soaked.

With the impact, Adams's door crushed in against him, knocking him across the seat as the grill of the yellow bus protruded into the Ford Crown Vic. Adams, lying on his side across the seat with his head against the passenger door, struggled for consciousness and noted a chemical that nauseated him. *Gasoline?* He had to get out of the car.

The scene was hectic with traffic backed up for blocks. The fire hydrant shot water fifty feet into the air, and there was a large commotion around the involved vehicles. The traffic accident of a school bus caused everyone in the area to visualize children inside the bus, and everyone panicked. They weren't able to see that the bus was empty except for the driver.

The few pedestrians that were present, along with the drivers of the other cars, watched four men get out of the rear of the white van and remove the drivers of both vehicles that were in the accident. The group of four men carried the two obviously injured drivers to the white van, pulled the rear doors closed, and the van left southbound. Although one of the men was the school bus driver, the other one appeared to the witnesses to be a policeman or security guard wearing a blue uniform.

On the east side of the street, rolling racks of clothing for sale lined the sidewalk separated by homeless tents. One of the patrons announced, "They must be taking them to the hospital."

In the van, one of the men continued to force a cloth over Adams's face emitting a strong noxious odor that filled the interior of the van. A second man removed Adams's handgun from his holster, then his handcuffs. After he pulled Adams's hands behind his back and handcuffed him, he struggled to take Adams's equipment belt off of him. Four leather keeper straps that secured the equipment belt, referred to as a Sam Browne, were a little hard to figure out for the men in the rear of the speeding and bouncing van.

As Adams was held down, incapacitated by the chemical the Russians called Agent 15, the driver of the school bus seemed to be forgotten by the group of men. After he was thrown into the back of the van, he slumped against one wall of the van with blood on his face. One of the other men in the rear of the van looked at him and announced, "He's fine. He's young, he'll be fine." The young Russian man who had stolen the school bus from the maintenance yard and smashed it into Adams's trapped police car, though, had his doubts. The Mercedes-Benz Sprinter van traveled west and north away from the scene.

LA Fire Department personnel from Station 10 were on the scene before the LAPD. As the paramedics approached the traffic accident, they were used to arriving at scenes that they didn't understand, scenes with a lot of chaos, but this was a new one, even for them. The few witnesses on scene told them the drivers of the two vehicles involved in the accident were not there.

As they looked inside the dark-blue Ford Crown Vic with the radio and other police equipment visible between the seats, red flags went up. This was a police car. Where was the policeman driving the car? The situation began to capture the attention of the entirety of the Los Angeles Police Department. By that time, the Sprinter van was well out of the area and heading toward the neighboring city of Glendale.

As Adams drifted in and out of the fog caused by the chemical on the cloth held over his face, he was being carried by two men and saw a building in the distance that looked familiar. The arched entryways of Glendale Community College. Why was he in Glendale? Was he being taken to a hospital?

He hurt all over and was nauseated by the chemical smell. As he tried to get the offending cloth off his face, he found his hands were handcuffed behind his back. Everything was cloudy, and it was hard to concentrate.

Adams realized he was being carried into a house. Inside, music was blaring so loud that Adams just couldn't grasp what was happening. Struggling to get loose of the two men carrying him, he was roughly dropped onto the floor in the living room. Adams tried to fight through the fog, to understand.

Adams's condition did not allow him to comprehend the passing of time or what was happening around him. As he gained some sense of his surroundings, he saw a young man standing in the room who appeared to be amused by his condition. The young man was handed the handgun that had been removed from Adams's holster, a custom-built Kimber .45 caliber handgun.

Adams realized he had been trying to get to his children, and he finally began to comprehend the dangerous situation he was in. He attempted to rise up off the floor and stand to face his captors. *Russians?* He stumbled and fell forward. He got to his knees but just couldn't get his feet under him yet. Adams was still weakened by the chemical and his hands were handcuffed behind him, hindering his balance. As he brought one foot up underneath him, he looked up at Aleks Antonov now standing directly in front of him.

Adams saw the large handgun pointed directly at him but felt no fear; it had never served him any purpose. Adams's faith was many times stronger than any fear he could imagine. He would fight.

Adams pushed off of his one stable leg and lunged at Aleks with the intent to knock him to the ground before he could fire the gun. Adams clumsily crashed into him, knocking him backwards and onto the floor. The music was blaring, but Adams heard the gun bouncing across the floor. The gun was loose. Adams used his momentum to land on top of Aleks and he searched desperately to find the gun.

Suddenly, two men and a large husky woman began kicking Adams, harsh, brutal blows to his stomach and his back. The woman was yelling at him in Russian. The beating, the blaring music, and the woman yelling in a foreign language pumped adrenaline through his body and the nausea went away. Adams tried to keep his head tucked in for protection while he looked for an escape route, the gun. *Strike, evade and escape.*

It was hard to see; Adams was still battling the chemical used to subdue him and the curtains were all drawn so that it was dark in the room. But there, only a few feet away, he saw the front door in the living room. That door was freedom.

Adams brought his feet under him and pushed through the female, hitting her with his shoulder as he lunged for the door. The loud woman was sent crashing backwards over a coffee table. He hit the door hard with his side and felt the doorknob in his hand behind his back. He twisted the doorknob and the door pulled open enough that daylight flooded in.

Adams knew if he could get outside, he could fight—he could escape. People would see the altercation and call the police. As he struggled through the door and onto the porch, he was pulled back by one of the men in the room who raised a handgun up over Adams's head and struck down with all his might. The gun impacted on the top of Adams's head, and the pain was blinding. The blood began immediately flowing from the injury and Adams fell face-first onto the floor. The room darkened again as the door was shut.

Adams tried to pull his hands up to his head to cradle the injury but couldn't release them from the handcuffs. The beating started again as Adams braced against the door to protect one side of his body. The female struck Adams with a wooden leg from the coffee table while the two men continued kicking him.

A young man and woman watched from the kitchen, not expecting this violence to erupt. Their instructions were to take control of two small children and keep them quiet inside the house; they were not told what the situation was.

Aleks Antonov was angrily yelling and pulled one of the men off of Adams as blood ran down his face. Adams's head wound was bleeding heavily, and the kicks and blows were taking a heavy toll on him. Aleks ordered one of the men to sit Adams up.

Adams raised his head and looked up at Aleks, who stood over him again armed with the .45 caliber handgun that Adams's abductors had taken from him. As Adams somehow pushed up to his knees, Aleks Antonov raised the gun and fired two rounds at point-blank range.

#

A massive response by the Los Angeles Police Department uncovered that an LAUSD school bus that had been stored at the Metro Bus Maintenance Yard was stolen and used in what appeared to be a planned and purposeful traffic accident to disable a Los Angeles Police car.

Through the hectic and convoluted investigation that followed, Lieutenant Jack Adams was found to have been spirited from the location by men in a van that had blocked his path prior to the accident. The worst-case scenario was feared: an abduction of a Los Angeles policeman by members of the ruthless Russian Mafia.

A canvas of all local medical facilities revealed that the victims of the traffic accident had not arrived. The threat by figures in the Russian Mafia group threatening the Gold Rush effort had to be the cause. The threatened police officer had been kidnapped, while his two children were being protected by the Orange County Sheriff's Department.

The Newton Division Patrol captain arrived quickly and even without the background information as to what the situation revealed, he took control and set up a command post to build a team of officers to canvass the area for witnesses. All he knew was that a policeman was missing from the traffic accident, and that was all he needed to know. Captain Billings went to work finding him.

Deputy Chief Steve Nelson was the first member of the command staff to show up at the scene. As the Newton Division captain briefed him, Chief of Police George Fuller rolled in with a stoic look on his face.

Although a field command post was set up at the scene in Newton Division, Chief of Police Fuller immediately ordered the LAPD RACR Division, Real Time Analysis and Critical Response, within the City Emergency Operations Center to coordinate all efforts to find and rescue Lieutenant Adams. As a section of Detective Bureau, RACR had access to incredible resources and the ability to coordinate responses by multiple agencies. The Los Angeles Police Department was put on a tactical alert, and the full force of the LAPD was directed toward the incident.

Commander Jelenick sat in his office in silence following his discussion with Segei Antonov. There was still no answer on his wife's phone. Hearing loud talking, he followed the commotion within the building to Chief Nelson's office. When he learned what was unfolding in Newton Division, he was still stunned by what had transpired and with worries about his wife. He was sure this situation with Lieutenant Adams missing or being abducted had to do with Segei Antonov and the Russian Mafia—the chess pieces that Segei talked about. Seeing no option but to play the situation out, he left for Newton Division.

When Commander Jelenick arrived at the field command post, Deputy Chief Nelson dispatched him to the Emergency Operations Center to provide staff assistance in coordinating the response to this situation. Truth be known, Nelson just wanted Jelenick out of the way. He had no patience for his incompetence right now.

Jelenick wanted to brief Chief Nelson on his personal situation, on his wife being held captive, but couldn't find the courage or the character to do the right thing. Instead, with his wife in danger and the threat of extortion consuming him, he quietly left for the Emergency Operations Center. His wife would be freed, and he would continue his upward path in the Los Angeles Police Department, and no one would ever know. Segei Antonov had even suggested an alternate path in politics.

#

Adams felt the .45 caliber rounds hit him and he was brutally knocked back to the ground. The two loud reports following the muzzle flashes were deafening, and the heat shooting from the barrel seared his skin.

The force of the rounds hitting him seemed to knock the air from his lungs, then the pain came. Adams had constantly prepared himself mentally for this moment, for maintaining the will to live and to fight back, but he could have never conceived what the impact of .45-caliber rounds would actually feel like. Planning and training for something rarely prepares you adequately for real life.

It did not register where the bullets had struck him. The trauma was brutal, more like being hit by a sledgehammer that burned and seared as it penetrated his body. As the brutal force drove him backwards, the immediate thought of death overwhelmed his thoughts. The surprise at being shot and the shock that began to overwhelm him only strengthened his resolve to fight back.

Through the chemically induced fog and the pain of his injuries, Adams forced one thought into his mind. *Never be a willing victim. Fight back.* The fight is never over, and he was still breathing. He would fight.

The other five people in the room froze in place. Aleks stood over Adams, holding the gun still pointed at him. "You are dying, policeman, but you'll die slow. Not now, but you will die later. You are the example, but one of many. Today, policemen will learn a lesson that we are not to be disrespected. Your Commander Jelenick has told us about you, policeman. About your undercover efforts to arrest us. You have made a large mistake that will not be repeated. The price you will pay will be long remembered and other policeman will learn—learn not to disrespect."

Adams was taken aback. *Jelenick burned the operation? Jelenick was responsible for all this?* Our past has a voice, and that voice always speaks to us at inopportune times. Oftentimes that voice is unpredictable.

Through the fog that Adams was fighting to escape from, this voice from his past spoke to him: Jelenick was a threat that brought the Russians to him.

"You will watch your family die today, policeman. They will be brought here shortly, and you will watch them die before you die. Then, the lesson will be learned."

The pain focused now on the gunshots to Adams's left shoulder. He couldn't get to the pain or move his body to ease the pain with his hands behind his back. Aleks said his family was being brought here? Adams knew his son and daughter were with the Sheriff's Department. *Did something go wrong? Were they abducted?*

Adams tried to force his body up, to get on his feet and face his captors. He wasn't dead; he would fight. Aleks ordered the group in the living room to take Adams to a bedroom. Each of the two men grabbed Adams's arms and dragged him down a hallway as Adams tried to get his feet underneath him. He knew he had to stand up in order to fight.

Adams didn't know how bad the gunshots were, but the pain was intense. He knew he was losing a lot of blood. Had the rounds hit his heart? The left side of his body was on fire. He had to fight against going into shock—he had to fight against giving up.

After being pulled down the hallway and into a bedroom, Adams was dropped onto the floor on his stomach. The female who had followed them down the hallway held her boot on Adams's neck and yelled at him in Russian. She was angry and stomped down hard on Adams's neck and back as he tried to roll away from her, the growing pool of blood under his body soaking into the carpet.

Adams saw a young female not yet old enough for high school being held down on a disheveled bed next him. She was being sexually assaulted by two men who were laughing at her and now laughing at Adams. Her hands were bound together in front of her with black plastic ties, and her wrists were bleeding. She was naked, her face was bloody. The look on her face told of her pain and her fear. It was one of hopelessness.

Adams looked for an escape point but saw that there were bars over the windows. He thought, *I need to get out.* The house was older, a single story with very low ceilings. The room was dirty. No personal items were visible. *A safe house? In Glendale?* He knew he was near the community college—he was sure he had seen it when he was dragged from the van and carried inside the house. That was where the Russian's apartment building was, in Glendale. His senses were clearing.

A report of shots fired was received by the Glendale Police Department, called in by a student of Glendale Community College who had been walking to class. He reported that he could not tell where the sound of the shots originated from but that there were two of them, and he believed they were close by. An unusual event in this part of Glendale, which was a quiet and highly desired area to live.

Adams knew he had to get his hands free. Aleks was right. He wouldn't die here—not now, and not today. It was time to fight, and he had to get his hands free and get on his feet.

Adams struggled to clear his mind of the chemical used to subdue him. He tried to focus on getting his hands free. He couldn't help himself or the young female being assaulted on the bed next to him without his hands. Adams convinced himself to focus on the pain of being shot. Use it. Let it hurt, let the pain keep him alert. He was losing a lot of blood and didn't have much time. He had to fight before his son and daughter arrived at the house.

Adams realized his Sam Browne was gone, along with the handcuff key lightly glued on the inside of his equipment belt where he could recover it in just this situation. Throughout his career, Adams had always planned for the worst and planned to survive and win. He would win this time.

Handcuffed or not, Adams was injured, there were multiple captors, and he needed weapons. Surveying the room for weapons he could use, he thought about the heavy pin on the back of his badge. *A weapon.* Looking at his chest he found his badge was gone, a trophy for one his captors. He'd be getting that back.

Adams was not carrying a backup weapon today. He had prepared for a long day of planning and briefings, choosing not to carry his backup until later in the evening, as it was heavy and uncomfortable. He wouldn't make that mistake again.

Then Adams remembered his boots. A handcuff key woven onto the laces inside his left boot that had been there for the two years he had been wearing them, and in every pair of boots since he had entered the Los Angeles Police Department. He remembered the small tactical knife secured with a clip inside his right boot that he was sure the LAPD would frown upon. His boots were on!

Adams tried to sit up to get to his boots and the female with her boot on his neck was pushed off balance, forced to step backwards. One of the men who had dragged Adams down the hallway kicked Adams on the side of the head, knocking him back to the floor and causing him to fight to keep consciousness. The beating that followed seemed like it would never stop.

Adams tried to turn his body to deflect the blows, but he was too disabled to be effective. The husky female was laughing now as she watched the beating. The gash on Adams's head was bleeding profusely, covering his face with blood. Adams's eyes were swelling shut and blood was running from his mouth and nose. The blood from the gunshot wounds continued to pool on the floor underneath him, and Adams knew he was getting weaker by the moment. He needed to fight back *now*. He needed to fight for his life. Adams needed to get his hands free and get on his feet. He tried to pull his legs under him again so he could stand.

The female began kicking Adams with her boots while the men in the room urged her on. She was hard-looking and spoke in Russian as she knelt and yelled at Adams. Her face came so close that Adams could feel her breath.

Adams was far from being done; he was still alive. He lunged forward with a headbutt that sent the Russian woman falling backwards and blood rushing from her nose. When the Russian men laughed and teased her, she stormed out of the room. That made the Russians break out laughing even harder.

Adams tried to catch his breath. He needed to get to his feet. He needed weapons, and he needed an escape route. *Strike, evade, and escape. Focus.* Only moments later, the woman returned with a large, heavy kitchen knife held in both hands. Blood ran down her face and onto her sweater. Without any comment, she held the knife over her head and thrust it down into Adams's back.

Segei Antonov waited impatiently in the comfortable private jet. The pilot had announced that their departure time was only moments away, but Segei needed to wait for Aleks to arrive. Segei ordered that the pilot report an unexpected delay in the departure time.

The driver of the limousine sat quietly in the car waiting for Aleks. No one seemed to pay much attention to the luxury Mercedes-Benz as it idled at the curb on the major boulevard.

In the safe house, the men in the room stopped laughing. They fell silent, unbelieving. Everything stopped. Adams felt the impact and the pain. The knife had penetrated deep into his back, glancing off his shoulder blade. Every movement of his body caused even more pain as blood flowed around the blade of the knife.

Leaving the knife in place, the female stepped back and cursed at Adams in Russian. Then she angrily yelled at the other men in the room while she pointed at him. She was not someone to be ridiculed.

Leaning forward with his knees underneath him and his hands behind his back, Adams ceased moving. Breathing slowly, Adams thought, *I'm still not dead, not yet. I'm not done yet. I need to get up.* Adams wasn't giving up.

Aleks walked into the room and saw the large knife in Adams's back. He exploded in anger and yelled, "He better not be dead! Damn it, what did I tell you? Not yet! Not until after his children are here! We have to wait."

Aleks pushed the woman hard against the bedroom wall, grabbing her hair and pulling her close to him. "I fucking told you not to hurt him, *cyka*! If he dies, so do you."

Aleks knelt next to Adams and pulled his head up. He could see that Adams's eyes were open, but they were full of blood. Adams was still breathing. "Ah, you are alive. But not for long, policeman; you are dying quickly. We are bringing your family here as we speak and once it's done, once you know, then it will be your time and your misery will stop. Then you will die also, and policemen in America will know who we are. They will know who I am. They will learn."

Adams thought that his son and his daughter had been taken to the sheriff's station. Something must have happened. He saw in his mind's eye a picture of his son and daughter being brought into the room with him, looking down at their father, handcuffed, shot and stabbed, beaten and bleeding. He could see tears in their eyes, and he could feel their fear. Then something happened. Something different.

Jack Adams would not allow his son and his daughter to feel fear. He knew he couldn't let this happen, and he wasn't done yet. Jack Adams ignored pain and denied fear. He hadn't even started to fight yet. Aleks Antonov had no idea what hell was coming his way.

#

Aleks thought about his power growing, about his father being proud of him. Aleks would have power, money, and women. Aleks would be feared by everyone. He called the phone number to the leader of the men he'd sent to Rossmoor, to the policeman's house. He wanted to know how long before the children arrived in Glendale, but there was still no answer. He was worried that Adams would die before he could kill his children in front of him. Killing the policeman as he sobbed and begged for his own life . . . Aleks would be a legend.

Aleks knew that the men at Adams's house must be busy completing their tasks, but he would know soon that the task was done. After that, Aleks's dream of gaining the status of Vor in the Russian Mafia, Bratva, would be realized. He would get the respect he deserved.

At the Emergency Operations Center, a liaison was created with the Glendale Police Department due to the apartment building populated by the Russians who were believed to be the source of these events. All events reported in Glendale were now online in the LAPD Emergency Operations Center.

The radio call of shots fired in Glendale was reviewed by the analysts assigned to RACR who believed it to be an event that should be addressed, albeit a long shot. However, Commander Jelenick came to another conclusion that the radio call was a routine issue and did not warrant assigning specialized resources to follow up on. It was not near the abduction site of Lieutenant Adams. Jelenick kept thinking, *Slow things down. That's what he told me to do. Slow things down.*

Aleks ordered that the young female be taken to another room. "She is young and valuable; she'll make much money. But marking her while you teach her and break her delays our ability to get her working. Do not injure her appearance. Take her to the other room. It is the policeman we are focused on today. She will be enjoyed later."

#

Police Officer Bob Burrell had been working in the Emergency Operations Center since its inception in 1980. His entire career with the Los Angeles Police Department had been spent coordinating responses to major emergency situations, and the EOC was his home away from home. Burrell had his desk and his tea pot situated exactly the way he liked it, and no one ever bothered him or questioned him. He had an assigned parking space. He was a fixture of the building.

Burrell, a Police Officer III, had always passed on taking promotional exams. He was happy where he was and had no desire to go somewhere else. He would live out his career as a policeman inside the EOC, setting his own schedule and his days off. There was never any drama, and no one bothered him.

Officer Burrell was adept at connecting the dots. That was his greatest value in the EOC—paying attention to the details. Burrell was not interested in where Lieutenant Adams was abducted. He wanted to know where he was being taken, and it was a good guess that he may be taken to the vicinity of Glendale. That's where the Russians lived. Since Adams wasn't at a hospital, he had to be somewhere.

A "shots fired" call in an area of Glendale that rarely had such a call was one of those dots that Burrell was willing to look at. As a matter of fact, he was drawn to it.

"Detective McClain, this is Bob Burrell at the EOC. I have a situation I'm not comfortable with. You have a second?"

Ron McClain was at the command post in Rampart Division, merely standing by until something happened, until Segei or Aleks was located. Gold Rush had been hit and they were investigating. The investigation into the murder of Detective Marks was being handled by Robbery Homicide Division and the Force Investigation Team that investigated officer-involved shootings.

They were looking to arrest people, to find Segei and Aleks Antonov. Now, Lieutenant Adams had been abducted. "You bet, Burrell. Where are we with this? Most of us are still in the dark." McClain was receiving bits and pieces of the kidnapping scenario and going crazy all the while.

"Detective McClain, I'm grasping at straws here. The van left with Adams and we're pulling out all the stops finding it. We're reviewing street and freeway videos looking for anything, but it takes time. If these bad guys live in Glendale, I've got to think they're in place where they're comfortable. That being the case, it wouldn't be beyond them to move Adams somewhere around there, somewhere they already have control over. So, this 'shots fired' call comes out over near Glendale College, shots heard, not seen. An area where there's never really shots fired. I know it's slim, but I want to look at it and I've been told to stand down by some Commander, some guy named Jelenick. He's here in the EOC with us."

Taking a deep breath to pause and think, McClain wondered what Lieutenant Adams would do. *Okay, here we go, over the deep end. Just like Adams would do it.* "Bob, send Major Crimes SIS to investigate it and cover the couple blocks around the call. The sound of shots probably wouldn't travel much farther than that. Have them find the needle in a haystack. It may be nothing, but it's the only thing we have until you guys review all the video cameras and come up with a direction they left or where they are. If nothing else, just keeping SIS over in Glendale may work out for us later."

"Okay, Mac, I'm good to go on it. It's the right thing to do, and if this guy wasn't here I'd have already done it. But he gave me an order, Mac." Bob Burrell had been around the LAPD for a long time and clearly understood how the command structure worked. He also understood what happens when someone in management gets involved who is either incompetent or a fool. He wrongly guessed Jelenick was only one of those.

"Bob, I'm giving you permission to do this. I'm just a detective and I can't overrule this guy, but we both know it's the right thing. I think we're both going to pay for this with some kind of insubordination beef, and Jelenick is the kind of guy to push it really hard, but you know Adams and you know the situation we're in. Is there anything you wouldn't risk to save his life? To save any policeman's life? I'll get Chief Nelson on the phone and run it past him. If he disagrees, I'll let you know and we'll pull Major Crimes back. No harm, no foul. But do it now."

Officer Burrell knew the path he was going to take. Hell, he would have done it even without someone telling him. "Fuck it, I'll get Major Crimes out there. Something comes up, let me know."

Burrell notified Major Crimes and laid out the long shot. A seven-detective Surveillance team was on the scene in just eleven minutes: two detectives on foot with backpacks walking the area like college kids, one on a bicycle, and four cruising in undercover Surveillance cars.

"Chief Nelson, it's Detective McClain. The EOC notified me of a lead in Glendale they want to look at, but apparently Commander Jelenick told them no. I advised them to go forward until we have something else to work on and I would seek your permission after the fact. If you disagree, I'll pull them back."

Deputy Chief Steve Nelson had a pretty even temperament most of the time, but every second counted and he had no time for anyone slowing things down or interfering. McClain had been trained by Lieutenant Adams. Adams was a rebel, but probably the most capable decision-maker on the Los Angeles Police Department; when shit hit the fan, that was the guy you wanted in charge. Nelson believed that just *had* to rub off on McClain. "Good job, Detective McClain. Keep me up on any new scoop. You doing okay over in Rampart?"

"Yes, sir. It's not the time for details, but I'll let you know if we need anything. Just get him back."

Meanwhile, Commander Jelenick was still reeling from his encounter with Segei Antonov. He and his wife, his whole family, were in danger. He needed to slow down the investigation into the Russians without appearing to interfere. He had to get his wife back. Segei said that all he had to do was slow things down and his wife would be spared. He was able to convince himself that the radio call of shots fired in Glendale had to be a routine call. How could such a random event be tied to the disappearance of Jack Adams? Calls of shots fired were an everyday occurrence in Los Angeles. He would take the first step and redirect LAPD efforts away from that call. It wasn't even in Los Angeles, so a routine investigation by Glendale was all that it called for.

Jelenick continued to work hard at convincing himself that the call was not involved with the Adams incident that had occurred in Los Angeles, but it was in Glendale where the Russians lived. He'd better not take the risk, and it would give him something to present to Segei Antonov should he be placed in that position. Should he need it to save his wife.

He still didn't know where his wife was. She was not answering her phone. He could use it to tell Segei he was slowing things down, just like he was told.

#

When Adams was able to stabilize his knees under him, his body leaning forward with his hands still handcuffed behind his back, he rested his face on the floor, on the carpet stained with his own blood. He just needed to catch his breath. He wished they would turn the music down; it was so damn hard to focus on what he had to do.

One of the men continued to laugh and verbally taunt Adams, laughing at the knife in his back. Roughly kicking Adams in the rib cage, he laughed again as Adams absorbed the blow and remained motionless, obviously dead, or at least dying. The two men and the female walked out of the room and down the hall. Adams was left alone in the room to die. He might have been dead already.

Adams had leaned toward the kick and absorbed it solidly on his rib cage. The crack of his ribs was loud and the pain shot through his body. His ribs, now broken, added yet another layer to the loss of Adams's ability to function. His mind kept repeating, *Fight.*

Adams sensed that he was alone. With his legs folded up underneath him and his hands forced behind his back by the handcuffs, Adams went about the business of unlacing the boot on his left foot. He had to contort, to stretch. It was painful. He had too many injuries, had lost too much blood. He was light headed and couldn't focus.

Unable to see with his eyes swollen and blocked by blood, and while in excruciating pain, Adams whispered aloud, "I'm not dying here, not today. Neither is that little girl. Neither is my son or my daughter. I'm coming for every one of you motherfuckers."

Adams raised his head and looked around the room. He was alone, but not completely. "For the Lord is my shepherd. Even though I walk through the valley of the shadow of death, I will fear no evil, for You are with me." Adams's faith was far stronger than his pain or his fears. Adams wasn't done yet.

The laces in Adams's boot slowly slipped through the holes until the small handcuff key dropped into his hand. Policemen placed handcuffs on a suspect with the keyhole facing upwards to make it easier for the officer to unlock them. With his fingers, Adams searched the top of his handcuffs for the key holes but didn't find them.

His left arm was numb, and he could barely manipulate his hand. Holding the key in his right hand, he found the keyhole on the underside of the handcuff on his left wrist. Carefully sliding the key into the Smith & Wesson handcuffs that he had carried since he was in the police academy, the well-worn lock coated in graphite turned easily and he heard the familiar clicking sound of the handcuff opening. His left arm fell forward, his hand dragging on the floor, but he had freedom.

Adams had escaped from the handcuffs, and it was time to fight back, but first he had to get on his feet. Pulling his hands in front of him was not an easy task. The two gunshots to Adams's left shoulder and upper arm had caused him to lose most function, but not all. Once he unlocked the handcuff on his right wrist, Adams whispered out loud, "Let's see what I'm made of. God give me strength."

Removing the folding tactical knife clipped inside his right boot, Adams deftly opened the knife as he had practiced a thousand times and cradled it in his left hand as he used his right to help him struggle to his feet. Holding on to the windowsill, he propped his body against the bedroom wall and slowly slid up the wall until he was fully standing upright. Blood stained the wall as he used it for support.

He found it hard to stand. He was lightheaded and his balance was slow in returning, but as he took his first step he became more confident that he could stay on his feet. He was standing now without holding on to the window or leaning against the wall. He could stay on his feet!

Adams considered how to stop the bleeding from the gunshot wounds. *Pressure on the wounds?* But he quickly decided that could come later; he was running out of time. He was weak, and he needed weapons.

Breathing alone caused his broken ribs to hurt terribly. Clearing the blood from his eyes and clearing a little of his vision, Adams backed up to the swinging closet door and pushed it shut with the heel of his boot. He felt the sharp pain when the knife in his back was captured between the door and door frame. Holding the door tightly shut with his boot, Adams willed his body forward as the knife slid slowly out of his back. The pain was overwhelming him, weakening him. When the knife was pulled from his body, he felt the blood pulsing from the wound and he became dizzy and nauseated.

Adams held the closet door shut with his boot, then slowly turned to recover the knife with his right hand. Adams was now armed. Not only with a small tactical knife, but with a large, heavy knife as well. He was ready for a battle, and he planned to go and find it. He was a warrior. *In your mind's eye.*

Adams immediately heard movement in the hallway. The loud music masked most other sounds, but he heard the unmistakable voice of Aleks Antonov yelling loudly, "Why did you leave him alone? He's not dead! Someone needs to stay with him!"

Aleks was frustrated with the lack of respect that the group of Russians were showing him. They were not listening to him, not obeying him. All of that would change soon.

Adams was free, and he was armed. Although gravely injured, Adams had just become a very dangerous man. He held the small black tactical knife supported against his chest with his left hand. The gunshot trauma to his left arm made most movement impossible. The larger and heavier knife was in his right hand, cradled over his broken ribs.

As Aleks turned to his left and stepped through the bedroom door, he was surprised by Adams crashing against him and pinning him against the doorjamb. Adams pushed upwards with his left hand to drive the small knife into the Russian's throat, but his wounds disallowed such a strong movement.

Aleks was surprised that Adams was not on the floor and not handcuffed. Aleks instinctively brought both of his hands up to protect himself and he grabbed Adams's left wrist, holding the small black knife away from his body.

Aleks understood his superiority over Adams; he accepted it. He had known it all along. Aleks smiled and said, "You waste your time, policeman. You are weak. Let's put this knife in your eye and bring you even closer to death. Let your children see their father in such agony before they meet their own end."

Aleks easily twisted the knife from Adams's hand and actually smiled. Aleks believed he was a powerful man, a man to be feared, and he would display that now. He squeezed Adams's throat and pulled him close. He felt the weight of Adams's body and knew that he was holding Adams up, that Adams was weak. Aleks moved the point of the small knife toward Adams's face in a taunting manner. Resting the point of the knife on Adams's cheek just below his left eye, he began to cut.

Aleks knew his actions at this moment would make him a legend, even more feared than he was now. Taking a man's eye in this manner would make him the most formidable of men.

As he squeezed Adams's throat, Aleks tilted the knife up to push it into Adams's eye. He searched for the fear in Adams's face, to revel in the victory over this policeman before he died. He would tell this story many times and his power would grow—but something happened. *Something different.*

Aleks was suddenly taken aback when he failed to find the fear that he expected. There was no fear in Adams's eyes. Only a calm, emotionless demeanor. With the knife pressed against his eye, Lieutenant Jack Adams calmly, slowly, and without emotion, told Aleks, "You threatened my family."

Adams had only just begun to fight. There was no fear in his heart and the pain was gone now. Looking directly into Aleks's eyes, Adams drove the large, heavy knife into Aleks's side just below his armpit then calmly said, "You'll never threaten them again."

As the knife pierced into Aleks's heart, Aleks was only aware of the blunt force trauma hitting the side of his body. His central nervous system immediately began to shut down and blocked most of the pain, but the trauma took his breath away, causing him to freeze in place, holding the small black knife in front of Adams's face as if it floated in the air.

Adams released his grip on the large knife and wrapped his fingers around Aleks's hand and squeezed. Squeezed *hard.* Adams pulled the small black knife away from his face and Aleks's eyes widened as the knife was turned toward him. Their faces almost touching, that fear that Aleks had searched for revealed itself in his own eyes. Aleks displayed fear with every fiber of his being and desperately looked for mercy, but he found none. Aleks Antonov was frightened. Aleks Antonov feared death. Aleks begged, "Stop, stop, stop."

Looking eye to eye, Adams pressed his forehead against Aleks's face. The small knife penetrated into the carotid artery on the side of Aleks's throat. The blood escaping was immediately forceful as Aleks attempted to stop it. Holding his hand over his throat, the look in Aleks's eyes told the tale. Aleks had no recourse but to wait for death to come, and he surrendered to it. He gave up. Aleks Antonov slumped to the floor, dead.

Adams knelt over Aleks's lifeless body, his eyes still open, and recovered his .45 caliber handgun from Aleks's waistband. He pulled the slide partially back to see that a round was chambered in his handgun, and releasing the magazine, he found he had seven rounds to fight with. Sliding his thumb to the side of the frame, Adams took the safety off.

Adams unpinned his badge from Aleks's chest and looking directly into Aleks's eyes, devoid of life, Adams said, "This is mine, asshole. You won't be needing it." Aleks Antonov was dead, and Jack Adams had just become a hunter.

Segei Antonov became impatient waiting for his son to arrive. The flight crew was anxious to depart, and Segei began to feel the pressure mounting. He feared that delaying the flight would draw attention to him from the airport authorities. He was avoiding the use of his cell phone and felt blind as he sat in the soft leather seats of the luxury aircraft, waiting, looking forward to returning to Russia where he would be met with a hero's welcome.

Outside of the Glendale house, Melissa Connor, one of the youngest Major Crimes detectives, was on foot carrying a backpack with her hair pulled back into a ponytail as she walked down the sidewalk in the immediate area of the report of shots fired. She turned her head left and right to throw her ponytail as she walked, then something glistening caught her eye. Something white. The driveway of the prewar house ran down the side of the house, terminating in a single-car garage on the back of the lot. But a very small piece of a fender of a vehicle parked in the backyard that was barely visible, poking out from behind the house, indicated that someone had driven down the driveway and turned left into the backyard and onto the grass. Someone driving a white van.

Detective Melissa Connor made a command decision. *Hit the house.* If it was the wrong house, they could apologize and move on. Shit happens. "6K33, white van secreted to the rear of the house. Loud music inside, no activity outside. I think we need to hit it. Let's hit it right now!"

"6K36, what do you have, Connor?"

"6K33, just a white van. Now get your ass up here and let's hit it." Melissa Connor was a decision-maker. A leader.

Inside, the hallway was empty as Adams stepped across to a closed door. The music in the house was still so loud that it was difficult for Adams to function, and it was a heavy weight on his shoulders. Entering the room surprised the two men who were continuing their brutal sexual assault of the young girl. The girl had initially fought back, but she had been beaten until she resigned to being victimized by the ruthless pair. The lesson had been taught, the lesson of submission.

The larger of the two men and the older of the pair, at about fifty years old, dove sideways to his clothing draped over a chair alongside a Glock handgun. Adams, holding his familiar Kimber .45 that felt like a part of his body in his right hand, shot the man just above the right ear. Crashing onto the chair, the impact sent the Glock flying against the wall.

The second man of about forty years old rose off of the young girl and spun around while still on the bed just as he heard the gunshot Adams had fired. Looking at Adams, he was clearly assessing his options. His pile of clothes folded on top of his gun were on the other side of the bed, near the dead man's Glock visible on the floor.

Deciding that Adams didn't look very formidable, his face pummeled and blood dripping down his left arm that hung uselessly at his side, the second man charged directly at Adams. Jumping from the bed and coming at Adams with both his hands outstretched, Adams pulled his handgun back close to his body and fired two rounds. Although each of the rounds struck the naked man, the velocity of his movement continued to drive him forward into Adams, causing both of them to crash to the ground.

Adams struggled to get out from under the man, knowing that the sounds of the gunshots would warn others in the house. He saw the windows of this room were covered by bars, and the only way out lay down the hallway and through the front door. He had to get out of the house before his son and daughter got there. He had to get outside to fight that fight.

As the SIS team formed up three doors down, the Surveillance detectives decided to get eyes on the van, possibly from a neighboring property. Suddenly, the unmistakable sound of a muffled gunshot was heard coming from inside the house. Then, only moments later, two more gunshots. An "officer needs help" call was broadcasted by the SIS team and an airship was requested. The team cautiously moved toward the house as quickly as they were able.

A few moments after Aleks had walked down the hallway, the female who had stabbed Adams heard what she thought were gunshots. She thought that Aleks had probably grown tired of this game and finally killed him. *Good.* Hard to tell because of the music, and she was sick of the noise now. The woman yelled above the music, "Aleks killed the policeman! Good. I'm done with this nonsense."

She walked down the hallway to tell Aleks she was leaving. She wanted nothing to do with the children who were being brought to the house. She was tired of this whole situation and just wanted to kill Adams and leave, to go back home. Killing policemen in America was out of bounds; it wasn't done. She thought Aleks was a fool who was trying to be a grown man, and she just wanted this to be over with.

As she stepped through the open door of the bedroom, Aleks lay motionless on the floor with a massive stream of blood pouring from the side of his neck. Aleks was dead, and Adams was gone. She looked up and saw that the windows were still closed; he had to be in the house. She turned back to the hallway and screamed for the others in the living room to help her, but she thought the music was so loud that they probably couldn't hear her. These young men were so stupid.

She opened the other bedroom door and stepped into the room. She saw first the girl on the bed, sitting cross-legged holding a blanket in front of her, then men on the floor in front of her. Adams, still struggling to get out from under the man who attacked him, kicked and knocked the woman's legs out from under her.

Lacking strength and the use of his left arm, Adams was immediately overwhelmed by the woman who dropped on top of him and began punching him and poking at his eyes. Adams retrieved his gun that had been partially covered by the second man's body. He pulled the gun up between him and the woman, firing one round, striking under the woman's chin. With a look of surprise on her face, she was done fighting. The large Russian woman would die in only moments.

The young girl on the bed was surrounded by the signs of death. Blood on the walls and bodies on the floor. When the blood from the female Adams had shot spread across the young girl's naked body, she placed her face in her hands and froze in place. She made herself invisible.

Knowing there was no time to waste, Adams found the will to stand. He pushed the two bodies from on top of him and pushed himself up to his knees. Adams was exhausted; it was hard to breathe. Somehow, he found his feet underneath him and stood one more time, but it took all his strength.

He went to the girl and helped her put her arms around his neck. "I'm a policeman. I'm here to help you. You can trust me." The girl looked at Adams but only saw blood. So much blood. Adams handed her his badge. "Here, this is my badge. I'm a policeman. You hold on to this and it will keep you safe, okay?"

As Adams pushed the young girl up onto his back, he felt her arms slowly pull around him and squeeze. The pain flushed through his entire body as he walked to the bedroom door with her clinging to him. She was tiny but right now it felt like she weighed two hundred pounds. He knew he had to fight his way out of the house, and he wasn't going without her.

Adams was not able to deploy his usual tactical acumen; he was not able to peer around the corner into the hallway in the manner that he had taught the officers who worked for him. Slicing the pie with his handgun was not working for Adams today. He was barely functioning, barely able to stay on his feet and mostly blinded, let alone carry the weight of the young girl clinging to his back. He became resolved to the fact that making this escape was going to mean blunt force trauma smashing down anything in his path.

As Adams stepped into the hallway as carefully as he could, gunfire broke out, striking the walls next to him and his right forearm. The blood flowed immediately and Adams was barely able to keep his grip on his gun. His left hand was useless, and his poor balance caused him to brace himself by leaning against the doorjamb.

The two men at the other end of the hallway continued to fire as they walked, shoulder to shoulder, down the hallway and toward the bedroom holding Adams and the young girl.

A young Russian, only twenty years old, sat in the living room with the young woman he had been hitting on for two weeks. They were told they only had to keep two children quiet, and they had no plans to involve themselves in this thing with the policeman.

Sitting on the couch with the music blaring, they heard the gunshots from the bedroom and saw the two Russian men working their way down the hallway to the rear of the house. When gunfire erupted in the hallway, they jumped to their feet and picked up guns from the coffee table. They waited in the living room for this thing to be resolved.

Two Major Crimes SIS detectives worked down the driveway to the rear of the house and saw the Mercedes-Benz Sprinter van. Peering into a side window on the passenger side, the blood on the floor of the van was clearly visible.

As the gunshots rang out in a continuous volley inside the house, the two detectives in the rear of the house forced the rear door open and stepped into a small room with a water heater that led into the kitchen. The kitchen was empty as they moved forward into the house.

The other five SIS detectives staged themselves at the front door and forced the door open. They entered the house in a line, one behind the other. The detectives immediately found themselves in a small living room with blood staining the floor. A lot of blood.

The detectives were convinced that this was where the suspects who had kidnapped Lieutenant Jack Adams had fled to. The first two detectives through the front door engaged a young man and woman who appeared surprised by their presence. The woman held a handgun in her left hand, while the man held a shotgun at port arms. The music was blaring, and the room was fairly dark with curtains covering the windows.

When the detectives ordered the two to drop their weapons, the female was standing behind the young man and her movements were not clear to the detectives. She immediately fired her handgun, striking the vest of Melissa Connor. The two detectives who had entered through the rear door and were now in the kitchen returned fire and shot her three times.

Connor absorbed the hit to her vest like she had been expecting it. She never even missed a beat and shot the young man who was holding the shotgun, knocking him to the ground. Still alive, the young man scrambled to regain his hold on the shotgun and raised it toward the officers. Connor and the detective standing next to her shot him four more times. Within four seconds of entering the house, two suspects had been killed in the living room of the Russian's house.

Major Crimes SIS detectives are among the elite, each one with a tactical background and a tested resolve to survive. Connor and the four other detectives who entered with her through the front door moved forward as they fired and literally ran over the top of both suspects as they fell to the ground, on a mission to get to Adams. The two detectives who entered through the rear door assumed control of the two suspects lying on the floor of the living room.

Adams's freedom was down that hallway and out the front door. Adams knew he was disadvantaged inside the house, and the next fight to rescue his son and daughter would be in the front yard. That's where he would rescue his children, and the two men shooting at him were in his way.

Adams struggled to maintain his grip on the gun in his right hand, blood streaming down his arm. He wasn't able to extend his arm now, so he held the gun against his chest for support and pointed it down the hallway. The young girl, clinging to Adams's back, whimpered as the shooting came closer. Adams would not lose this fight. He would push down the hallway and over the two men blocking it. *Blunt force trauma.*

Stepping back up to the door, his handgun cradled against his chest, Adams leaned his chest forward through the door and fired two rounds down the hallway as the two men were only steps away. He shot one of the men squarely in the chest and watched him stumble, then pitch forward onto the ground. The second man fired twice more just as Adams was able to fire again, snapping the man's head back before he fell forward.

The five detectives who had kicked open the front door and the two detectives who came in the rear had come together in the living room and pushed aggressively forward to the hallway, where they saw the backs of two men firing randomly down the hallway.

They seemed to understand that Adams was holding them off. As the detectives fired down the hallway at the two armed men, both men were knocked forward to the ground with .45-caliber bullets. The two men were hit from the front and the rear, and both would die in the hallway.

Before moving further down the dark hallway, the detectives immediately called out, "Adams? LAPD Major Crimes. Adams?"

The slide on Adams's handgun was locked back. *Out of ammunition.* He slid it into his waistband and an invisible hand helped him somehow to overcome his pain and fatigue and kneel down to pick the Glock up from the floor when he heard the voice calling his name. Holding the Glock in his right hand cradled against his chest and pointing it toward the door to the hallway, Adams was ready for the next gunfight.

"Adams, this is Major Crimes! This is LAPD, Lieutenant. Can you step out into the hallway? We need to know it's you, sir."

Carrying the young girl on his back and the music still blaring, Adams ignored the muffled yelling from the dark hallway and pointed the barrel of the Glock in front of him as he peered around the corner. He could only see from one eye. The two men he had just shot were lying dead on the floor. Adams didn't know that they had also been shot by the SIS detectives.

Suddenly, the music stopped. One of the detectives in the living room pulled the plug.

Adams held at the bedroom door and committed to moving down the hallway to the front door of the house. Holding the Glock tightly against his chest, his finger on the trigger, it was now or never. He would fight his way out, and anyone standing in front of him would die.

SIS Detective Kirk Wilder, who had the nickname "Top Flight," took a risk—a large risk. He revealed himself at the mouth of the hallway, holding his badge out in front of him, his gun held to his side as Melissa Connor stood behind him with her gun pointed down the hallway over his shoulder.

Detective Wilder announced, "LAPD, don't shoot! Jack Adams, it's LAPD, Lieutenant! Don't shoot. The bad guys are dead. Step out into the hallway, Lieutenant, we need to know it's you, sir."

Adams heard yelling as he leveled his handgun in front of him and pushed around the corner to fight his way down the hallway and kill anything blocking his path. He wouldn't stop until he was out of the front door to fight the next fight. Adams began putting pressure onto the trigger as he fought through the pain and brought the front sight of his handgun up to the forehead of a man blocking his path.

In the darkness of the hallway, Detective Melissa Connor saw the blur of a man she did not recognize, a man in dark clothing charging down the hallway with a gun in front of him. A gun pointed directly at them. She didn't initially see the young girl on his back who was clinging so tightly that she was hidden. Connor brought her gun over Wilder's shoulder, clicked the flashlight on, and took aim at the center mass of her target. The chest of Jack Adams.

Detective Wilder was a large man who filled the mouth of the hallway. He knew Adams, but he didn't recognize the bloody face of the man charging down the dark hallway. Wilder wasn't sure it was Adams as he faced the Glock that was pointed at him, but he chose to act on instinct and made a life-threatening decision. "It's okay, Lieutenant, don't shoot! We're LAPD, sir. Major Crimes SIS. Don't shoot! We've got you, sir."

Adams stepped on the two Russian men laying in the hallway as he engaged the people standing in front of him, blocking his path. With his finger on the trigger, Adams looked over the top of the sights to see a man holding an LAPD badge. With the Glock pointed forward and his finger still on the trigger, he continued to push down the hallway until he was sure. He wasn't stopping until he got out the front door.

Detective Connor's vision was partially blocked by Wilder and she struggled to keep her gun downrange and on the "suspect" without endangering her partner. She pressed on her trigger and anticipated the recoil of the large .45-caliber handgun, as she had practiced countless times. Tight grip, control the recoil, and hit your target accurately and effectively. Overwhelm your target with effective firepower limiting their ability to fire back.

Adams took one more step and in that half of a second…Connor released the trigger and let out a loud sigh. *My gun didn't fire.* For the rest of her life, Connor would wonder why her gun hadn't fired. She was pressing the trigger.

As Adams came within just a few steps away, Detectives Connor and Wilder couldn't believe what they saw. Lieutenant Jack Adams was unrecognizable, and there was a child clinging to his back. "Are there any more back there, Lieutenant?"

Adams spoke, but it was difficult. "They're all dead."

"Step this way, Lieutenant. We need you to clear two more shooters."

With the young girl on his back, Adams continued to step over the two men lying in the hallway and made his way to the LAPD detectives. Melissa Connor took Adams's right arm and directed him over the next two bodies on the living room floor and out of the front door. "Carried him" is probably a better description. Two Glendale police cars with red lights flashing and sirens blaring skidded to a stop at the curb in front of the house as a Glendale police helicopter dropped down to hover over the house.

Adams had made it to the front of the house for the next fight. "My son and my daughter, the Russians have them. I need a magazine for my Kimber." More than anything else in the world, Adams needed to protect his family.

Melissa Connor looked confused. "I don't think so, sir. They're fine, Lieutenant. They're safe with the Sheriff's Department. Who do you have here?" The detectives helped the young girl down from Adams's back and covered her with one of their shirts, but she held on to Adams's waist and couldn't be pulled away. Adams struggled to stay on his feet even with Connor's help.

A second helicopter, one from LAPD, arrived overhead and numerous Glendale and Los Angeles Police vehicles continued arriving along with the Glendale Fire Department. It wasn't long before two news helicopters also arrived and circled the scene from a higher altitude.

Adams challenged Detective Connor. "The Russians said they have my kids. Give me another magazine!" Lieutenant Jack Adams stood in front of that house in Glendale looking down the street, looking for the next fight. Looking for targets.

"Stand by, Lieutenant. Here, sir, take this." Connor handed Adams a fresh magazine from her own Kimber and immediately got on her phone to the office of the Orange County Sheriff.

Adams slid the Glock into his pocket. He felt for his Kimber with the slide locked back. Leaving it in his waistband, Adams released the empty magazine and stripped it out. He pushed the fully loaded magazine in and seated it, then slid the gun out of his waistband and released the slide, loading the gun. *In your mind's eye, the fight is never over.*

Detective Melissa Connor disconnected the call. "Lieutenant, your kids are at the sheriff's headquarters. They're safe. The Russians were lying to you. They're okay, sir. Your family is safe, Lieutenant."

Lieutenant Jack Adams struggled to stay on his feet and began to stumble. Connors believed he was dying and tried to hold him up. He had lost too much blood—the trauma to his body was too great. Adams appeared to be losing consciousness as Detectives Melissa Connor and Kirk Wilder helped him to the ground just as the paramedics got to him.

Melissa Connor leaned close to his face and whispered. "It's okay, Lieutenant, you did good, sir. They're all dead."

Adams looked into Connors's eyes and whispered, "Where's Segei?"

In your mind's eye, Adams wasn't done yet. Then his eyes closed.

#

The Major Crimes detectives cleared the rest of the house to find the body of Aleks Antonov, two other men, and a woman in the rear bedrooms. Eight bodies.

When the paramedics arrived, they immediately recognized the advanced trauma and degrading condition Adams was in. They put Adams and the young girl on gurneys and began an immediate transport. Time was of the essence.

As the Fire Rescue ambulance left the location with flashing red lights and the siren blaring, the paramedics began to work on Adams as his blood pressure dropped dramatically. "We're losing this guy—something is sideways. Get that IV moving, we need volume!"

In Adams's absence, the long crime scene investigation at the Glendale house began with the Glendale Police, Los Angeles Police, and FBI. Special

Agent Bill O'Reilly pulled in with a much different attitude than he normally wore. He was serious. He was angry, and he was driven. Bill O'Reilly rallied thirty-one agents who arrived on the scene in Glendale, initiating a Russian organized crime task force.

At the yellow tape, a large group of people assembled to watch the events as they unfolded. This was a fairly novel event in this neighborhood, which rarely experienced any police action at all. The tall man dressed in a dark suit maneuvered closer and closer to the action. He watched Lieutenant Adams being loaded into the Fire Rescue ambulance, then the young girl being loaded into a second ambulance. Listening intently, he heard one of the firemen remark to a Fire captain, "Everybody inside has been pronounced. Six males and two females." That was all he needed to hear.

He walked slowly away from the yellow tape and sat in the Mercedes-Benz limousine before he called the man sitting alone in the private jet. "Eight people. I'm sure Aleks also. They're all gone; there's no arrests. The policeman and a little girl were taken to the hospital, but Aleks is gone. The police killed everybody."

#

At the EOC, Commander Stans Jelenick listened with horror. Jelenick thought, *How did this happen?* There would be questions. *Where is Elana?*

At the last minute, Elana Jelenick had been invited to spend the day with Yvonne Sokoloff. Kostya Sokoloff had sent a car to pick Elana up and bring her to the Sokoloff home in Pasadena.

It was a larger home with a very formal European design that did not fit in the upper-class neighborhood of modified craftsman homes. It simply didn't fit in Pasadena. Although most in the area appreciated the landscaping on the large lots their homes were built on, the Sokoloff home was designed to populate every available inch of land. The driveway was designed to showcase the cars parked at the residence for the benefit of the neighbors.

When Elana arrived, Yvonne hugged her. "We are so glad to have you, Elana, my friend. Kostya has offered his friendship to the Jelenick family. This is a very important event for all of us. Many good things are in our future together."

Yvonne asked Elana to spend the entire day with her because Kostya had called Stans into negotiations with powerful men who could help his career. Yvonne asked Elana to leave her phone on the entryway table with everyone else's; it was their family rule. She also told Elana not to bother Stans with phone calls because they were in very important meetings. "These are the men that make things happen, Elana. This is how these things get done. These men can help Stans to be in control at the police department. They are powerful allies, and you must help Stans to accept their friendship. You must encourage him."

Yvonne smiled and took Elana's hands. "I wanted to spend more time with you, Elana. While the men are discussing great career enhancements, I wanted to discuss your career also. You are such a talented artist, my friend, and you also need friends to do these things."

The afternoon passed and Elana thought that dinner was incredible, but she grew increasingly uncomfortable and wished to return home. Sitting on the patio, an employee of the Kostya house approached with an urgent phone call. Yvonne stepped away out of Elana's earshot, then appeared animated and upset during the conversation.

As she returned to the table on the patio where Elana sat, she had a look of grave concern on her face. "Elana, friends in Glendale have been arrested. Close friends. Arrested by Stans and the police department. Kostya has raced off to his office to confront this, and he is angry and upset. I think he is angry at Stans. There is much danger to all of us, I think. You must go with these men and they will take you to Stans."

Two men escorted Elana to the waiting black Mercedes-Benz idling in the driveway. Elana paused before getting in the car and looked back at Yvonne for support. Yvonne offered no expression as she turned and closed the door. Elana Jelenick was never heard from again.

CHAPTER FORTY-THREE
THE FIGHT IS NEVER OVER

Glendale Fire Rescue transported Adams to Glendale Memorial Hospital, a trauma center. A black Mercedes-Benz followed the ambulance clear to the hospital entrance. When the driver saw two plain police cars parked at the ambulance entrance to the emergency room, he turned and parked in a nearby parking lot. The four officers from the Glendale Police Department SWAT team walked alongside the gurney as Adams was wheeled into the hospital.

Adams was unconscious upon arrival, the loss of blood overwhelming him. As he was wheeled into the emergency room, he was taken directly to a surgical suite that had been prepared prior to his arrival. Two hospital security personnel were already posted inside the surgical suite.

From Rampart Division, Detective McClain dispatched eight LAPD Gang officers to Glendale Memorial Hospital to provide security for Lieutenant Adams. Four of the Gang officers posted at the emergency entrance and the main hospital entrance, for effect. The other four posted in the hallway outside the surgical suite with the four Glendale SWAT officers.

The trauma team leader stood at the foot of the bed with the chaplain as a team of trauma nurses immediately began cutting Adams's clothes off and washing blood away to get a visual on his injuries. The primary physician, standing at the head of the bed, began calling out Adams's vitals for record management. The trauma nurses hung fluids and the IVs were converted to large bore free-flowing lines. The trauma team leader was continually communicating his commands for X-rays, a CT scan, and other services as the medical evaluation and life-saving procedures advanced. As the extent of Adams's injuries were revealed, the surgical team grew. It was seven hours before Adams regained consciousness.

#

Segei Antonov sat quietly after receiving word that his son, Aleks, had been killed by the LAPD, by Lieutenant Jack Adams. Segei had delayed the jet departing for Russia as long as he could. There was nothing more he could do, and he gave the pilot the order to take off. The engines spooled up and the doors of the hangar were opened. As the jet pulled onto the tarmac, Segei fully realized that he was leaving America and leaving his son Aleks. Segei did not feel pain or sorrow; he felt vengeful. Something had been taken from him, and someone had to pay for that. Once the jet was airborne, Segei continued a series of international telephone calls to pave the way for his return to Russia. The effort to restrict Segei's passport was not implemented in time to stop his return to Russia and by the time he landed, FBI Special Agent Bill O'Reilly had a lot on his plate as his newly formed Russian organized crime task force began seizing real estate, businesses, and bank accounts. The IRS agents on the task force were swamped, and everyone was working overtime tying everything together.

#

Lieutenant Jack Adams appeared to rest comfortably. Robin, the ICU nurse caring for him refused to leave his side even for a moment. She had a son who was a military policeman in Afghanistan, and she camped out in Adams's room and pored over every detail of his medical records. She was stymied by some of the items in Adams's possession when he had been brought into the hospital.

A handwritten note for his son and his daughter. But then, something different. "Detective McClain . . . in the lieutenant's shirt pocket? When they stripped his clothes off, it was in his pocket."

Ron McClain knew what she wanted to ask. He didn't quite understand it, either, but had a little bit of a handle on it. It was pretty deep, a South Central Los Angeles policeman thing.

"Detective McClain, that old bullet? It looks really old. Why does the lieutenant have that in his pocket? It scares me to think about it. I asked my son and he said that he's heard about things like that from the older combat guys."

McClain looked at the tarnished .45-caliber bullet. "Robin, the lieutenant told me once that it reminds him, every day, that we're vulnerable. Men like him, Alice, they don't feel fear and they need to be reminded that they're vulnerable, that they can be hurt. Maybe it's so they don't do stupid things . . . run into a bullet, or something. Lieutenant Adams fights really hard every day to go home to his kids. His son and daughter mean everything to him. I think it helps him to stay safe and get home to them."

McClain set the tarnished .45-caliber bullet on the nightstand next to Adams's bed.

Later in the day, Adams opened his eyes and saw Alice, the ICU nurse, standing next to his bed taking his vitals. She seemed concerned. Then he saw his son and daughter sleeping next to him. The deep breath he took hurt a lot, those broken ribs. The nurse stepped closer and put her hand on Adams's chest. "You're in the hospital, Mr. Adams—Lieutenant Adams. Don't be afraid; you'll be groggy for a bit, but you're doing fine. I heard what happened. We all heard what happened, and it's all over. My name is Robin. I'm your nurse, and this is Glendale Memorial Hospital. You're out of surgery and you're doing fine, everything is fine. I just love your children; they are so precious. God bless you, Lieutenant Adams."

The three LAPD Gang Detail officers standing in the room protecting the lieutenant, along with the two standing guard in the hallway, had already briefed the medical staff of the security procedures in place. The two LAPD SWAT units parked at the entrance to the hospital, and the two parked at the entrance to the emergency room visibly warned everyone that there was a very serious law enforcement presence there.

The nurse merely looked over her shoulder at the older officer to signal him that Adams was awake. "Lieutenant, it's McClain. I'm right here with you. Your son and daughter are doing fine. They've been asleep for a little bit, but you're the one we're worried about."

"Where's that little girl, Mac?" Adams's speech was slurred.

"They took her to Glendale Adventist, sir. She's a mess—they really hurt her. I've got a security detail on her. She's a wit and I don't want anything happening to her. She's going to struggle through this, I'm afraid."

Adams took another deep breath and felt the pain. His mind was clearing. "I killed the Russian from Gold Rush, Mac. He's one of the assholes in that house."

McClain and the rest of the law enforcement team had quite a bit of time to keep piecing things together. "Yeah, we found that out, Jack. We've been interviewing one of the Russians from the Gold Rush hit and one we arrested after they hit your house. Looks like a group of them actually came to your house, but we were a step ahead of them. They're small-time, but it looks like they planned to hit Gold Rush and hit your family, along with taking you out. There's nothing about hitting any of us, only you. Looks like they didn't know who the rest of us were, but they got your name from the press. Somehow they linked you to being in charge of Gold Rush. We're not sure about how Aleks or his father, Segei, plays into this yet. One of them is calling the shots, or maybe it's both of them."

"That little Aleks asshole talked about making a statement, making an example of us so that the police will leave them alone. But this ain't Russia, Mac." The LAPD ran blue in Adams's veins.

McClain smiled, as Adams was slurring his words and clearly not fully coherent yet. "Agent Bill O'Reilly brought the FBI's Organized Crime Detail in, Jack. I understand they've hit the ground like a tornado. They're targeting everyone in that apartment building and every one of the players, even the dead guys. They're throwing a really big net. I've never seen the FBI respond to anything we do like this."

"He's a friend, Mac. Bill is a good man, someone we can count on. He's a street policeman."

McClain's mouth fell open. "Wow! You've never referred to anyone in the FBI as a policeman, Jack. That's quite the compliment coming from you."

"Like I said, Mac, he's a friend . . . wait. Mac? Mac? What about Jelenick?"

"What about him, Jack? He was over at the EOC fucking things up like he always does. But the guys over there worked around him. I'll tell you about that later." McClain didn't think it was time yet to have these discussions with Adams.

"No, Mac. Jelenick burned us. How would Aleks even know his name? Jelenick burned us, Mac. He told the Russians about Gold Rush—that's how they knew."

McClain struggled to understand whether Adams was coherent, whether he even understood Adams correctly. "I need to get Chief Nelson in here, Jack. Is that okay with you? He's been here for hours. He's outside talking to one of the neurosurgeons."

#

Commander Stans Jelenick stood in the EOC after learning of the rescue in Glendale. He realized his order to stand down on that information had been disobeyed. His wife was not answering her phone, and he did not know where she was. When his cell phone rang with a blocked number, he was compelled to answer. The call came from the private jet still in US airspace.

"Commander Jelenick, we had an agreement, and that agreement has been violated. My son is presumed to be dead at the hands of your policemen. Our agreement is terminated, as is our friendship."

Jelenick recognized the voice of Segei Antonov. When the phone call abruptly disconnected, Jelenick knew that he was in jeopardy, though he didn't yet know what the full extent of that jeopardy would be.

#

Deputy Chief Steve Nelson listened to what Detective McClain told him, but was apprehensive about jumping to conclusions. Lieutenant Adams was still in recovery, still using medication. Acting on intuition, he briefed Chief of Police George Fuller and recommended they personally hear it from Adams.

Adams was talking with his son and daughter when the two chiefs came into the room. The two children didn't seem to be fazed in the slightest at Adams's appearance; to most people, he was unrecognizable. Adams sent them to the couch near his bed to look at books the nurses had brought for them. "Chief Nelson, Chief Fuller, good to see you sirs."

Adams appeared fatigued. It was hard for him to talk due to his injuries. His face displayed the results of multiple fractures and sutures; both eyes were swollen almost completely shut. It was hard for the two men to look at him, even though his children didn't seem to care at all.

Chief of Police Fuller was the first to talk. "Lieutenant, the doctors are going to brief you on your condition, because I wouldn't even know where to start. Thank God you're much better than you looked when they brought you in, but you still look like shit. You've been through a lot, but you're going to be okay. You have some healing time in front of you. We have a lot to talk about, Jack, but we'll save that for another time. We're still piecing this together, but we'll have a better handle on it very soon."

Adams had to smile at a memory. "I broke my nose in baseball when I was little. My dad teased me a lot. He told me not to worry about it because I never was very pretty."

Chief Nelson stepped closer to the bed and put his hand on Adams shoulder. "Jack, you're going to be fine. You have all of us behind you. Your injuries are serious, but you're tough and you'll get through it. Chief Fuller said we'll have time to talk about this later, but Jack, I have to ask you something now."

Adams already knew what was coming. "In that house, sir. The Russian asshole shot me, then he said Commander Jelenick told them about Gold Rush. He said Jelenick rolled on us. That's how they knew. How would he even know who Jelenick is, Chief?"

Chief Nelson's face twisted into a terrible frown. "Jack, are you sure about this? They're still giving you meds, Jack. A *lot* of them. Can you be sure?"

"I'm sure, Chief. It's hard for me; there was a lot. But I'm sure. He was going to kill me, Chief. He was just waiting to kill my family first. He said they had my son and my daughter and they were bringing them there to kill them. Then they'd kill me. He wanted it to be an example for other policemen not to mess with them. Why would he tell me something about Jelenick that wasn't true? I was dead to him, Chief. There's no reason to tell me that. He thought I was already dead. How did he even know Jelenick? It was true, Chief. What he said about Jelenick is true. Where is he?"

A shudder raced up Chief Nelson's spine. "They never had your son and daughter, Jack. I guess the Russians went to your house after Orange County sheriffs had already picked them up. We'll talk about that later. Somehow, we think that Aleks never knew that it didn't pan out the way they had planned. But this thing about Jelenick . . ."

Adams remembered something. "Jelenick interviewed the father, Segei. We learned about the hit on the wire and picked the father up. Then Jelenick released him before anyone else knew he was gone. Jelenick knows him, or the father told Jelenick something to convince him to roll on us."

Chief Fuller stepped forward and interceded in the conversation. "Okay, we'll work on this, Jack. You have my word—we'll figure it out. You rest and we'll get on this. Be safe, Jack."

The two chiefs stepped out into the hallway to discuss a plan to isolate Commander Stans Jelenick. The chief of police of the Los Angeles Police Department was now a very angry man.

#

Thirteen-year-old Jemma Gasparyan was taken to Glendale Adventist Hospital. She had a broken wrist and was treated for serious internal injuries. The swelling and bruising on her face would heal with time.

Two Glendale Police Department officers had been assigned to stay with her during her stay at the hospital. After McClain initiated a constant LAPD security detail, four LAPD Gang Detail officers arrived and relieved Glendale PD. One female uniformed officer was stationed in Jemma's room, two officers were at her door positioned in the hallway, and one stood at the elevator to watch people coming and going.

When Glendale Police officers Larry Terrill and Vern Peters were relieved by the LAPD officers, they headed for the station. They were assigned to twelve-hour shifts and were sorry to see the overtime stop. When they stepped off the elevator in the hospital lobby and headed for the doors, there were raised voices at the information desk. "I'm sorry, sir, we can't give that information out."

The young man seemed angry. "She's my sister and I want to see her. Where is she?"

As the two Glendale officers passed the information desk, Larry Terrill stopped. Intuition. He turned around and asked the young man, "What's your name?"

The young man was identified as Michail Lebedev, a thirty-year-old Russian immigrant requesting the room number of Jemma Gasparyan. "I don't know her. Someone asked me to deliver flowers, but I don't know the room number. I was going to buy the flowers here at the hospital and take them up to her."

"Detective McClain, this is Officer Morgan from Northeast Division Gangs. I'm on the security detail at Glendale Adventist. Glendale PD just identified a Russian guy trying to get the victim's room number. Something about she was his sister, and then something about he was delivering flowers. But he didn't have any flowers. The FBI is sending an agent over to pick the guy up. I think it might be a hit on the victim, so we're doubling the security detail here."

McClain put everyone on alert at Glendale Adventist Hospital and then put a security detail on Jemma Gasparyan's house. The danger wasn't over yet; the Russians were still in play.

McClain stepped out of Lieutenant Adams's hospital room to speak with Rand and Andrews. "You guys float the hospital. If they're trying to hit the girl while she's in the hospital, you know they're here trying to hit the lieutenant, and that's not going to happen. I'll keep two on the door and two inside the lieutenant's room. We've got SWAT on the two entrances and they'll respond inside if we need them, but I'm going to request another full squad to beef up what we already have. Stanford and two of his Surveillance guys are almost here. Right now, you two are hunters. If they're here, you find them."

Michail Lebedev could not explain why he'd said that Gasparyan was his sister, nor could he identify the person was had supposedly requested him to deliver flowers. One lie led to the next, and he was held for Special Agent Bill O'Reilly. The weight of the Federal Bureau of Investigation fell on him like a ton of bricks. O'Reilly proved to be a pit bull that didn't let go. Ever.

McClain walked through the hospital lobby to get a feel for things. He was approached by a very attractive young woman in gray slacks and a white buttoned shirt who was being followed by a cameraman. "Hello, Detective McClain. You work with Lieutenant Adams, don't you? I'm Candace Morgan."

"Hi, Miss Morgan. I can't make any statements right now. We're too early into this."

"No, that's not why I'm here, Detective, although I'd love to get that statement as soon as you're able. It's something else. When I got to the shooting scene in Glendale, it was pretty hectic. Different police departments, feds, the fire department—a mess. But someone caught my eye, not even sure why. He was a bystander out in front of the house watching everything, but there was something else. I'm not even sure what that means, but there was something else. Detective, I just saw that same guy in the parking lot by the emergency room entrance. He's a big guy, dark hair and dark complexion, wearing a black suit and a white shirt. He's driving a black Mercedes-Benz with the windows all blacked out."

McClain turned his back on Candace Morgan and keyed the microphone from his police radio. "35G11 to 5K3. Paul, what's your ETA to the hospital?"

"5K3, pulling in now. Two of my units are only five minutes out."

"35G11, possible Russian player in a black Mercedes outside the ER. Black suit and white shirt. See if you can locate him, or the car."

Paul Stanford cruised the parking lot looking for the car and the Russian. Stanford held his .45-caliber handgun in his lap as he quickly drove the aisles. "5K3 to 35G11, I'm pretty sure I've got the Mercedes but it's empty. Only one possible in the lot and it has dealer plates on it, but the cars empty. Dealer plates come back to an invalid number. Another bogus DMV paper plate."

"35G11, 5K3. Put your two units on the car and be prepared to block it. Keep eyes on it and if it moves, block it and hold the driver. I need for you to be on foot in the hospital, Paul. Find this asshole."

"5K3, roger that."

Paul Stanford abandoned his car and entered the hospital through the emergency room. As he turned left at the end of the hallway and walked through the lobby, he observed a tall dark-haired man in a black suit approaching the "Heart" elevators. Stanford followed as the man hit the elevator button and waited for the doors to open.

Mike Rand and John Andrews left Adams's room and headed for the lobby. They stepped into the Heart elevators and hit the lobby button. When the elevator door opened at the lobby level, Rand and Andrews stood face-to-face with a tall dark man in a black suit. They saw Paul Stanford in the lobby standing twenty feet behind the tall man. Stanford had a serious look on his face, and he was holding a large handgun at his side.

As the man looked at the two large uniformed officers, the nonverbal exchange revealed the tension. Rand stepped forward. "Who the fuck are you?"

Viktor Timoshenko, the driver of Segei Antonov, was a dedicated bodyguard and enforcer. A problem solver. A fixer. When he received the call from Segei to finish what had been started and to avenge Aleks's death, Victor Timoshenko knew he was on a one-way mission. Succeed or die. He knew death by the police would be more merciful than death by the Bratva, but he was used to such assignments.

Timoshenko stood silently looking at the two officers, deciding how best to kill them and get to Adams's room. He was armed with a handgun in a shoulder holster under his left arm and believed he could draw and shoot both officers before they could respond. Timoshenko's left hand was in his pants pocket holding a pointed knife. He calmly brought his right hand up and unbuttoned the single button on his suit jacket. "Excuse me, officer?"

Mike Rand knew. Intuition. Rand charged forward in the blink of an eye, crashing into Timoshenko and knocking him backwards into Paul Stanford. Rand never saw the knife that pushed into the side of his right thigh as the three men tumbled. John Andrews stepped to the side and drew his handgun.

Rand ignored the pain of the knife and fought to control Timoshenko and handcuff him. The Russian was brutal; his blows were hard and hit their targets with precision. Timoshenko was an effective fighter, but he had never had to engage a man like Mike Rand. Rand took the blows without flinching and hit the Russian back with powerful force. The altercation was so violent that Paul Stanford had been knocked away from the two combatants.

Stanford yelled for everyone in the lobby to leave through the lobby doors. He tried to find a way to help control Timoshenko but couldn't find a way to intercede in the violent confrontation.

Andrews watched helplessly, but knew he had to maintain a cover position with his handgun. He continually scanned the lobby for other suspects. *Watch your back.*

Timoshenko forced himself on top of Rand but couldn't get to his gun under his jacket. He was able to get his hand on Rand's gun in his holster, but Rand effectively rolled to his side and pinned his gun between his body and the floor, holding it in the holster. Timoshenko pulled the small knife from Rand's leg. The pain was terrible but Rand knew to fight for his life, punching violently at Timoshenko's face. Andrews couldn't see the knife; it was on the other side of the two men. As Timoshenko raised the knife, three shots rang out.

#

Karen Aoki had knelt in the chapel for over an hour. She needed time to herself, time to think before visiting Lieutenant Adams. Her injuries were healing and allowed her to get around fairly well now, but her ability to return to full duty was questionable at best.

The commotion out in the lobby drew her out of the chapel doors where she immediately saw two men fighting on the floor. She saw Andrews with his gun drawn only a few yards from the fight, then recognized Rand fighting with the other man. The large man on top of Rand raised a knife as if to thrust it down into Rand's face or chest. Aoki drew her handgun from under her UCLA sweatshirt and placed three .45-caliber rounds in the middle of the man's back in a pattern the size of a golf ball. There was no time to think, no time to assess other options—just protect Rand. She drew, fired, and watched

Timoshenko straighten up from the impact. The knife fell to the tiled floor.

Rand reached up, grabbed Timoshenko by the throat, punched him in the face, and threw him off to the side. Andrews turned and scanned the lobby to find the rest of the suspects, but again, suspects who never came.

CHAPTER FORTY-FOUR
A HERO'S WELCOME

Deputy Chief Nelson ordered Commander Jelenick to his office. No small talk—just the order. As Jelenick hung up the phone, he realized this conversation with Chief Nelson was the next step in his demise.

"Chief, how is Lieutenant Adams?" Jelenick hoped that his personal involvement had not been discovered. He had to play his cards right and hoped he would be able to weather this without anyone knowing. All he had actually done was make one decision about a "shots fired" call in Glendale. It wasn't even in Los Angeles. All he wanted was to get home and hopefully reunite with his wife. It had been almost twenty-four hours without any contact with Elana. All he wanted was to know that she was okay.

Deputy Chief Nelson was all business. "Stans, I need you to listen carefully to me. You have been identified as the source of the leak to the Russians. The arson attack on Gold Rush and on our officers, the death of Officer Mark, as well as the attack on Lieutenant Adams and his family, have all been traced back to you." Pulling no punches, Deputy Chief Nelson then sat in silence staring daggers at Jelenick.

Nelson and Chief of Police Fuller decided that an investigation into what Lieutenant Adams had told them would take too long. Present it to Jelenick as a fact and see what the response was—that was the plan. They would either jeopardize the investigation or solve it on the spot. The risk had to be taken, as time was not their friend. Fuller assigned the task solely to Nelson. Fuller wanted to remain as the reviewing manager to make final decisions.

Deputy Chief Nelson threw out the police interview tactic of pretending he already had the answers. Watching Jelenick's response, he knew the allegation was true.

"They have my wife. They have Elana."

Jelenick laid out the story as best he understood it. He told Deputy Chief Nelson that he had been advised by Segei Antonov that the information came from Elana. He and Elana had discussed many of his police efforts throughout the years. "Don't you talk to your wife, Chief?" Somehow, the information about Gold Rush had probably been leaked to one of Elana's friends.

After Jelenick revealed the possible danger his wife was in, Deputy Chief

Nelson initiated another EOC activation and a full-scale investigation using all the resources of the Los Angeles Police Department and the FBI. Still, Elana Jelenick could not be located.

#

After almost eleven hours, Segei Antonov's private jet landed at Pulkovo Airport in St. Petersburg. Segei tried to gain information on his son's death and the events that preceded it by staying in touch with his family in Glendale but it proved difficult, as the FBI was rapidly scooping people up in their investigation. The information was spotty, and most of the information was gleaned from the media reports that followed the events nonstop. Candace Morgan went international.

Segei strode through the St. Petersburg airport, which had been very specifically designed by Grimshaw Architects to provide a face of Russian prosperity to international visitors with a flair for Italian and French art and architecture. Probably not an honest depiction of Russian society, but it gave Segei a sense of calm and safety after losing his son to the LAPD and personally escaping his assured arrest.

Segei hoped that the young girl and the LAPD Lieutenant Jack Adams were now dead. They had to be sacrificed to educate American law enforcement. To teach them. Although it wasn't exactly the message he had planned to send or the way he had planned to send it, the result would still get the attention of American policemen. His plans for the future would send new and violent messages to all the policemen involved in his son's death, along with their families. Segei planned to orchestrate the violence from his home in Russia.

The pressure placed by the FBI and the restrictions now on Segei's passport made it difficult for him to manage his return. Segei paid a handsome fee to grease the skids and move through the administrative tasks of returning to Russia. He was well versed in taking advantage of Russia's easing of visa requirements for European nationals visiting Russia, and he moved through customs with that group of travelers. It's only a matter of money—and threats, of course.

After clearing customs, Segei confirmed his reservation at the Lotte Hotel in the heart of the city on St. Isaac's Square. Upon returning to St. Petersburg, he desired to first visit family and then those he answered to. Tovarisch. His plans to retaliate against his foes in America were beginning to take shape. He couldn't sleep on the plane and spent the time planning his revenge. Each person involved in the death of his son would pay a heavy price. Each would be made an example of, and American law enforcement would take notice.

Segei hadn't eaten since the day before his arrest but couldn't bring himself to eat during his flight. Upon landing, he directed his driver to take him directly to Palkin, his favorite restaurant. He would enjoy his country, relax, eat well, and resume his position of power in Russia.

When Segei finished the long-bone ribeye steak, his favorite, he ordered dessert. Deluxe Palkin ice cream with Glenfiddich Palkin Edition whiskey. He would treat himself and begin his return to Russia with luxuries he had missed while he was in America.

Halfway through dessert, Segei ordered Raf coffee and leaned back in his booth, extending both his arms out. He leaned his head back, closed his eyes, and realized how fatigued he was. He had not yet communicated with his wife about the death of their son.

As he opened his eyes, he was startled by a man simply standing at his table staring at him. This did not appear to be the waiter with his coffee. Yuri Ambov of the Tambov Gang stood emotionless in front of Segei's table and shot him four times at point-blank range. Yuri Ambov calmly walked around the table, leaned over Segei, and pushed a knife into his chest before slowly walking out of the restaurant.

Ambov left the restaurant and sat in the rear seat of what appeared to be a black government vehicle waiting at the curb. Segei Antonov died in St. Petersburg. Not exactly the hero's welcome he had expected.

The photograph of Segei Antonov with a knife left in his chest was prominently displayed in the Russian media.

CHAPTER FORTY-FIVE
THE MAYOR'S PHOTO OP

Adams's time in the hospital was hard on him. He was content to finally be out of the hospital and home with his son and daughter. The security detail on his house by Metropolitan Division initially made everyone in the neighborhood apprehensive, but now they were just another part of life in Southern California. Los Angeles was a violent city, and it made sense that the violence occasionally spilled out into the neighboring communities of Orange County.

Adams's first venture away from home was to attend the funeral of Detective Jay Mark at Harbor Lawn-Mount Olive Memorial Park in Costa Mesa, only minutes from Adams's house. Performing the unbelievably dangerous job of a Los Angeles Police Officer, Jay Mark left cover and a place of safety during a tactical situation to keep two women safe. Both women were now on the path to prison for his murder, embroiled in a federal investigation of transnational organized crime.

Adams was driven by officers of Metropolitan Division, but purposely stood alone in the rear of the crowd. The sound of bagpipes haunts every policeman and every fireman. The sound is sobering. The world becomes quiet and dark while time stands still. The bagpipes bleed the story of the lives of those heroes who work the streets of our cities.

Two days after the funeral, Lieutenant Adams had a fairly lengthy meeting with the FBI Assistant Director in Charge, Los Angeles. The FBI was considering entering the world of gang investigations and enforcement by replicating the model developed by Adams. Adapting intelligence-based investigations to street gangs was garnering a lot of attention in the law enforcement world, and the FBI was eager to get on the bandwagon.

Some weeks had gone by, and Lieutenant Jack Adams was mobile. His injuries allowed him to drive, even though his primary doctor advised him not to. The security detail was pulled off and life began to return to some semblance of normalcy in the small community of Rossmoor.

As a result of the traffic accident with the Russians, Lieutenant Adams's police car was destroyed and sent to Salvage. He had an opportunity to choose from multiple new cars, but he chose another Ford Crown Vic. Old habits die hard, and he wasn't happy with the Chryslers that were being purchased by the city. Detective McClain and the six officers in Adams's unit were in and out of Adams's house so much that they began to know the neighbors. They even brought Adams his new car.

Today was the long-planned day for the mayor's photo op, and Adams's first drive in his new car. Mayor Hernandez had worked with his speech writers to modify the plan for his photo op. He wanted the LAPD undercover operation to benefit his message that crime was down in Los Angeles and that he was personally creating a safer place for people to live by removing guns from the hands of criminals. A lie, of course, but it was the perfect precursor to selling the need for stronger gun laws.

Senior Editor Kevin Dolinski was prepared for the lead story on the nightly news long before the press release and photo op by the mayor were even announced. The spin on gun control was going to make the chief of police really angry, but his efforts to support anti-gun lobbyists were successful in many ways. The partnership between Dolinski and Mayor Hernandez would open the floodgates for new money rolling in, and Mayor Hernandez was now in Dolinski's pocket.

Inside Pershing Square, using the amphitheater as a backdrop, Mayor Gilliam "Gilly" Hernandez stood in front of a table decorated with guns from the undercover LAPD operation, Gold Rush. He stood close to the table, wanting to give the press plenty of time to photograph him and the guns.

The mayor was accompanied by Chief of Police George Fuller and FBI Assistant Special Agent in Charge Mark Burton when he announced that a joint LAPD-FBI task force had successfully targeted transnational organized crime operating in Los Angeles as well as trafficking in illegal guns. "With great pride, as your mayor, we have made the streets much safer by removing these illegal guns that were being used against each of you and your families. And you have my guarantee that I will continue to seek legislation that supports our efforts to uphold a safe and peaceful Los Angeles."

Candace Morgan had received her running orders from her editor, Kevin Dolinski. She stood to the side of the staged table of guns and made the plea for stronger control of gun ownership. Shelley Givens of the *Los Angeles Times* received her direction from Deputy Mayor Sarah Holly as to the photographs to be published in tomorrow's edition of the *Times*, on the front page. A uniquely orchestrated presentation.

Chief Fuller did not appear happy as he stood on the stage next to the mayor. The downside of the responsibility to publicly support the person who appointed you to your job . . . even when you don't.

Adams struggled through traffic on the way to downtown Los Angeles, then parked his brand-new car at the Consulate General of Japan. He walked down the street to Pershing Square and was met with a large media crowd around the amphitheater. No real people, only the media in an area that was cleared of the homeless the day prior. A completely staged, preplanned, practiced presentation for the unsuspecting and easily fooled citizens of Los Angeles.

Adams was waved toward the steps leading to the raised platform by Deputy Mayor Sarah Holly. He ignored Holly and elected to stand in the audience between media cameras to watch as the mayor took credit for all their literal blood, sweat, and tears. Adams didn't want to be a part of the spectacle. This was the mayor's show, and he relied on the chief of police to be on the stage, although silently. There was no need for Adams to be in front of the cameras.

Lieutenant Adams couldn't understand the large smile the mayor held on his face. He couldn't understand the mayor's untruthful comments about his personal support for the Los Angeles Police Department, or of his personal involvement in the efforts put forth at Gold Rush. He couldn't understand the mayor's lies about the greatness of Los Angeles and how safe the city was. You only needed to look one block in every direction to visibly recognize the mayor's lies.

Adams had to walk away. His wounds seemed to be slowly healing and he was able to function on his own well enough, but the pain was never absent. He simply accepted that everyone had aches and pains; he shouldn't be any different. It would take a bit for him to return to full duty, but he believed himself to be a lucky man with time to spend with his family. *A little mandatory vacation time.*

As Adams walked away from the press conference, he thought about the ugliness of Los Angeles politics, of Los Angeles politicians. Adams found his car and wandered slowly up and down the streets of downtown Los Angeles, sightseeing. He parked in the red zone on Cesar Chavez and walked into the tourist restaurant row on Olvera Street for taquitos and guacamole.

Adams sat quietly and questioned his future with the Los Angeles Police Department. He was in no hurry and had no plan on how to spend the rest of his day, but ultimately he found himself walking through the ominous glass doors at LAPD Headquarters to see Deputy Chief Nelson. Adams was sure the press conference was over now.

On this day, after listening to the press conference with Mayor Hernandez, Adams saw no point in continuing his efforts and sought out Chief Nelson to tell him. Being a policeman had become a failing occupation. He began to wonder whether he should have become a fireman instead.

Walking down the hallway and without thinking about it, Adams walked right past Chief Nelson's office. As he stopped at the next door and peered in, he saw Commander Jelenick seated at his desk.

A little time had gone by, and Jelenick was still waiting for the administrative decisions about his actions. About his lack of courage and weak character. Oftentimes, command staff are not relieved from duty pending the outcome of administrative investigations in the same manner that those in lower ranks endure.

Truth be known, those decisions had already been made by the rank and file of the Los Angeles Police Department. If no one will follow you, you're no longer a leader. In this new role, Jelenick was now an outsider relegated to a position in which his rank no longer had any meaning. His authority no longer extended beyond the walls of his office, and he was the only person within those walls.

Jelenick had accepted that his wife would never be located. That she was dead. He constantly wondered what her death was like and if it was his fault or hers. In the end, he still tried to minimize his own role, even in his wife's death. Unsurprisingly, he still considered whether there was a path to climb further up the LAPD ladder. If he could develop enough sympathy with the right people over his wife's abduction and probable murder, he may still have a chance.

As Adams stepped into the office and walked toward Commander Jelenick's desk, he never gave a thought as to why he was even there. Some things happen without consideration and without intent. Some things just happen naturally.

Jelenick stood and scowled, clearly not understanding his place in the department any longer. Jelenick's wife had been abducted and probably killed because of Adams's undercover operation. Jelenick knew that he should have taken over for Adams. To make the situation worse, Jelenick's goal of moving further up the ladder was clearly being sidelined because of the man standing in front of him. It was all Adams's fault.

"Lieutenant Adams, I never thought you'd have the courage to face me again. Your future on this department is over, Lieutenant. I suggest you move on of your own accord and not make me have to do it."

Jelenick moved around the desk and pointed to the door of his office. "Get out of my office, Adams. And don't you ever walk in here again without being invited. Do you understand me?"

Using his right arm, which was only somewhat usable, Adams punched Commander Stans Jelenick three times. The punches were vicious, fueled by the unbridled anger of a man seeking justice. Adams knocked Jelenick to the ground, unconscious, with a broken nose and cheekbone.

Adams calmly looked down at Jelenick and took a deep breath. Jelenick's office was very quiet and very peaceful at that moment. His ribs still hurt when he breathed, hurt a lot. He noticed significant blood on the bandages covering his right arm now. He must have broken the stitches open. Nothing made much sense lately, but Jelenick sprawled out on the ground and bleeding gave Adams a sense of peace. If nothing else, some wrongs had been righted.

Making his way back to Nelson's office, Adams found Lieutenant Moss dutifully at her desk. "Hi, Jack. Didn't know you were coming in today. You're supposed to be recovering at home, but man, Jack, you still look awful. Chief Nelson isn't back from the press conference yet. Aren't you supposed to be there? You look a mess. How are you feeling?"

Adams wasn't really in a mood to talk anyway. "That's okay. Just stopped in to say hi. I'll stop in later."

Adams turned toward the door to the hallway and paused before stepping through it. Turning around to face Lieutenant Moss, Adams remarked in almost a whisper, "By the way . . . Commander Jelenick isn't feeling that great. You might have someone look in on him."

Moss smiled at the attempted humor, but then her expression changed to one of concern as she looked at Adams with an expression of disbelief. Adams casually walked toward the elevator as Lieutenant Moss ran down the hallway.

Adams opened the trunk of his car, which was illegally parked at the curb, and committed to straightening everything up. All his gear had been thrown from his old car into the new one without much thought put into organization. He opened one of his duffel bags and found a long-sleeve San Diego Fisherman's Landing T-shirt that he pulled on to hide the blood soaking through the bandages on his arm, then drove to Glendale even though he probably shouldn't have been driving. He refused to take pain medication, but driving with one arm probably wasn't advisable anyway.

The gunshot wounds didn't seem too painful now, but his whole body ached. The stitches closing the trauma in his back bothered him while he was driving, but it was his ribs that hurt the most.

After the meeting with the FBI, he was enthusiastic that the war on gangs would escalate to a much more effective level nationwide. Today, he felt that he just had to see the mayor's photo op and then get a couple things done. Sitting at home wasn't working out for him, but he hadn't planned on the excursion to LAPD Headquarters.

As he pulled into the driveway of the beautiful home set on a hillside, he watched the front door swing open and saw thirteen-year-old Jemma Gasparyan standing in the opening. Jemma had been released from the hospital to return to her parent's home, where she now refused to leave. Even stepping outside to the front porch was hard for Jemma.

As Adams climbed the steps and stood on the porch, Jemma recognized him and cried. The first time the two had met since the abduction. Jemma wanted to speak, but no words came out. Adams wanted to tell her so much, but he was at a loss just as much as she was. They looked at each other in silence and communicated what words couldn't say.

As Adams bent forward to be face-to-face, Jemma handed Adams the badge she had been carrying since the assault on her, then slowly placed her arms around his neck and hugged him strongly. The injuries and bruises on her face were largely faded. A man and woman approached from inside the house and although Adams had not met them, he knew they were the parents. The fear and the pain in their eyes told Adams everything. The same look Adams had seen in so many parents' eyes. The look of pain that becomes a part of who they are for the rest of their lives. Ruined lives.

The Gasparyans wanted to visit Adams while he recovered, but so far they hadn't been allowed to visit him. The security detail around him had built a solid wall that did not let anyone through.

Adams held his hand up to stop their approach. It wasn't the time for this conversation. Adams stood and squeezed Jemma's hand before he left.

#

Pulling into Fish King, one of Adams's favorite spots, he decided to treat himself to a snack of ceviche and take a little time to think, kill a few more minutes. He wasn't really hungry after eating on Olvera Street; he just didn't seem to be in a hurry to do anything today. Punching Commander Jelenick probably wasn't the best decision he had made lately. He should probably have given that a little more thought. Maybe he could blame it on the pain meds. Anyway, he was glad he did it, and he'd do it again. If his other arm wasn't in a sling, he could have hit him much harder.

Adams decided to head for home a little while later but found his car veering off track toward Karen Aoki's house. Once they lowered the boom on him for assaulting a police commander, he may not have as much freedom to move around as he did now. *Better to get socializing out of the way.* "You all healed up yet, Karen?"

"Hi, LT. You're all the hero and everything! Oh my God, you still look terrible. How's that little girl, sir?"

Adams thought about that for a moment and realized she'd never be a little girl again. She'd never live a normal life. She was broken.

"Damn, Lieutenant . . . Detective McClain just called me and asked me if I've seen you. You're not answering your phone, LT. He told me about you beating the shit out of the commander and now everyone's looking for you. They should make you chief of police if you don't go to jail."

"Don't get too excited, Karen. I'm sure the Department will make me pay for it; nothing is free. I'm doubting they'll ever put me back to work, but just between you and me . . . it felt pretty damn good."

"They won't fire you, Lieutenant Adams. You're the best we have. There's no way they would fire you. But, LT, I bet they suspend you, like, forever. For six months, I bet. I heard they had to take the commander to the hospital and he was going into surgery. He's fucked up, sir."

Karen Aoki was one of those rare people that Adams genuinely enjoyed talking with. "Yeah, well, it must have been a lucky punch."

"Just remember, LT. Remember what you taught us: in your mind's eye. It's just some vacation time, sir, and we can hang out together. We can heal up together. I can be your physical therapist and your personal trainer."

"Yeah, I'd like a little vacation. Maybe take my son and daughter to Mammoth. But I doubt I'd survive you being my personal trainer. A man can only take so much, you know. I hear that Russian didn't do so well when he met you."

"I was watching everyone's back, LT. I learned my lesson. Too bad for him."

"See ya around, Karen."

"Be safe, Lieutenant. You ever need me to whip you back into shape, sir, just give me a call."

CHAPTER FORTY-SIX
IT ALL ENDS IN YOUR MIND'S EYE

Adams's visit into downtown Los Angeles last week had predictably stirred up a lot of problems. He didn't look forward to his meeting today, but it was time to get it over with. Commander Stans Jelenick had undergone surgery for his injuries and was recovering at home. His nose had been repaired without much fanfare, but the fracture of his cheekbone resulted in some ongoing concerns.

As Adams slowly ventured down the crowded, dirty, and unkept roads of downtown Los Angeles, the shadows crept out of the dark alleys and pulled in behind him, even in the daylight. *Something rare, something different, even for the shadows.*

Chief of Police George Fuller was in a serious mood. He sat at his desk looking across at Lieutenant Adams and Deputy Chief Nelson. His own career was on the line after Mayor Hernandez had made it clear that his job was in jeopardy. But more importantly, his ability to lead the Los Angeles Police Department had been jeopardized. Chief of Police Fuller knew he could receive his walking orders at any moment and fully expected to be retired before the end of the month.

"Why aren't you apologizing, Lieutenant? Why aren't you trying to save your job, even though the chance of that is nil? You're looking at a Board of Rights and termination. The absolute best you could hope for is a six-month suspension and demotion to sergeant or policeman. Most probably criminal assault charges, probably a lawsuit for damages."

Adams was prepared for this conversation. He knew that sitting in front of the chief of police was just a formality of what was coming. "Whatever you decide, Chief, I'll accept. If you'd like me to sign a resignation and avoid all that, I will."

Chief Fuller expressed a concerned and fierce look before loudly yelling to the outer office, "Lieutenant Dawson! Print out a resignation letter for Lieutenant Adams."

Jim Dawson peeked around the doorjamb. He just so happened to be standing just outside the door. "I don't want to, Chief, but I'll do it. It's a form letter on the computer, takes two minutes. Are you sure, Chief?"

Chief of Police Fuller stood up behind the desk. Placing both hands on the desk and leaning forward, he spoke in a loud voice, even for someone who was angry. "Lieutenant Adams, I'm the Goddamned chief of police of the Los Angeles Police Department and appearances be damned, I will do the right thing. Do you understand me, Lieutenant?"

"Yes, sir. My answer is still the same. I don't apologize, I don't beg, and I'll accept whatever your decision is." After punching Commander Jelenick, Adams had walked out of the commander's office knowing his fate was sealed. He knew that everything that followed that moment was merely foreplay until the boom fell. He knew his pension wasn't enough to support his family, but he figured he could get another job somewhere. He'd figure that out. The tentative part was criminal charges. He didn't think he'd do any time, but a criminal record of assaulting your boss can really mess up your efforts to find another job.

Lieutenant Jim Dawson walked tentatively into the office and placed a freshly printed resignation letter on the desk of Chief of Police George Fuller. As he walked out of the chief's office, he closed the door behind him. This was one of those things that needed to occur in private. Once the door closed, it was unusually dark in the office as the shadows slipped in and engulfed the entire room.

Quietly, Adams stood, turned the paper toward him on the desk, and saw his name in all capital letters and bold print. Adams signed the document and gently placed the pen down on the desk. *That wasn't too bad.*

He unpinned his police identification card from his shirt front and set it on the paper he had just signed. *That hurt a little more.*

Then Adams removed the badge hanging on his belt and held it in his right hand. This turned out to be the hard part. This was unexpected; laying that badge on the chief's desk was tough. Lieutenant Jack Adams stood looking down at the badge in his hand while the rest of the room faded out.

Adams had carried the badge of a Los Angeles policeman for many years. It had become a part of who he was. This wasn't his job; this was who he was. Who he had always desired to be. A protector.

The shadows suddenly surrounded him and held him fast in place. Minutes went by and there was total silence in the room as each of the three men were lost in their own thoughts. Adams knew what he had to do but just couldn't get it over with. The shadows held him and he stood, frozen, looking down at his badge while the shadows blurred out the rest of the room.

Chief of Police Fuller was the first to speak. He had just made a decision that would most probably end his own career. A decision he hadn't planned on. "Lieutenant Adams, you're out of uniform. And why does your badge always look like shit? Don't you ever polish your gear? Get that shit squared away and get back to work, Lieutenant. With all this shit you stirred up, you and your crew will be in court for months."

Adams was lost. *What just happened?* "Chief?"

Chief of Police George Fuller spoke in a softer tone. His demeanor changed with his new and unexpected decision. "I never expected to be in this job very long anyway, Jack. If you hadn't punched that son of a bitch, I would have. I think he'll be fine, anyway. I heard you hit like a girl. But I'm keeping this resignation letter in my desk, Lieutenant. I'm betting it will be useful in the future. This is my insurance, and if you give me the slightest reason, Adams, the slightest fucking reason, I will sign this thing so fast your head will spin. Now hit the streets, Lieutenant Adams, and get out of my office before I do throw you off that balcony."

With a look of confusion, Adams turned and walked slowly to the closed door. He stopped, turned to face the two chiefs, and replied, "Thank you, Chief Fuller and Chief Nelson. But about Segei Antonov . . ."

He tried to finish his comment, but his mind just wouldn't allow it. Jack Adams was not finished with the Russian investigation. Policeman or not, Jack Adams was intent on not allowing Segei Antonov to threaten his family. It was time they met, and Adams was planning to find him and introduce himself.

Chief of Police George Fuller took the lead. "Jack . . . this case has received a lot of press. State Department notified me that you purchased a ticket to St. Petersburg. That's a suicide mission. Los Angeles policemen are not in the revenge business, Jack."

Adams was resigned to his fate. "It's not revenge, sir. I can't let him threaten my family, it will never end. I'll take the fight to him. I'll find him."

"Jack, Segei Antonov was murdered in St. Petersburg. He was shot and then stabbed as he sat in a restaurant. Apparently, he was not appreciated by the Russian Mafia assholes he worked for." Although Chief Fuller seemed to enjoy telling Adams that Segei was dead, the concerns he held about the State Department notification haunted him.

"He got off easy, sir."

Adams lingered for just a moment, then softly closed the door behind him.

Chief of Police George Fuller was dangerously candid when he confided in Chief Nelson, "Steve, lucky for us that bastard is dead. I'm sure Adams would have ended up making that trip to Russia he's talking about."

"I get it, George. Would you want Jack Adams coming after you? Segei threatened his son and his daughter. Ignorant bastard. None of us like to believe that monsters like that really exist. The part that scares me even more is that none of us like to admit that sometimes we turn into monsters ourselves in order to police monsters."

Fuller stayed way out on that limb. What the hell, he was already out there. "It's a hypothetical, Steve. Segei Antonov is dead, and Adams didn't go to Russia. There's no law against buying a ticket. It's a hypothetical and I can live with it. I hope you can, too."

Nelson saw a lot of jeopardy in the decision. "But it looks really bad, George. How do we square it with the State Department?"

Suddenly, a large smile appeared on the face of the chief of police. "What is it that Adams is so fond of saying? 'Yeah, well, I don't work for them.' Let's don't worry about the State Department, Steve. Let's just take care of our house, because I'm not acting on a hypothetical."

After Adams walked out of the chief's office, Fuller moved his own chess piece. "Steve, call Jelenick at home and get him in here. I've got another resignation letter in my desk drawer, and it's got that bastard's name on it."

Nelson didn't expect things to go this way. He expected the traditional and called-for response: sacrifice the lieutenant. "Are you sure about all of this, George? I'm behind you one hundred percent, but I don't know if I'd have the courage to do it."

Chief Fuller took a deep breath and leaned forward with his elbows on his desk. "It's the right thing, Steve. Even after what Adams and his family went through, his punching Jelenick was wrong, and my decision is not sending the right message to the department. I'll be persecuted by the mayor and the City Council, but it's still the right decision, so whatever comes my way, well, I'll weather it. If Gilly fires me, I hope you'll be the next to step in, and that's a good thing."

The chief of police seemed to get lost in his thoughts as the reality of his decision began to set in. "Steve, I never realized how hard of a job this is until I actually sat behind this desk. We all want to be the boss until we are. But it's not really the job. We know what we're doing; we've been doing this all our lives. It's the politicians and the press who think they can manipulate us. When you're the one sitting here, Steve, be flexible where you can, but don't let these people cause you to lose your way. It's not worth selling your soul. When you're the chief of police, do the right thing and accept the consequences. Life always goes on."

#

Dawson watched as Adams walked slowly out of the chief's office and closed the door behind him. Adams stood still with his back braced against the door for support, trying to figure out what just happened. "Jack, I'm so sorry. I didn't want to print that shit out."

Adams took a deep breath and remembered what his father had told him as a young boy: *"When you don't know what to do, just start somewhere."*

Adams looked at Dawson and tried to muster his best tone of authority. "Yeah, well, we're not doing that, Jim. I've gotta get back to work. See ya, Lieutenant Dawson."

"What? You're not serious, Jack? You're walking?" Dawson was amazed. He was already geared up to accept the firing of Adams, fired for doing what everyone else wanted to do but didn't have the courage to.

Adams pretended to know what to say, but he was still as amazed as Dawson was. "Someone has to get the job done out there, Jim, and you're goofing off in here."

Standing with his mouth open, Dawson asked, "Why do you do this, Jack? And why do you support these officers so much? These officers are not your personal responsibility."

Adams's answer came easy, unrehearsed. It had always been clear to him, and it still was. "People need help, Jim. That never seems to change, but it's getting worse. People are afraid and we're all they've got. Times have changed, and they're afraid to fight for themselves anymore. We've broken their backs by prosecuting people who fight back to protect themselves. The politicians don't allow people to stand up for themselves anymore, so we are all they've got. They want to convince everyone that the government will take care of all of their needs, even if they have to put them in jail to convince them. And these officers? Damn. They either lose or give up most of the good things in their own lives to protect people. Because when they go to work, they have to put on a bulletproof vest. Because no matter how hard the liberal element in our country tries to convince everyone that they are the bad guys, they don't give up. Every one of them is a hero, Jim. We owe them."

Adams stepped out of LAPD Headquarters followed by the shadows that flowed out into the sunlight and disappeared. Adams just stood and looked up at the sky. He still wasn't used to the sun being in his eyes. *What just happened?* He still had a job, and Segei Antonov was dead. Everything he had prepared himself for just turned upside down.

On his way home, Lieutenant Adams pulled into the driveway of Jemma Gasparyan's house. Jemma actually stepped outside onto the porch today and her injuries were barely visible. Adams handed Jemma his badge for the second time and said, "You keep this, Jemma. It will keep you safe. I can always get another one."

It was much easier surrendering his badge to Jemma than it was laying it on the chief's desk.

"Hello, Lieutenant Adams, I want to tell you something. Thank you so much for your badge—it's just perfect!" Jemma began. Adams ignored his pain and knelt down on his knees in front of her and held both her hands. "I want to be a policewoman, Lieutenant Adams. I want to help people."

"You can be anything you want to be, Jemma. See it in your mind's eye."

Jemma Gasparyan threw her arms around Adams's neck and hugged him. Occasionally, we come across someone in our life who amazes us. Someone with such strength of character and such courage that they change our lives. But that's another story . . .

God Bless the Protectors

Almighty God, Protector of all Mankind

Give special guidance to police officers

So that they may be protected from harm while performing their duty.

Lord, I ask for courage to face and conquer my own fears,

And for the courage to take me where others will not go.

I ask for strength of body to protect others,

And strength of spirit to lead others.

I ask for dedication to do my job, to do it well,

And dedication to my community, to keep it safe.

And please, Lord, through it all,

Be by my side,

For my faith is stronger than my fear.

*Dedicated to the men and women of law enforcement,
the true heroes of our society.*

**Lieutenant Gary Nanson, Retired
Los Angeles Police Department**

#

Made in the USA
Monee, IL
13 March 2023

513fe488-4b11-4839-a56f-ad32ecf4253eR01